Reality In Check

EMILY BANTING

Reality In Check
Copyright © 2023 Emily Banting
Published by Sapphfic Publishing
ISBN: 978-1-915157-12-6
First edition: August 2023

This is a work of fiction. Names, characters, business, events and incidents are the products of the author's imagination. Any resemblance to actual persons, living or dead, or actual events is purely coincidental.

CREDITS:
Editor: Hatch Editorial

1 3 4 5 6 7 8 9 10

ABOUT THE AUTHOR

Emily Banting is an award-winning and bestselling author of contemporary sapphic romance featuring LGBTQ+ characters and plenty of British humour. History obsessed, she throws her sapphic leading ladies into historic buildings and environments at every opportunity and strongly believes in representing women over forty in literature.

www.emilybanting.co.uk

FIND ME HERE

I love to hear from my readers. If you would like to get in touch you can find me here…

www.emilybanting.co.uk

Or follow me here…

facebook.com/emilybantingauthor
instagram.com/emilybanting
twitter.com/emily_banting
bookbub.com/authors/emily-banting
goodreads.com/emily_banting
amazon.com/author/emilybanting

ACKNOWLEDGMENTS

It seems only a few months since I wrote my last acknowledgements, in fact, it was about a year ago. Broken Beyond Repair's success blew me away for a little bit and it took a few months to get back into writing.

Beginning again is always a daunting prospect, especially with a book that will likely be judged against the success of its predecessor. Reality In Check, although similar in some respects to Broken Beyond Repair, is also entirely different, and it wouldn't be what it is without a lot of people standing beside me. One of them particularly I couldn't have done it without.

Conny, you've held me in one piece the last few months. If there was such a thing as human glue, you would be it. You've stuck me back together countless times and I can't tell you how much I appreciate you always being a tap of a screen away despite being at such a geographical distance. You are the best of friends and I value you and your musings more than I can say — and definitely more than you could cope with! Thank you for your patience, for listening to my ramblings, and for making me laugh every day.

Sarah, thanks for picking me up off the floor and dusting me off in my hour of need. Dropping everything for someone you didn't even know speaks to your huge heart and generosity. You've always encouraged me, given me a good kicking, and even the odd much needed slap. Thanks, buddy!

Thank you to my beta readers for laying your eyes on my first creation, to all my early readers, new and old, for your speedy reading and valuable opinions, and to my ARC team for always volunteering so eagerly.

Jess, you have worked your usual magic tricks on my words. It was an honour to finally meet you this year — even at a height of 500 feet!

Catherine, thanks for being so much more than a weekly escape from the crazy, and for always cheering me on from the sidelines — something you seem to excel at!

And thank you to all the readers for the epic proportions of support with Broken Beyond Repair. Your love and passion for it was the driving force behind getting this book finished. I hope you adore Arte and Charlotte (and Rodin!) as much as I do.

I can't finish without mentioning Maddie, my black Labrador, for all the cuddles and crazy things that inspired Rodin.

For Conny

For always being there, night and day,

and in the moments between.

CHAPTER 1

Arte Tremaine peered up at the cloudless sky. From inside the warm taxi, she could be fooled into thinking Britain was enjoying the height of summer. The thick, khaki parka and matching beanie she'd hastily bought when she entered the country a couple of weeks ago told another story.

She tossed her phone to the seat beside her, unable to concentrate on the small text of her favourite book, *Fingersmith*. If the turmoil of Victorian England couldn't distract her today, what could? She had half a mind to ask the driver to pick up the pace, impatient as she was to reach her grandmother's hotel and get to work. The other part of her screamed for him to slow down as fear of what awaited her consumed her.

Looking out over the familiar South Downs landscape brought her a momentary distraction, until memories surfaced, moistening her eyes and cinching the knot in her stomach. It had sat there like a heavy stone since she received the phone call in Rome — a call that had said everything in her life was about to change.

How did one prepare for death? It was hard enough when it was expected, but when it had come for Gran when she was 1,900 kilometres away, the guilt churned inside her like sour milk.

She had thought there would be more time. Time to make plans and decisions, arrange things, and to say goodbye. Goodbyes were always spoken, but you never knew if a garden-variety goodbye would become the final farewell — another of life's cruel twists.

A text message caused her phone to vibrate against the seat. She picked it back up and stared at the image of her metal sculpture on display in Rome's National Museum of Twenty-First Century Art. She couldn't seem to muster the pride she was sure she would feel under normal circumstances. It was a piece her gran had advised her on and encouraged her to make subtle changes to improve over the years. Arte had lost herself in its creation for hours at a time, forgetting about the world around her. It was the biggest achievement of her life, and now Gran wasn't around to share in it.

Taking a deep breath, she pressed her hands against her stomach and slowly blew out. Believing the knot would ease after her gran's funeral, its continued presence three days later niggled at her.

In the back of her mind, she always hoped this was her future, even though she knew it would be bittersweet, coming with the death of her gran. Was she even ready for that future to become the present? Teaching a room full of students was one thing; now she was about to enter a whole new level of responsibility. Inhaling another deep breath, she told herself she was ready for her new life; it was just another adventure.

A little voice undermined her own reassurances.

Then why do I feel so scared?

Had she lost the adventurous spirit of her younger self by working nine to five for years? Was it something that could even be lost, or did it simply lie dormant, waiting to be reawakened? It didn't feel like something was waiting to be awakened. At the moment she wanted to curl up in a ball and fall asleep, not face everything she'd left behind all those years ago.

She may have been back in England for a couple of weeks, but she was already missing her small apartment in Italy — a place she knew she'd never return to. How could she feel homesick when she was actually returning home? Not that she'd called it that for about seventeen years. Was it even home if the people that made it feel like one were no longer there?

To her relief, the taxi finally came to a stop. She didn't feel comfortable left alone with her thoughts at the moment; they had a habit of overwhelming her.

The taxi driver looked at her in the rearview mirror. "Cheer up, love. Nothing's ever as bad as it seems."

She forced a smile as she paid him. He meant well.

Arte shut the door and dropped her hefty rucksack by her feet, clinging on tightly to a white boutique gift bag. The sound of dogs barking filled her ears, and she closed her eyes as the taxi drove away. The chorus of canine voices echoed like distant thunder, lighting her face as they transported her back to her childhood visits to the kennel.

"Arte Tremaine! Is that you?"

Arte opened her eyes to see a tall figure with a bob of dense, grey hair, wearing a tweed coat and wellies. Her long stride brought her across the courtyard from a late Victorian house in no time.

Squinting against the low winter sun, Arte could make out a much older version of Jenny, the kennel owner, to the one she remembered. She sighed quietly to herself, annoyed at the ravages of time and how fragile life was when set against it.

"Hi," Arte called back, tightening her plaid, lambswool scarf around her neck to rebuff the biting wind.

Looking her up and down, Jenny shook her head. "I dare say a few summers have passed since you used to come and play with the dogs in the holidays."

"More than a few," Arte replied with a smile.

Jenny's face dropped as she asked, "You've come for Rodin?"

Arte nodded, feeling her smile edge away, too, despite the desperation to cling on to it. A smile, even if brief, was an unfamiliar feeling of late.

"He'll be happy to see you. He's been pining. They always seem to sense when something is wrong."

"It won't be me he wants," Arte replied, only to wonder how Rodin was going to react.

Jenny looked down at the concrete drive. "No, I expect not. I'm so sorry about your gran. She may have been a neighbour but she became a good friend over the years. I was sorry not to make it to her funeral last week. I'm packed to the rafters. The Christmas period is so busy, it has me run off my feet. I can't wait to get the decorations down in a few days."

Arte placed a hand on Jenny's folded arms. "She would have understood you putting the dogs first."

Jenny nodded with a sniff. "You know, the first thing she did was call me to collect Rodin. She hadn't even called herself an ambulance. I did that."

"No, I didn't know that." It sounded typical of Gran to put her Labrador first, even when she was moments from death.

"I arrived as they were putting her into the ambulance. 'Look after Rodin' was the last thing she said." Jenny took a deep breath. "She drifted away after that."

Arte blinked, trying to focus on anything except the sudden urge to cry. She took in a shaky breath, her chest heaving as she tried to push the threatening tears away.

"I'm sorry, love. You don't want to hear all this."

Arte gave Jenny's arm a light pat. "No, I do. It's not easy to hear, that's all."

Realising Gran's loss was not her own to bear felt oddly comforting.

"Come and pop your bags in the office; we'll freeze out here," Jenny said, beckoning Arte towards a wooden cabin on one side of the courtyard. "So, where have you been hiding all these years? Your gran said you'd spent time travelling, and last I heard you were teaching in Rome."

"Yes. I travelled around Europe for a while after I graduated from university. Did a bit of work in hospitality to boost my travel funds and eventually ended up in Italy.

I studied there and loved it so much that I stayed on to teach."

"Any plans to return? Only" — Jenny held the office door open for Arte and then followed her inside — "when your sister rang to check on Rodin, she mentioned you would be reopening the hotel."

Arte rested her rucksack against the wall and set the white boutique gift bag next to it. Stuffing her hands into her pockets, she shuffled her feet. "That's the plan," she replied, keeping her tone as upbeat as possible.

She had to keep upbeat. There was nothing about the plan that didn't scream madness, yet it was all she and her sister had. Sophie had suggested selling the hotel; with three children, she could use the money. Being almost five years older, Sophie had already left university and was living with her husband and high school sweetheart, George, by the time their parents died. Arte was just finishing college, though, so she moved in with Gran and then spent the holidays with her during her university years. They were already close, but their unexpected time together only tightened their relationship.

Sophie had given Arte six months to get the hotel up and running again. If she failed, they agreed they would sell it, though 'agreed' was a loaded term. Selling the hotel was not an option for Arte. The hotel was the beating heart of the family, with Gran at its centre. Arte's mum had grown up there, she'd spent a lot of her own childhood visiting, and it had even been her home at the worst point of her life. Beyond her personal attachments to it, it was where the whole family would convene every year for special occasions and for Christmas — well, all Christmases save the one that had just passed.

Arte rolled her shoulders and stretched her back to dislodge any lingering thoughts of the past from her mind before they overwhelmed her.

"Well, I, for one, am glad to have you back in the neighbourhood," Jenny was saying. "Your gran would be ever so pleased you're taking it on and keeping her legacy alive. She was always so proud of you, especially your artistic talents. She was chuffed you were following in her footsteps."

Legacy. The word Arte had used to convince Sophie to let her make a go of running the hotel. She'd never appreciated before how heavy a word it was. It held a weight of expectation, and she had to hope in the future it didn't turn into a weight of burden as she feared it had for her gran.

"As soon as the hotel is up and running, I aim to put some time aside for my work again. Combine the two if I can."

Jenny shifted uncomfortably. "When was the last time you visited the hotel?"

"Last spring."

"Prepare yourself. There may be a little more work than you bargained for. The last time I went up there, it wasn't in the best condition, and it was always… a little dated. Ratings haven't been great of late either, but she was determined to keep going. She was nothing if not a hostess."

Arte's stomach lurched, but she nodded confidently. "I'm expecting to get my hands dirty." She was expecting to get them very dirty. Jenny was right; the place was dated. It had been in dire need of updating for at least twenty years. "What about you? Any plans to retire?" she asked, moving the subject away from the hotel before her stomach knotted entirely.

"I've thought about selling the business. I know I'm getting too old for it, especially carrying sacks of dog food around. My great-grandfather built the house, though, and I don't want to be the one to sell it. Sadly, I've no one to pass it on to."

Arte knew that problem. With no intention of having kids, if she made a success of the hotel, there would only be her niece and nephews to inherit her half.

"Right." Jenny clapped her hands. "Let's fetch Rodin."

Arte followed Jenny across the courtyard to a single-story building. Although the exterior was exactly as she remembered, it was unrecognisable on the inside. A once exposed concrete floor was now tiled throughout with slate. The breeze-blocked kennels with barred doors — which resembled prison cells and had intimidated her as a child — were now tiled with sliding glass doors. As she followed Jenny down the corridor, she peered into them, noticing miniature beds made from metal frames, small televisions, and artwork on the walls. A pair of eyes and a wagging tail stared at her from each of the luxurious rooms she passed.

"You've made a lot of changes since I came here last," she commented.

"I had to up my game. Gone are the days of treating dogs like animals. They are members of the family and require five-star accommodations." Jenny chuckled. "Your gran made the art for me."

Arte flashed her a weak smile. She always felt Gran's artistic talent was wasted, and here it was adorning the walls of dog kennels. The hotel had always been Gran's priority, though. She had referred to it as her canvas, and it had been quite something back in the day. If a guest enquired about one of her paintings, she would offer to sell it to them, then paint a new one to put in its place. Whether it was really enough to satiate her passion for art, Arte had to wonder.

Jenny stopped by a door and opened it. A black Labrador shot out and pounced at Jenny, then noticing Arte, leapt toward her with wild panting.

Arte crouched to greet him; fearful he would knock her over if she remained standing. "Hello, boy! I've missed you," she said, wrapping her arms around his neck and lapping up the affection from the dog. He pressed his cold, wet nose against her ear, sending a shiver through her.

Jenny reached inside the kennel and unhooked a lead from the wall.

"You'll be glad to get back to your own bed, won't you, Rodin?"

At the sound of his name, Rodin approached Jenny and nosed her leg. He sat and looked up at her with his triangular ears poised, waiting for attention. Instead, she hooked the lead onto his collar and passed it to Arte.

"He's all yours now."

Arte took the lead; she was now a dog owner. For the first time in her thirty-eight years, she was responsible for another beating heart; tied to a crazy fluff ball who would look to her to provide exercise, food, entertainment, and love.

Her gran had a black Labrador by her side for as long as Arte could remember, and although she had never owned a dog herself, she knew well enough how to care for them. As long as they had a meal in their belly, a sofa to sleep on, and a good walk each day, they were content. It would be strange to have to consider someone else before she did anything, though. Even something as simple as leaving the house would bring its challenges. She would need to be aware of how long she was gone. When was the last time Rodin went out to do his business? When was she going to be back? Could she take him with her? Would it be too hot, too cold? What if she forgot about him and left him somewhere?

She loosened her scarf, puffing out a breath as she followed Jenny back across the courtyard. It would be fine; they would both get used to the new routine in time.

"How much do I owe you?" Arte asked as they re-entered the office.

"Oh, don't even think about it."

"No, you must let me pay you," Arte insisted. "You've had him almost a month."

Jenny raised her hand. "No, I'm more than happy to have helped a friend in her final hour of need."

Arte didn't feel Jenny left any room for negotiation and, not wishing to appear ungrateful, thanked her for her generosity.

"I'd better be heading off to see what awaits me," Arte said, lifting her rucksack onto her shoulder.

Jenny scooped her car keys off her desk. "Let me run

you over to the hotel. You can't lug all that up the road with Rodin."

"Are you sure? I don't want to put you out."

"I insist, and you're going to need this." Jenny picked up a large book from her desk and handed it to Arte. "It's last year's reservation's diary. I grabbed it when I collected Rodin. There weren't many cancellations to make."

"Thank you." Arte sighed as she placed the diary into the white gift bag and followed Jenny out to the car. "She was always quiet out of season. I'd tried to persuade her to only open for the peak season to save on staffing costs, but she wouldn't hear of it."

"She was fond of her staff. She wouldn't wish to make them redundant during the winter months. They're all locals, you know," Jenny said, opening the back of the Land Rover for Rodin to leap in.

"Yes, some of them came to the funeral," Arte replied, immediately pushing any memories of that day aside.

They drove to the hotel in silence, the only sound coming from an excitable, panting Rodin. As Jenny negotiated the narrow lanes, Arte recalled the multi-coloured tulips that had been in bloom the last time she came, when the air was warmer with the promise of summer to follow. Gran had collected her from the station in town, and they'd spent the weekend celebrating her eightieth birthday and Arte's thirty-eighth. It had struck her then how her gran, who had always been full of energy and zest for life, was starting to slow. Her thoughts had drifted to that weekend many times in the last month; she wondered if she should have done more, visited more often, or returned permanently to help her. Gran was the only family she and Sophie had left; it was their duty to look out for her. Inevitably, you never knew it was too late until it was.

Now the weight of her gran's ashes pressed heavily into her lap. How could a woman, who had influenced Arte's entire life, who was larger than life itself, be reduced to two kilograms of ash? Why the funeral director saw fit to present the bereaved with the ashes of a loved one in a gift bag, she had to wonder. She and her sister had agreed that Gran would have wished to return to the hotel; it was her home from the moment she'd married their grandfather. It was his wedding gift to her, knowing it was her dream to open her own hotel. They had then set about restoring it and converting it.

The familiar wooden sign for Hotel Aloysius came into sight up ahead. One of the wooden posts had rotted so badly the sign was sitting at an angle. She mentally added a new post to her to-do list. As they drove through the tall, wrought iron gates, the hotel came into view. Arte had always hoped one day it would be hers, even if only partly, yet it did nothing to prepare her for the feeling of seeing it for the first time as its owner.

The beautiful Queen Anne building stood with the same grandeur as it had for more than three hundred years. Its symmetry created a pleasing uniformity for the eye. The red-brick walls contrasted with the lighter, carved-stone quoins, and the central, triangular pediment was set perfectly against the hip-tiled roof with its wide eaves, dormers, and tall chimneys. The white sash windows with their small, square glazing were framed in stone.

Growing up, Arte hadn't appreciated how opulent Hotel Aloysius was — it was just her gran and grandfather's home. In her teens, she became interested in art and began looking at things differently, particularly old things. As her appreciation for the building's history grew and she took in its beauty, she realised she never wanted to be without it. Her gran loved the place even more than she did, if that was possible. It was woven into their DNA as much as their shared love of art. Now Arte was going to put her heart and soul into saving it. Hotel Aloysius was not failing on her watch.

Jenny followed the drive around to the left of the circular lawn that lay in front of the house and stopped outside the front door.

"Thank you, Jenny. Not just for the lift but for being here for Gran when I..." Arte stopped as the next word caught in her throat like a fishbone.

A subdued expression played upon Jenny's lips as she nodded. "Good luck. You know where I am if you need anything. Pop down and visit us. Rodin is always welcome to come and play."

Hearing his name, Rodin bounced about in the back, rocking the vehicle.

"Thanks," Arte replied as she stepped down from the old, beaten-up Land Rover.

Retrieving her belongings and Rodin, she waved Jenny off to the sound of loose gravel under rubber tyres.

"Just you and me now, boy," Arte said to the black dog, who was sniffing at the front door.

The pair of brass doorknobs didn't hold the shine they once did. Gran always kept them glistening and the doorstep swept, citing how important first impressions were. As Arte unlocked the door, she realised dull doorknobs were likely to be the least of her problems.

Rodin bolted off into the dimly lit building before the clip of his lead even had time to close. The sound of paws pounding up the wooden staircase resonated and then echoed above her as he ran through the rest of the building, searching for something he would never find.

A musky, wooden smell hit her as she entered; the building was going to need some serious ventilating. Arte shivered as she set her rucksack down on the black-and-white-tiled floor. Opening all the windows and doors in such a frigid winter wasn't something she would relish, but it was unlikely to create a noticeable temperature difference with it being so cold inside. She eyed the old stone fireplace. Unsure of the state of the hotel's central heating, she had a feeling she would be making good use of it.

Keeping a firm grip on Gran, she opened the window shutters on either side of the door to illuminate the reception area. As she placed her keys on a large, white doily on the centre table, a warm tear ran down her cheek. She was hoping to get through the day without tears, even if she knew it was an impossible task. She had thought it would take more than one of her gran's beloved doilies to set her off. Retrieving a tissue from her pocket, she wiped her eyes as Rodin pottered back into the hall, his head and ears down.

She picked up a piece of dusty potpourri from a metal bowl on top of the doily and sniffed it; the scent was long gone. The bowl was her first foray into sculpting during her first year studying art at University College London. The sides of the bowl were in the shape of petals; it was a surprise to see them all still welded together. It was this bowl that had lit the fire in her belly and ultimately driven her across Europe, in the direction of Rome, where she gained a master's in sculpting a few years later.

Rodin flopped down on the rug in front of the fireplace and rested his head on his paws. A soft whine came from him as his eyes drifted over to the reception desk beside the front door. Arte walked over to the Victorian walnut pedestal desk and sat down, placing Gran on top of the red leather inlay. She smiled as her eye caught a small, framed picture she'd drawn as a child. It was a little faded, having sat there for thirty-odd years, but her gran and grandfather were still clear enough to see, standing outside the hotel with a black Labrador between them.

The tear-off desk calendar beside it showed the day before her gran's death. Not wanting to correct it or even look at it, she opened one of the desk drawers and placed it inside. Noticing a reservations diary for the new calendar year she pulled it out. Flicking through the next few weeks, Arte was relieved, yet also concerned, to see there were no bookings at all. The hotel was quieter than it had been in its heyday, but to have no reservations was unusual. Had Gran been ill and not told anyone? She decided to take some comfort that her gran had bought the diary in the first place, so she must have expected to make reservations.

She examined the previous year's reservation diary that Jenny had given her and flicked through it to find only a handful of bookings per week since the summer months. She placed both books into the drawer. It wasn't the time to be thinking about guests, nor would it be until she could carry out a full assessment of the repairs the hotel needed.

Resting her cheek on her fist she surveyed the room, taking in the enormity of the challenge surrounding her and the eerie silence. Where impatience to get started once lay, now sat dread.

The brass reception bell caught her eye, and before she could stop herself, she pressed it. The familiar, high-pitched ding of the bell echoed around the room, searing through her body and transporting her back in time. She sank back in the chair with a sigh. Time had moved on and people with it, but some things never changed. The bell had been there at the beginning of Gran's journey; here it still sat at the beginning of her own. It had picked up some marks over the years, just like the building, just like Gran — and just like Gran, its shine never dulled.

Rodin looked around the room as if expecting Gran to enter. He directed his confused, brown eyes at Arte and then rested his head back on his paws with a whine. Arte rose and went to him. She sat down beside him on the cold tiles, stretched her legs out, and tucked an arm around his furry tummy. He lifted his head and rested it on her legs.

Examining the familiar cracks in the black and white tiles that lay before her, she could hear her mother's voice telling the story of how Arte had taken her first steps across them to the fireplace, determined to reach the black Labrador Leo, who had once lay there.

Rodin let out another low whine.

"I know, boy; I know. I miss her too."

If only she could make Rodin understand that Gran hadn't left either of them willingly. A wave of grief hit her square in the stomach as she imagined what had happened that morning, how scared her gran must have felt at what was happening to her. She wiped her face as tears flooded from her eyes, and she pulled Rodin a little tighter into her side.

"You've got me now, and I've got you, and we'll get this done for her."

CHAPTER 2

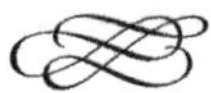

Arte woke the next morning to the sound and sensation of her phone vibrating. The bed was strewn with the piles of paperwork she'd been looking through before falling asleep under the weight of them. A sleeping Rodin lay peacefully beside her.

"Rodin, I told you there was no sleeping on my bed."

He opened a drowsy eye to look at her and then closed it again.

Shifting some papers, she found her phone half wedged under the dog. Her sister's name greeted her on the screen.

"Why are you ringing so early?" Arte groaned down the phone.

"It's not early; it's seven a.m.," Sophie's voice came back. "Five a.m. is early, the time I have to get up."

Arte decided not to rise to the bait and instead rolled her eyes as she often did at Sophie.

"You said you'd call yesterday to let me know you'd arrived," Sophie continued.

"I forgot." That was true; she had.

"Then you didn't answer my text last night."

"I was asleep." A lie. She hadn't been asleep when the text arrived, just too exhausted to get into a text conversation with Sophie about how the hotel was when she hadn't even had a chance to fully assess it.

"Or this morning," Sophie added.

"Again, asleep. Until you just woke me."

"Well, sorry for worrying about you. Annabel, stop hitting your brother!" Sophie hollered.

Arte pulled the phone away from her ear and winced. She rubbed at her face and sat up, waiting for Sophie to return to their conversation.

"So, everything is okay then?"

Unsure how to answer, Arte hummed back. "When was the last time you actually came to the hotel?"

"Last spring, same as you, for your birthdays. Remember?"

"Why not more recently?" Arte asked.

"Because I have three kids. It's different for those with no responsibilities, who swan about in foreign climes."

Arte swallowed her sister's bitterness and refrained from biting back.

"Why? What state is it in? If it's that bad, we should just sell it. You know I could use the money right now. I have a mortgage, kids, universi—"

"Everything's fine; we'll be open in no time." Arte said over her. She'd heard Sophie say all of this a million times since she'd returned from Italy. Feeling the need to slip in some words of reassurance — despite how false they may be — she added, "It's nothing a good clean won't sort. I can make a success of this, Sophie. I just need the time we agreed to."

"I don't have the luxury of time, Arte! My children are growing an inch by the day. I've had to buy both the boys new football boots this week. Despite Archie being two years younger than his brother, his feet decided they had to be exactly the same size. We rely on hand-me-downs," Sophie squawked.

Arte knew this only too well. Most of her childhood wardrobe had consisted of her sister's old clothes, and Sophie had questionable tastes back then. One summer her gran had laughed so hard at what she referred to as Sophie's rags. After that, she made a habit of buying Arte a new outfit each time she visited.

Sophie finally hung up, seemingly satisfied that everything was okay for the moment. Arte took a deep breath, exhausted from their five-minute conversation. She'd stayed with Sophie since returning from Italy and was now on the far reaches of her tolerance level. Having lived alone for so long in the peace and serenity of her small Roman apartment, it felt like a different world at her sister's house — a loud and busy world. Even so, it had been nice to spend time with her niece and nephews, whom she hadn't seen in a while.

The uncomfortable sofa she had slept on sprang to mind, and Arte snuggled down deeper, grateful for a warm, comfortable bed and the knowledge that at least one mattress wouldn't need replacing. That said, it wouldn't matter how comfortable the mattress was if Sophie pulled the rug out from under her. She would need to ensure that wouldn't happen and do her best to keep Sophie onside.

Arte stretched out and considered the shape of her day. One of her first tasks would be to check over Gran's car and see if it started. Then she would need to get herself insured and drive into town to get supplies. Her stomach growled at the thought of food; a bacon roll wouldn't go amiss right then. The ready meal she'd picked up in the small supermarket at the train station barely counted as an evening meal, and she had been too preoccupied with worry to stock up on snacks or think about breakfast.

The second task was to check the heating, though with no guests she could forgo the expense of putting it on. The small, portable radiator she had found had warmed her bedroom well enough, and the rest of the time she would be working and therefore unlikely to need it.

The cold English air came as a shock after the milder Italian winters, especially as Sophie was stringent with the heating during Arte's Christmastime stay. She could still hear Sophie's voice echoing off the tinsel and ornaments, shouting at various family members to put another jumper on if they were cold. It had at least offered a brief period of acclimatising between Italy and the Arctic temperatures inside Hotel Aloysius.

With those tasks complete she would need to focus on the arduous job of formulating and executing a plan. Based on the brief look she'd taken into each room following her arrival, they would all require a full assessment. She had later regretted the quick glance as she lay awake at one a.m., entertaining rotating thoughts of, 'What the fuck am I doing?', and, 'It will be fine; I can do this', whilst combating the memories the rosewater scent in her gran's room had evoked. The bed was unmade, presumably left that way from when Gran had woken that last morning. Arte couldn't look any further; her eyes were full of tears by then. She had grabbed Rodin's bed from beside the door and retreated to her room.

Although the hotel wasn't in a dire state, it was severely neglected and would require an inordinate amount of effort from one pair of hands to get all the work completed by the spring. It was obvious her gran had reduced the number of rooms she was booking out to those on the first floor, but all the rooms would need to be in use eventually if the hotel was going to pay for itself. The three bedrooms in the attic space were clearly being used for storage. The room Arte had always used had fewer things in it, and with the bed clear she decided she would set up camp in there.

Rodin jumped off the bed and walked over to the bedroom door. Realising that lie-ins were not a luxury for dog owners, Arte reluctantly pulled herself from her warm haven and pulled a hoodie over her pyjama top.

"Let's find you some food."

She made her way down the small staircase to the first floor and then down the grand cantilever staircase. Her fingers and thumb nestled into the groove on either side of the smooth, mahogany handrail. There was a time when her hand was too small to fit around it, and she'd simply glide down the top of the well-worn surface. When she was even smaller than that, she was told she would hang on to the spindles for dear life, frightened by the sheer size of the staircase. As she grew older and braver, she would copy Sophie, who would impishly put one leg over the banister and slide down, until one day Gran caught them and told them they would 'do themselves a mischief'. A peaceful, contented expression settled upon her face as she recalled the memories.

Rodin careered down the stairs in front of her, colliding with the kitchen door as he reached the bottom. He nudged at it with his nose and sniffed. As soon as she opened it, he rushed off to a cupboard and pawed at it.

"I guess that's where Gran keeps your food."

Her furry companion inhaled his biscuits whilst Arte filled the kettle. Feeling a cramp coming on in her cold, bare feet, she stepped into a pair of her gran's wellies by the back door. She cursed her lack of foresight to pack some slippers, being rather preoccupied when she got the call and having hurriedly packed her suitcase. She was roughly the same size as her gran, but wellies generally came up larger, and as she wasn't wearing socks, they swamped her. She was grateful for any protection from the cold, tiled floor and pushed away the thought of walking in Gran's shoes — they were always going to be too big to fill.

Arte stepped out into the garden only to be immediately nudged aside by Rodin, who ran off onto the lawn to do his business. Taking a lungful of clean, country air, mixed with a tinge of manure blowing across from the neighbouring farm, it was a world away from city life. Rome was beautiful, but the traffic pollution was at dangerous levels and among the worst in Europe. She wasn't going to miss that. As she exhaled, her breath condensed in the cold air.

She headed back upstairs with a mug of black coffee despite not being a huge fan. Her years in coffee-mad Italy hadn't changed her British tastes, but without any fresh milk — another thing she'd forgotten to pick up — black tea was a big no-no. Her gran always believed in fresh milk in the rooms and despised the little milk portions often used in hotels to save money.

A packet of individually wrapped biscuits was going to have to satisfy her appetite for now, even though they were a month past their 'best before' date. They were nothing compared to Gran's famous shortbread. During Arte's childhood, they were in constant supply, and the hotel would be filled with the smell of freshly baked biscuits. She couldn't recall when Gran had stopped making them and replaced them with the packets.

As she reached the top steps, she skipped the last one automatically, knowing it creaked. Not that it would wake her gran, not anymore. Rodin brushed against her legs as he raced past her on the narrower attic staircase. The realisation that he would never leave her side caused a smile to form on her lips, not the tightening in her stomach she expected.

As she climbed back into bed, she didn't even bother to tell him off when he jumped on beside her. He wouldn't have listened anyway. Her gran had said that Rodin liked a nap after his breakfast. He looked at her with his big, brown eyes and burped. Sniffing out a laugh, she stroked his soft ear, which made him groan with pleasure. Fifteen hours in and they were already a dynamic duo.

Tempted as she was to cuddle into him and go back to sleep, she resisted the urge and instead looked at the paperwork scattered across the duvet. She was doubtful it was going to look any less bleak than last night. The amount of administration that needed to be done on top of all the paperwork for her gran's estate, which Sophie had kindly delegated to her, was unbelievable. Although they were both executors, Sophie had said it would be easier if one of them dealt with everything, then suggested as Arte had nothing else to do, it should be her that did it.

She picked up a pile of unpaid bills, and a wave of nausea washed over her. Every creditor would need phoning today to explain the situation. Hopefully, she would be met with compassion for her situation. It wasn't her fault, and she was going to do her best to sort it out. If only she had known how bad it had gotten, if only Gran had reached out to say she was struggling, if only Arte had noticed she was struggling. Life was full of 'if onlys', and her gran had clearly been hiding her problems.

At this point, she needed a miracle, ideally in the form of a lottery win — if only she bothered to play it.

The faint sound of the reception bell rang out. Rodin leapt from the bed and was out the door in a blink of an eye. Realising she must have forgotten to lock the front door last night, Arte followed, stopping by a mirror for a glance at her dishevelled appearance. Her unexpected guest would have to take her or leave her as she was.

The bell sounded again as she stumbled down the narrow attic staircase. Who on earth could it be at this ridiculous hour? She hoped it wasn't guests looking for a room for the night, or she'd have to turn them away.

A glance from the window overlooking the front of the hotel halted her on the main staircase.

"What the actual—"

The oval drive was packed with people rushing about and odd-looking vehicles. She caught a name on the side of a double-height truck with lots of windows.

"Facilities UK?"

A man wheeled a large, black case along the path below the window, heading for the front door. Arte jumped the last steps two at a time and belted through to reception.

A woman passed her with a clipboard in hand.

"Excuse me," Arte said. "We are closed."

"Yes, I know, for filming," the woman said as she continued past her.

Filming? Filming what and with whose permission? She tried to get the attention of a young man as he passed her carrying what looked like lights. He either didn't see her or ignored her, she wasn't sure which. As more bodies filed into reception with their arms full, she was about ready to burst with rage.

"Will someone please tell me what the hell you're all doing in my hotel!"

It achieved the effect required as everyone froze and turned to look at her. A youngish man, who looked to be in his late-twenties, stepped through the front door and headed straight for her. Dressed in an exquisitely fitted navy suit, with a side parting and quiff in his light brown hair, he looked quite resplendent. Everyone else continued with their business, bringing what appeared to be equipment boxes into the hall.

The man approached her with his arm extended. Arte

responded by folding her arms, so the man dropped his to his side and slapped on a smile.

"Sorry, you should be expecting us. Is Mrs Hardcastle around?" he asked, surveying the room.

"No, she isn't," Arte replied, even more confused now they were asking for her gran. "Can I help you and your... people?"

"We're from the show; we did agree on today. If I could speak to Mrs Hardcastle... She *is* aware of everything."

Arte folded her arms and clenched her jaw. She didn't see why she had to explain to perfect strangers where her gran was. What business was it of theirs? Whoever they were.

"Can you please explain what you are doing in my hotel?"

"Your hotel?" The man's tone changed immediately. "We understood it to be Mrs Hardcastle's."

"I'm her granddaughter; it has been... passed to me. She..." Arte couldn't get the word out.

"I'm so sorry," the man replied, sensing what she couldn't say. Any initial sadness fell from his face as it broke into a smile. "Mrs Hardcastle, she was... not like most people you meet. I only met her once, but I liked her. She was... unique."

Arte couldn't help smiling with him. "Yes, she was."

"I'm Wilf — erm, Fred. Call me Freddie." He offered his hand again. "I'm Charlotte Beaufort's PA, and I help out a bit during filming. I'm an all-round general lackey."

Arte unhooked her arms and took the hand he offered.

"Charlotte Beaufort?"

"Yes." He met her eyes with confusion. "Do you really not know who we are?"

"No."

"*Hotel SOS*. Your grandmother arranged for us to help get the hotel back on track," he elaborated, examining her attire. "Why don't you get dressed, then come and find me? I'll talk you through it all."

Had Gran sent her the miracle she needed?

CHAPTER 3

Charlotte's foot hesitated over the brake pedal as the traffic light she was hurtling towards changed from green to orange. Flicking it to the accelerator pedal instead, she pushed it to the floor, and the car shot through as it changed to red. Already running late thanks to heavy traffic out of the city that morning, she needed to make up time.

She would have stayed in a hotel nearby, but as filming was only a one-hour drive from the city, she'd decided to come from home instead. The avoidance of a subpar hotel and the absence of Gideon — who was abroad on a business trip — had made for a pleasant evening, so pleasant she'd drunk one glass too many of Château Lafite Rothschild and gone to bed far later than she should have. Now all that remained was a dry mouth and a cloudy head threatening to turn into a headache.

Pressing her temples with her thumb and middle finger, relief came in an instant, though it was a pose she couldn't sustain when the satnav instructed her to pull off the main road into what looked like a dirt track towards no-man's-land. Making her way up the narrow lane, she winced as mud spray hit the car. As the lane narrowed further she gritted her teeth, sucking in a long breath at the row of savage brambles scratching the car's paintwork. Not that it mattered; she had staff to sort it.

A rumbling from her stomach reminded her she'd skipped breakfast. Rifling through her handbag on the passenger seat she felt for a packet of Beaufort Hotel complimentary biscuits. She always kept a pack or two in there; someone had to quality-check what was being given to the guests. A flash of blue in the corner of her eye pulled her attention back to the road. Slamming her foot against the brake, she came to an immediate halt, stopping a gnat's nipple short of a blue tractor that had appeared from thin air. Tooting her horn, the farmer gesticulated back and drove off along the lane in front of her.

"Bloody countryside."

Did tractors seriously go this slow, or was the farmer trying to make a point?

After what felt like ten miles but was more likely half a mile, the tractor turned down a farm lane. She pressed the accelerator, and her car careered over a clunky cattle grid, taking her by surprise. She was too busy frowning at the farmer and his farewell finger to have noticed it.

As she rid herself of one encumbrance, her phone rang through the car's audio system bringing her another as the word 'Mother' flashed on the screen. Her automatic internal groan was soon replaced by an adrenaline rush as she realised her mother may have news of the acquisition.

"Hello, Mother," she greeted her.

"Lottie. Where are you? Are you in the car?"

Despite years of asking her mother to refrain from referring to her by her childhood name, nothing had changed — except Charlotte had given up asking. Her mother knew how she felt, so she was clearly ignoring Charlotte's request, and no amount of reminding was going to do anything except tell her mother how much it annoyed her.

"Yes, driving to a location. We start filming at a new hotel today."

"Oh good. Well, I was just calling to let you know our bid was accepted. Contracts are being finalised. Beaufort Hotels has another feather in its hat."

"That's great news. I'll be happy to take on the acquisition from here, you know; free you up and all."

"No. I'll deal with it myself," her mother snapped. "I've worked hard to bring this about; it's too important to get wrong."

Charlotte let out a silent, exasperated breath as her leather gloves tightened around the steering wheel.

"I feel like I'm being underutilised," she replied, forcing herself to keep her tone upbeat, not wanting her mother to realise she'd rattled her. Especially when that was likely her intention.

"You have your little television show to concentrate on. This needs the full attention that only I can give it."

Annoyingly she was right; it would require someone's full attention, but even when she didn't have her 'little' television show — so little that it had earned her several awards for entertainment — there was always an excuse as to why she couldn't be brought onto a project, manage a renovation, or oversee an acquisition.

"What is it this time?" her mother continued.

"An old country hotel," Charlotte answered, wincing as her mother's howls of laughter filled the car.

"Oh Lord, built from timber and wishes, I expect, and no steel in sight."

"No doubt," Charlotte agreed. "I'll try and get into the office after filming finishes tomorrow."

"Don't trouble yourself. I've got to go; the car is here."

"Keep me posted on your progre—" Her mother had hung up. "It's not like I'm the managing director of Beaufort Hotels," Charlotte hissed, smacking the wheel with her palm. "This fucking show." It had been holding her back for years.

Charlotte could appreciate a historic building a little more than her mother, though at a distance and only when someone else was paying for the upkeep. One thing she and her mother did agree on was keeping them off the Beaufort Hotels property portfolio; it didn't make financial sense to have them.

Modern city hotels were better, and the buildings made for reliable long-term investments. The staff tended to be more reliable and easier to come by, the occupancy rate was higher all year round, maintenance costs were lower, and the guests had lower expectations when it came to interior design. The rooms needed to meet a high standard, which Beaufort excelled in, but not individual design like they would in a country hotel. They were essentially cut and paste, which meant furnishings and decor came in bulk at an excellent price. One of her first jobs as managing director had been to renegotiate all the contracts for the interior design team, saving the business thirty-three percent.

It was important to remember she was a hotelier first — or at least the managing director of a hotel empire — not just a television celebrity. It had been far too long since she'd carried out any boots-on-the-ground work or dealt with customers face-to-face who weren't threatening to sue them for one ridiculous reason or another. She missed having interactions with satisfied customers; it gave her a buzz like nothing else.

After graduating from Ecole Hôtelière de Lausanne in Switzerland, the oldest and most prestigious hospitality school in the world, she had spent some of the happiest years of her life running one of her father's new acquisitions, Beaufort Mayfair. He had always believed in her. When she questioned the level of responsibility he was placing in her hands so early on, he had simply replied, "I didn't send you to the top hospitality school in the world to start you off pot washing." If he believed in her, who was she to argue? As it turned out, his instincts were correct, and Beaufort Mayfair rose to the top of Beaufort Hotels. Its turnover and profits increased faster than any other in the company. It seemed hotel management was in her blood.

When her father passed away suddenly, she was moved into the Beaufort Hotels' headquarters in London by her mother, who took over as CEO. It wasn't unexpected. Charlotte had known at some point she would move to HQ. When the time came, however, whilst grieving the loss of her father and mentor, it wasn't a move she felt ready for. She needed familiarity in her surroundings, not a new and challenging environment.

Despite her reservations, within a year, Charlotte had worked her way into a seat on the board of directors. It wasn't until a few years later, after she disagreed with her mother about how a negotiation should be handled, that her mother informed her she had only been given the position to back her up against the all-male board. She'd then gone on to question what use Charlotte was to her if she couldn't even do that. Since then, Charlotte had spent her early career proving her worthiness to the board, who knew full well what her mother did, and why. They certainly had no qualms in telling her so.

Over the years, faces on the board changed, and with fresh blood coming in, she now commanded their full respect. Proving herself to her mother, even at the ripe age of fifty-one, was an ongoing task with ever-moving goalposts. Even becoming a household name wasn't enough to impress her. The production company initially offered the presenting role to her mother, only for her to decline. She claimed it wasn't a suitable role for a CEO, but knowing the exposure of a television show would be good for business, she volunteered Charlotte. Now Charlotte lived in hope that her mother would step down soon and allow her to take over as CEO. Then she could stop presenting *Hotel SOS*.

The car emerged from a dense woodland into an undulating patchwork of fields, hills, and valleys, like a work of art. It couldn't have been a starker contrast to where Charlotte had come from only an hour ago.

A sign for boarding kennels caught her eye, and beside it was a directional sign for Hotel Aloysius.

What hapless hotelier awaits me this time?

CHAPTER 4

After dragging Rodin away from *everyone,* Arte shooed him upstairs to their attic room to dress herself. He launched himself onto the bed and curled into a tight ball. She couldn't blame him; the house was freezing. A search of the bed revealed her phone, which she tapped multiple times before placing it on the bedside table.

"Have you bum-dialled me?" came Sophie's voice through the speaker.

"What the hell is *Hotel SOS*?" Arte asked, shivering as she hooked her bra together.

"It's a reality TV show. Why?"

"They're downstairs setting up."

"That's fast work, even for you."

"Ha," Arte retorted as she hopped around the room, pulling on a pair of knee-length socks, only to fall onto the bed.

"Are we assuming Gran applied to be on the show and didn't tell us? Are things that bad?"

"Yes," Arte admitted with a sigh. She could hardly hide it any longer when a TV show called *Hotel SOS* was literally in reception.

"You said everything was okay" — Sophie paused, apparently to check her watch — "only fifty-seven minutes ago. A lot has happened in fifty-seven minutes."

"Okay, I admit the hotel might not have quite the charm we remember, but it's not falling down."

"That's not as reassuring as you think it is, Arte."

"Gran was obviously hiding the fact she's been struggling from us. I can only guess she didn't want to worry us by asking for help," Arte said, ignoring Sophie and the overwhelming desire to go back in time and be there for her gran.

Sophie hummed her agreement. "I called regularly, and she always sounded fine. Though… the last time I saw her was September for my birthday, and she insisted I meet her away from the hotel. She took me to that new spa hotel in town for lunch. Do you think she was keeping me away so I couldn't see what state the hotel was in?"

"That, and I think she was checking out the competition. Sorry, Soph, I should have been more honest earlier. I was hoping I could sort it out, and I can, I promise."

"You always were like Gran."

Arte would have taken that as a huge compliment, especially coming from her sister, but, this time, perhaps not. Her gran was always honest, but when times were tough, it could make fibbers of even the most virtuous.

"Tell me the worst," Sophie continued.

"The debt," Arte said, lifting the pile of unpaid bills

from the bed. "We both know what little funds Gran had left. If she'd have paid her bills, she would have been forced to close. I guess she was hoping *Hotel SOS* would be a turning point."

"Then we better hope that, too, assuming you're not going to tell them to walk?"

Rodin jumped from the bed. Clearly he hadn't been as asleep as she'd thought, if he'd heard the magic word.

"Language! Rodin's listening."

"Sorry. You need to get down on bended knee and beg for all the help we can get. They usually do some rooms up. See if you can get them to do the drawing room; it was screaming to be modernised in the nineties. Think how much we could save on carpet alone in a room that size."

"Sophie!"

"What?"

"I've literally just said hello. I have no idea about their intentions or anything. I'm not about to start negotiating to save money."

Or am I?

"I better come down soon," Sophie decided. "I'll see when George can babysit."

"Babysit… his own kids? Seriously, Soph?"

"You know what I mean."

She did know, and Sophie meant exactly what she'd said.

"George is obsessed with the show. Or more Charlotte Beaufort, the presenter. She's quite the stunner. She's married to a man, though, so don't go making a fool of yourself and chatting her up."

Arte made a face at the phone as she pulled her

dungarees on. Dating was hardly on her list of priorities at the moment anyway. "How do you know some random woman's marital status?"

"It says it on her Wiki page," Sophie replied. "You should watch an episode; she's quite formidable."

"Formidable. You know there are multiple meanings to that word?"

"You make your own mind up as to which applies to her. Watch some clips on YouTube; they also have reruns on whatever channel airs it. I have to get to my Pilates class. Report back later."

"Enjoy your class." Arte tried not to level any sarcasm in her reply.

With her dungarees clipped over a thick jumper and her beanie pulled over her head to stave off hypothermia, she left her room hoping Rodin wouldn't notice. She'd only got as far as the top of the stairs before she heard scratching on the door. She retraced her steps and let him out. "Good call, boy. It is your house but do try to behave."

Rodin rushed off to bother the nearest person he could find that smelled of food as Arte made her way back into reception in a more decent state than when she left it. The young man, who was now wearing a headset with a microphone, was holding the front door open.

"Ah, there you are. Good, I'm glad you didn't bother doing your own make-up. I'll get one of the girls to sort you out."

Her own make-up? She wouldn't even know where to start. The only times her lips were red was when they were smothered in ketchup.

"Do you have a doorstop?" he continued.

"No, it encourages people to leave it open." Gran always hated draughts. And people who left doors open.

"I'm sorry, I didn't catch your name before." The man strained as he dragged a black equipment case to sit in front of the door.

"Artemisia."

"Artemi—"

"Just call me Arte," she said, making sure to clearly indicate the two syllables: the 'AR' and the 'tee'. She was used to people only making it as far as the 'I' in her name.

"Eccentric parents?"

"You could say that. Wilf — erm, Freddie? Right?" Arte winced, hoping she'd remembered correctly.

"Since we're sharing long and complicated names, I'm Wilfred…Wilf to most people and Freddie to Charlotte and anyone else on the show."

"Okaaay."

"Not my choice," he said, then looked around and lowered his voice before continuing. "I think Wilf might be triggering for her."

A formidable woman with a trigger. Colour me intrigued.

"Let's sit for a moment and I'll run you through everything. Charlotte's on her way."

Arte followed him to the old church pew by the window overlooking the drive, feeling more like a stranger in her own home as more faces appeared in reception and then disappeared into the other rooms.

"So we'll start filming once Charlotte arrives," Freddie began. "We film her arrival, introduce the two of you, and then she'll look around the hotel. We don't need you for that part. Charlotte will then appear to deliberate overnight, but we already have a plan in place for you."

"A plan. Can I see it?"

"In good time… tomorrow. We film it, so we'd rather capture your reaction as it happens."

She had her own plan. What if their plans didn't match her own?

"Then what?" she asked, still confused by what the show was about. She'd seen shows in the States where a team would come in for a few weeks and renovate the place. So far, she hadn't seen so much as a paint tin or a screwdriver waved about.

"We give you guidance to execute the plan. We've booked a couple of filming dates over the coming weeks to tie in with the design team. They make over a bedroom and one other room. Charlotte and the film crew will be here for some of it. A copy of the schedule was emailed over to your grandmother; I'll make sure you get a copy. That all sound okay?"

"I guess." It certainly answered one question: why there were no reservations in the diary for the foreseeable future. "What about permissions? It's a listed building."

"We work on a lot of historic properties. Nothing that needs doing here will require permission; we're only redecorating, not restructuring. We'll peel back a layer, two at the most."

Arte crossed her fingers that an eighteenth-century wallpaper would be hiding behind one of them.

"How do you know what needs doing?" she asked. "Have you been here already?"

"The research team visited a few months ago. They

measured up, took photographs, and gave an assessment of the condition. Then our design team produced their plan."

"What does this Charlotte do?"

Freddie laughed. "She's the presenter. She brings everything together and gives it meaning. She *is* Hotel SOS."

"Did Gran contact the show for help? She didn't mention anything to me or my sister."

"Yes," Freddie replied, seemingly unfazed by all her questions.

"And when did you meet Gran?"

"In the summer. Charlotte sends me as a scout when the production team make the rounds on applications. Your gran had a remarkable spirit about her; I can see you take after her."

Arte's forehead furrowed. "You've just met me."

"And already I can tell. What does that say about you?"

Was the guy trying to chat her up? If he was, he was getting ten out of ten for cheese.

"Did she say why she applied to be on the show?"

Freddie leaned against the back of the church pew and crossed a leg over the other. "She said the hotel was slipping and needed modernising, which was beyond her abilities and vision."

Beyond her vision? Her abilities, perhaps. Gran was the most artistic of all the family; if she could lose her vision, what hope was there for Arte when she got older?

Inhaling a deep breath, the aroma of bacon lit up her senses. Her rumbling stomach reminded her that regardless of this morning's stampede, she still had work to do, and the first job was going to buy groceries.

"I need to go out for supplies. I'm starving, and I haven't had a cup of tea today. I only arrived yesterday, and the cupboards are bare."

A loud voice echoed through the room. "Does anyone know who the owner of this dog is? It's trying to devour the catering van."

"Catering van?" Arte perked up at that. "I thought I could smell bacon. I'm so hungry I thought I was imagining it."

Rodin shook himself loose of the woman holding his collar and bounded over to Arte as if he wanted to tell her all about his exciting time.

Freddie patted Rodin. "Cute dog. You're welcome to help yourself to any meals or drinks you'd like whilst we're here. Just you, though; not him."

"Free food, hot drinks, and you want to fix my hotel? You're like a fairy godmother."

Freddie looked out of the window beside them at the sound of a booming car engine coming around the drive.

"No. She would be your fairy godmother!"

Arte stood up to get a better look at this so-called formidable woman whose arrival had sent every head in reception into a spin. Freddie appeared beside her as she noticed a head of spiralling, ash-brown curls appearing from the car. The woman turned and looked up at the house, her curls bouncing above the shoulder line, sculpting around her neck. Her long, chiselled face held the glow of a light tan, and even at a distance, Arte could see her eyes were the very deepest brown.

Freddie lips curved up. "She's wearing the Vivian Westwood coat I adore. I warned her it would be cold in here."

The long, black, double-breasted jacket reminded Arte of an old police coat.

"Wow! She's…"

"…quite something isn't she?" Freddie finished for her.

Realising she'd said that aloud, she quickly followed it with, "Got a nice car. I was talking about the car." To be fair, the black Bentley Continental was pretty stunning too.

"Yeah, yeah. I believe you. I can spot a fellow rainbow-flag waver when I see one protesting too much." He winked and sprinted off outside.

Arte looked down at the colourful, stripy jumper her gran had knitted her years ago and shrugged. That confirmed he hadn't been hitting on her, and why he'd drooled over a Vivian Westwood.

Her gaze fell back to the figure of Charlotte Beaufort appearing around the side of the car, better pleased with herself than her surroundings, balancing expertly on a pair of heels. Freddie joined her and ushered her to one of the production vans. A sign saying 'Make-up' on the door became visible as he opened it for her.

Sophie had been annoyingly correct about one thing: Charlotte Beaufort was a stunner.

CHAPTER 5

Having spotted the catering van when she arrived, Charlotte headed straight for it the moment she stepped out of the make-up van. She wasn't working on an empty stomach. If the owner was old, she would likely spend the entire day having to shout. As the bacon sizzled on the griddle, she took in the house before her.

Hotel Aloysius had one thing going for it: it was beautiful, but no doubt rotting from the ground up. She would never understand hotel owners who clung to a dream even after it had turned sour. It made no business sense to pile up the debt and let the place disintegrate — literally, sometimes — hoping something would come along to turn it around.

She was sure the show only encouraged them. Why bother making good business decisions when someone would come along and save your incompetent arse when it all went wrong? The number of applications for the show had increased every year since it began. Some of them were genuine cases, of course, due to illness or disagreements over the management in family-run establishments, but most of them were cases of poor management and complacency. She could even believe some of them thought any publicity was good publicity, which was certainly not the case.

Many hoteliers believed the hotel industry was simply a matter of feeding and watering guests, and then changing a few sheets. That couldn't be further from the truth. It was a business, and like all businesses, it needed an effective advertising and marketing strategy, long-term goals and projections, investment, and, most importantly, a competent leader.

The show was about slapping a plaster on a hotel with some interior design, pointing out the faults to the owner, and trying to establish an effective management plan. The latter always fell on deaf ears. It was inevitable when the person wasn't an effective leader or business manager and should have stuck to washing sheets.

She admired her Bentley, only for her face to fall flat. It was in dire need of washing to remove the brown spray up the side of it. That wouldn't happen in the city. Even though it would be tough to bear the filth, there was no sense washing it until filming wrapped. She sighed as she realised she hadn't changed her deep pile floor mats for her all-weather set. Looking down at the catering van, she noticed how clean it was. All the other vehicles were clean too.

A slender woman stepped out from the hotel, admiring the Bentley as she passed it slowly. She was a curious-looking creature in a pair of black dungarees, a bold move for any woman over the age of twenty. Her long, blonde, wavy hair cascaded out from under a beanie and over her shoulders onto a stripy knitted jumper. She didn't recognise her as one of the usual crew. In a pair of dungarees, she could be a member of wardrobe. They often dressed on the eccentric side whilst believing themselves to be at the forefront of the fashion industry.

As the woman neared, Charlotte found the look grew on her; it kind of suited her kooky cuteness and added an element of authenticity to her overall appearance. The way she carried herself with such uninhibited expression served as a reminder to Charlotte of the beauty and strength that comes from embracing one's true identity. She pushed the unhelpful reminder aside, and suddenly aware she was staring, she turned her attention to the server passing her a bacon roll. The woman in the dungarees appeared beside her and ordered the same and a cup of tea.

Charlotte took her in again out of the corner of her eye. She was a fraction shorter than Charlotte's taller-than-average height, but then again, she wasn't wearing heels, just a pair of beaten-up Doc Martens. Her flawlessly sculpted face, smooth skin, and vibrant sky-blue eyes glowed, creating a harmonious symphony of beauty that was hard for Charlotte to ignore.

"Are you a brown sauce or a ketchup woman?" Charlotte asked, as she smothered her bacon in brown sauce and cursed her lack of casual conversation skills.

"Brown, of course."

Her smooth, breezy voice made Charlotte smile. She

passed the woman the bottle of brown sauce as the server offered up a roll to her.

"Good choice." She watched as the woman covered her bacon in sauce and took a bite as if she hadn't eaten for a week. It made Charlotte's smile tighten. "Why are none of the vehicles covered in mud and scratches? I've driven through miles of barren countryside to get here."

"There's another route in from the main road. It's much longer, but the road is wider. There's no farm traffic, so it's cleaner too," the woman replied through her mouthful.

"Bloody satnav, they're a waste of time; as is this place, no doubt." Charlotte sighed as she looked up at the building. "Another shithole of a hotel run down by some incompetent idiot who's failed to invest for years in a historic property. And somehow that's my problem."

Charlotte was expecting a laugh or at least some amusement to reach the woman's lips. Did she not have a sense of humour?

"I'm Charlotte Beaufort, I've not seen you before. Are you a new crew member?" Charlotte asked as she took a sip from her paper cup,

The woman wiped her mouth with a serviette. "No, I'm the owner of this shithole of a hotel. My dead grandmother would be the incompetent idiot who failed to invest in it."

Charlotte choked on her drink and began coughing as the woman marched off.

"Shit."

Why hadn't she started a conversation about the car instead? That would have been a safe topic. She appeared interested in her Bentley, and Charlotte could have spoken at length about it — and probably bored her to death.

That was a reason she didn't chat people up — not that she was chatting this one up she told herself. She could command a lecture theatre or meeting room when she was talking about business, but put her face to face with someone on a social level and her tongue failed her. Social chit-chat wasn't a skill she'd developed when she was younger, not with her mother to do it for her.

The only reason she'd got together with Gideon was because he had done most of the talking at the charity dinner where they first met. It had been held in the Guildhall in London, and her mother had been so delighted to receive an invitation from his family that she took Charlotte along. She later found out her mother's sole intention was to introduce her to the most eligible bachelor in the city.

Their courtship read like a fairy tale, though the only thing she lost was her mind when she agreed to marry him, not a glass slipper. She should have trusted her instincts that wealthy men bought and sold everything. Unfortunately, she realised too late that she, too, had been bought. Not for any financial sum — it wasn't as if her mother needed the money — she had simply been passed as property from one to the other.

Thankfully, she had enough of her mother's blood in her to put her foot down when he insisted she give up work and become a high-society wife. Despite his protestations that she was embarrassing him, and that he would be the laughing stock of the City, she stood firm. She pitied the other wives and made it clear to him that she would continue along her career path until she decided to stop.

Gideon was charming at the beginning, annoyingly so. The repetitive flattery was irritating — Charlotte knew how beautiful she was from all the attention she received from suitors — and the barrage of gifts he sent her she threw in a drawer. After they were married, both stopped. The gifts went first; he'd already bought her, so they were no longer necessary. When he realised she had no intention of giving him children, the flattery stopped too.

The subject of children should have been discussed prior to marriage, though Charlotte had felt it was obvious that if she wasn't giving up her career for him, she wouldn't be giving it up for children either. Meanwhile, Gideon presumed that, as the woman, whose sole purpose in life was to bear children, it went without saying that he expected her to bear his.

Although they remained married, it was in name only. She had agreed to blame their lack of children on a medical issue. It was not so much an agreement, really; Gideon had declared it so, and she was forced to go along with it. Due to their families' status and connections, divorce was not an easy option. Although it wasn't ideal, they agreed to remain legally married until such time as one of them wished to remarry. Not that she hadn't thought about leaving many times over the years since; it was just easier to stay.

Now Gideon slept in a separate bedroom and went about whatever business he wished to undertake, and she did the same. She knew he was seeing other women; as for herself, she preferred to focus on her work. On paper they were married; she and Gideon would attend family and social events together as man and wife; and someone else got to deal with his sexual demands. She saw it as an advantageous position that kept unwanted attention at bay.

She had no wish to take on another man who only wanted a beautiful woman on his arm and massaging his ego. Men didn't do a lot for her anymore anyway, but pursuing any female interests was challenging. Women were difficult to chat up. They would rarely recognise another woman hitting on them and would assume it was just friendliness. You would need to become quite obvious to get the message across, and that wasn't her style.

In the kind of society she frequented, which hadn't progressed much past the nineteenth century, there was no hope of discreet liaisons. Even if a woman was interested in women, they were required to keep up the pretence of a happy home as she was. With most of them being good wives, having plenished their husbands and nannies with multiple children, it wasn't worth the risk to lose it all for a frisson.

She took the last bite of her bacon roll as Freddie appeared beside her.

"There you are. They're waiting for you."

"Let's walk and talk then," Charlotte said, throwing her serviette in the bin. "Why wasn't I informed earlier that the owner wasn't an old woman and instead a woman in her…" How old was the woman she'd just insulted? Younger than she was, that was for sure.

"Sorry, we've only just found out. She'd never heard of the show. She'd never heard of you either." Freddie jogged beside her, trying to keep up with her long stride. "Have you met her then?"

Charlotte's stomach churned at the thought of their encounter and decided not to answer that question. "At least we can use the excuse that she didn't know we were coming for me not to stay... if conditions don't allow. Have we had the figures for the last quarter yet?"

"We're only three days into the new quarter."

"Exactly! Chase them up; a few days is more than enough time."

"You've had an email from Mrs Boughton."

Charlotte groaned. "What now? Would she like me to sign over a hotel to her in payment for the fact she fell down the stairs because she wasn't looking where she was going?"

"No, actually; she's accepted your offer."

"How decent of her. Seven days' full board at a Beaufort Hotel of her choosing. Bloody woman was after a free holiday. Tell Malcolm to make her sign something prior to booking to confirm she won't be going to the press." Charlotte looked up at Hotel Aloysius. "Right, let's get this over with."

CHAPTER 6

Rodin's ears dipped as Arte took the last bite of her bacon roll. Wiping her mouth with the serviette, she stuffed it into her pocket.

"Sorry, boy. You've had your breakfast. I need to eat too."

Rodin looked down at the floor and lolloped off. She was of no use to him now. Movement outside the window caught her eye. Charlotte Beaufort was striding towards the house.

Insufferable woman.

She couldn't believe her initial thought of Charlotte Beaufort had been that she was attractive. Gran always told her never to judge a book by its cover. This was a case in point. Charlotte's pages were littered with rudeness. Opening her up would likely reveal torn pages, dog-eared corners, and tea stains.

Why had she waited for the queue at the food van to go down? If she had gone when Charlotte Beaufort headed into make-up she could have avoided her — and her insult. To top it off, her parched mouth reminded her of the tea she left behind. On the plus side, if it could be referred to as such, at least she didn't have to wait until later to find out what Charlotte was like or what she really thought of the place. How dare she brand Gran an incompetent idiot. She never met her. It was so typical of the rich and famous to pour scorn on those they considered beneath them.

Arte could just make out Charlotte's grey skirt suit. She hadn't noticed it before; she was too distracted being insulted. As Charlotte drew nearer, Arte caught sight of the tightly fitted waistcoat accentuating her large breasts. A throat cleared behind her. It took a second to pull her eyes away. When she did, she regretted it as they fell on something far less appealing — a short, greasy, balding man.

"Hi, I'm the director, Mike. Are you Arte, the new owner?"

"Yes. How did you know?"

Mike's head twitched. "You're the only one I don't recognise."

"Oh, of course."

How embarrassing!

"And Freddie filled me in," he said, suddenly shivering and rubbing his arms.

"Michael." A low, soft growl came from behind them.

Mike turned to find himself under the scrutinising glare of the woman herself.

"Ah, Charlotte, I thought I *felt* your presence," he said dryly, shivering again. "Have you met Arte, the new owner of the hotel? Her grandmother passed away recently."

Arte looked up, ready to meet Charlotte's gaze and soak in the embarrassment she must be feeling, but the glow of Charlotte's deep brown eyes burned straight back into Arte's and remained fixed there. There was no remorse to be found, just an air of arrogance.

Removing a black leather glove, Charlotte extended her hand to Arte. "So I hear. I'm sorry for your loss… Arte."

Okay, so she was going for outright avoidance.

Arte hesitated before reaching out to take it. "Thank you."

They shook hands. Charlotte extracted hers almost immediately, leaving Arte with an uncomfortable urge for more of its warmth and softness, not to mention a need to hear that alluring, posh voice again. She groaned internally at her body's betrayal.

"Freddie, would you show Arte where make-up is?" Mike asked.

"Of course." Freddie held out an arm to show the way.

"I'm fine like this, actually. Thank you."

The curl at the corner of Charlotte's lip didn't escape Arte's notice. Did she disagree?

Mike opened his mouth to speak, only to close it again. Reopening it, an 'ermm' stuttered out, followed by what felt like a snappy 'fine'.

Rodin appeared between them all, whipping his tail against everyone's legs.

"Whose dog is this?" Charlotte cried, stepping backwards as if she'd trodden in something foul.

"He's mine."

"Can he be yours somewhere else?"

Unsure if it was a question or a statement, Arte decided a firm response was necessary. "No, this *is* his home." Arte refrained from adding 'shithole of a home' as Gran's voice gently reminded her, *If you can't say anything nice, don't say anything at all.* Charlotte could have benefited from a few of Gran's words.

"Michael? A word outside, please." Charlotte had already turned on her heels.

"Of course. Can we get the vans off the drive, people? We're shooting the arrival shortly," Mike yelled.

Two men scurried out the front door ahead of them.

"Poor Rodin, the mean lady doesn't like you either," Arte whispered to the dog as she ruffled his ear. "What's her problem with dogs?" she asked Freddie.

He shrugged. "She's just not a fan."

As Charlotte and Mike disappeared out the front door, Arte took the opportunity to disappear herself. She had work to do, regardless of the kerfuffle going on.

"I'd better go and sort the heating out; none of you will be any good to me frozen."

"I'd help, but I'm useless with that sort of thing. My ex was a plumber" — Freddie paused for a moment and then continued, his tone sullen — "so he did all that."

"No worries. I'm sure I'll sort it," Arte assured him, concerned she'd just surfaced something painful for him.

"Take this," Freddie said, extracting a card from his top pocket. "In case I can help with anything else, or you have any questions and need to find me."

"Thanks. I'll send you my number back in case you need me. I'll be hiding until you all leave."

"Good luck with that." He chuckled. "There isn't a crevice Charlotte won't poke her nose in…" He softened his tone before continuing. "…just to warn you."

"Consider me warned," Arte replied, realising she'd need to find a minute to return to her room and give it the once-over. She wouldn't put it past Charlotte to berate its level of tidiness.

Arte flashed him a smile, told Rodin to stay where he was, and headed to the kitchen, now anxiety-ridden about what was required of her. At least the show wasn't live. If she wasn't comfortable with something, they could reshoot, couldn't they?

Housed in a small lean-to extension on the side of the hotel, the boiler house was only accessible from outside. Arte's heart sank as she realised it was the same boiler she knew had been last upgraded in the early nineties. It was well past its time. The glowing orange light gave her some hope; it at least indicated power. She pushed the light in, and the boiler whirred up, only to whirr down again a moment later. The obvious thing to check first was the oil level.

Making her way across to the oil tanks outside, she leaned over the containment wall to check the gauge. Her heart sank as she saw the tank was empty.

Great! More expense I can ill afford.

Raised voices nearby caught her attention. She could just make out Charlotte's perfectly clipped tones.

"…don't care that her grandmother just died…"

Arte strained to listen further as Charlotte continued.

"…it's business as usual."

What was business as usual? And what effect would

Charlotte not caring her grandmother had died have on that?

A sneaky peek around the side of the oil tank brought Mike and Charlotte into sight, making their way around to the front of the hotel. Charlotte looked back, her eyes taking in the hotel and then falling on Arte. After an initial look of confusion, she appeared to send a half smile in Arte's direction. Arte held her breath for a moment and stopped herself from ducking back behind the oil tank. That would look ridiculous, like she'd been caught listening outside the staffroom door at school.

Returning to the boiler house, she spied a tarpaulin covered log pile beside it, and was relieved she could at least make a fire. As for hot water, the immersion heater in the attic cupboard would have to suffice — if it worked!

Whilst outside, she took the opportunity to tackle the next job on the list: giving the car a once-over. Her gran had kept it in the old tithe barn on the grounds, which stood beside a smaller building that was once a dairy. The barn was constructed from oak beams and inlaid with brick, capped off with a tile roof. It pre-dated the main house by a couple of centuries.

As she opened the large central door and stepped inside, light poured in from a hole in the roof. It was in worse condition than she'd remembered, as was Gran's car, which had a number of scrapes and dents along it. The reliable Volvo estate choked into life on the second attempt. Now, she not only needed to get used to driving a car again, after having driven a Vespa for years, but also to driving on the left side of the road.

She took a moment to wander around the large barn, extracting a tired piece of paper from her back pocket as she went. Unfolding it carefully, so as not to add to its small tears and creases, her eyes traced over the faint pencil lines of a rudimentary sketch. The same warm, fuzzy feeling of excitement washed through her as when she'd first drawn out her grand plan for the barn to become a studio, back in her teenage years when she'd first developed her passion for art and sculpture. The addition of windows and glass front doors in the exterior would allow light to flood the dark space.

Inside, she'd laid out a basic floor plan, assigning one end as a work area and adding a mezzanine floor and staircase. She'd taken inspiration for this from art galleries she'd visited with her gran as a child, hopeful that one day she, too, would be able to proudly display and sell her work. At the other end was a seating area and kitchen, where she'd envisaged having a sofa bed and being able to live amongst her work.

The sketch needed some serious updating. It required a more formal plan to be measured out and laid down before the time came — if it ever came. She hadn't appreciated as a child that such a dream would be almost impossible to fulfil, and now as an adult, all she could see was a giant pound sign hanging over it.

Despite how far away it felt from her grasp, she was not giving it up. One day, if the hotel became successful, she could convert the barn, buy new tools, and begin creating again. She'd gifted her electric sculpting tools to some of her students in Italy, knowing they would make effective use of them. Some of the tools were too big to transport anyway, and the smaller ones would require new power sockets. It made no sense to pay to ship them with the rest of her belongings when she would have no time to use them. She needed to focus fully on the task of fixing the hotel — at least for the foreseeable future.

There wasn't a soul in sight when she returned to reception, aside from Rodin. He was lying in front of the fireplace, looking exhausted, reminding her to light the fire. Raised voices outside drew her attention to the window. The crew appeared to be standing around, and cameras were set up on one side of the drive in front of the production vehicles. What on earth were they doing? On the other side, she could see Charlotte's car drive in and pull up outside the front door. Arte pressed her nose against the cold windowpane to get a better look.

"Cut!"

The sound made Arte jump. All faces turned in one direction. Her eyes followed them to find Mike, who was staring and pointing at her. Charlotte appeared from her car and glared at her, too, hands on hips. The impenetrable stare was only broken by Freddie sprinting past the window. He sprang through the front door.

"You're in the shot," he explained. "You need to move."

"Oh, shit. Sorry."

How fucking embarrassing.

Moving away from the window, she caught a glimpse of Charlotte's car reversing back around the drive to the entrance.

"Do I need to be outside?"

"Only if you want to watch. Otherwise, stay away from the windows."

Watch? Watch Charlotte Beaufort give her another death stare. No, thank you.

"Can I go upstairs and work?"

"Yes, bu—"

"Stay away from the windows. Yes, I get it," Arte cut in.

"No. I mean, yes, that, but we'll need you shortly. Nothing big, just to greet Charlotte in reception. They'll take an hour or so to move all the equipment inside and set up."

Freddie placed a hand on her shoulder. The concern she felt at the realisation she was going to be filmed must have spilled out over her face.

"Charlotte's a natural. Go with the flow and follow her lead."

His reassurances did nothing to calm her sudden nerves. She nodded nonetheless and let out a breath. "I've never been on television before."

"You'll be fine; don't overthink it. Imagine it's just you and Charlotte alone, having a conversation."

Given the result of their brief conversations so far, that was little encouragement.

"Text me when I'm needed. I'll work in my room," Arte said, feeling a sudden urge to retreat to safety.

"Good idea."

"Come on, Rodin."

Rodin followed her out of reception and up the stairs to

the halfway landing. She made a quick check out the window before crossing. Charlotte's car was at the top of the drive. Assuming it was all clear, she darted across and up to the safety of her room. She could at least make a start on her extensive list of phone calls. It would be a useful distraction from her impending moment in the spotlight.

CHAPTER 7

Charlotte strode through the front door of the hotel, towards a cameraman set up beside the reception desk. "Today I'm at Hotel Aloysi—"

A sudden flash of movement in the corner of her eye brought her to a stop. Something lifted her skirt, and cold wetness smeared itself across her leg.

"Seriously!"

The pesky black Labrador sat in front of her and stared up, his tongue hanging from one side of his mouth, drool dripping from it.

"Cut!" Mike yelled, the delight on his face showed how much he was enjoying her discomfort.

"Rodin, come here, boy! Sorry," Arte said, scurrying into the room. She dragged him away into a room beside reception and closed the door behind her. Charlotte could still hear her scolding the dog: "You can't go shoving your nose up a pretty lady's skirt, Rodin! It's not cool. Did Gran not teach you any manners?"

Charlotte choked back a chuckle before realising she'd

been referred to as a pretty lady. Of all the words Arte could use to describe her, Charlotte hadn't expected those.

"Let's go again," Mike shouted, two inches from her ear.

Retracing her steps to her start position outside, she waited for the hum to die down and prepared herself for the inevitable call to action from Mike.

"And... action."

Opening the door she entered reception with a feigned expression of delight on her face.

"Today I'm at Hotel Aloysius, meeting another hotelier who's in need of some help from the *Hotel SOS* team."

Reaching the reception desk she tapped the bell, and on cue, Arte appeared from the next room.

"Hello, I'm Charlotte Beaufort," she said, extending her hand as Arte approached her.

There was something in Arte's piercing eyes she hadn't noticed from their formal introduction earlier. Her eyelids had been narrowed at the time, likely because she was pissed at her — and quite rightly. Now, her pupils were dilated like full moons; there was a sincerity to them.

There was a feeling of kindness about her in general, a sweetness even; her shabby hippy appearance exuded a softness she found refreshing. Charlotte was so used to sharp suits and shiny shoes in the office. Her mother's were so pointy at the toes that Charlotte was sure she only wore them to keep members of the board in line. She wouldn't put it past her to weaponise them under the table to get them to agree with her. Charlotte would be surprised if Arte had ever worn a suit in her life and imagined there was a pair of dungarees tucked away in

Arte's wardrobe for every occasion — even bedtime. She moistened her lips to disguise her amusement at the thought.

"Hi, I'm Arte. Welcome to Hotel Aloysius."

Arte took her hand and shook it, holding it a little longer than expected, though it wasn't like Charlotte was letting go either. An unexpected sensation came from the back of her hand as Arte's thumb brushed it. It threw her for a moment as their eyes met in an intense stare. Realising she was supposed to be speaking, she couldn't for the life of her remember what to say.

"Cut!" Mike yelled. "Charlotte, are you with us?"

"Sorry."

What had come over her?

"Let's go again, people," Mike groaned.

A few retakes later, and it was done. Like a mouse, Arte seemed happy to retreat into the shadows. It was for the best; Charlotte didn't need the dungareed distraction making her fluff her words. As Arte reached the doorway Freddie stopped her and gave her a carton of milk, which she thanked him for with an overzealous embrace.

What on earth!

Charlotte stiffened, a slight pang of something — which definitely wasn't jealousy — washing over her. That would be ludicrous, feeling jealousy for a woman she'd hardly shared a Scrabble board's worth of civil words with. If Arte was eyeing Freddie up as a potential love interest, she was going to be disappointed.

Pushing the weird pang aside, she opened the schedule the production manager had sent to her phone and set about finding her way around the hotel. She always gave a place a once-over before they began filming and worked up a script in her head for each room they would film.

A check of the bedrooms revealed peeling wallpaper, mismatched furniture — not only in styles but decades, possibly centuries — faded curtains, and worn carpets. By chance, she happened upon the laundry cupboard. Her heart sank at the sight of faded patterned bedding. There wasn't a single white set in sight. The towels were worse, if that was even possible. A quick feel confirmed her suspicions that they, like the bedding, had been washed a thousand times.

The en-suite bathrooms were dated, too, with dripping taps, and cracked tiles. One was even sporting an avocado toilet, basin, and bath. Her hand shot to her mouth at the sight of a shower curtain; there was likely more microbial life on it than on the toilet seats.

The attic en-suite bedrooms weren't in such a bad state. Being in the eaves there was little vertical space for them to be suffocated by dated wallpaper. Instead, they benefited from an abundance of exposed beams that gave off a romantic feel. One of the rooms was clearly Arte's; the dog bed and what appeared to be a hasty tidy were obvious giveaways. Charlotte chuckled at the lump in the bed — no doubt where the hotelier had shoved everything — but soon felt a quick retreat was in order. She didn't feel comfortable imposing herself in Arte's space.

Bracing herself as she descended the stairs and entered the kitchen, she was surprised to find it fitted out with commercial catering equipment. On closer inspection, though, she found that it was tired, and that some of it could do with being replaced. The rest of it needed a thorough cleaning. It certainly wasn't adequate for catering a dinner service any time soon.

Next to the kitchen, she discovered the dining room, which backed neatly onto reception. Luckily, its walls were covered in the same wood panelling as reception, which had thankfully been left alone. With double doors out onto the garden and a bar in one corner, it appeared to be a more versatile room than just a dining area. The room would be perfectly serviceable for breakfasts, afternoon teas, and evening drinks.

Double doors led her through to the drawing room, which, in contrast, was another wallpapered nightmare suffering from the same problems as the bedrooms. Running the full depth of the house, it had windows on all three sides and patio doors in the centre which led to the side garden. It was a beautiful room full of potential. Charlotte drew a curtain back to let more light in, revealing an original and rather impressive marble fireplace. One thing was definitely proving to be true with this property: history didn't date; sadly everything else did. The carpet was almost threadbare in places, and the furniture needed burning. Beside the fireplace, where the carpet was lifting, revealed what she suspected might lay underneath: original wooden flooring, often a saving grace in every cash-strapped hotel of horrors.

Taking the door on the other side of the fireplace, she found she'd looped back into reception. It was one area of the hotel that was in a better state, even more so with the fire now blazing in the hearth. She'd already spied several problems which would need addressing, though. The mantel was chock full of trinkets, a strange array of ornaments, ceramic pots, and odd bits of metalwork. It ruined what was otherwise a rather beautiful fireplace. They would need to go. The tatty doily and dusty potpourri on the centre table were enough to induce vomiting, not a warm welcome, and on the reception desk sat a small, framed drawing of a man and woman that looked like the work of a child.

None of these items were suitable in a hotel, let alone reception. A threadbare rug lay as a trip hazard, partially covering a beautifully tiled floor. With a few minor changes, Charlotte thought, the room would be warm and welcoming, making it a great asset to the hotel.

What wasn't an asset were the random inspirational quotes dotted around the building. Whether they were for the benefit of the staff or the patrons, she wasn't sure. They certainly didn't fit within a historic hotel. Arte's gran was more than a little baffling in her tastes. Should she be grateful that none of them read, 'Live, Laugh, Love'?

It was a shame there was no framed quote from Bill Gates on his view of hospitality: "Your most unhappy customers are your greatest source of learning." She'd read the reviews of the hotel; it didn't appear that Arte's gran had. She probably couldn't use the internet, or perhaps she believed her inspirational quotes would save her. Charlotte rolled her eyes at herself, hearing a bitterness she so often heard in her mother's voice rippling through her own. She spent too much time with her mother and on the damn show. There was nothing intrinsically wrong with an inspirational quote; some might be true, even if they were cliched.

Life wasn't so easily fixed by a quote, though, was it?

Was that what she was missing from her life? A bit more 'be yourself' and all her problems would be resolved? She inwardly snorted. If only that were possible.

The exterior of the hotel was also lacking. The sign by the entrance needed burning along with the furniture. Not only was it broken, but it hardly created the correct impression of a hotel with the Aloysius's potential calibre. The window frames, although passable, were flaking and would benefit from stripping and repainting. The parts of the roof that were visible appeared to be in one piece and in good condition, although appearances were often deceptive.

Overall, it was an epic amount of work for one grieving person to do alone — if Arte was alone. That seemed to be the case. There was no sign of anyone else about, and she behaved like she had the weight of the world on her shoulders. There was a sadness about her, which was unsurprising if she just lost her gran. Hotel Aloysius would be full of memories for Arte, but the only way the place was going to save itself was by expelling its contents and starting again. Almost everything needed to go. How was she going to explain that to the beanie-headed beauty? She let out a long sigh, knowing there was only one way she could; the way she was contractually obliged to do.

By mid-afternoon, after a few hours of filming various locations around the hotel, Charlotte cradled a steaming paper cup of coffee beside the catering van, desperate for its heat and caffeine. Although her head felt clearer than it had this morning, she was flagging. Filming always took a lot out of her, more so in recent years. She refused to blame her age and instead laid it at the door of disinterest; her heart wasn't in it anymore.

The black dog bounded across the lawn from the front door, chasing after a tennis ball, his owner close behind. Collecting his toy into his mouth, he pottered over in Charlotte's direction. Paying no attention to the catering van, he stopped in front of her and dropped his ball. When she didn't respond, he nudged the ball with his nose, causing it to collide with her black patent leather Vera Wang court shoe.

What is it with this dog? Can it not take a hint?

She didn't want to encourage the animal, but she was aware Arte was observing her, possibly judging her actions. Her phone rang from inside her pocket. Quickly answering it with relief, she walked along a narrow path leading off the drive, only to find the animal following her.

"Charlotte? Are you there?"

Gideon, damn. She should have checked who was calling before answering it.

"Yes."

"Will you be home this evening?"

What Gideon actually meant was, 'Will you be back to make dinner?' It was a rare occurrence that they were home together, but when they were they would share a meal — one she cooked. It allowed them time to update each other on what they were doing so they weren't caught out in social situations, and also to confirm dates of events the other needed to attend. Annoyingly it required them to keep abreast of each other's schedules to some extent. He took more interest in hers than she did his; he was the one who was incapable of feeding himself. She was in no hurry to be fulfilling what he saw as a wifely duty.

"Not out with one of your lady friends this evening?" Charlotte said, knowing full well it would annoy him.

"I've just got off a twelve-hour flight from Thailand," Gideon snapped.

It was more likely he'd been sucked dry in Thailand than he was suffering from jet lag.

"I'm away filming," Charlotte responded sharply, suddenly realising she was wandering into a small, ruined chapel. As she turned to take it all in, she realised the dog was no longer following her.

"You could have said."

"You were away."

"I told you I was coming home today," Gideon growled. "You could have messaged or left a note."

"Why?"

"Why?" he mimicked her indignantly.

"Yes, why?"

His silence pleased her; his change of tone when he finally spoke, less so.

"Because it would have been polite, considerate even, for Christ's sake. I know we don't exactly have a conventional marriage, Charlotte, but we can at least be those things. You don't always have to play the heartless bitch."

Now it was her turn to be silent as his words ate into her, dissolving her confidence.

"You haven't forgotten we are expected at my parents' house this weekend for my father's birthday?"

How could she forget the sheer delight of her in-laws'

company? The thought of sharing a bedroom with Gideon and playing happy families had haunted her for weeks. His parents would spend the weekend as they always did, doting on their grandchildren from Gideon's younger brother whilst repeating what a shame it was that Charlotte couldn't bear children.

"No, how could I forget?" she hissed.

Another awkward silence ensued. Taking it as an opportunity to bring the call to a close, she confirmed she would return tomorrow and hung up.

Leaving the enchanting, ruined chapel, Charlotte retraced her steps to the reception, where she walked in on Freddie and Arte in conversation.

"Well, normally Charlotte stays the night, but as you aren't open…"

Right now, a three-course meal and a bottle of wine, followed by a spa bath and eight-hundred-thread-count Egyptian cotton sheets was in order. Not eight-hundred-wash coarse sheets, a microwave meal, and a dripping tap to encourage her insomnia.

Stepping in to prevent Freddie from digging a hole she couldn't get out of, she approached the pair.

"I won't be staying this evening. We've descended on you unexpectedly, and you're not prepared."

"I can be prepared if you would give me five minutes," Arte replied stiffly, her top lip twitching.

How could she explain that there was no possibility of Hotel Aloysius being prepared to her standards in five minutes? Five months would be pushing it.

"I insist," Arte ground out through clenched teeth.

"So do I. I couldn't possibly put you out." Charlotte turned to Freddie and glared at him.

"They have one room left in the spa hotel in town, the honeymoon suite," he replied.

"Perfect. That settles it then," Charlotte said, her eyes sparkling with a sense of accomplishment.

"No, it doesn't. How is it going to look if you don't stay here?"

"It will look like it is, unfit for human habitation." Catching the shock on Arte's face, she quickly clarified. "Which will make for a better show. A real rags-to-riches story."

The hurt and anger didn't leave Arte's face, though they did leave Charlotte with a bitter taste in her mouth. It wasn't like previous hotel owners hadn't pulled similar faces at her in the past, but somehow this face felt different. She had a feeling it would be staying with her.

CHAPTER 8

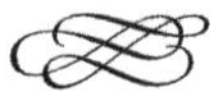

Arte woke rather disorientated the next morning. With one leg hanging off the bed, she couldn't even feel the other.

"Rodin, you bed hogger."

The dog lifted his head and looked at her, allowing her to pull her numb leg from under him.

"Come on. I've got plans for you today, so you don't go sticking your nose in inappropriate places."

Although reluctant to turf Rodin out of his own home and even more reluctant to satisfy Charlotte with his removal, it was for the best. Arte knew she would be on camera for much of the day as Charlotte presented her thoughts and the plan of action, so it would be harder to keep an eye on him.

Thanks to the thoughtful Freddie, she could at least have a cup of tea with milk before they set off. Breakfast would have to wait until she returned. By then the caterers should be on site and she could devour another bacon roll, this time without the insult. They'd kindly donated the leftover chicken jambalaya from the previous day, which she'd enjoyed before turning in for an early night. With only today's filming to get through before they left, she intended to survive off the catering van again until her grocery delivery arrived in the morning. She needed every minute of every day available to work on the hotel, so it was sensible to have everything delivered that could be.

A member of the crew arrived in a white box van as she was locking up. She recognised the boom operator from the previous day. She unlocked the door for him and dragged Rodin from the flowerbed, where he was behaving rather suspiciously.

A walk across the crisp, frosty fields shook out any remaining cobwebs. Seeing Rodin trotting around the fields to investigate all the scents they offered lightened her mood… at least until he plunged face first into a cowpat as they walked through a farm and began gobbling as much of it as he could before she got there to tell him off. She climbed the stile at the bottom of a hill, watching Rodin as he pushed his rounded tummy through a gap in the fence, and crossed the road to the kennels.

"Thanks for taking him for the day," Arte said as Jenny stood to greet her in the warm office.

"That's no problem. I said he's welcome here anytime, and I meant it. I've no spare kennel for him, only a comfy sofa I'm sure he'll like. He can help me with my paperwork today."

"He'll love that. He likes being helpful."

Her mind shot to him shoving his nose up Charlotte's skirt. Amusing as it was, she could see Charlotte was uncomfortable with the dog around. She'd even appeared to fake a phone call to get away from Rodin when he asked her to play ball the previous afternoon. Poor dog, he was only trying to be friendly.

"So you really have *Hotel SOS* up at the hotel?" Jenny said. "I thought I was hearing things when you rang last night."

"They turned up out of the blue yesterday morning. Apparently, Gran was expecting them."

"That woman who presents it is something else," Jenny said, shaking her head with some gusto.

"Charlotte Beaufort."

"That's her. Wouldn't hurt her to be nice. People are down on their luck and need a bit of help, and then she comes along and is rude to them. If she starts on you, make sure you don't take any of her nonsense."

"You can rest assured I won't, but I do need all the help I can get. I've gone through Gran's accounts, and there has been little income over the last year. It's clear she was living off what savings she had. I've managed to put off some of the overdue bills for a little while, but I can't put off paying them forever."

"You pay whoever threatens you with court action first and then whoever shouts at you loudest."

Arte hoped it wouldn't come to court action or a shouting match. The people she'd rung were local suppliers who provided Gran with goods and services over the years; they were sad to hear of her passing. One or two had asked for a payment date, so she'd given them one. Whether she'd be able to stick to those due dates was another matter. The small amount of money Gran had left her and Sophie was still tied up in probate, and with few savings herself, Arte would need to work hard to get the hotel open as soon as possible.

"If I'd have known she was struggling so much, I would have tried to contact you or your sister, but you know what she was like."

Arte nodded. "She was proud of the hotel."

"At least she wasn't too proud to ask for help from somewhere."

"Even from a bunch of strangers?" Arte questioned, feeling the truth like a punch to the stomach.

"I expect she didn't want to worry you girls. You've got your own lives to lead."

That was her gran all over, a minimum-fuss kind of person.

Jenny bent down to pet Rodin and shot back up immediately. "What a whiff, Rodin!"

Arte scrunched her face. "Yeah, sorry about his breath."

"Hmm, cowpat or a cat deposit?"

"Cowpat. Though I wouldn't put it past him having had both this morning; he was sniffing in the flower beds as we left. I'll never understand why they love eating other animal's poo so much yet run a mile from their own as soon as it hits the ground."

"That is one of life's mysteries." Jenny laughed.

Arte gave Rodin's ear a stroke. "It's a good thing you're so cute and forgivable. Well, I'd best be on my way. The crew will be descending shortly. I'll be back for you later, Rodin, I promise. Be good for Jenny."

He tried to follow her until Jenny held him back. Arte could hear him barking for her as she crossed the courtyard and wondered if it was a mistake bringing him to a place where he likely had felt abandoned for some weeks. She joined the road, trying to suppress her guilt. It was important that he realised she would return for him.

The booming of a car engine sounded behind her as she turned the first corner of the narrow lane. Stepping aside into a passing place, she turned to see Charlotte's car coming up the road. It appeared to slow for a minute, so much so, Arte wondered if Charlotte was about to stop and offer her a lift. The answer came as the car shot off up the hill. Arte couldn't stop herself flipping her the finger.

It was a magnificent car, despite the addition of a fresh layer of mud up the side. The driver was less magnificent. Coming via the quicker, muddier route again, it appeared Charlotte valued her time more than the cleanliness of her car. No doubt she would make that someone else's problem.

On her return, the hotel was a hive of activity. Grabbing a cup of tea and a bacon roll from the friendly catering lady on her way past, Arte headed into reception. Charlotte was nowhere in sight. Arte assumed she was with the crew, filming around the hotel or garden. It was tempting to earwig on the filming, but Freddie had said Charlotte would give her assessment today, and Arte didn't need an appetiser before the main event. Although it would bring the advantage of no nasty surprises, it wasn't as if she didn't know what needed doing. A good clean, a bit of redecorating in a few of the rooms, and she would be open for business.

Freddie appeared and sat himself down on the church pew beside her.

"Morning."

"Hi," Arte replied, swallowing her mouthful of breakfast.

"Raring to go?"

"No, but yesterday wasn't as bad as I thought. It doesn't actually feel like you're on camera."

"It's always worse watching yourself back. That makes for Cringe City."

Arte made a mental note to never watch the episode when it aired.

"With so many takes, it kind of distracts you from what's actually going on," she said, catching some brown sauce with her tongue before it dropped onto her lap.

"Yeah, that was unusual," Freddie said, rubbing his chin. "Charlotte never has to retake. I wonder what got to her?"

Arte would never look at television in the same way again after yesterday. It had taken six takes to get the introductions right. Each time they had to make it look like they hadn't been introduced a few hours prior; it was so false. She was relieved the retakes weren't down to her, and Charlotte was the one stumbling over her words.

Suddenly, the woman herself appeared before them like an apparition, looking refreshed, glowing almost, no doubt thanks to her night in the honeymoon suite of the luxurious spa hotel, where she was pampered and waited on hand and foot. Arte pushed the thought of the spa hotel away quickly. It made her want to throw it all in, and as that was never going to happen, it did nothing other than deflate her mood. Positivity and proactivity were required now. This job was going to be an arduous physical task. It didn't need to be mentally draining too.

"Can I take it that the animal has found a more suitable accommodation for the day?" Charlotte asked.

"I dropped *Rodin* at the kennels," Arte replied, looking up at the woman whose presence felt even more domineering from a seated position. "I don't want him to feel unwelcome in his own home. You might have seen me as you passed."

Charlotte stiffened at the remark. "A dog has no place in a hotel. It is a professional work environment and a place for guests, not pet hair and odd smells."

Arte was glad Rodin wasn't there to hear that. What sort of person didn't like dogs? She could understand if a dog had bitten Charlotte in the past, yet she didn't react with fear whenever Rodin was near her. Likewise, she hadn't sneezed, so it wasn't an allergy. She simply appeared intolerant to them — and *shithole hotels*.

"When I open, I will be welcoming dogs just as much as their owners. It's what people expect from country hotels."

Charlotte examined Arte for a moment, opening her mouth to speak only to close it again. She finally said sharply, "They don't, however, expect a host smothered in sauce." She turned on her heel and headed for the front door.

Arte wiped her face with a serviette. She nudged Freddie with her elbow. "You could have said."

Freddie chuckled. "I would have done if I was staring at your face as intently as she was to have noticed."

Arte wanted to ask for clarification — Had she been staring, or *staring* staring? — but what did she care what Charlotte Beaufort thought of her anyway? The sooner she was gone, the better. She could say her piece, send in whoever was helping, and then be done with the woman.

A quick Google of Charlotte before bed had told Arte that she was part of the Beaufort Hotel empire, which owned fifteen hotels dotted around the UK. Not a single one was in the countryside. In fact, every one of them was a modern, cold metal box. Admittedly some of them were architectural masterpieces, and one was the winner of a design award, but they didn't have the heart and soul of Hotel Aloysius. Likely because their owner had none either.

Within the hour, Arte was cleaned up well enough to be presentable for television and found herself sitting opposite Charlotte on the sofa in the drawing room. A fire was blazing in the hearth, and the coffee table between them held a tray with an empty teapot, two cups and saucers — mere props. A shame, as she was gasping for a cuppa to calm her nerves.

Arte hadn't appreciated how much sitting around and waiting there was to do in the name of television; it only encouraged nervousness. In the time they were sat there, as cameras were repositioned and lighting meters thrust in their faces, Charlotte had only managed to aim the briefest of false smiles in her direction.

In an attempt to distract herself, Arte examined Charlotte, who was tapping furiously at her phone. Today she was dressed in a similar style to the previous day but without the waistcoat. A white silk blouse had taken on the job of restraining her assets. She crossed her legs, distracting Arte for a moment with a flash of stockinged inner thigh.

Get a grip.

Arte shifted in her seat and looked away.

"Are you all right?" Charlotte asked, lifting her nose from her phone.

"Perfectly. Thank you," Arte replied, pinning the woman with a stare.

Having spent a lot of time studying eyes, Arte found Charlotte's particularly striking. With the structure of the bones around the eyes considered to have a direct link to their attractiveness, Charlotte's larger orbiture — height and width — was considered to be more attractive than a smaller orbiture.

Realising she was still staring, Arte looked away, only to look back a moment later to see Charlotte's eyes still fixed on her. An odd flutter caught in Arte's chest, and she was grateful for the stern voice that came over the general mutterings in the room.

"Quiet, please."

Arte knew by now this meant they were about to call action. She forced herself to sit up, only to realise it wasn't a position she could hold comfortably, and so she quickly slumped back down again before the camera rolled. Charlotte placed her phone in her jacket pocket and looked over at Arte again, leaving her with that odd fluttering sensation again. What was that?

"And action," Mike's voice came over the perfectly still room.

"So, Arte, I understand you've recently inherited the hotel from your late grandmother."

Arte nodded as she tried to regain her focus to answer. "Yes, my sister and I did. In the last few days, in fact."

"I've had a good look around your… establishment, and sadly it is in a rather poor state of repair. You have only six rooms on offer, assuming you will be taking one. Even at full occupancy, there is a limit to the income this will bring in. Until you can find a reason to charge higher rates, I suggest we start by going back to basics."

Basics. Could she be any more patronising?

"There are ample, decent-quality restaurants in the surrounding towns that can provide your guests with evening meals," Charlotte continued. "There's really no need for you to offer a dinner service. This will help keep your costs down. With a comfortable drawing room and small bar, you could offer guests evening drinks. You could even supplement this with afternoon teas. In fact, it would be best if we moved forward thinking of it more as a bed and breakfast, depending on your abilities to provide breakfast, otherwise guesthouse may be a more accurate description."

Abilities? Is she serious?

Any fool could provide breakfast. Even if it was a simple continental offering. It said 'Hotel Aloysius' at the entrance, didn't it? Even with a broken post and at an angle, it still said that. Was the woman blind? It was a hotel, not some scaled-down version of one. She was glad her gran was ensconced in the wardrobe of her attic room so she didn't have to listen to this.

"Now, let's turn to your bedrooms. The biggest room on the first floor will make a suitable superior suite."

Arte felt her body stiffen at the suggestion. "That's Gran's room." Her reply came out sounding like it came from a whinging, pubescent boy.

Charlotte's face twitched. "Sentimentality has no place in business."

Before Arte could react, let alone get a word of reply in, Charlotte continued.

"All the rooms are in an awful state. The wallpaper is peeling, and the carpets are not only a trip hazard but a biological hazard."

Arte opened her mouth to dispute such an appalling suggestion, only to find nothing came out.

"However, they have the benefit that they are hiding some beautiful wooden floors, which you could utilise to save on the cost of re-carpeting. Every room requires full redecoration and new furniture. Some of it is so old it could be back in fashion… if it were in better condition. We're going for the modern country with a shabby chic feel, but less shabby and more chic. This brings me to the laundry. It will all need replacing with plain white sheets and towels."

Arte clenched her teeth to stop herself from calling the woman a bunch of expletives that would result in a retake or being arrested. Gran had always taught her to ignore bullies, not to feed them.

"Now, the en-suites… these, too, will need to be ripped out and replaced with modern, white suites, ideally with separate showering facilities. Where necessary, shower screens, not curtains are to be used. Curtains harbour bacteria… as you may have noticed."

Was she implying that Arte had noticed and simply ignored it? Her forehead and armpits were beginning to moisten. Charlotte's insinuations were making her blood boil.

"The place has been rather neglected this past month, through no one's fault," Arte slipped in as calmly as she could whilst Charlotte took a breath.

The comment appeared to throw Charlotte off script for a moment. To Arte's annoyance she soon recovered.

"You have a lot of work ahead of you to get it up to the standard required by today's guests. We will assist by transforming the largest bedroom into a superior suite. You can then use it going forward as a template for the rest of the bedrooms. We will also redesign this drawing room. It will make a great asset to your" — catching Arte's fiery eye, she paused before saying — "accommodation."

"Thank you," Arte replied, silencing any disgruntlement she felt at having to appear grateful when the woman had just insulted her *again*. As if the room wasn't already an asset, for fuck's sake.

"Before we do anything, there needs to be an element of decluttering. Then we can move our design team in. I would suggest you start with the reception area; it's no place for doilies or trinkets."

Was she implying that Arte's sculptures were trinkets? The movement of a crew member in the corner of her vision reminded her they were filming and to clench her teeth instead of opening her mouth. This needed doing; there was no way she was sitting through retakes of Charlotte repeating the things she'd said.

"Take down the painting above the fireplace," Charlotte continued, barely drawing breath, "and add a mirror. With the narrow windows, it will help reflect the light and make the room seem bigger, more welcoming. The wood panelling, although a great asset to the room, brings with it an element of darkness. We need to lighten it."

Make it welcoming! Was she suggesting that the entire time Gran had run the hotel it hadn't been welcoming?

The cheek!

"You only get one chance to make a first impression," Charlotte finished, a glimmer of satisfaction dancing in her eyes.

"Trust me, I am well aware of that."

Arte's face must have backed up the sentiment behind her words, as Charlotte pulled herself back a fraction and her eyes widened.

"Start with a thorough clean," Charlotte said, recovering herself.

Arte clenched her teeth. She said she'd only arrived the previous day, hadn't she? Now Charlotte was insinuating on national television that Arte lived in filth. With a deep breath, she tried to muster as much enthusiasm for Charlotte's suggestion as she could.

"It's at the top of my to-do list. I've only been here two days, and you've kept me rather busy." She finished with a flat 'fuck you' smile.

Charlotte shifted uncomfortably in her seat. "Now, let's turn to your brand."

Arte caught herself before the groan that was escaping her lips became audible. She had hoped they were coming to the end of their little 'Charlotte explains how shit everything is' chat.

"Now is a good opportunity to bring a fresh look to the hotel. A new website and a new name should be your priorities. Something that's less of a mouthful. The signage needs modernising to create some element of curb appeal for any passing traffic."

"My gran named the hotel after my grandfather. I'm not changing it."

"Yes, well, we can discuss that when the time comes."

"You can discuss it all you want; the name isn't changing," Arte said, folding her arms and glaring at her.

Charlotte cleared her throat and soldiered on. "As for inside, you need a bit of uniformity to bring everything together. Get some art on the walls and take down the inspirational quotes." She flexed her cheeks up in a forced smile and added, "As cute as they may be."

"Art?" Arte probed, almost growling. *Bring it on.*

"Yes, *art*."

"They already have… *art*."

"This may be a country ho— lodging, but that is not an excuse for being chintzy. Clients expect a certain level of accommodation, more so with a country hotel, and a hotel you are not."

Charlotte's eye twitched, and she looked down. Arte noted a look of what could have been remorse, then realised it was more likely to be wind than remorse when it came to Charlotte Beaufort.

"Annnd cu—"

"Are you for real?" Arte snapped before Mike had even finished wrapping the take. "What the fuck was that?"

Charlotte cast a thoughtful eye over her for a moment; Arte was hopeful there may be an apology on its way.

"I merely express what I see."

Trying to gain control over her anger and her thudding heart, Arte took a deep breath and stretched out her clenched fists. She wanted to make her point and make it clearly, not sound like a crazed, ranting woman. She shifted forward in her seat so she could direct her words towards Charlotte and not the crew, who were busy with their equipment.

Looking directly at her, she hardened her jaw and said, "Those inspirational quotes are there because my gran believed in lifting people up, not knocking them down. You should read some. They might teach you something about working with others and being polite. The general rule is if you don't have anything nice to say, don't say anything at all."

Charlotte's eyebrows rose; she gave no reply. Taking it as an opportunity to air a few more of her grievances, Arte continued.

"You knew I'd only just taken this place on, so why did you try to make out that I'm happily living in some disease-ridden cesspit? You're mean, plain and simple."

She wanted to call her a bitch but refrained. She wasn't lowering herself to Charlotte's level; she could be angry and polite… *ish.*

Presented with yet more silence, she fired again.

"And you really hate art?"

"Is that a question or an observation?"

Arte's narrowed eyes appeared to answer for her as Charlotte continued.

"I don't hate art; I just don't like this" — Charlotte looked around the room — "version of it. Eclectic art is rarely good art. The mixture of styles relies heavily on the eye of the artist to bring everything together. Not all artists can achieve it."

Arte opened her mouth only to find it flapping about like a fish, with no sound coming out. What was it about this damn woman that made her speechless? To her horror, Charlotte had finally found her voice.

"Anything constitutes art these days. You could stick a ten-thousand-pound sign on a dead bumblebee, and someone would buy it. It undermines the whole industry. Wasn't that what Andy Warhol said? 'Art is anything you can get away with'?"

Ouch.

That one she did have a response to.

"You don't believe that the beauty of art is in the eye of the beholder then? Even if you don't like something, surely even *you* can still appreciate it?"

Charlotte's lips tightened. "That's a very romantic notion. Let me guess, are you an 'artist' yourself?"

She wasn't even going to dignify that remark with an answer. Charlotte was clearly baiting her, and she wasn't going to be drawn into an argument over art with someone who had no taste. A change of direction was in order.

"Was it your intention to speak to my gran like that? You know that would have killed her, right? She put her *all* into this place, and she'll continue to live on through it, I'll make sure of it. It might not be what it once was, but you could at least leave her with some dignity now she's dead."

Arte stopped while she still could. Her throat was tightening, talking about her gran, and she could feel herself slipping into an emotional rant.

"Your gran applied for the show knowing exactly what

it entailed. It seems the only person living in ignorance here is you."

"What's that supposed to—"

Freddie appeared behind Charlotte. "You have to take this call."

"Not now, Freddie," Charlotte replied, waving him away with her hand and keeping her eyes fixed on Arte.

Freddie placed the phone in her hand. "Yes, now."

Charlotte finally turned to look at him; something in his expression seemed to force her to lift the phone to her ear. Arte watched as Charlotte listened and her mouth opened with either surprise or shock.

"I understand," were the only words she said before standing, handing the phone back to Freddie, and rushing from the room.

CHAPTER 9

"What's going on?" Arte demanded. Her whole body was itching with rage, and she wasn't finished with Charlotte Beaufort, not by a long shot.

Mike appeared beside Freddie with the same question on his lips.

"Charlotte's had to leave. Family emergency," Freddie informed him.

"We have everything we need from her anyway," Mike said. "We'll need to do some external shots once everyone's cleared off the site. We'll be back in a couple of weeks, as per the schedule, to start work on the larger bedroom, and tackle this room. In the meantime," he told Arte, "I need you to declutter. We're not a clearance service. The design team will send you a list of things that you need to complete before we come next so they can access the space they need to. Ensure Freddie has your contact details."

He was gone before she could reply.

Clearance service.

Cheeky bastard. He was as bad as Charlotte. She had a mind to tell the lot of them to piss off.

"So she won't be back?" Arte asked Freddie. Although she was pleased to see the back of her, she would rather have said her piece. She felt like Charlotte had got off scot-free.

"Not until next time," Freddie confirmed.

"You know, for a moment there I was glad my gran was de—" She couldn't even finish her sentence. "No one has ever made me feel glad someone else was dead until just then, when she decimated my hotel. Sorry, lodgings, guesthouse, bed and bloody breakfast!"

Freddie looked around as the room fell silent. All heads had turned toward Arte.

"You need some fresh air. Let's take a walk," he said, pulling her up off the sofa.

"Rodin. I need to collect him from the kennels now she's gone."

"Okay, let's go," Freddie said.

"Hadn't you better go with your boss?"

"No. She'll ring if she needs me for anything. Grab your coat and I'll meet you outside."

Having retrieved her coat from her room, Arte found Freddie waiting by the catering van, where he was being handed two disposable cups. She coughed as the freezing air filled her lungs.

"Here. Tea, right?"

Arte took the cup between her gloved hands. "Thanks."

"Hopefully it will calm you down a bit."

"Unlikely. How do you work for her?" Arte asked as they made their way down the driveway. "You seem so nice, and she…"

"I only *seem* nice?"

"Sorry, that came out wrong. You know she drove right past me this morning on my way back to the hotel? She didn't even offer me a lift."

"I would guess she didn't want your muddy shoes in her car. I wouldn't take offence."

"She shouldn't come to the countryside if she doesn't like mud," Arte grumbled as her eye caught the broken sign at the entrance. Perhaps it could do with replacing entirely.

"She's okay, you know. Once you get to know her."

"That's a ringing endorsement from someone who had to change their name because of her."

Freddie snorted. "I'm sure she had good reason, and Freddie is still part of my name, you know."

Arte found herself tilting her head to concede the point.

"She's been good to me. She helped me when I needed it… I owe my life to her in a way."

Arte found that hard to believe.

"She's a good sort," Freddie continued, pressing the point as if realising he wasn't convincing anyone. "She can rub people the wrong way sometimes, but that's because she spends too much time with her mother." He stopped and turned to Arte. "Oh, please never repeat that to anyone, ever, especially since she's just had a stroke. Oh Lord," he said faintly. "Karma's going to bite my arse for that."

Arte's jaw dropped. "Her mother had a stroke! No wonder she rushed off like that."

"I'm sure she'll be fine. A nuclear weapon couldn't take Claudette down."

Claudette. With Beaufort as a surname, Arte knew from her travels the family must have roots in France.

She continued down the road, curiosity eating away at her. "Do you mind me asking how Charlotte saved your life?" Freddie's silence made her instantly remorseful. "Sorry, you don't have to answer that. I just can't see how Charlot—"

"Would carry out such an act of kindness?" Freddie smiled gently. "It's not that unbelievable if you really know her."

His tone forced another apology from her. "Sorry, forget I asked."

"It's okay. I can sense I'm in safe hands with you. Remember I mentioned the plumber boyfriend?"

Arte nodded.

"He was the first boyfriend I introduced to my parents when I came out. He was also a lot older. I'd had boyfriends my own age before then and never gelled with any of them. We were only fooling around and experimenting. Johnny I was serious about, and he helped support me in coming out. My parents didn't take it very well, calling it a phase, you know, the usual bullshit. So I introduced them to Johnny to show them I was serious. Big mistake. He was thirty, so they assumed he'd groomed me. It fed into their theory that I couldn't be gay, and I was made to believe I was, by him."

"That's ridiculous."

"They threw me out, so of course, I went and lived with him… I had nowhere else to go."

"How old were you?"

"Eighteen."

"Twelve years." The words slipped from Arte's lips in answer to her mental arithmetic.

"It's a gap that feels wider than it is when you're young. No one bats an eyelid when you're both over thirty."

"Sorry, I didn't mean that to sound judgemental. It's true enough."

"Well, everything was fine for a while… until it wasn't. He, erm…"

Arte placed a hand on his arm. "You don't have to tell me. I don't need you reliving an old trauma to satiate my nosiness." She regretted ever asking him. The last thing she wanted was to upset him so she could judge Charlotte's actions.

"It's okay. It was a long time ago, but it still catches in my throat." He continued after a deep breath. "About a month after I moved in, I was made redundant from my first job. It was only an admin job, but it was important to me. It gave me purpose when I felt like I had none. It was something to focus on other than my parents throwing me out." He kicked a large stone from the centre of the road into the curb. "It also gave me that link to my old life. It was the only bit of continuity I had."

"I can see that," Arte added.

"Anyway, Johnny was earning well enough and suggested I take a bit of time off, look after the house, and take some time for myself. I had every intention of looking for a job. I applied for a few and didn't hear back. I kind of gave up. I didn't need to work as such, so I kept myself busy with the house and cooking for Johnny. I even started organising all his accounts for him. He was self-employed. Great with a spanner, useless with a spreadsheet." A wistful smile tinged with sadness crossed his face briefly. "One day his sister turns up on our doorstep, saying his dad was dead, and they buried him a month ago. The news completely floored him. He was estranged from his family as well and hadn't seen his parents for about eight years. He hoped that one day they would reunite, and to hear that it would never happen really hit him hard."

Freddie paused again. Arte braced herself, feeling something worse was to come.

"That's when he began drinking and became violent. He hit me a couple of times, told me I was useless, and that I did nothing other than sit around all day."

Arte's heart sank at his words. "Could you not leave?" she asked, realising as soon as she said it that life wasn't that simple.

"Every time I tried to leave, Johnny apologised and promised he would do better, only to revert back to being abusive again. I wanted to believe him, I really did. Every time. Leaving wasn't exactly easy either. Like I said, I didn't have anywhere to go. I'd lost touch with old friends. I had no job; I was financially dependent on him. Above everything I wanted to help him; I loved him. It broke my heart to see him like that. Then one night he'd been drinking; it was his dad's birthday. I managed to get him up the stairs, but then as we got to the top, he became difficult and pushed me away. I went flying down the stairs, breaking a few bones on the way. That sobered him up enough to call an ambulance."

Arte's eyes widened. "Was he arrested?"

Freddie shook his head. "I told them I fell. He had enough problems without me adding to them. One nurse took pity on me. I opened up to him. He made me realise I had to leave for my own safety. They got me a place in a shelter. I left everything I owned behind. I only had the clothes I'd gone to the hospital in. I was twenty, living in a shelter, hiding from the man I loved, nursing broken bones and unable to seek refuge with my family."

"Did you not contact them?"

"And have them think they were right all along? No way."

"I'm sorry that happened to you. You had so much to cope with at such an early age. How does Charlotte fit into this?"

"Ah yes, Charlotte. The reason for your interest in my sob story of a life."

Arte opened her mouth to object as he nudged her with his elbow to indicate he was teasing.

"Once I healed, I started applying for jobs. The admin job I'd had was at a hotel, dealing with customers and bookings, the usual stuff. With the experience I'd picked up helping Johnny, I chanced my luck and applied to be Charlotte's PA. I was surprised to get an interview and even more surprised to get the job. I'm sure she took pity on me."

Arte almost spat out a laugh but held her hand to her mouth in time. "Charlotte, taking pity on someone. I'm sorry, but I still find that hard to believe."

"I was honest with her. I told her everything I've told you, and then she did more than give me a job. She gave me a home."

Arte blinked. "A home?"

"Yes, a hotel room, with all meals included, until I got back on my feet."

"Oh... wow... that's, erm..." Arte stopped herself from continuing with her random thoughts until she was able to order them. "She did save you."

"Remember, it is a TV show. Don't judge anyone until you really know them."

Arte knew that; of course she did. But it would be difficult to forgive some of the things Charlotte had said. They hadn't even been filming when they'd first met, and she had insulted her, so any blame apportioned there was thinly spread.

"She said some pretty hurtful things. Did you hear her tell me to throw everything away?"

"Did she? I heard her say that some things weren't suitable for the hotel, and you should declutter."

Arte sucked in a silent breath. What had she said exactly? That it wasn't a hotel. Well, it wasn't at the moment, and Charlotte was right that Arte couldn't afford a chef. With Arte being no culinary master herself, it did look as if bed and breakfast might be a better fit until she could afford one. Charlotte was also right about the condition of the rooms; they had seen better days twenty years ago. The carpets, however, were nowhere near being a biohazard — not quite anyway. As for the brand, there was no way she was changing the name, although the signage could do with replacing rather than fixing up.

Had she been too sensitive? Charlotte had got Arte's back up from the start; it was inevitable that things were only going to go downhill from there. Regardless, there were no excuses for the way Charlotte had phrased everything. That she could have done with a lot more consideration and care, particularly given the circumstances.

Arte stopped, and Freddie turned to her as soon as he realised she wasn't beside him.

"Is she right? Everything she said about the hotel, is it true? Have I been trying to ignore the depth of work that needs doing, hoping I could whack a plaster over it and move on?"

"Who would blame you if you were? Only you can decide if she's right. It's your hotel. When was the last time you visited a hotel that wasn't yours?"

Arte shrugged and strained her brain to recall but was unable to.

"Things change constantly, and standards only get higher. Customers expect and demand more. They also shout about any grievances on the internet, which you might have noticed has also changed things in the industry. Never before has the customer held so much power to destroy a business with a couple of taps on the keyboard."

Arte nodded. She knew what he was getting at. "I saw the reviews."

"Take comfort that the negative ones were only directed at the hotel itself and not your gran's hospitality. They seemed quite delighted with her. I expect a lot of people refrained from leaving a negative review about the condition of the hotel *because* of her. The hotel we can change."

"I can't change Gran not being here, though."

"You are her. The next generation, at least. Continue to do what she did on the personal level, and you'll be fine. You'll be more than fine, you'll thrive, even more so with a rejuvenated hotel."

"Bed and breakfast, you mean," Arte snarked.

"Baby steps, remember? Do you have any idea how much a chef costs these days? Once everything is back up to spec, I'm sure it'll be a hotel in no time. You'll see the standards expected when you stay at one of the Beaufort Hotels."

"What? They expect me to stay in one of her hotels?"

Freddie nodded. "It's part of the show, I'm afraid. I expect it will be Beaufort Mayfair. It's a stunning hotel, the best in the company, and Charlotte's pet. That's where I stayed."

Pet. The thought of Charlotte having a pet anything was laughable. Although a black cat might suit her.

Intrigued yet slightly nervous at the prospect, Arte replied, "I'd better get Rodin booked in for a night at the kennels whilst I'm there then."

A clicking of claws against tiles followed Arte into the drawing room, where they were immediately dulled by carpet. That was going to be the soundtrack to her life now, especially if all the carpets were going to go.

Although a large room, the drawing room had always

been her favourite in the hotel. The draw of cosy sofas surrounding the fireplace in winter was difficult to pass up. She placed the logs she was carrying onto the hearth, hoping they would get her through the rest of the afternoon and evening, and then collapsed onto the sofa with a sudden sinking sensation. Rodin jumped up on the opposite sofa and curled into a ball. If she did have to buy new sofas or if the show supplied them, she was going to have to stop Rodin from helping himself to them.

Her phone vibrated against the wooden coffee table.

"Hi, Soph," she answered.

"How's it going? Have they started ripping it apart yet?"

The word 'ripping' caused Arte to wince. She didn't like the idea of anything going, let alone ripping it out. The carpets, though, would likely cling on for dear life.

"No, I have to declutter apparently."

"Well, you were going to do that anyway, weren't you?"

"Yes, but now I have to do all of it in a few weeks before they return. It's a huge amount of work."

"I'm sure you'll manage it," Sophie replied, some essence of genuine encouragement in her voice.

Arte braced herself for the regular comment of 'you have nothing else to do', but this time Sophie surprised her.

"I'd better try and come down quite soon then."

"Yes, that would be useful. We need to decide what to do with Gran's personal belongings."

"So… tell me all about Charlotte Beaufort. Is she as hot in the flesh as George would like her to be?"

The question caught Arte off guard. "Oh, erm, yes, she's, erm…"

"Wow. She must be quite something if she's got you tongue-tied."

Engaging her brain finally, Arte added, "Yes, she's very beautiful to look at." There was no denying that. "The rest of her leaves a lot to be desired. She's rude, and opinionated, and rude, and downright…"

"Rude? Yes, you said that, and you know that's kind of her M.O."

"What? How could anyone's M.O. be being rude?"

"You have heard of Gordon Ramsay."

"Of course. Is he rude, though, or does he not take any shit? Charlotte was downright rude."

"Have you not watched an episode yet? You should. She's like that with everyone; you're not special. Though don't watch the older ones, she's not really rude in those. It seems to be an art she's perfected over time."

"Okay," Arte replied, intrigued.

"Hold out, yeah? Charlotte Beaufort may be rude, but we'll take her rudeness if she wants to help transform the hotel. Do as she says if you want to make a success of this."

Arte wanted to dispute needing *Charlotte bloody Beaufort* to make a success of it. She didn't need some toffee-nosed rich bitch telling her what to do. She had always planned to make a success of the hotel without her and still could if she chose to — although she wouldn't be able to do it so quickly, nor whilst gaining the hotel some exposure and potentially saving her thousands of pounds.

Arte sighed.

"I'll take that as a yes then," Sophie said. "Sorry, I have to go. I'm out with friends tonight, and I need to get dinner prepared before I go. Speak soon and just remember that it was Gran's idea to call them in. If she was cool with it, then you can be too."

Before Arte could even say goodbye, the line had gone dead.

Sophie's last words sat with her for a minute. They were true enough, and words she was going to have to remember. She hunted down an episode of the show online, choosing one from the first series. She knew what the current Charlotte Beaufort was like; now she wanted to meet the original incarnation.

One episode later and she could see what Sophie had meant. Charlotte wasn't rude in the earlier series; in fact, she was really sympathetic, understanding, and kind. She was completely incomparable to the version Arte had come to know over the last two days. What could have happened over the years to make her change so much?

One episode led to another episode, which led to another. Arte's eyes were drawn on each of the opening titles to Charlotte extracting herself and her long, shapely legs from a tiny sports car. They were distracting. Why did she have to be so infuriatingly attractive?

Skipping through each series, she noticed a change in Charlotte's behaviour around series three. She was still none the wiser as to the cause. Nothing had changed with the show's format. Charlotte had just become a little more forthright and more honest. She'd stopped sugar-coating. The hoteliers didn't even seem to take offence to it, though there were a few tears in some episodes.

Daylight fell to dusk before she realised the time. So much for having her afternoon back to get some work done. Arte picked up her phone to distract herself from the thought of Charlotte Beaufort, her tall, hourglass figure, and her chestnut curls, but without thinking, she found herself googling her. Soon she was flicking through countless images of Charlotte, looking gorgeous in stunning dresses at various events. With every passing picture she could feel herself getting warmer. She fanned herself with her hand.

There was a man on her arm in most of the photos. He was equally as tall, with a full beard and deep-set eyes, but he was no match for Charlotte in looks. Photographs of the pair in their younger years appeared happier and more relaxed. In more recent photographs, with the more familiar-looking Charlotte, the pair seemed distant. Their happy expressions looked forced and hollow, and their body language was just plain awkward. A look on Wikipedia informed her that his name was Gideon Black, a London financier, whatever that was. The page went on to describe the power couple and their successes, various charity donations, and the Beaufort empire. It also told her Charlotte was fifty-one. She didn't look it.

Arte turned her phone screen off and rubbed her eyes. She needed to get that blasted woman out of her head, not drool over pictures of her in revealing dresses on the internet.

CHAPTER 10

The door banged behind Charlotte as she charged down the long corridor, its length appearing to extend the faster she went.

"Eleven, eleven, eleven," she repeated, fearful of forgetting the room number.

Her head flicked from side to side in search of it. Catching sight of a '9' on a door, she slowed her pace and stopped outside its neighbour. With a deep breath, she mentally prepared herself for what awaited her inside and what it would mean for her future.

Opening the door she was greeted by a curtain and the low hum of voices behind it. She pushed it to one side, surprised to see her mother sitting up in bed with her talon extended to her unwavering assistant, Janet, who was rifling through a handbag.

"Sometime today, Janet, if you please."

"Mother, you're…"

"Fine, yes. Janet, I told you not to contact anyone. Why is she here?"

Janet stopped rifling for a moment. "Sorry. The doctors insisted I give them your next of kin."

"And since when do they pay your salary? You answer to me only. What do doctors know of anything?" She slapped her fingers into her palm and extended it again. Janet dove back into the bag, retrieving a brush and placing it into the awaiting hand.

"Mirror!" Claudette demanded with a roll of her eyes.

"What happened?" Charlotte asked. The momentary relief at seeing her mother very much in her usual state had already passed.

"Oh, nothing, I'm fine," Claudette said, looking into the mirror Janet placed in front of her on the overbed table. "It's all a fuss over nothing, and you know how I hate fuss."

"They said on the phone they suspected you had a stroke."

Claudette ordered her long, white pixie cut into place with a few twitches of the brush. "A mini-stroke, not an actual stroke; there is a difference. A clear distinction in the fact that the former is not the latter."

"That's still serious. I should take over the business. It's time I gave up the show so you can step back and take things easy."

"You'll do no such thing!" Claudette screeched.

"You've had a mini-stroke, Mother!"

"If that. I just have a headache, that's all. There's no need for anything to change. I'll take the weekend off, if you insist, and I'll be back at work on Monday."

"You have the Women in Business award ceremony tomorrow night," Janet added quietly.

"Well, that won't do any harm," Claudette mused. "I'm bound to win. It will do wonders for the endorphins."

Charlotte looked to Janet in disbelief, only to be met with the smallest of noncommittal shrugs. She'd find no ally in Janet. She was there to do what her mother demanded, not what she needed. It was surprising she was still her mother's assistant after twenty years. Not only must she have the patience of a saint, but the skin of a rhinoceros. How her nerves weren't in shreds from managing her mother's whims was beyond Charlotte's comprehension. Even when she was in a pleasant mood — which was rare — it wasn't something that came naturally to her.

"A mini-stroke is a warning, Mother, not an inconvenience designed to ruin your weekend plans. Surely you need to stay here for a few days?"

"They've said she needs to stay for twenty-four hours for observation," Janet said softly, "but as she's functioning with no impairment, she's fine to go home after that. They'll refer her to a private specialist going forward."

"Exactly," Claudette added smugly. "If you're going to insist on being here, Lottie, at least make yourself useful and fetch me some bottled water. I'm not drinking this." She jabbed a finger at the jug of water on the table.

"Why don't I go," Janet said, "leave you two to have some time together."

"No! Lottie can go. Take this away."

Charlotte removed the water jug from the table, curbing the temptation to pour it over her mother. As she closed the door behind her, she overheard the words, "She's no use to me. Never has been."

The words seared through Charlotte's body, almost knocking her from her feet. She'd always felt that her mother didn't appreciate her, not just in their work environment but also in their personal life. To hear it directly from her lips, expressed with such coldness, and at such a time when normal families pulled together, it burned. There was nothing normal about her family, and nothing normal about her mother.

Steadying the water jug with her free hand, she walked along the corridor towards what looked like a nurse's station. She smiled weakly at a passing doctor as he did a double take, something she was more than used to. Her thoughts raced through all the moments her mother had said something spiteful or embarrassed her. She remembered them all like they were yesterday, the pain etched into every fibre of her being.

Armed with a bottle of spring water, she returned to her mother's room. The curtain was still pulled across, but between the gaps, she could make out the doctor she'd passed in the corridor.

"It keeps her busy and out of my hair, distracts her from biting at my heels for my job. You know what children are like. Who knew it would become so successful?" Claudette crowed. "Though Michael, the director, is a personal friend. He's worked wonders on it. I've even given him a little direction over the years."

The pride and joy in her mother's voice at being a personal friend to such an odious man made Charlotte nauseous. The anger from all the hurtful things her mother had said over the years came coursing back through her, giving her the urge to finally burst open and say everything that was weighing on her mind.

But she couldn't.

Of all the times she'd willed this strength to come forward, of course it had to come now, when her mother was at her weakest. She would be the worst person on earth if she expressed herself now, tempting as it was to let out years of the hurt and pain her mother had caused her.

With a deep breath, she stepped around the curtain, flashing the bewildered doctor a thin veneer of cheerfulness. "Here we are, Mother," Charlotte said as she opened the bottle of water. Droplets splashed onto a magazine as she poured it into a glass, any attempts at controlling her shaky hand failing.

"Oh, you are clumsy, Lottie. She was always clumsy as a child you know, doctor."

"I have to go now, Mother," Charlotte said as she screwed the lid back on the glass bottle. "As I'm not nee—"

"No, not needed. I'm fine. Janet can help me with anything, should I need it."

Janet flashed her a brief and subdued smile.

"Goodbye, Mother," Charlotte said, turning her back on her.

"Oh, before you go."

Charlotte swept around far too quickly for her own liking. She chastised herself for hoping that this would be some acknowledgement or even, possibly, a thank you.

"Don't tell anyone about this."

Unable to even muster a reply of agreement — What

was the point? It hadn't been a question, more of a demand — Charlotte manoeuvred herself around the curtain to the door.

"Sorry, can I have a quick word before you go?" the doctor asked as he followed her out into the corridor.

Charlotte refrained from saying no or adding that she didn't care. She did care, and it was time she stopped. Her care was unwanted, unnecessary, it seemed, and, most hurtful of all, unrequited.

She'd stayed in an unhappy marriage — no, she'd been *coerced* into a marriage because her mother persuaded her that it was necessary for the family name, and then she'd stayed. All not to disappoint someone who clearly held no respect for her as a businesswoman, much less as her child. What had she done to make herself such a disappointment in her mother's eyes? She'd never put so much as a step out of line. What had it all been for?

As she exited the hospital into the biting air, the doctor's words replayed in her head. A mild stroke occurs before 15 percent of all strokes; up to one in four people who have a mild stroke die within a year; one-third of all people who have a mild stroke then go on to have a more severe stroke within one year. The details of the facts would soon fade; the underlying feeling that her mother would become worse if something didn't change would remain with her. It was enough to make her blood run cold. She steadied herself against a railing, hoping it would stop her head from pounding and spinning enough for her to remember where she had parked the car.

An ambulance zoomed past her, its siren wailing. It was so loud she stepped back instinctively. The sound still resonated in her head long after it had passed, joined by tooting horns on the main road.

Spotting a sign for the car park, she waited at the crossing for the lights to change. A boy racer zoomed past, his bean-can exhaust vibrating loudly and emitting a cloud of smoke around her. By the time she'd crossed the road, coughing up a lungful of smoke along the way, she felt so sick she vomited beside her car as she reached it. It didn't make her feel any better, and why would it? She fumbled for the keys in her handbag, desperate to be in the safety of her car.

She'd always loved the city. Its vibe, its busyness, had always made her feel alive, even part of something. Did the city make her feel alive in a good way? Or was it a place where she could hide, keep busy, and stop herself from focusing on her car crash of a life?

It felt so different to the silence of the countryside she'd been in hours earlier. She could feel the city grasping her around the neck and suffocating her. Her hand reached up to check, but then she felt foolish; of course nothing was there.

A parking ticket attached to the windscreen caught her eye and reminded her she'd been in so much of a rush she hadn't thought to pay for parking.

"Fuck!"

She ripped it off, throwing it into the passenger

footwell as she slid into the driver's seat and slammed the door.

She rested her head against the steering wheel. Taking a deep breath, she leaned back in her seat and let out a scream — a scream she'd been holding inside for years, if not decades. It was aimed at Gideon, Michael, and her fucking mother. What she'd do to be free of all of them, free of the lies and the pretence. She wanted to go back to the beginning and do it all again the way she wanted. Tears ran down her cheeks at how much she hated the reality of her life.

She was the managing director of the most luxurious chain of hotels in the UK, and it meant nothing. She had no real position, no power. She'd been held back from managing yet another acquisition, with the excuse that the show needed to be her priority. All she did in that was crush people. Most people just took it and accepted it as part of the gig. They were in it for some free work and a shove in the right direction, but not Arte. She hadn't asked for any of it; she didn't know who they were or what to expect, and all Charlotte had done was crush her after she'd lost her grandmother.

Fucking Michael.

So much fell into place now that she knew her mother had given him 'direction', as she had called it. Charlotte knew exactly what that direction was and what it had led to. Although it had done wonders for the show over the years, the same couldn't be said for her.

Why had she spent her life being loyal to the wrong people? Not one of them had shown her any respect, and by following their orders, she'd become a monster. She was sure she wasn't one, not deep down. Mean? Absolutely. She couldn't even offer Arte a lift that morning in case she dirtied her interior, and it wasn't as if she would be cleaning it herself. There was no reason for that except meanness, and mean was exactly what Arte had called her. An element of it was required by the show. Normally it didn't bother her, not until the pain on Arte's face earlier that day and the anger in her words had given her a hard slap around the face. She was almost relieved to get the phone call just so she could get away.

Somewhere along the way Charlotte had lost herself, failed to keep herself in check, allowed herself to be weak. She hadn't always been a mean person, and for Arte to be the one to call her out hurt. She didn't care what most people thought of her, but it didn't sit right with her that Arte thought she was that person. Despite her family's appalling taste in art, she seemed like a good and honest person. Probably the most honest, upfront person she'd ever met. She was a force to be reckoned with, and that intrigued Charlotte, leaving her with a hunger to know her better. Even Freddie had seen something in her. The two of them were getting along swimmingly; after two days they were already hugging.

Charlotte couldn't even remember the last time someone had hugged her; her mother made no physical contact with her ever. As for Gideon, he wasn't a hugger, not even early on when their marriage was a pretence of mutual interest. The realisation that she likely hadn't been hugged since her father had died winded her. She'd felt so angry at him for leaving them so soon. For changing everything by leading them into this life in the first place.

They were happy before he decided he wanted to play Monopoly for real. If he hadn't died when he did, she would never have been thrown to Gideon by her mother. She wouldn't have felt the need to shore up her social standing with her husband beside her; Henri Beaufort was powerful and well-respected, and by extension, so, too, was her mother.

The thought of spending the weekend with Gideon's parents made her stomach retch again. She pressed a tissue, moistened with tears, against her lips to stifle the impulse. The rhythmic thumping of her blood pumping began to thunder in her ears as her vision blurred and her chest tightened, leaving her gasping for a breath. Resting her head on the steering wheel again, she took short breaths, trying to calm herself and fix her mind on something pleasant. She couldn't think of anything. Nothing positive. Not one thing in her life.

A vision of Arte in her dungarees, walking towards her across the drive, filled the darkness behind her closed eyes. It brought some relief until she recalled the conversation they'd had after. The weight of her words burdened her with regret. She couldn't even blame the most unforgivable part on a script.

She had to fix it, all of it, before it was too late. She was young, well, sort of. There was still time for her to start again, wasn't there? She knew one thing. She had to try. Drying her eyes and regaining control over her lungs, she began to formulate a plan. She didn't want to go home. With the pick of any hotel room she desired, being alone with her thoughts — which would begin by telling her to open a bottle of wine, then another — was not a good idea.

She could go anywhere, but there was only one place she wanted to go. She needed to be busy, and she needed to be rid of the guilt that was eating at her. A check of her watch told her Gideon was unlikely to be home for a few hours. She started the engine, cracked the window open, and headed home.

After an hour of frantic packing, she placed a large Louis Vuitton holdall onto the passenger seat and climbed back into the car, pleased to have avoided Gideon. What she had to say to him she did not want to say in person.

As she drove through the electric gates, the phone rang, Freddie's name flashed onto the infotainment screen.

"Ah, Fred—"

"How's Claudette?" her PA butted in.

"Oh, she's fine, couldn't be better. Look, I need you to arrange the collection of my belongings from home. Have them taken to Beaufort Mayfair. They're all packed up and by the front door. Immediately, please."

Not that Gideon was one for violence, but she didn't want to risk him holding her belongings hostage. It would be best to have it all done before he returned from work.

"Okay. Are you heading to Mayfair now?"

"No. I'll be in touch when I'm ready."

She hung up and dialled Gideon before she could change her mind as she'd done so many times before. Getting as far as packing bags was a new level of achievement. Now, she just had to say the words.

"I'm divorcing you."

Well. That came out easier than she'd anticipated. Was part of Arte's frankness rubbing off on her?

"What?" Gideon's disbelieving voice came through the car's speakers.

"I'm not sure I can make it any clearer, Gideon. We should have done this long ago; we both know that."

After a moment's silence he said, "What do I tell my parents tomorrow?"

"Well, I'd start with that if I were you. Get it over and done with."

"No one has ever divorced in my family, Charlotte. You know that."

"I don't care, Gideon. I literally don't give two flying fucks about your fucking family. You can tell them that as well if you like, because I don't care." She fought back the tears that were forming in her eyes, though she was pleased to note they were happy tears for a change.

"What if I need to get hold of you?"

"I'll have Freddie send you my solicitor's details."

She hung up. She had nothing further to add and no wish to hear him grovelling for her to spend the rest of her life in a miserable marriage to satisfy his miserable family. They were her past; she was looking to the future now, and she was in the driving seat, quite literally. It was time to make some changes.

CHAPTER 11

Arte sighed as the ding of the reception bell sounded over an episode of *Hotel SOS*. Although burglars wouldn't ring the bell, she really needed to remember to lock the door. Rodin leapt from the sofa, where moments before he had lain snoring, and scratched at the drawing room door. He was unlikely to offer any level of protection against unwanted guests, except a puddle of drool to slow them down. As Arte opened it, he bolted into the adjacent room.

Nothing could have prepared her for the figure standing by the reception desk.

"Charlotte! What are you doing here? They finished filming hours ago."

"Yes, I know," she replied, fidgeting her hands.

Something in her manner prevented Arte from restarting the conversation they had been having when she'd left. Recalling Rodin to her side, in case that was the cause of Charlotte's distress, she asked, "How's your mum?"

"Fine. She's always fine, even when she's not."

There was no good way to respond to that.

"I… erm…" Charlotte stared at Arte with a glazed expression.

"Are you okay? Do you want me to call someone? Fredd—"

"No!" Charlotte snapped, shaking her head. "Thank you," she added, more politely.

The offer seemed to bring her out of her daze, and after an uncomfortable moment of silence, she said, "I'm sorry. I… erm, I don't like the way we left things."

What the hell?

Had Charlotte Beaufort travelled all the way out of the city when her mother had just had a stroke to come and apologise? Not that she had apologised, Arte shouldn't get her hopes up, yet Charlotte was definitely standing in her hotel reception for a reason.

"Would you like to sit down? The fire is on."

Charlotte nodded. "Yes, thank you."

"Go on through," Arte said, dropping into host mode. "I've just opened a bottle of wine. I'll fetch you a glass." The woman looked like she could do with a bottle, not a glass.

Rodin seemed torn between whether to follow Charlotte or his mistress. Realising Arte was heading for the kitchen, his choice became a no-brainer.

Returning to the drawing room, Arte and Rodin found Charlotte seated where she'd been only hours before. Thankfully, the laptop with her face paused on it was facing away from her — that would have been embarrassing. Arte placed the wine glass on the table and shut the lid.

Rodin stared at their guest as if he was in as much disbelief at her presence as Arte was. She was surprised Charlotte hadn't requested he be removed. She was even more surprised when Rodin manoeuvred himself between the table and Charlotte's legs to jump onto the sofa beside her. Since she didn't flinch at the contact, it was unlikely a physical issue she had with dogs.

Charlotte watched Rodin in disbelief. "You let him sit on the furniture?"

"No, Gran did. Have you not heard the phrase 'You can't teach an old dog new tricks'?"

"Hmm, indeed. I'm all too aware of that."

"Don't worry, he won't bite you. Drool on you, yes," Arte said as she filled the glass, scraping around for anything to say to break the awkwardness. When Charlotte didn't reply, she decided to stop the pussyfooting and get straight to the point. "Look, I don't mean to sound rude, Charlotte, but may I ask what are you doing here? We didn't exactly hit it off on a personal level, or on any level in fact, and we are out of hours for the show."

"Let's say I've come to test out the hospitality?" she answered, taking the glass Arte offered her. "Thank you."

Arte watched as she gulped its contents. "Well, I don't think it's quite up to your standard."

The comment seemed to catch Charlotte off guard.

"I may have left you with the wrong impression, which is something else I've come to rectify, if you will allow me."

Arte blinked and remained silent. This she had to hear.

"My mother clearly has no use for me, and I need to be useful somewhere. It might as well be here. God knows you could use the..." Charlotte paused and chewed at her bottom lip before continuing. "I'd like to be here if you'll have me. I'm sure your accommodation will meet my needs."

Arte was sure it wouldn't, yet she was reluctant to turn her away. Charlotte was clearly in distress over something; maybe shock was setting in from rushing off to be with her mum only to find out she was fine. Whatever it was, her manner sparked enough intrigue in Arte to agree to her staying — in good time.

"And if it doesn't? Am I going to find you telling the world about it on television?"

"No. I'd rather we keep my visit between us if you don't mind."

Arte inclined her head in agreement.

Charlotte continued. "I would hope that any feedback I give would be seen as constructive."

"If you can refrain from being rude, it may be."

"I only speak the truth. I haven't said anything that isn't true."

"I understand there will need to be some changes, but you could use a little tact. A lot of tact, in fact!" Arte replied loudly and firmly.

Charlotte's expression moved from shocked to pained, but she remained silent. Arte felt a pang of remorse for raising her voice at her when she'd clearly had a difficult day — not that it excused her behaviour. Arte wasn't one to kick someone when they were down, no matter how angry she might be at them. She softened the blow by following it with an almost playful "Why do I get the feeling you're always right?"

"Because I am," Charlotte replied, a satisfied grin creeping its way onto her lips. "So, have you got a room, or are you going to make me beg?"

The thought of Charlotte begging for anything was something Arte would pay top dollar to see.

"Really?" she asked instead.

"Yes. I'm sorry that we got off on the wrong foot, I truly am. I'm here to make amends. I'm sorry about your grandmother, and for your situation. It must be difficult."

Bloody hell, this evening is full of surprises.

"You're welcome to stay, but I'm pretty sure any room I have won't be up to the standard of a spa hotel's honeymoon suite."

"Well, let's start making it up to standard, shall we? I have the whole weekend free, and you'll be amazed to hear that when it comes to hotels, I like to get my hands dirty."

"Consider me amazed on both counts. Aren't you some kind of busy executive when you're not a television star?"

"Yes. But even busy executives get the weekend off, very occasionally."

"And your mum really doesn't need you?" Arte asked cautiously.

"No. I couldn't be more unwanted if I tried."

That was more of a loaded answer than Arte had expected. She'd got the impression from Freddie that Claudette was a bit of a character, but for Charlotte to feel unwanted… that was something else entirely.

"I'd better open another bottle of wine then." She for sure was going to need it if she was going to have Charlotte for company this weekend.

"That I can help with. I picked a few things up on my way here. I thought it might be rude to turn up empty handed, and the least I can do is make you dinner."

A glint of mischief danced in Arte's eyes. "So you *do* have some grasp on rudeness then."

Charlotte conceded the point with a small nod. "I'll fetch everything from the car."

"I'll meet you in the kitchen," Arte said, following her to the door. "And just to warn you, I've eaten out a lot in Italy. I sincerely hope this meets my standards."

"Hmm… well, I do love a challenge," Charlotte said with a wink as she left the room.

Arte had to steady herself with a hand on the back of the sofa before making her way through to the kitchen. What the hell was that wink?

It was optimistic thinking on Charlotte's part to believe she would be welcomed back to Hotel Aloysius, let alone that Arte would want to have dinner with her or even let her stay. Yet the optimism hadn't been misplaced; she was here, after all, when she could be anywhere else and at a time when she should be with family. Charlotte must have felt worse about her behaviour than Arte could have imagined — or perhaps she was desperate.

Another thought occurred to her then. Maybe Charlotte was just someone who was used to getting what she wanted and didn't expect anyone to say no to her. The anger Arte was desperately trying to contain bubbled up again. She pushed it down; now wasn't the time to air her grievances. She'd ensure there was an opportunity to do so in an adult and civilised manner. At the moment, the thought of a home-cooked meal had her stomach aroused.

Charlotte appeared minutes later with two bags of shopping, which she heaved onto the work surface and proceeded to unpack.

"You bought your own tea?" Arte said with surprise, though she realised almost immediately that it wasn't that surprising. If Twinings wasn't good enough for her, what on earth was she going to say about the bed sheets that were so far away from Egyptian cotton they could be extraterrestrial?

"I watched my assistant give you milk. I wasn't taking any chances on the tea front. Anyway, I don't expect you to keep my favourite. If you kept the right sort of tea, you wouldn't have a need for the milk."

Arte picked up the metal tea tin to examine it. She struggled to hold in a grin as she said, "Oh, you're a tea snob. I didn't see that coming."

"'Connoisseur' is the word I think you are looking for," Charlotte replied with a grin to match.

"'Mariage Frères'," Arte said, reading the name on the side of the tin.

"Perfectly pronounced. You speak French?"

"*Un peu*. Enough to know Beaufort means 'beautiful fortress'." Arte felt herself die inside the moment she finished the sentence. Had she just called Charlotte beautiful? No, there was no way she could interpret it like that. It was a direct translation, not an observation of her unexpected guest.

"And did you know that the French have a longer

history with tea than the British?" Charlotte asked, skilfully moving the subject back onto tea as a subtle rosy hue graced her cheeks.

"I did not know that," Arte replied, only noticing the hint of flirtation in her voice when it was too late.

"It was introduced into France by the Dutch in the seventeenth century, years before it ever arrived in London," Charlotte explained. "It was typically used as a health tonic. It turned out to be nothing more than a fad introduced to court by Louis XIV and it never quite gained the popularity that it did in England."

"You sure know your French history."

"When it comes to tea, I do."

"Can I take that to mean you're not born-and-bred French then?" Arte asked, taking it as an opportunity to do a little nosing.

"No, I was born in Kent. I only ever went to France to visit family. Can I assume you spent time in France?"

"I travelled a lot when I was younger, mainly around Europe. I picked up a little of everything. I'm fluent in Italian, well, almost. I've just moved back from there."

"That explains the healthy tan."

Charlotte had noticed the tone of her skin. She was paying close attention.

"Why were you in Italy?" Charlotte asked as she continued to unpack the shopping bags.

"I taught there."

"Is this where you tell me you're an art teacher?" Charlotte chuckled as she extracted a bag of onions.

"Yes, it is, actually."

The onions slipped from Charlotte's hands; Arte's hand shot out and caught them.

"Are you serious?"

The look of horror on Charlotte's face gave Arte enormous pleasure. "Yes."

"And your name is Arte? Is that short for something?"

"Yes, Artemisia."

"That's… beautiful. Is that after some Greek goddess or something?"

Arte chuckled and tried not to blush. If she'd had a pound every time someone asked that, she would not be worrying about money right now.

"Artemisia Gentileschi was not a Greek goddess, no. She was the daughter of a painter and became a successful artist in her own right. She was the first woman accepted into the Fine Art Academy in Florence. If you think my name is odd, my sister is named after Sofonisba Anguissola. Like Artemisia, she was fortunate enough to have a father that believed in educating his daughter in fine art. She was mentored by Michelangelo and later became a painter in the court of King Philip II of Spain."

Charlotte frowned. "Artistic family or eccentric parents?"

"Both. My gran instilled art into my mother growing up, and then she instilled it into me. My father was an artist, too, so it's in my blood. Although it seems to have skipped Sophie; she's a beauty therapist — well, she was until she had children."

"That still sounds pretty artistic to me. I'm sure your parents must be proud of you for taking over from your grandmother. Wouldn't they rather you had progressed your career as an artist?"

"They might well have preferred it if they were alive. They died when I was a teenager."

"Oh, I'm sorry. That must have been a horrendous experience for you."

"It was, but I still had Gran. I had to come and live here for a short time before I went to university. Then I'd return during the holidays and help her out."

"So, she wasn't just a grandmother but a mother figure too."

"Yes, I guess she was." Arte hadn't quite appreciated that before now.

"It explains your attachment to this place and your passion for art."

Arte nodded, feeling it was an opportunity to air at least one grievance. "You do know that a dead bumblebee represents more than the dead body of a bumblebee. It is art. Its value is only *debatable* for those who intend to buy it and then only established by the market."

"It depends on how you value art."

"There is only one true way to value art, and that's by what it brings to the person looking at it, its meaning. I suspect you see its value in the purchase and resale price." Arte ended her sentence with a harsher tone than she had intended.

Charlotte paused. "There's no need to take things so personally. Just because I don't like your gran's art doesn't mean others don't. It doesn't mean there is no value — either intrinsic or monetary — in it. It means it's not to my taste."

"Why not say that then?" Arte bit back.

Charlotte's silence indicated that Arte had her on that one.

They unpacked the rest of the shopping in silence. Charlotte kept some ingredients to one side, which Arte assumed she was going to cook.

Despite her simmering temper, as Charlotte slipped her suit jacket off, Arte couldn't help admiring the white silk blouse again. They were designed for women with Charlotte's figure. The light reflected off every crease as it curved around her breasts. Complemented by a navy-blue, knee-length skirt, stockings, and heels, it was a look that snatched Arte's breath.

The sound of Charlotte clearing her throat snapped her out of… wherever she was heading to with that image.

"Here," Arte said, rushing towards the kitchen door and nearly falling over Rodin, who was right behind her. She unhooked her gran's apron from off the back of it and passed it to Charlotte. "I'm thinking you don't want to get that blouse dirty."

Nice save.

"Thank you," Charlotte said, placing it over her head with a knowing grin.

Maybe not.

"Let me tie that for you."

Why did I say that? She's capable of tying her own fucking apron.

"Thank you." Charlotte turned her back to Arte.

Arte stepped forward, suddenly aware it was the closest they'd been to one another. She was so close she could smell a hint of musk perfume, now light after dissipating throughout the day. The evening was a perfect time to enjoy the fragrance of perfume, when a woman's natural scent blended with it to make a unique aroma.

Picking up the cotton ribbons, she tied them loosely so as not to touch Charlotte, then let the bow fall onto the top of her curvaceous backside. Before she could stop herself, she lifted Charlotte's curls out from under the cotton neck strap and began adjusting the metal clip. She noticed goose pimples appearing on the pale skin of Charlotte's neck, and Arte wondered if the room was colder than she realised.

"Are you done?" Charlotte asked, turning around, leaving only millimetres between them.

Stepping back, a little more than flustered, Arte replied, "Yep. What's for dinner?"

Charlotte swept her hair into a ponytail and secured it with a band from around her wrist. Arte was so distracted at how gorgeous Charlotte looked with her hair up, she didn't even hear the answer.

CHAPTER 12

Arte entered the kitchen the following morning to find the washing-up drying on the draining board. The aroma of the previous night's meal still hung in the air, causing her stomach to cry out for even more of Charlotte's delicious food.

Although Charlotte was nowhere to be seen, her car was still outside. As she made herself a much-needed cup of tea, she discovered that the kettle was already hot. Not that she had expected her to do a runner after pleading so hard to stay, Arte mused as Rodin scoffed the food in his bowl.

She hoped Charlotte had had a comfortable night; having suggested the room she knew had the best mattress, she couldn't have done more to ensure she would. She'd even let Charlotte pick out her own sheets and duvet from the laundry cupboard. It amused Arte to watch her sifting through them to find the least horrendous of the bunch. They were still bad, as Charlotte had insinuated. She must have really been desperate to stay if she was going to tolerate them.

Nothing further had been discussed over dinner as to why she was there, so Arte decided to steer clear of the topic and try to enjoy the evening. They had conversed congenially whilst they ate, discussing places in Europe they had visited. Charlotte had told her a little about her time in Switzerland at what she boasted was the best hotel school in the world. She spoke with such pride about her education that it made Arte wonder why on earth she was a television presenter; it couldn't allow time for running hotels.

After they had decided to call it a night, she convinced herself there was still time to watch a few more episodes of *Hotel SOS* in bed, the earlier ones at least; they were preferable. She was becoming quite addicted to the satisfaction a good hotel transformation could bring. She was sure it had nothing to do with watching Charlotte tour a bevy of hotels in exquisite, form-fitting outfits.

She followed Rodin outside into the brisk air, armed with a mug of Charlotte's tea — which admittedly was rather nice. Something immediately caught the dog's attention, and he was away. Arte finally discovered him again, ball in mouth, following Charlotte as she paced back and forth in front of the hotel.

Charlotte was dressed in a pair of dark blue jeans that were perfectly sculpted to her muscular legs. They were complimented by a thick, plum jumper, making her quite the contrast to the corporate Charlotte Arte was used to seeing. Her face, normally softened by her smooth curls, was hardened by tight, damp curls. Holding a mug in one hand she was speaking into a mobile held in the other.

Arte stepped back into the coverage of a bush so as not to intrude on her conversation. Charlotte neared her, rooting her to the spot.

"I want nothing from him; he can keep the house. It was never mine anyway. Have the paperwork sent to Beaufort Mayfair. I will be living there for the foreseeable future."

Rodin must have caught Arte's scent, as he bounded over, forcing her to walk out casually and not appear as if she had been earwigging from behind a bush.

Charlotte acknowledged her with a nod and then turned away. "I've got to go now. Thank you."

Arte watched as Charlotte placed the phone in her back pocket. Her shoulders lifted and then drooped.

"Everything okay?" Arte asked, aware Charlotte had just declared she was moving to a hotel. With paperwork involved, it sounded like she was getting divorced.

Charlotte turned to face her. She opened her mouth to speak only to be drowned out by the sound of two skip lorries coming down the drive, wheels crushing into the gravel.

"I didn't order these; they must have the wrong address," Arte said when they finally came to a stop. "I couldn't afford one, let alone two. I'd best tell them."

Charlotte grabbed her shoulder to prevent her from marching over to the first driver, who was hopping out of his vehicle. "Consider it payment for my weekend stay."

Arte gawked. "You ordered these? That's a generous payment, especially for my rooms."

"Call it part of my apology too," Charlotte said, squeezing Arte's shoulder before removing her hand.

"Thank you, for your apology and your skips," Arte said.

Fine creases appeared at the corners of Charlotte's eyes when she smiled in acknowledgment, and Arte realised for the first time just how big, and beautiful, her smile was.

"Tell me, how did you intend on clearing out without skips?" she asked.

"I was going to use Gran's car and take things to the recycling centre." That was a teeny lie; her intention was to hide everything in the old tithe barn until she'd decided what to do with it all, making it appear as if she was conforming to the show's requests. That was going to be a challenge with skips on the drive and Charlotte Beaufort at her side for the next two days.

With the lorries relieved of their skips and despatched it was time to get on with the day, which had started the same way since the day she'd moved in.

"Would you like to join me for a dog walk?"

Rodin bounded across the lawn, his ears pricked at their corners having heard the magic word. He was keen, but the twitching on Charlotte's face said she was less so.

The twitching slowed, and she smiled, a little too forcefully, and replied, "Sure."

"There are some wellies you can borrow. Gran always kept some spare for unprepared guests. I'm sure you'll find something in your size. Be sure to check them for spiders first."

Charlotte shuddered.

"Would you like me to check them for you?" Arte teased.

"Are you mocking me?"

"Not at all," Arte replied, holding the laughter back as much as she could. "Do they not have spiders in the city?"

Charlotte pulled her lips to one side and narrowed her eyes by way of reply.

"Sorry." Arte chuckled, unable to withhold it any longer. She hooked a thumb back at the front door. "So, wellies, or are you going to traipse around the fields in your trainers?"

"I'll risk my trainers. I can't stand wellies; they always rub, and I have no need for blisters."

"Suit yourself. I'm putting some on."

A klaxon rang out from Charlotte's pocket. She retrieved her phone, glanced at it, and stuffed it back where it came from.

"You're not going to answer it?" Arte asked, intrigued to know to whom Charlotte would assign such a ringtone.

"Clearly not," Charlotte answered, sweeping past her. "Let's get this walk over and done with. We have much work to do."

Arte caught up to her and followed her inside.

"Thank you for dinner last night. It was definitely up to standard."

"I'm delighted you approve."

"I haven't had such nice food since I left Italy. Sophie's cooking is…"

"Sophie?" Charlotte stopped and turned, causing Arte to have to do a quick bit of manoeuvring to avoid walking into her.

"My sister. I stayed with her until Gran's funeral."

"Ah. Yes, of course, Sofonisba."

Ah? Why did that sound like an 'ah' of relief? Who had she thought Sophie was? A friend? A girlfriend? There was no way Charlotte could know Arte was a lesbian. Unless Freddie had said something to her, though it wasn't as if he knew for sure; he had insinuated that he knew, but she hadn't confirmed it. And even if Charlotte had worked it out, why would she care if Sophie was a girlfriend? Unless...

No, not even possible.

Charlotte was married to a man. *Married to a man and moving into a hotel for the foreseeable future,* a little voice teased. Arte shut that train of thought down before it could leave the station. That still meant nothing.

"So you think you're cut out to run this place?" Charlotte asked as they walked down the drive five minutes later. "You know it's more than a full-time job."

"Gran managed it."

"Did she? My being here is proof she didn't. Helping out in the holidays is a bit different to running a place like this single-handedly in your—"

"I'm thirty-eight and quite capable of running a hotel... or *whatever* it becomes."

"I see you have come around to my way of thinking."

Arte gave Charlotte a slight nudge with her shoulder. "There's no need to gloat."

Charlotte gave her a nudge back as they stopped by a stile leading into a field. "Not gloating; simply pleased we are making progress."

Rodin careered off into the open space as soon as Arte let him off the lead.

"Is your sister not interested in running it with you?" Charlotte asked.

"No, she'd rather we sold it, and she's too busy…" Arte couldn't complete the sentence. She had no idea what kept Sophie busy other than a routine of exercise classes and lunches with friends. Perhaps letting the cleaner in and out of the house kept her schedule tied up.

"Does she work?"

"No. Her husband, George, has a job in finance."

"Why does she want to sell then? Does she need the money?"

"Apparently. I don't expect she's any different to anyone else who has a bit of money in that they never have enough to keep up with their neighbours and friends. They spend most of their time trying to outdo each other with the latest car, which they don't own anyway, and earning bragging rights by sending their kids to the best schools that they can't afford."

"And you don't want to sell the hotel because it's beneath her to get a job and she wants to keep up with the Joneses."

"Well, I wouldn't say that, but yes, exactly that," Arte said, catching Charlotte's eye and smiling.

The klaxon sounded from Charlotte's coat pocket again, and again she proceeded to ignore it. Once it had stopped she said, "Why does the countryside have to be so silent? It's unnerving."

"It's not silent. You're drowning it out with your

inappropriate footwear and an annoying ringtone you are clearly ignoring." Arte stopped, one eye on Rodin, who was sniffing a bush further up the field. She took hold of Charlotte's forearm. "Stand still for a moment and listen."

Arte prayed Mother Nature wouldn't let her down. The middle of winter was not a great time to listen to the wondrous noises it would offer in the spring and summer, but soon, a rustling came from the undergrowth beside them. Arte gripped her companion's arm. Charlotte seemed more amused by Arte's response to what they were hearing than what they were hearing itself.

Arte leaned toward her, grateful Charlotte was wearing shoes that didn't require her to rise up on tiptoe to whisper in her ear. "The countryside is alive and thronging, just quietly. Sometimes you have to stop to hear it. It also has the advantage of less light pollution when you want to stare up at the stars."

A chorus of twittering came from the hedgerow as a sparrow flew onto a branch, looked in their direction, then hopped along and disappeared into the shrub. Arte caught Charlotte's eye and, realising she was so close she could hear her steady breathing, stepped back in a fluster.

"Less air pollution is always useful when you want to live those few extra years," she added, resuming her normal volume. "What do you dislike about the countryside?"

"I don't dislike it. Not everything is black and white. I don't find it very convenient, that's all."

"Convenient?" Arte laughed. "What convenience do you require from the countryside?"

"It's miles from anywhere useful. There are fewer shops and amenities. "

"I'm surprised you noticed. Don't you have Freddie to fetch everything your heart desires?"

Charlotte ignored the dig. "It's filthy, smelly, and this mud is too much to bear," she groaned, pulling at her foot to retrieve it from the soft earth she'd sunk into since they'd been stationary. Grabbing hold of Arte's shoulder for balance, she added angrily, "Have you brought me through the muddiest field you could find as punishment for not accepting your offer of spider-ridden wellies?"

"As much as I would love to admit to such trickery, I can't. This is nature in all her glory."

Rodin ran towards them just as Charlotte extracted herself from the mud.

"I take it you're a self-professed city woman then?" Arte asked as they continued on.

"Well, I find the city more—"

"Convenient?"

"Yes," Charlotte replied. "Convenient."

"It must be annoying then when the show takes you out into the sticks."

"I bear it as best I can," Charlotte said. "I understand you'd never seen the show or heard of me before we arrived."

"Correct. I've seen a couple of episodes... very recently," Arte confirmed, refraining from admitting she'd spent the previous day watching as many as she could. "You give quite the performance, much like you did with me yesterday."

"It is a performance. It's not me," Charlotte added, a tone of desperation seeping into her usually eloquent voice. "Not the real me. The show made me change — well, act…" She thought for a moment and then settled on, "No, change is right," with a defeated sigh.

Arte shook her head at Charlotte's sudden declaration. "Are you saying this… icy exterior is fake? You're not really a bitch?"

Charlotte's eyes widened as her mouth formed an O shape. "Bitch?"

Arte regretted her word choice immediately.

"That's a strong word. I speak the truth without the bubble wrap. It may come across as a little mean, I admit."

"A little mean! Have you conveniently forgotten what you said when we met? That felt bitchy, and you weren't even on camera. That was all you."

Charlotte's shoulders dropped as quickly as her eyes rolled. "I… I was trying to impress you."

Arte stopped and took Charlotte in. "Impress me?"

"Yes."

"But you didn't know who I was. Why were you trying to—" The penny dropped, and rather than brushing over what she thought Charlotte might be trying to say, Arte's mouth opened and words spilled out. "Oh… like, *impress* me."

Charlotte's darting eyes in every direction but towards Arte, answered for her.

Seriously!

Arte wrinkled her face. "You seriously need to work on impressing people. Anyway, I thought you were married… to a *man*."

"A person," Charlotte corrected her. "Their gender doesn't define my sexuality."

Was this some kind of random proposition? There was a lot there to unpack, but it didn't feel appropriate to dig deeper at the moment, especially when Charlotte was already steering the conversation back around to where it had started as well.

"Please believe that it's not me," she continued.

"I believe you."

Relief swept across Charlotte's face, her eyes turning almost glossy. "You do? Why?"

"Because you're here. The woman who was here before wouldn't have come back and apologised for what she said, she would have meant it. So the only conclusion is you're not that woman. Well, that is, unless you just needed a bed for the weekend. You seem to be running from something."

"I am not running! Do I look like someone who goes around apologising in an attempt to get a bed when I have thousands at my disposal?"

"Fair point," Arte conceded.

It begged the question, though: Why did it mean so much to Charlotte that Arte believed her?

"It does leave me wondering why you say things you don't mean," Arte ventured. "You strike me as a strong, independent woman."

"Michael suggested — well, he did more than suggest, if I'm honest — that I approach the problems with a little less sympathy. Ratings were slipping. He said if we were going to save the show, something had to be done, and I couldn't have the show fail. I needed it to be a success, so I went along with it. I didn't say anything that wasn't true. It's my job to paint a stark reality. It is reality television. What I should have seen as a character, a role to perform, I kind of allowed to take control of me. I think we all have this mean-spirited part of ourselves hidden deep within us that can get a little out of control if we allow it."

That was true enough. Too often people mixed with the wrong sort and would undergo complete personality transplants.

Charlotte continued to press her point. "When you're at the top of a male-dominated industry, you need all the help you can get. I admit it has gotten a little out of hand on the show. Someone should have been keeping it in check."

"Why didn't you refuse? Say no, that you didn't want to be part of that?"

"No one says no to Michael; I wasn't as strong then as I am now. It was such a gradual change that I barely noticed it over time. Michael would ask me to say things, and I guess in some way… I was groomed. He was clever about how he got what he wanted. I thought being meaner might impress my mother, but I've since realised it may have all been at her suggestion anyway. She and Michael go way back."

"Why would being mean impress your mum?"

Charlotte laughed. "To people like my mother, it's not mean. It's showing knowledge and power."

"Can't you do that in a way that doesn't come across as mean?"

"I'd like to; I was. At least, I hoped I was early on."

Arte bent over to pick up the ball Rodin had dropped at her feet; she caught Charlotte's eye as she threw it. "Yeah, you were."

Charlotte startled. "I thought you'd only watched one or two."

"Okay, I've watched a few… series."

A corner of Charlotte's mouth lifted. "Fast work indeed. Anyway, it doesn't matter what I want; the ratings are all that matters."

"And do you still need the show to be a success?"

A silence followed until Charlotte finally said, "I'm beginning to wonder that myself."

Rodin returned, dropped the ball at Charlotte's feet, then sat and looked up at her. Arte bent down to pick it up only to find Charlotte had beat her to it.

"You were impressive when you said no to Michael about the make-up," Charlotte said, throwing the ball. "I think you broke him."

Rodin sprinted off after it.

Arte's face fell in surprise. "I thought you were mocking me."

A look of disbelief crossed Charlotte's as she turned to Arte. "Seriously?"

"You smiled."

Charlotte's hand reached out and settled on Arte's arm. "*With* you, Arte. Never at you."

Arte sucked in a breath at the gesture of solidarity she had completely mistaken for a sneer.

"I have tried to push back," Charlotte added. "Like when you overheard me talking to Michael."

"You said you didn't care that my grandmother had died."

"You thought I didn't care?" Charlotte's grip on her arm tightened. "I was angry at Michael. He told me I couldn't go softer on you because of it; he wanted business as usual."

"Oh," Arte whispered, realising she'd grossly misinterpreted the conversation she'd overheard. Had she completely misread everything about that day?

Realising she was still holding Arte's arm, Charlotte let go. "So, no make-up? I wish I could make such a stand. Not all of us can be as naturally pretty as you."

Choosing to wash over the compliment, not knowing quite how to deal with it, Arte said, "My face is my face. If someone doesn't like it, then they shouldn't look at it. I don't see why I should change it. 'Love who you are,' that's what Gran always said."

Charlotte's lips simmered with amusement. "I know. It's in a frame in my room."

"Okay, you were right. They do need to go," Arte relented.

"Your gran sounds like she was a wise woman."

"The wisest." Contentment settled on Arte's face at the thought.

"Despite her questionable taste in how she shared her wisdom."

"Yes, I think you've made your point." Arte nudged her shoulder playfully against Charlotte's. "We should head back. I have a grocery delivery coming soon."

"Stocking up on milk to ruin your tea with?"

"I'm not even going to dignify that with an answer,"

Arte said, head held high as she climbed back up the hill ahead of Charlotte.

"Probably best. Save your energy for throwing things in a skip."

Arte knew what that meant. It was time to tackle Gran's room.

CHAPTER 13

Arte's hand hovered over the doorknob of her gran's room. If she grasped it, she'd need to turn it, and turning it meant opening the door. Then she'd have to see inside again, see everything as her gran had left it. Smell her gran's familiar scent of rosewater again.

The welcome weight of a hand pressed into her shoulder and squeezed. A tingling sensation swept through her body. Although it was a pleasant feeling, it did nothing to strengthen her already weak knees.

"Are you okay?" Charlotte asked.

Arte nodded, determined to keep any tears in check. She was not crying in front of this woman. "I'm not sure I can do this."

"Why don't you tackle it another day?"

Arte shook her head and swallowed. "If not now, then when? I can't put it off. It's top of the interior designer's list, and it's not exactly going to get easier, is it?"

Charlotte's only response was another light squeeze of

her shoulder, which resulted in the same pleasant, but distracting, feeling.

Focus, damn it.

"I've only been in to grab Rodin's bed. I'm not sure what I was expecting. Everything's as it was that morning."

Arte turned to face Charlotte, causing her hand to slip. Instead of letting it drop completely, she held it against Arte's upper arm and gave it a soothing rub — so soothing, in fact, that Arte had to use all her strength not to bury herself in Charlotte's arms and ask her to hold her. She sensed Charlotte wasn't a natural hugger and wouldn't appreciate it.

"Would you like me to go in and strip the bed?" Charlotte asked. "Tidy up a bit?"

Arte felt her mouth gape open at the unexpected gesture and quickly closed it; it would take the edge off, certainly. "Would you mind?"

"Not at all. You go find some boxes."

"Thank you."

Charlotte patted her arm, flashed her a sympathetic smile, and disappeared into the room as Arte backed away down the corridor. Charlotte was full of surprises, kind ones at that. When Arte returned, precariously balancing a number of boxes and a roll of black bin bags, she found the bedroom door open.

She stood in the doorway and took it all in as natural light filled the room. The mattress was stripped, the duvet folded at the foot of the bed with pillows on top. It had been years since she'd been into Gran's room properly, but in that time, it hadn't changed a bit. All the photographs were in the same places as she remembered. A large, framed, black-and-white portrait of her gran and grandfather on their wedding day sat in pride of place on the bureau. A smaller, sepia photograph of Gran with her siblings, who had all passed away long before she had, sat beside it.

"I'm sorry if the show has made you deal with this sooner than you would have liked," Charlotte said, spotting her in the doorway.

"It's okay. Out with the old, in with the new, and all that. A fresh start," Arte said, hoping she might even convince herself.

Rodin brushed past her legs and curled up in a ball where his bed used to be. If he could do it, then so could she. With a deep breath, she stepped over the threshold and placed the boxes on the bed. Looking around at the mismatched art on the walls, the ornaments, even the wilting, brown-about-the-edges peace lily that had sat on the windowsill since forever, made the room feel like it was waiting for Gran to walk straight back into it.

A framed print beside the door caught her attention. She took it off the wall and passed it to Charlotte. "Here; you should have this."

"'Always be a little kinder than necessary'," Charlotte read aloud. "Is that a hint?"

"It's more than a hint. It's a demand," Arte said, picking up the roll of black bin bags and tearing one off. "If we're going to be friends, you'll need to live and breathe it."

Arte clocked Charlotte's reaction as she shook open the bag. A smile had crept across the woman's lips, a smile which Arte could sense she was fighting to keep hidden.

"Okay, I'll see what I can do. Sounds like a lot of work. This friendship better be worth it."

"It will be," Arte replied, biting her lips to hide her delight at Charlotte's reaction. "Right, time to throw things away. Where to start?"

"I didn't tell you to throw it away. Just because it doesn't belong here doesn't mean it belongs in the bin. Only rubbish belongs in the bin."

"We should start with those then," Arte replied, pointing to a row of handcrafted ornaments on the windowsill.

"Did you make them?"

"Yes, those *trinkets* are mine," Arte confirmed, swapping the bin bag for a box.

Charlotte rolled her eyes. "I see I'm not going to live that one down. Is this yours as well?" Charlotte lifted a glazed clay pot and examined it. Noticing writing on its base, she read aloud, "From the potato peeler extraordinaire."

Arte cringed and took it off her, placing it in the box.

"Modest. I'm going to need an explanation on that."

"It's what Gran called me. When I would come and stay during the school holidays, I would peel potatoes for dinner service. One day she caught me shaping a potato instead of peeling it. I thought I was going to get in trouble; instead, she taught me to sculpt. I have her to thank for my abilities. She saw a talent in me and nurtured it. Art has fed my soul from an early age. It allowed me to express myself, especially after my parents died."

"It must have been a source of great comfort to you. I'd like to see some of your creations," Charlotte said, smirking at the rudimentary, wooden carving of an animal she'd picked up next. "I'm assuming they've developed beyond this, whatever species it is."

Arte put the box on the floor and took the carving from her with a wry smile. "Yes, they have, actually. I was twelve when I made that. And it's a rhino, thank you!"

She took out her phone, scrolling through her photos until she found what she was looking for.

"Here, flick through these," Arte said, passing her the phone.

Charlotte swiped through images of sculptures. "These are impressive, Arte."

Arte moved to her side to point to a partial face constructed from small fragments of metal welded together. "This mask is on permanent display in the entrance to MAXXI in Rome."

Charlotte turned to look at Arte, her forehead furrowed. "Seriously?"

Arte nodded. She was proud to be able to show she wasn't a brainless idiot who was taking on more than she could chew with a rundown hotel.

They stared at each for a moment, though it felt longer to Arte. It was enough time for her heart to beat faster and cause a little light-headedness.

"You do have talent," Charlotte said, as she handed the phone back and stepped away. "Which begs the question, why aren't you selling your art?"

"Because I'm not making any. Teaching has taken up a lot of my time, and that feeds my soul just as much as creating art. I nurture creativity and innovation. I encourage mistakes and experimentation. Helping others to express themselves is a gift. You can teach so many skills through art; I really believe it educates the soul."

"And what inspired the mask?"

"I started it after my parents died, when I realised I wasn't coming to terms with it. I put it away, but then, over the years, I'd get it back out to add to it. Gran said, 'If your heart is broken, make art with the pieces.' You could say it was a journey in the making."

"Like grief is a journey?"

"Yes." Arte beamed at Charlotte. "I actually called it 'The Grief Mask'. I'm not even sure it's finished."

"If it represents your grief, it's unlikely to ever be finished."

The soft expression on Charlotte's face and the words she spoke made Arte's breath catch in her throat. She never expected Charlotte to be so deep and meaningful. Had she been so blinded by prejudice?

"So, how did it end up at MAXXI?"

"The mother of one of my students, who happens to be the museum's director of exhibitions, saw it and asked if she could display it."

"I'm sure they wouldn't have asked to display it unless it was worthy. These art galleries have exacting standards."

A hint of a blush coloured Arte's cheeks. She was reluctant to agree with Charlotte's reasoning yet she was grateful for it nonetheless.

Removing more of Arte's creations from the windowsill, Charlotte placed them into the box on the floor. "It must have been nice to have a positive female role model when you were growing up."

"My mum was great, but Gran was my rock. I'm not sure what would have happened to me if she hadn't been there. Sophie would have been fine, she'd met George by then, whereas I was at a vulnerable age, still trying to find my way in the world."

The familiar klaxon sounded from Charlotte's phone.

"Are you going to ignore that all day?" Arte asked.

"If it continues to ring, then yes."

"If that's the ringtone you use for them, then I'm not sure I'd want to talk to them either."

"It's my mother, if you must know."

Arte frowned. "Shouldn't you answer it if she's unwell?"

"If she can use her phone, then she's fine."

"Why doesn't she leave a message instead of calling constantly?"

Charlotte chuckled. "Mother doesn't leave messages. She's too important. She made it quite clear at the hospital yesterday that I'm unwan… not needed. I can't see why she needs to call."

"You did run away," Arte said, hoping that she would confirm it this time. It was quite the compliment to her if Charlotte had run to her of all the places.

"I'm fifty-one. I don't run anywhere."

"Is this not a little mean, ignoring your mother?"

Charlotte scoffed. "You've not met her."

That was true enough, and she wasn't sure Claudette Beaufort was someone she'd want to meet either. She must have some redeeming features, though; everyone had at least one, didn't they?

"Was your mum always... problematic?" Arte asked, determined to keep her mind engaged on anything but the task at hand — emptying a set of musty drawers.

"Not that I recall. She changed around the time my father died — I was twenty-eight then. It hit her harder than I think she'd ever care to admit. There was so much to prove back then as a female CEO, despite her having had as much input as my father in the running of things since Beaufort's inception."

"And that affected your relationship?"

Charlotte nodded and took a deep breath. "As she floundered, she pulled me from a position in the business I loved and thrived at, to use me as a boardroom chess piece. By that time my confidence and business experience had flourished, and I was no longer the child she thought she could manipulate. I hadn't worked hard in my career to become someone's pawn, and I made that clear. I said I would support her on decisions I agreed with and fight her on the rest, like any other board member."

Arte had taken it for granted that everyone had a loving and supportive family behind them. The world was hard enough to navigate without those closest to you taking advantage. But even with that in mind, Claudette did sound like a piece of work.

"I'm sorry," Arte said. "That sounds difficult."

"I expect it's better to have your family alive and not have a good relationship with them than... the alternative."

The words scorched into Arte's core, and the tears that

had sat waiting on the sidelines since she'd entered her gran's room ran down her cheeks.

Not wishing to put Charlotte in an awkward position or make her feel that her words had upset her, she said, "I'll fetch some more boxes," and left the room, cursing her brittle voice.

CHAPTER 14

Arte dabbed her eyes with a tissue. She'd done well to hold herself together so far, but now she felt herself crumbling into a thousand pieces, a feeling she knew all too well. Opening the back door of the kitchen, she let the cool winter's air surround her and fill her lungs.

Charlotte appeared behind her, making her jump.

"Are you okay?"

A nod and a hum were Arte's reply. She didn't want to use words in fear they would tremble and give away her fib. She wiped her eyes again and blew out a breath.

"I'm sorry. I didn't mean to upset you," Charlotte said. "I'm not exactly versed in thinking before I speak; you may have noticed."

Arte laughed and sniffed. "Yes, I had." Something that had been hugely irritating only a day ago was already something she was learning to appreciate in Charlotte's character, now that she'd seen her in a different light. In a world full of dishonesty, straightforward people like Charlotte, were rare.

"I think we should take a short break and have some tea," Charlotte said, walking over to the kettle. "Grab some chairs, and we can warm ourselves up by the fire in reception. Rodin's already hogging it."

Arte nodded again and left the kitchen to follow out her instructions. It was nice being told what to do for a change; not having to think. It had been a long time since anyone had taken care of her — too long to even remember when. She rubbed her hands together in front of the fire to get some feeling back. The flames licked at the hearth, appreciative of the logs she'd thrown to it. Keeping a fire going in the reception area was just about taking the edge off the frosty day. Centrally located in the building, it acted like a beating heart, warming its extremities.

Some familiar markings in the stone legs of the large fireplace caught her eye. She reached for them, running her fingers over the small lines that had marked her and Sophie's heights throughout their childhood. The family would gather round for an annual measure during their Christmas visit. Her grandfather would mark with a pencil first, which he always kept behind his ear, and then chisel them in with a small 'A' or 'S' beside it. She looked for the year when she finally became the taller of the two. Sophie had sulked for the whole of the Christmas holidays. Eventually they outgrew the fireplace, and the measuring stopped.

She turned her attention to the dancing colours of the fire, grateful for its warmth. Patting her eyes with a tissue, she took some slow breaths, hoping to restore herself to normal before Charlotte brought the tea.

"Here you go," Charlotte said, appearing behind her with two mugs.

Too late.

"I'm really sorry I upset you."

"It wasn't you really; it's been building. I've been trying keep it at a distance, even though I knew I couldn't keep it there. I knew it wouldn't be easy coming home."

Charlotte sat on the chair beside her. "So you do see this as home?"

Arte nodded. Yes, she did. As much as she'd tried to avoid thinking of it like that over the years, she could no longer deny it.

"This place has been here from the beginning, despite the people that have gone from my life. First my grandfather. Then, shortly after, my parents."

Charlotte's hand reached for her leg. It brought some comfort and made her feel less alone.

"Can I ask how your parents died?"

The note of caution and concern in Charlotte's voice kept Arte from brushing the question off like she normally would. It felt like Charlotte was asking because she wanted to support her better, not just to be nosey like a lot of people did before they went on to pity her.

"Carbon monoxide poisoning. They died in their sleep," Arte replied, taking a cautious sip of tea. It burned her lip as much as her words had done.

Charlotte blew out a breath and rubbed Arte's leg with her hand. "I'm sorry."

Arte forced a flat smile to try and express some gratitude.

"I take it you weren't with them?" Charlotte asked, caution still in her tone.

"I was staying at a friend's house for the weekend. We were going to a concert. I didn't expect my love for Dido to save my life."

They sat in silence for a moment. Arte expected Charlotte was taking it all in.

"It must be odd to have a near-death experience without the near-death experience."

Arte nodded. "That took some coming to terms with. Staying away from home was not something I did very often. We were a very close family… back then." She inhaled deeply as images from the memory appeared in her head; she tried to push them away as she exhaled. "It felt like fate really, like a higher power was watching over me — not that I'm religious. In my head I still play through all the different paths that could have led me to being in the house that night. It's difficult to get your head around how fragile life is. One wrong move, and it's game over."

"It's a scary thought which can no doubt spiral if you let it. Why do I get the feeling that's exactly what you do?"

Arte pulled her lips tight in amusement that Charlotte had guessed correctly.

"So, you're not religious but perhaps a little spiritual?"

"A little. Another thing that rubbed off from Gran. I think to be an artist you have to be. The only thing we can be sure of in this world full of uncertainty is that we don't know everything."

"When I first laid eyes on you, I thought you may have

grown up in a hippy commune. I was even more convinced when you told me to play nicely."

Arte laughed, trying not to focus on the phrase 'laid eyes on'. "I'm glad you didn't say 'cult'. We preferred to call ourselves an 'artistic community', actually."

Charlotte chuckled. "Oh, so you did?"

"No!" Arte laughed. "Mum and Dad didn't want us to grow up like that, so we had the standard upbringing. Not that we didn't have close ties to our community. My parents just wanted us to have an average childhood. You know, playing in the woods with school friends, out on our bikes, watching the streetlights switch on so we knew when to go home. It suited Sophie more. I wouldn't have minded living with other artists. There's something wholesome about a group of like-minded people coming together in a space and sharing their passion. After Mum and Dad died, we lost touch with them. Sophie had never been that close to the community, and for me it hurt too much to be amongst them..." Arte took a deep breath. "I struggled... more than I'd care to admit... and there were too many reminders of everything I lost." She looked around the room. "A bit like this place. One big reminder of the past."

In her mind, she could see her family stood round the huge Christmas tree Gran insisted on placing in the corner of reception. It was always haphazardly decorated — or 'decorated with love, not a ruler,' Gran would say if anyone teased her about it, which most of the family did. With a flash it was gone, replaced by the image of her gran at the reception desk, furiously licking her fountain pen to make it work better, her crooked, soft fingers doing the best they could to hold something so small.

Arte blinked away tears, though she held on to the vision of the woman with powder-white hair, her skin wrinkled by time but still with a twinkle in her eye and mischief in her face. All the memories were there, etched into the very fabric of the building, waiting for her to find them where she left them. She couldn't hide from them anymore; they were part of her fabric too.

"I can see it would be," Charlotte added, her voice forcing Arte back to the present. "So you never mixed with your artistic community again?"

"No. I thought it would get easier, but the longer you stay away, the harder it gets. It was simpler to tell myself I was too busy, but I know what you can lose when you're busy keeping busy. I packed my past and grief away into boxes and went to university for three years. After that I floundered a bit, with nothing to focus on. That's when Gran suggested I take some time out and travel Europe. A 'grand tour', she called it. A way to find myself and inspire my artistic talents further. Then I found my way to Italy and decided I would complete a sculpting Master's, kick the can of life down the road a little further. When I realised funds were low and the bills were piling up, I managed to gain a teaching position and stay on at the university in Rome. As it turns out, I'm rather good at it, and I enjoy it immensely."

"I'm not surprised you are a good teacher. You have patience and kindness. You seem able to communicate effectively, especially when you see something you don't like. There's a nurturing spirit about you. Teaching probably gave you back that sense of community too."

Arte nodded, hoping the heat from the fire would cover her blushes. "You're right."

A look of satisfaction washed over Charlotte's face. "Where was Sophie in all this?"

"Off living her life. Don't get me wrong, it affected her, too, but she had George and work to focus on. She's always been a little on the selfish side," she admitted. "I'm not sure she stopped to consider what Gran lost. I think she must have thought, as she was older, it was something more familiar to her and she would cope. Plus, Gran always had a way of making it look like she was coping. I mean, look at this place." Arte held out her hands.

"Honestly, I've seen worse."

Arte offered up a smile of appreciation at Charlotte's attempts to make her feel better, futile as they were.

"So it was just me and Gran. I try not to hold any ill will against Sophie. I honestly believe she thought we had each other. She became kind of distant, and then with me living abroad, we just grew apart. We'd check in occasionally with each other and Gran. Try and visit when we could. Perhaps not enough."

"I guess that was her way of dealing with the grief," Charlotte offered.

Arte nodded. "Some families would pull together over losses like ours, but we kind of pulled apart."

"You all had to deal with it the way you needed to deal with it. It must have been hard for your gran to let you go."

"I know she didn't want me to go. She was struggling,

too... if not more." Arte stopped, realising her voice was wobbling. She swallowed. "She lost her husband and her daughter in a short space of time. Not that she ever let me see that, but I knew. I felt the change in her. I just wish I'd had the chance to thank her properly, for letting me go when I needed. It was probably one of the hardest things she had to do."

The memory of their emotional farewell by the door behind them now came to mind. Saying goodbye to her gran that day had marked the beginning of a new adventure, one that had terrified but also excited her. It was a familiar feeling to how she felt now, to think how far she'd come from that twenty-one-year-old, who had gone full circle and returned, ready to take on a new challenge and begin another new chapter. Hopefully this time she was a stronger, more confident person.

"I dare say you made her proud."

"I hope so." Arte sniffed, trying to hold back her tears. "Today would have been my first day back after the Christmas break. Right now I would be surrounded by young adults with a thirst to learn about the artistic world. Here I am, face to face with grief, and alone yet again."

Charlotte squeezed her leg. "Did you have anyone special to help you in Italy?"

"No, nothing serious," Arte replied, placing her hand on top of Charlotte's without thinking. "I kept myself busy with art. It's my constant."

"Why come back at all then?"

"I needed to start unpacking some of the boxes I stuffed my grief into, and to stop myself from doing it again. I should have returned long before now to exorcise my demons, to face the reality I'd been hiding from. Leaving may add distance, but it doesn't solve your problems. I was young and naïve to think so. Now, I have the added weight of guilt at abandoning Gran. So I'm back, to face the past and fulfil a lifelong passion."

"Passion? I see obligation, guilt, but…"

Arte patted Charlotte's hand. "Can I show you something?"

"Of course," Charlotte said, gesturing for her to lead the way.

Arte led her around the side of the house to the old tithe barn, excitement building in her at the fact that she was about to share her idea for the first time with someone who knew about business — that is, until she realised Charlotte may think it was an awful idea. Then a wave of nausea hit her.

Opening one of the large, wooden doors, Arte asked, "What do you think?"

Rodin trotted off, sticking his nose into anything that looked of interest, as Charlotte gawped up at the high, timber-frame roof.

"Okay, what am I missing here?" she asked, pursing her lips. "Weddings?"

"God, no! Everyone does that. Have you never heard of a unique selling point?"

The sides of Charlotte eyes furrowed, but a smile played on her lips. "Then what?"

Arte's face illuminated as she answered. "An art studio?"

"A studio?"

"Yes. It's a childhood dream. You said yourself I need

to find a reason to charge more." Arte removed her sketch from her back pocket and passed it to Charlotte. "Here, take a look."

"How does that increase revenue?" Charlotte asked as she unfolded the piece of paper and stared at it.

"I'll teach. I can't compete with a spa hotel anyway," Arte replied. She strode to the other end of the space and began gesticulating as she spoke, hopeful she could get her latest incarnation of the studio across effectively. "At this end I want a teaching area that I can combine with a workshop. Above would be a mezzanine floor and a staircase coming up from where you are by the door."

She turned and began walking back towards Charlotte. "This central area would be open plan, maybe with a galleried landing against the back wall coming off the mezzanine to make full use of the height. It will be somewhere to display and sell my work. I could even bring in other artists and create a gallery, bring back a bit of that community feel. Artists could come for a five-day course with a reduced nightly rate at the hotel. It will help with the low midweek occupancy." Arte returned to Charlotte's side and put her hands on her hips. "So, what do you think?"

Charlotte's face had drifted from bemusement to shock. "This is a very ambitious plan, Arte."

Arte grinned. "I know." No matter how daunting the hotel felt to work on, the thought of renovating the barn did nothing but light a fire in her belly. "Think about it with your heart and not your head for a moment, if that's even possible."

Charlotte's playful narrowing of the eyes told Arte she'd taken the dig on the chin.

"You sketched this all out when you were a child?"

Arte nodded. "I never thought it would be possible. I always assumed Gran would reach a certain age and then sell the place, but she always seemed to hang on… until she didn't."

"Did she know of your plans?"

"Oh, yes. I never stopped talking about it."

"Perhaps she hung on for you, hopeful that one day you would return and make it happen."

"You mean she kept the place going and died here instead of a comfortable retirement home so I could realise my dreams one day?"

"Sorry. I…" Charlotte trailed off, looking down at her feet.

"It's fine. I know what you meant," Arte said as she headed back to the door. Knowing her gran, Charlotte probably wasn't far off the mark.

Charlotte followed slowly behind, still taking in the space and the sketch. "You're impressive, Arte. I think I may have underestimated you."

"Oh, I know you have. Wildly underestimated," Arte said with an air of smugness as she closed the door behind them.

Charlotte handed the sketch back, her face radiating unmistakable admiration.

"Now I see that passion," Charlotte said, "and why it's time for you to face your demons."

"Yes, it is, and also time we got back to work," Arte

said, finding her mood higher now that Charlotte thought she was impressive.

With the last of the knick-knacks removed from Gran's room, all clothing and shoes bagged, and personal effects boxed, it was time to deal with the removal of the furniture. A flimsy, fibreboard wardrobe was first to be launched into the skip, followed by a bedside table and various other odds and ends. Only the bed and an Edwardian oak bureau remained.

"This was my great-grandmother's," Arte said, rubbing the top of the bureau with affection.

"And not skip-worthy. Can you repurpose it anywhere?"

"I could use it in my room. I need a desk and somewhere to hide all the bills."

Charlotte gave her a look of disbelief. "You want to get this up that narrow staircase?"

Arte shot back a pair of pleading puppy-dog eyes.

"Okay," Charlotte sighed. "Up we go then."

They carried the bureau to the bottom of the narrow staircase; Charlotte then lifted it from behind as Arte guided from the front, taking it one step at a time. Rodin barged his way past, knocking them off kilter.

"Does he always do this when you're trying to get upstairs?" Charlotte asked, rebalancing herself.

"Every time. If there's room for one, there's room for Rodin, too, in his head."

They heaved the bureau up the last step and into Arte's room.

"Excuse the mess," Arte said, knowing full well there was no mess, as she'd made a point of tidying whilst watching *Hotel SOS* before bed. It was best said, though. People had varying standards of tidiness, and Charlotte struck her as a woman with a label maker who would likely still think it was a state.

Having carried countless boxes of personal possessions, photographs, and paperwork down to the sitting room for Arte to work her way through at a later date, they reconvened in her gran's bedroom, now a barren landscape of threadbare carpet and faded wallpaper.

"I could do with a lie-down after that," Arte said, perching on the side of her gran's bed.

"We should. The mattresses could do with testing out," Charlotte said.

"Charlotte Beaufort, are you propositioning me?" Arte teased.

"Oh, I only mean… erm, we should lie on them to see if any are salvageable," Charlotte added.

Arte couldn't help feeling a flutter of sadness at such a quick rebuff.

"This one definitely needs to go," Charlotte said, joining her on the bed and bouncing.

"Gran loved a soft mattress."

"I prefer hard."

"Me too," Arte said, catching Charlotte's eye.

Amused faces turned sour as both their noses twitched.

"Oh, Rodin!" Arte groaned. "Have you let one rip?"

Rodin scurried from the room and lay down outside the door with bashful ears lowered.

Charlotte wafted her hand in front of her face. "The downside of being a dog owner."

"Mattresses?" Arte asked, trying not to choke on the stench.

"Lead the way."

Tempting as it was to invite Charlotte to test out her own mattress, she knew it was fine, and she wasn't about to invite herself into Charlotte's room to test hers. Arte took her at her word that she'd had a comfortable night's sleep. After testing the next three mattresses and condemning all of them, they entered the last bedroom and lay down beside each other.

Arte arched up and looked over the bedframe. "Where did Rodin go?"

"I didn't see him follow us in."

Flopping back down on the comfortable, firm mattress, Arte turned onto her side and faced Charlotte. "Thanks for helping me today. I wouldn't have gotten through it on my own. And… thanks for listening."

Charlotte turned to face her. "You're welcome. I've enjoyed it — well, as much as anyone can enjoy helping someone clear out their dead loved one's belongings. It's also been nice getting to know you a little better."

Arte's face tingled. "Likewise." She smiled and looked up at the ceiling, too embarrassed to hold eye contact. "You know, I was born in this room. Quite by accident."

"I'm not sure anyone is born by accident, Arte. Not even you."

"I mean I was early. My family were staying here for

Gran's birthday. I was a little birthday surprise for her — and my parents."

She imagined how the room must have looked at that moment all those years ago, with her first breath being taken and then everyone taking a turn to hold her. Goose pimples rose on the nape of her neck.

"Really?" Charlotte pulled her face back. "You share a birthday with your gran."

"Yep. We would have joint celebrations whenever we could."

Her chest tightened as she realised she wouldn't be sharing another with Gran.

"Didn't that bug you when you were little?" Charlotte enquired. "Not getting all the attention?"

Arte turned back to Charlotte. "Of course not. I loved sharing it with Gran. Anyway, she'd always let me blow the candles out and have the first slice of cake."

Their eyes locked across the mattress, causing Arte's heart to skip. She desperately wanted to reach out and touch Charlotte's hand, where it rested an inch from her own. The urge to have some form of physical contact with the enigmatic woman was overwhelming. As she was about to move her hand, the door crashed open, followed by a panting noise. Immediately she was grateful for the interruption. What had she been thinking?

"Ah, there you are, Rodin. We were beginning to wonder what had happened to you," Arte said, sitting up.

Her attention was pulled back to the door by the appearance of her sister's pointed features and bleach-blonde, shoulder-length hair, sitting atop a smart, slim-fitting, navy wool coat.

"Sophie!"

"Here you are." Sophie stopped when she clocked Charlotte. "Sorry, I'm not interrupting something, am I?"

They both shot up off the bed at that, feeling even more foolish as Rodin bounced excitedly around the room.

"No, of course not," Arte said, straightening out her clothes only to realise the action made it look even more like Sophie had interrupted something. It didn't help that Charlotte was frantically smoothing her hair with her hands.

"I had hoped to be here earlier; it's been so crazy at home. Still, George will cope until tomorrow evening."

"I didn't realise you were even coming this weekend."

"I said I would," Sophie said, placing her bag on the end of the bed and removing her gloves and an enormous scarf.

"No, you said you'd come soon," Arte insisted. "You didn't specify when. I could have prepared a room for you."

"You must be Charlotte," Sophie said, ignoring Arte and extending her hand.

Charlotte took her hand and gave it a brief shake. "Yes. Hi."

"She's helping me this weekend."

"Golly, I didn't realise you gave the full service," Sophie said, folding her arms. "I was under the impression you went in, tore the place and the owner to shreds, and got out as quickly as possible."

Arte caught Charlotte's expression. She clearly didn't appreciate the assessment, which, to be fair, felt accurate.

"Well, yes, normally... we..." Charlotte looked to Arte for help.

"They're testing a new format."

"Without cameras?" Sophie said, arching an eyebrow as she looked around the room.

"Yes, can't see it working myself. Why don't you take this room? I think it was the comfiest mattress. Wouldn't you agree, Charlotte?"

"Yes, definitely; memory foam and everything," Charlotte said, manoeuvring herself towards the door. "I'll make myself scarce."

As soon as Charlotte had left the room, Sophie rounded on her sister. "Well, well. I come to help you and find you in my bed with Charlotte Beaufort of all people."

"Soph, it only became your bed a second ago. You don't need to say it like that." Though she had to admit she liked the way it sounded.

"Like what?" Sophie protested.

"Like we were doing something in *your* bed."

"I didn't say it like that; you interpreted it like that. I told you she was married. To a man."

"Not that it makes any difference, but she's getting a divorce *and* she's bisex—"

Arte stopped herself, realising she'd outed Charlotte. Not that she'd had confirmation of her sexuality, even. Bisexual was a wild stab in the dark.

"Oh, the plot thickens," Sophie cooed. "And she came all the way here to tell you that?"

"Of course not."

"What's she doing here then? I thought you found her rude and opinionated."

"I don't know; she turned up unannounced. She apologised for the way she said things, and I've realised I seriously misjudged her. She's been really helpful, Soph. I couldn't have tackled Gran's room without her."

"I could have helped you. We could have done it together."

"You weren't here, and I didn't know when you were coming. If you learnt to communicate a little better, I could have been prepared," Arte said through gritted teeth.

Sophie pulled herself back and fell silent.

Taking a breath, Arte continued. "We were just finishing up for the day. We packed up all Gran's belongings. Perhaps you could drop her clothes and shoes at a charity shop when you head home. Her personal effects are in boxes; we could go through them together in the morning."

Sophie nodded her agreement.

"I'll leave you to unpack then. You know where the laundry cupboard is."

Arte left the room and set off in search of Charlotte. She found her stoking the fire in reception, Rodin by her side. She couldn't help the soft smile that broke across her lips; he was really taken with her.

"I'm sorry," Arte said as she approached them. "I didn't know she was going to turn up today."

"What does it matter?" Charlotte replied, far too casually for it not to have mattered. "It's good she's here. I should lea—"

"No!" Arte almost shouted. "No, I want you here." She paused before continuing, realising she was overstepping.

"Sorry. I just mean, more hands are always useful. You've been so helpful."

"Well, I won't deny you my hands if they are so useful to you."

Arte did a double take at the comment.

Charlotte leaned the poker against the fireplace and added, "If you're sure I won't be in the way?"

"No, you won't be," Arte replied as convincingly as she could. She was nowhere near ready for Charlotte to leave. "Anyway, who's going to make dinner if you leave?"

"Ha. I see where my hands are particularly useful to you. I'll make a start then."

"Thanks."

Arte fanned herself as she watched Charlotte heading for the kitchen, followed by her four-legged assistant. They were just friends. New friends at that. But if that was true, why had she pleaded so hard to make her stay? And why was she so relieved when she agreed?

CHAPTER 15

Charlotte sipped from her glass of Chateau Latour, grateful that she had thought to ransack the wine cellar after she'd packed her bags. She was quietly enjoying the richness of its expressive fruit aromas and wood perfumes as she listened to Arte and Sophie chatting — or, more accurately, bickering — on the opposite sofa. She'd noticed over dinner how strange their relationship was; they either seemed to be at odds with each other or completely immersed in reminiscing about their childhood. There was no middle ground.

She'd heard sibling relationships could be challenging; even so, she would have appreciated a sibling, they could have taken some of the heat from Claudette off her own back. At least her mother had made the right decision not to have any more children after Charlotte. One child out of duty was bad enough; to have had more would have been unpardonable. It was a shame for her father, though, who had adored children. Charlotte had been the centre of his world, and every spare moment he'd had he'd spent with her.

When it came to the Tremaine sisters, something had shifted since Sophie had arrived, right at the moment when Charlotte had been lying beside Arte on the bed in room 4. Arte, who had begun to relax since she'd opened up about her gran, now seemed on edge. Charlotte hoped it wasn't her presence clashing with Sophie's that had caused it. She had tried to leave right away, but Arte had practically begged her to stay. A smile crept onto her lips at the thought.

She had been sure Arte was going to reach out and touch her hand on the bed — she had done so in front of the fire, after all — but she had since convinced herself it was nothing more than her overactive imagination. The hand twitch before Sophie burst in was pure fantasy, a lustful delusion. Although they were getting along well and the word 'friendship' had been thrown about, along with a bit of banter, Charlotte doubted Arte felt it was as flirtatious as she did.

...or did she? Arte had quite clearly understood Charlotte's intention when she explained that she'd been trying to impress her outside the catering van at their first meeting. And, more importantly, Arte hadn't said she wasn't open to being impressed, nor had she expressed a disinterest in Charlotte for being a woman. She'd simply suggested Charlotte work on how she tried to impress someone, which sounded like an open invitation to try again. With her.

Whatever it was, in the day since she'd zoomed back out to the country, it felt like an elephant had taken two feet off her chest. Arte wasn't like any other friend she had — not that she had many. There was something about her that drew Charlotte towards her, especially once Arte had shared details of her life and the tragedies that had befallen her. To find someone like her, a woman of substance, with depth, experience, and passion, was rare.

Charlotte had become acquainted with lots of women in Gideon's social circles, and she would trust none of them to look after a dead cat, let alone a secret. Being a working woman, she was always on the outside, never around to luncheon with them at the latest trendy restaurant or play tennis with them at their country club. Charlotte was not a lady of leisure, to her relief. The very idea of it was enough to induce a panic attack. What did those women do all day except sit around and talk? Their lives must be like a Jane Austen novel, with fewer carriages and even more heaving bosoms, no doubt heaving for their tennis coaches rather than their dull husbands.

Realising she should at least keep one ear on the conversation in the room, Charlotte tuned back in.

"I'd like to know why Gran didn't tell us about the show. You would have thought she'd have told you at least, being her favourite."

There was so much bitterness loaded in Sophie's voice that, internally, Charlotte was pleading for Arte not to take the bait and react.

"I wasn't her favourite. Gran would never have a favourite," Arte protested.

Sophie ignored her. "I suppose you did live with her for a few years; it was more than I had with her."

"Over the holidays, yes, because our parents died, if you remember."

"More wine, Sophie?" Charlotte asked, feeling the need to disrupt the violent flow of the conversation.

"No, thank you, Charlotte. I'll finish this and go to bed. I have a feeling we'll be rather busy tomorrow. It's lovely though."

Charlotte refilled Arte's glass, earning her a tender smile that made her light up inside.

"She has French heritage," Arte said.

"Ah, that explains it… and you can cook. You can visit anytime you like, Charlotte."

Charlotte gave a thankful glance at Sophie, only to find her winking at her sister. Arte had the appearance of someone who wanted the sofa to swallow her up. What was that about?

The conversation moved on to which sister was the better cook. Following some heated debate, they finally agreed that neither of them was as good as their gran had been and proceeded to recall some of her best dishes. Massaman curry was crowned the winner. As the pair bonded over their childhood, Charlotte regarded Arte and her dungarees. Today's pair were khaki and matched perfectly with a long-sleeved, black T-shirt. She'd nearly embarrassed herself by saying something that morning, only for the noisy skip lorries arriving to interrupt her.

Charlotte was quietly pleased when Sophie went to bed and left the pair of them to chat. Arte had a calming effect on her, and she was enjoying being alone in her company. For Arte to have taken Charlotte's apologies as genuine and to have seen her for who she really was said a lot about her — even if Charlotte herself was grappling to work exactly who she was.

Arte was curious, not the usual type of woman her gaze would fall upon. It had a habit of falling on tall, beautiful, unobtainable, straight women. Not that Arte wasn't beautiful in her own way; it shone from every part of her, from her confidence to travel abroad alone, to living in another country, learning a new language, and sharing her creative passion with others — all when she must have been at her lowest, trying to cope with her grief. Even her unconditional love for Rodin was admirable. Then there was the way she'd stood up to Charlotte and pointed out how she could do better; Arte made her want to do everything better, to be more honest.

Charlotte had spent much of her life trying to impress people by being someone else, but Arte only seemed impressed by her when she'd been herself. Her passion and ambition for a long-held dream was admirable. It had brought her back to a place that held painful memories, and yet she'd sought out only the good ones. Her plans for the barn were more than ambitious, falling closer to impossible, considering the work and investment needed to bring the accommodation up to specification and then make it profitable. Throw in a barn renovation on top, and it was nothing more than a pipe dream — a pipe dream with the potential to rip out Arte's heart if it failed.

It at least explained why Arte was so enamoured with the hotel and so determined to make it succeed. The hotel wasn't the end goal of her grand plan; that barn was. It was a way back to her art, a chance to fulfil a childhood dream despite everything she would need to face when she returned. It was also brilliant. The light in Arte's vibrant blue eyes and the energy exuding from her as she walked around the space had been hypnotic. It had warmed Charlotte's heart to feel Arte's passion for her dream, and, if she was being honest, it had made her a little jealous.

"Are you okay, Charlotte?" Arte asked. "You seem miles away."

"Yes, fine." She gave Arte a reassuring smile. "Things are quite intense between you and Sophie."

"They can be. It's only sibling rivalry. You should tell her that your performance on the show is just that, a performance. She'd understand."

"Is it a performance? I know I said it was, but have I not become that Charlotte Beaufort?"

"Only you can answer that."

Charlotte pulled her lips to one side, not wanting to consider how much the show had changed her over the years.

"I seem to have gained respect from your sister based on her current opinion of me."

Arte met her with a frown. "I'm sure she'd respect you either way."

"It's not a good idea that too many people outside the show know anything. Sometimes people prefer to see the worst in others."

"How many do know?"

"My mother. Then only Gideon and Freddie, as far as I'm aware." It stung to think they were the only three people who really knew her, but in fact, they didn't know everything about her.

"Freddie's not your typical personal assistant."

"No. I took a chance on him and never regretted it. When I asked him why he wanted the job, he was honest, which was more than the others could say. They told me what they thought I wanted to hear. He was the only one that came as himself. I respected that; I needed that."

"You want others to be themselves, yet you don't set the same standard for yourself?"

Arte made a valid, albeit annoying, point.

"I'm trying to change that. I suspect you may have heard I'm divorcing my husband."

Arte's fidgeting fingers and darting eyes confirmed that she had overheard her conversation from behind the bushes.

Charlotte continued. "It was an arranged marriage of mutual tolerance."

"I didn't realise arranged marriages were a thing in our culture."

"They are in high society when it's convenient for both parties' parents. Don't get me wrong, we liked each other to begin with. The thought of fulfilling parental wishes at the time was important to us both, but it was all very rushed. If we'd spent more time getting to know each other, we would have realised we were completely incompatible." Charlotte paused. "Why do my standards matter to you anyway?"

"I think we should all live our lives the way we want to," Arte answered. "Be the best version of ourselves."

"I get that, bu—"

"I like this version of you," she admitted. "I think you

do too. You certainly seem happier and more relaxed than you did yesterday."

That was true. In the last twenty-four hours, she'd ditched her husband and confessed her true nature to a rather cute stranger who was beginning to make her body and mind feel things they hadn't felt in years.

She gave Arte a brief smile to acknowledge her observations but remained silent.

"So you employed Freddie because of his honesty?" Arte asked, taking a sip of wine.

"I also noticed he was wearing a Pride pin on his jacket," Charlotte replied, relieved the conversation was heading back to its original starting point. "I knew then that no matter what happened I was safe with him."

"He told me what happened, and what you did for him."

The two of them have gotten close.

Charlotte waved her hand casually. "It's what anyone in my position would have done."

"No, it's not, Charlotte. I don't think anyone else would have done that at all. They wouldn't have made it past the Pride pin for a start. When you can't even get past other people being different from you, you don't offer them a safe haven. He says you saved his life."

Charlotte turned her attention to the flames dancing in the hearth. "That's somewhat of an exaggeration,"

"I don't think it is. He doesn't. Why can't you accept the compliment? There is an immense amount of kindness in you, Charlotte."

Charlotte fanned herself with her hand.

"Too hot, or are you about to pass out from the compliment?"

"Both? I would move away from the fire, but there isn't space." Charlotte looked at the sofa-hogging Labrador beside her.

Arte patted the seat next to her. "Join me."

That was an invitation she didn't have to think about. As she joined Arte, she watched her tuck her legs up onto the sofa and reposition herself to face her. Charlotte kicked her shoes off and mirrored her, resting her arm on the back of the sofa.

"One of the things I missed most about England were the fireplaces," Arte said. "If you were lucky enough to have a fireplace in Italy, then there were few opportunities to use it."

"Do you miss Italy?"

"I miss the shutters blocking out the morning light. The food, the wine, the easiness of society. Everyone's a little more relaxed."

Charlotte raised an eyebrow. "And kinder?"

Arte let out a little chuckle. "Yes. I won't miss the wacky electrics, the small baths, or the noisy backdrop of vehicles driving over cobble streets, though. There is no better place than the English countryside. What more could anyone want than a fire roaring in the hearth, the trees creaking outside, owls hooting, and wind whistling through the gaps in the window? Though the latter would be preferable in a property I don't own."

"Okay, I admit there may be a charm to the countryside. It's particularly beautiful around here."

"We're just inside the South Downs National Park. I

hope to take advantage of its popularity when I open, especially with walkers."

Hearing one of his trigger words, Rodin dropped his front paws onto the floor, leaving his back end on the sofa. He stretched out, walking forwards until his back paws dropped onto the carpet. He pottered over to them and jumped onto the sofa between them.

"He's quite taken with you, despite your obvious dislike of him," Arte teased Charlotte as she rubbed his ear, making the dog groan.

"I don't dislike him," Charlotte sighed. She'd known the topic of dogs would be raised sooner or later.

"You could have fooled me."

"I adore dogs, but I prefer not to be around them," Charlotte said, stroking Rodin's back.

"Who on earth loves dogs but prefers not to be around them?"

Her sullen expression must have led Arte to her conclusion. "Oh, you lost a dog, didn't you?"

Charlotte gave a reluctant nod and felt Arte's hand come to rest on hers on the back of the sofa. Their eyes met over Rodin, and Arte offered her a sympathetic smile, causing a wave of comfort to rush through Charlotte. She turned her focus to telling the story Arte appeared so keen to hear.

"A husky called Wilf. He was actually named Wolf, but I struggled to pronounce it properly when I was little, and everyone ended up calling him Wilf. He didn't seem to mind either way." Charlotte smiled at the memory. "We became the best of friends; he was fiercely protective of me. It broke my heart the day he died. I didn't get to say goodbye. I didn't even know he was ill. I came home from school one day expecting to be greeted by him as usual only to discover I'd never see him again. You take it for granted that things will continue forever as they are, that things that are there will always be there. It was a life lesson that things can change in a matter of hours — or even minutes, when it came to my father's death."

Arte's fingers slipped around the side into Charlotte's palm, effectively holding her hand.

"I know that well enough. I thought Gran would be around forever, until one day she wasn't. By then it was too late for goodbyes."

Charlotte hoped to offer some empathy as she tightened her fingers against Arte's. They sat in silence for a moment, alone with their memories but physically bound.

"So I take it when Freddie turned up for the PA job and said his name was Wilf..."

Charlotte noticed a smile twitch at the corner of her new friend's lip. "Yes, go on, smile that even I have triggers," she teased.

"You are a softy, aren't you?" Arte remarked, narrowing her eyes playfully.

"Don't tell anyone. I have a reputation to uphold. I find keeping myself at a distance from the things I could 'love' the best course of action. Good decisions are rarely made when emotions are involved."

Arte chuckled. "Okay, not a total softy then."

"I believe it's healthy to have walls."

"Walls, maybe. You could forgo the barbed wire and the alarm system, though. Have you considered that you're spending time with the wrong people or haven't met the right ones yet?"

"There could be some truth to that," Charlotte replied. "It's certainly something I'm considering changing."

"Maybe you've already started," Arte said, stroking Rodin with her free hand. "You have to open your heart to love in the right places, knowing the price you have to pay for it." She paused and took a breath. "I'm prepared to exchange all the future pain of losing Rodin for all the love and cuddles I get before that time comes. I wasn't always prepared; I've spent most of my adulthood being quite guarded, pushing people away to protect myself."

Charlotte gave a sympathetic nod. "You lost a lot at a young age."

"We all lose someone along the road, and no child should lose a parent that young, but protecting myself didn't make me happy. In fact, I missed out on a lot of… romantic experiences with good people, some of whom backed quietly into the shadows. Others stayed to try to make it work, only to fail. When we lose someone we love, we feel like we're going to die too. That feeling forces us to adjust our perspectives. It took a long time for me to do that, and it has taken a lot of therapy to get me to this point where I can accept love for what it is — often a form of delayed pain. We'll always face pain in our life, so why not take the good with the bad? Love is worth all the hurt in the end."

"That's… quite a good perspective to take, considering."

Rodin rolled onto his back, offering his tummy for a tickle, which his mistress obliged. It allowed Charlotte a moment to get her head around everything Arte had shared. She found herself joining in with her free hand, not wishing to break away from Arte's hold.

Arte cleared her throat. "Believe me when I say you're missing out on so much to guard your heart when it doesn't need guarding."

"Are we still talking about dogs?" Charlotte murmured.

"You tell me. And while you're at it, can you tell me why you're here? You said you wanted to apologise. You could have done that and been on your way or even said it the next time we met."

"Well, at the moment, a famous film star is encamped in my usual penthouse suite at Beaufort Mayfair."

Arte quirked an eyebrow. "Seriously? One of your many other rooms not up to your standard?"

Charlotte exhaled. There was no escape from Arte's questioning, and she deserved the truth.

"I needed to convince you I wasn't the person you thought I was, not deep down anyway. I sensed it would take a little time."

"Why is it so important to you that a complete stranger knows the real you?"

Charlotte had wondered that herself. Why had shame at her behaviour burned inside her more than it usually did after filming? Having spent more time with Arte, she now knew. Her gaze fell to their hands, where Arte's fingers were now stroking and playing with Charlotte's as if they had a mind of their own. The feel of her warm, soft fingertips against her skin made her heart pulse hard. She looked up at Arte and their eyes locked. The tender encouragement in Arte's forced Charlotte to be honest.

"Perhaps I was hoping you wouldn't remain a stranger."

Arte's delight at her declaration was palpable, despite her attempts to bite her lips and pull them to one side to hide it. She reached for her glass on the table, causing her hand to slip away from Charlotte's. Still feeling the sensation of Arte's touch against her skin, Charlotte was eager for its return.

Arte took a couple of gulps of wine and returned her glass to the table. "Well, I, for one, am pleased you came back. I would never have got as much cleared without you."

A sly smile appeared on Arte's face, lighting her eyes. There was something about it that hijacked Charlotte's ability to control her own senses.

"Oh, I see. I return with my heartfelt apology, hoping to make amends, and you saw it as an opportunity for a bit of free labour," she teased.

"You're getting a bed and a very comfortable, serviceable room for two nights in return." Arte grimaced. "Yeah, okay. Maybe I should have stopped after 'bed'. It all seems a little unfair for you to be turned out of your home and into a hotel."

"It was never home to me, and I left very willingly," Charlotte admitted. "It was Gideon's home. I moved in when we married. I have thousands of rooms at my disposal, yet here I am at fifty-one, feeling effectively homeless. Beaufort Mayfair is the closest thing I have to a home. My father trusted me with it straight out of university. He said the best training to run a hotel was to run a hotel, and I didn't let him down. It was his latest acquisition, and I built it up from nothing, single-handed. Those years were the happiest of my life. Working on the front line is exhilarating, and getting instant rewards for your efforts is a hell of a buzz. My mother tried to fight it; even back then she didn't believe in me."

"I'm sorry. I've only known you a few days, and I wouldn't bet against you."

Charlotte's face tingled. She hoped it wasn't turning the colour of beetroot.

"And I'm sorry about your divorce," Arte added. "It can't be easy."

"It's high time I started living my life on my terms, and I'm determined to do it." A chill swept over her as she realised at some point she was going to have to tell her mother. Was that why she was ringing? Had Gideon told her? It was unlikely. He was probably expecting Charlotte to change her mind and return home. Making it public wouldn't be at the top of his list, although she wouldn't put it past him to request her mother order her to return to him. She wondered if he'd even told his parents or if he'd decided to make an excuse for her absence instead.

"Good for you. I'm just surprised you're starting it at a shithole of a hotel, not a five-star luxury spa with a bottle of champagne."

"I'm beginning to see the charm behind it." Forcing herself to make eye contact with Arte and ignoring the pounding in her chest, she added, "And inside it."

Arte nodded. "Good save."

Charlotte's lips tightened. "I thought so. Don't get me wrong, it is a shithole too. That, we can work on."

"I'm so holding you to that," Arte simpered,

"Be sure to."

As their amusement settled, Arte asked, "It was never your ambition to be a television star then?"

"Certainly not, but I find enjoyment in making something of nothing. It's the only part of the show I enjoy. You can't beat the satisfaction of turning a business around, working with people to help them give the best hospitality they can. It gives me that connection to running a hotel that I miss since I moved to headquarters."

Even with mild enjoyment she still bore a grudge against the show every day it held her back at Beaufort Hotels — not to mention how it had turned her into a monster.

"My life is the show now, whether I like it or not. I don't get much input at work."

"Is this why you needed the show to be successful and why you went all mean? It's all you had?"

"Perhaps. I was shoehorned into it by my mother. It was good for business, I'll give her that. Yet I've always felt it's held me back from progressing at the company… from taking over." Her mother's words resounded in her head. *What use is she to me?* Charlotte pushed them aside.

"Can you give up the show? Or would that not solve the problem?" Arte asked.

"How do you mean?"

"Isn't your mother the problem rather than the show? You said it was her idea that you do the show, and it resulted in you having to step back from the business side when you were working your way up. Sounds to me like someone kicked you back down."

Charlotte scrunched her face. "No… she says I'm not ready."

"Sounds to me like she's not ready."

What?

Charlotte's mind spun with a whirlwind of thoughts and emotions. Had Arte hit the nail on the head? Was her mother, not the show itself, holding her back? Did her mother not believe she would ever be ready? She found with devastating clarity that she could quite believe it.

"Why did I not see that?" Charlotte said, closing her eyes and shaking her head.

"See that your mum has been sabotaging you? Why would anyone want to see that? Is this not another reason why you are here, ignoring her calls? You're sulking. Did you see her illness as an opportunity to strike, only to be told no?"

Charlotte's eyebrows shot up at the suggestion, only for them to drop immediately as she realised there was a vein of truth to the last part.

"I'm not sulking, just like I'm not running. My father always had the intention that one day I would take over from him as CEO. He told me before he died. Now my mother's had a stroke, or a mini-stroke, whatever the fuck that is. Now it's my turn."

"For what?"

Charlotte shot her a questioning look.

"A heart attack? A stroke? To take over the company? All of the above?"

Arte's words sat with her for a moment as she digested

their meaning. There was nothing to say she would suffer the same fate as her parents. Was there?

Shifting uncomfortably in her seat, Charlotte said, "I've chosen my path."

"Have you? Or are you simply fulfilling a family legacy?"

"Isn't that what we're both doing? Shouldn't you be off creating art?" Charlotte asked, trying to divert the focus away from herself.

"I haven't cast that future aside. I have a job to do first, a job I've chosen to do. I'm working towards getting back to what I want in life. But you… do you even know what you want, or are you blindly walking down a path someone else has laid for you?"

Am I?

"Sorry, it's not my place to question you," Arte said, seeming to realise she may have overstepped. "I get the feeling you're not one to open up easily."

"You would be right."

"It's my face apparently, why people overshare with me. Not that you *are* oversharing, I mean. Unless you feel you are?"

Charlotte shook her head. She did feel she'd overshared, but she didn't regret it. She felt Arte might be the only person in the world that truly knew her — a rather depressing thought — but perhaps that was because she'd been honest for the first time in forever. Realising Arte hadn't finished, she braced herself for more from her beautiful, insightful host.

"You said it was time you started your life. I would urge you to think about what you want from it, not just personally but professionally. Make sure it's your path, not someone else's. You've spoken passionately about one thing this evening, and it wasn't being a CEO. That part you spoke about like an entitled brat," Arte said, poking a finger at Charlotte's arm playfully, as if to soften her words. "You're obviously good at what you do. You're adding immense value to my business… and to me. You deserve so much more than being unwanted. If you'll never be good enough for your mum, then perhaps it's time you think about walking away."

Walk away? Is she serious?

"I worked hard for my position," Charlotte replied indignantly. "I helped build the business up."

Arte shrugged matter-of-factly. "If you think it's your destiny, find a way to make it work. But stop basing your value on other people's opinions, especially those who aren't worthy of having one. What do you enjoy most about the business? Do that. If something doesn't work for you, then it's up to you to change it. Don't wait around for others to acknowledge you and see your worth. You get one life; you don't owe anyone any of it."

Even though she didn't hugely appreciate Arte's simplistic view of her life, Charlotte responded with a warm and amicable expression. As the intriguing artist was the only person taking any interest in it, she wasn't going to tear her to shreds for her opinions. Arte appeared to be genuinely concerned for her; another attractive quality to add to the already extensive list Charlotte was tallying.

"Can I ask who the famous person is that's sleeping in

your bed?" Arte smirked. "Is it Goldilocks? She has a habit of doing that."

Charlotte snickered. "No, but you're not far off, and she appreciates discretion. So no, you can't ask."

Arte seemed satisfied and didn't enquire further, much to Charlotte's relief. She reached out to the sleeping dog beside her and stroked his soft nose. He eyeballed her and then went back to sleep as she continued to pet him. She was partly annoyed at herself for lowering her barrier and letting the black Labrador leap over it with boundless enthusiasm, and partly chuffed she'd made a new four-legged friend. He was gorgeous.

Reminding herself that only heartbreak would ensue from letting even a little bit of Rodin into her heart, she stopped and picked up her wine glass to busy her hand. Taking the last sip, she realised she was more light-headed than she wanted to be, and with the bottle empty it was a good time to call it a night. It was only ten o'clock, but it had been a physically and mentally exhausting day, and there was a lot to digest from their conversation. She was unsure how she felt about any of it, but she knew she was best left alone with her thoughts.

"I'm going to head up," Charlotte said, extracting herself from under the paw resting on her leg.

"Oh, okay. Goodnight."

There was no mistaking the melancholy in Arte's voice. Charlotte resisted the urge to stay. As much as she wanted to spend the rest of the night in her company, it was late.

She left the room feeling she would be missed — something she hadn't felt in a long time, if ever.

CHAPTER 16

A warm fizz shot through Arte's body as the sound of shuffling feet entered the kitchen behind her. She sensed immediately that they belonged to Charlotte and not Sophie. It was the sound of someone who'd consumed a few glasses of wine and gone to bed with a lot on her mind, not the sound of someone who routinely rose at dawn. Rodin's tail whipped everything within reach as he greeted the newcomer.

"Morning," Charlotte said through a yawn.

Knew it!

"Morning. Toast?" Arte asked, knife already lined up on a loaf of bread.

"Please," Charlotte replied, joining Arte and watching her cut a slice. "Although, perhaps not, if that's how you butcher bread." She picked up a wonky wedge and examined it. "This makes me question all your artistic skills."

"It's bread."

"And there's a wrong way and a right way to cut it."

"The wrong way and your way, you mean?" Arte playfully snarked.

"Sorry if I prefer my toast in slices rather than… what do we call this, a doorstop?"

Arte passed the knife to Charlotte and took the wedge of bread from her. "Fine, you can cut your own." She turned to place it in the toaster only to find Sophie beaming from ear to ear by the door. "Oh, morning. Didn't hear you come in."

"Clearly," Sophie replied. "Morning, Charlotte."

"Morning."

"Cut me a slice, too, please. I know only too well that Arte's artistic talents don't extend to the kitchen."

"You can talk," Arte shot back.

Sophie glared at her. "I'll have you know I have no complaints at home. Just from ungrateful houseguests."

Rodin pawed at the back door, pulling their attention over to him.

"I'll take him," Charlotte said. "Pop those slices in the toaster when you're finished please, Arte."

"Okay," Arte replied, watching Charlotte in disbelief as she opened the back door. "Take a—"

"Bag. Yes, I know."

She would hardly acknowledge Rodin in any positive light a few days ago, and now she was cleaning up after him. Charlotte Beaufort was an enigma, and a rather attractive one at that, dressed in slim-fitting black jeans and a grey wool jumper.

"Coffee, Soph?"

"No, thanks. I've already had two this morning whilst you were lounging in bed. What on earth is this?" Sophie asked, picking up Charlotte's box of tea from the work surface as soon as Arte pulled it from the cupboard. "Mariage Frères."

"Charlotte's swanky French tea. It's actually quite nice; just don't tell her I said that."

Sophie clucked as she set the tea tin down. "You two are like an old married couple."

"Shut up. I barely know her."

"Yet you've spent the weekend with her, shared a bed with her, and she's outside cleaning up after your dog. It's not about the time; it's about the feels. Anyway, I've seen how she looks at you. She's keen."

Arte overlooked the bed-sharing comment. Sophie was being obtuse, and she wasn't going to allow her sister to bait her. She was too distracted by the thought of how Charlotte looked at her.

"She doesn't look at me like anything," Arte said, popping Charlotte's perfectly sliced bread in the toaster and trying to hide her elation.

"She does. You can tell because it's the only time she smiles."

That comment, which couldn't possibly be true, made Arte's heart skip in her chest.

"She's married."

"Divorcing, you said," Sophie snarked. "Anyway, someone's marital status doesn't stop them from having an enormous crush on someone. I can see it all over social media… Chart."

Arte pulled a face. "What?"

"You know, your couple name."

"No. Absolutely not. I'm not a tween, and you know that sounds like 'shart'."

Sophie laughed. "Oh, I remember the kids doing a few of them."

"Yeah, thanks for that image, Soph. Why are we even talking about this? She's Charlotte Beaufort, television star, millionaire, and soon-to-be CEO of a vast hotel empire. I'm Arte, owner of a bed-hogging, farting Labrador and part owner in a run-down hotel I can't afford to fix."

"Don't forget artist extraordinaire."

Arte shot her a look of bemusement. "You know that's kind of the second time you've complimented my artistic skills this morning? Are you feeling all right?"

"Yes, but don't get used to it. I suppose it is an unlikely match. Only two days ago you were on the phone slagging her off."

Arte twitched and clocked the door. Even though she knew Charlotte wasn't in the room, the last thing she wanted was for her to hear she'd been rude about her behind her back.

"I was not *slagging* her off," Arte whispered. "Just letting off steam about how rude she was. That's all water under the bridge. She's not as icy as she makes out."

"Or is it being around you that melts her edges and makes her all moist?" Sophie said with a wink and a nudge to Arte's side.

Arte was about to nudge her back when her phone beeped.

How's the clearing going? F

"Who's that?"

"It's Freddie, Charlotte's assistant," Arte said, fingers flying over the phone as she responded.

Great, especially with the help of someone we both know.

Sophie glared at her. "Why is he texting you?"

"He's asking how the clearing is going." Realising that explanation hadn't quite answered her question, she finished with, "We're kind of friends. Oh, he's ringing me now. I better take it."

"I'm going to make a start on Gran's stuff. Join me when you're not too busy with all your new friends. You can bring my toast and some of Charlotte's tea," Sophie said, her voice laced with playful teasing.

Arte returned Sophie's sassy expression with an equally matched one as she answered the phone. Freddie's voice greeted her before she was able to speak.

"Are you serious that Charlotte is with you?"

"Hello to you too. Yes. I'd hardly make up something like that, would I?"

"Is she okay? Can you put her on? I need to speak to her right now."

"She's fine, Freddie. She's just taken Rodin outside for his..." It didn't feel quite right to finish that sentence.

"I'm sorry, what? Are we talking about the same person? Charlotte Beaufort is staying at your—"

"Shithole of a hotel?" Arte offered.

Freddie's voice dropped. "Charlotte didn't say that, did she?"

"Yes. To my face, the first time we met."

"Wow. Okay, that explains a lot. I was going to say 'inferior establishment', but she seems to have termed it only the way Charlotte would. She's been with you since...?"

"Late Friday afternoon."

"She must have come straight to you after she told me to collect all her belongings from her house. I was already a little concerned, and then Claudette rang me this morning demanding to know where Charlotte was and asking why she's not been answering her phone. I've just tried to call her, and she's not picking up for me either. I was really worried; she never ignores my calls. When I phoned Gideon he said he didn't know or care, and said..." Freddie went silent, then added, "She's divorcing him," in a whisper.

"I know," Arte whispered back.

Freddie continued, not registering her comment. "I hope she's not having some sort of breakdown. I guessed she wasn't happy in her marriage, and Claudette is something to be contended with but — wait, what? You know?" He groaned. "Of course, you know. Why wouldn't you know when she's spent the weekend helping you clear out your nearest and dearest's effects and has gone to take a dog, that she apparently couldn't stand forty-eight hours ago, outside for a shit!"

The high-pitched strangle in his voice as he finished, and the subsequent breathlessness coming back down the phone, had Arte concerned.

"Are you okay, Freddie?"

"Yes. I'm fine." A long, deep breath followed. "But if Claudette finds out about the divorce, I'm not sure any of us will be fine ever again."

Arte was now finding herself intrigued to meet the

woman who appeared to have the ability to put so many people on edge.

The back door opened, and Rodin thundered in, still on his 'I've just done a poo' high. Charlotte followed.

"Hang on a second, Freddie."

Charlotte's face dropped at the mention of the name, and Arte realised it might have been a mistake to let on to where Charlotte was. Despite her protestations that she wasn't on the run, something was obviously afoot.

"I might have just told Freddie where you were," she whispered, one hand over her phone.

"Arte!"

Arte winced. "What was the harm? You said you weren't running." She offered her the phone. "He wants to speak to you."

"Tell him I'll ring him back from my phone. I left it upstairs."

"Freddie, Charlotte says she'll ring you back in a minute."

"I'll ring her," he said. "Make sure she picks up."

"Will do."

After Freddie hung up, Arte studied the phone. That wasn't the usual chilled Freddie she'd come to know and like.

"He says he's calling you and you have to pick up," she reported.

Heading for the door, Charlotte said, "I don't have to do anything I don't wish to, and I'm not running."

"He's worried about you," Arte said, as seriously as she could. "Most people don't just drop off the grid and ignore their phones."

"I'm not most people," Charlotte stated firmly, causing Arte to recoil.

Charlotte's face softened immediately, as if she regretted her harsh tone.

"That's something I'm beginning to realise," Arte replied with a warm smile, hoping it would dilute the sudden tension.

The comment was met with a twitch of amusement at the corner of Charlotte's mouth as she left the room.

Arte pushed away the same fuzzy feeling she'd felt in her stomach when Charlotte had entered the kitchen. Hunger. It had to be hunger… but for what?

The toast popped up, annoyingly snapping her from where her thoughts were wandering.

Charlotte was feeling the effects of a busy day, one too many glasses of wine, and lying awake at night, playing over what Arte had said on the sofa. Why would she not want to be CEO of Beaufort Hotels? It was in her blood, pumping through her veins.

Having convinced Freddie she was fine, he'd still insisted she call Claudette back immediately. When she did, her mother informed her she was taking some time off after all, insisting that nothing else had come from the hospital tests. Even so, a few weeks of rest were in order, and she needed Charlotte to take over temporarily as CEO.

Her unexpected announcement left Charlotte wondering how she'd come by that decision. She was unlikely to have made it voluntarily, so she suspected her mother had been given further stark warnings from the doctors. Everyone was to be told she was on holiday, and her medical blip, as she called it, was to stay between those who already knew.

It was time, Charlotte thought. This was finally her opportunity to impress and prove not only to her mother, but to the board, that she was ready. She was going to give it everything she had.

As she carried her bags down the stairs, she met Sophie on her way up.

"Leaving us so soon?" Sophie asked.

"Afraid so," Charlotte replied.

"I hope it's not on my account. My sister seems to rather enjoy your company."

A subtle expression of joy appeared on Charlotte's lips, despite her attempts to prevent it. "The feeling is mutual."

"You two make an effective team. I'm not sure she and I would have whipped Gran's room into shape as well as you did."

"Sometimes it helps to have someone on the outside. I hope the show helps you get the fresh start you need."

"I hope so, too, for Arte's sake. She has a little more invested in this than I do," Sophie said with a sigh as she looked up at the staircase. "I'd sell it tomorrow if it wasn't for my little sister and her big dreams. There are too many ghosts here for my liking."

Charlotte frowned. "Ghosts?"

"Memories of the past. Some of us don't like to cling to them as much as others. I hope we'll meet again, Charlotte. My husband is an… enthusiastic fan."

"Well, I wouldn't want to disappoint."

"Oh, I don't think you're capable of disappointing anyone," Sophie said, as she continued climbing the stairs. "Safe journey."

If only that were true.

Arte didn't look surprised to see her with her bags packed as she appeared from the kitchen. Following Freddie's phone call, it was inevitable that things would change and Charlotte would need to return to normal life. Arte gave her a resigned smile and followed her to the car.

"It seems I can't hide any longer," Charlotte said, placing her bag down beside it.

"I thought you weren't hiding."

"I said I wasn't running; I didn't say I wasn't hiding," Charlotte said with a smirk. "I've spoken to my mother; it seems I'm to take over as CEO." Charlotte raised her eyebrows in an 'I told you so' manner, refraining from adding the word 'temporary' in front of 'CEO', which was in fact all she had been granted so far. She was sure once her mother had had some time away, though, she wouldn't wish to return. By the time she and Arte met again Charlotte would be fully instated. She was sure of it.

Arte nodded. "So I was wrong. Your mother isn't standing in the way. I'm pleased for you. You can go and fulfil those dreams."

Charlotte noticed her phrasing, which seemed to acknowledge they were *someone's* dreams, if perhaps not her own, but decided not to respond. She'd already reached the unfortunate conclusion that Arte had been right about her mother being an obstacle in her path. What she was going to do about it was another question entirely.

"Oh, you mustn't forget your tea," Arte said. "I'll run in and fetch it."

Charlotte stopped her with a touch to her arm. "No need. You keep it. I know you secretly enjoyed it." She refrained from adding that it would be something to remember her by.

Arte rolled her eyes and shrugged. "Okay, you got me."

"I meant to give you this earlier." Charlotte pulled a business card from her pocket.

Arte's face lit up.

"It's the contact details for one of my laundry suppliers. Mention my name and you'll get a huge discount."

The light in Arte's face extinguished immediately but was soon replaced with a look of appreciation. "Oh. Great. Thank you. That's really kind of you."

Charlotte inclined her head at the acknowledgement and reached back into her pocket, suspecting Arte had been hoping for something else. Taking out her phone she opened it and handed it to Arte.

"Put your number in."

Arte took the phone. "Oh, okay."

The delight radiating from Arte's face did not escape her notice as she passed the phone back. Charlotte tapped on it at great speed, and a beep sounded from Arte's pocket.

"Now you have mine. Just in case you need to reach me… anytime. I guess we'll see each other next at Beaufort Mayfair, to film that segment of your episode. I hope you will join me for dinner during your stay."

"I'd like that," Arte said as she reached forward to hug her.

The unexpected, tight embrace sent Charlotte's heartbeat off the charts as she absorbed the feeling of Arte's breast pressed against her a little too much. A warming sensation surged through her, leaving more than her extremities tingling. She took a moment to take in the scent of her, the shape of her, and how all-consuming it felt to be held so firmly by Arte, until social etiquette forced Charlotte to step back. Their eyes met momentarily, until Arte's turned away as she tucked a loose strand of hair behind her ear. What Charlotte would give to know what was going through the curious artist's mind. All that filled her own was a longing to be back in that hug again and to enjoy the connection with another human being — with Arte.

"Thanks for coming back and for all your help," Arte said. "I'm not sure I would have gotten this far without you. I don't think I would have even filled a single skip. Oh, what am I saying? I wouldn't even have the skips!" She took a breath. "It was nice to spend time with you and get to know you better."

"Likewise. Thank you for letting me stay. It's been a breath of fresh air getting away from my life and those in it for a few days. It's... brought a new perspective on things."

"I'll send you an invoice for all the psychotherapy. Or should I send it to your mother?"

Charlotte's lips tightened as she got into her car, placing her sunglasses on in an attempt to defy the low winter sun.

Lowering the window and her sunglasses, she said, "I look forward to seeing you again very soon, Arte."

With a glance in the rear-view mirror as she drove away, she saw Arte hurriedly withdraw her phone from her pocket.

As Charlotte turned onto the main road, she realised she had not prepared herself for how much she didn't want to leave the shithole of a hotel and its sweet new owner behind. She was excited about Arte's overly ambitious and totally unachievable dreams. It had been a long time since she'd had a project like that, and just the thought of it sparked a little flame in her belly.

CHAPTER 17

Following Charlotte's departure, Sophie assisted Arte with marking up every piece of furniture in the building to indicate what would be staying and what would be going. Everything that was going and required two people to lift they dealt with as a priority; the rest they left for Arte to attend to at a later date. They made great progress, even agreeing on what to do with Gran's possessions without argument. Sophie took some items for herself and the children to keep, and the rest they sorted into piles for either the charity shop, the skip or for storage. By the time Sophie left, Arte knew she had a grasp on things that she hadn't had two days before, when Charlotte had come knocking. Even the knot in her stomach had gone, though she couldn't pinpoint when.

As the week progressed with only herself for company, though, her mood dropped. Without the distraction of Sophie, and only the clicking of Rodin's claws and his bored yawns for company, she was left with an overwhelming feeling of loneliness at Hotel Aloysius.

Loneliness in the shape of Charlotte. The only thing keeping her going was knowing she would see her again soon. She'd taken to drinking wine in the evenings. Sitting in her usual seat, she would close her eyes and pretend Charlotte was beside her to help fill some of her emptiness, recalling some of their — what she'd felt to be — flirtatious banter.

A moment's distraction came when her belongings arrived from Italy. They had taken the longer route, by sea. She was pleased to see her art books had made it in one piece, along with her drawing pads and pencils. The few sculptures she'd decided to ship were relatively unharmed, too, with only one having taken a knock. Her immediate thought was to fix it, but then she remembered she didn't have the equipment anymore, a thought which left her feeling even more empty. Was she even a sculptor without her tools?

With the urge to do something creative, she sat down with her sketchbook to lay down a more formal design for the barn, only to see the outline of Charlotte appearing beneath her pencil instead. She put the book down and returned to work in room 4, where she found herself lying on the mattress, pretending Charlotte was next to her again. That was the final straw. She promptly took Rodin out for a walk in the freezing rain to shake the memory of Charlotte. It didn't work. She just imagined she was walking beside her, her alluring, plummy voice in her ear. By the time she returned home, Charlotte was still firmly fixed in her mind, and she and Rodin were both cold and damp.

"Oh, Rodin, I can't be falling for Charlotte Beaufort," Arte said as she cuddled him beside the fire.

Rodin stared at her with his big, brown eyes as if to say, "Too late, mistress, you already have fallen" before closing them. The thought made her whole body tingle with a mix of lust and apprehension. She had to admit she was pining for her. Well, if she couldn't shake Charlotte, then she would need to feed herself *more* Charlotte. She sighed and opened her laptop, knowing that while it was not the solution, she was unable to stop herself.

Three episodes of an early series of *Hotel SOS* made her feel even worse. The overwhelming urge to be near Charlotte and connect with her, like they had at the weekend, was unexpected and suffocating. She missed their mundane exchanges over dinner, their friendly banter, their heated discussion, their subtle touches, even Charlotte's warm, musky, woody scent, which lit up her brain like nothing else.

She was still undecided whether to reply to the message Charlotte had sent her when they'd said goodbye. It didn't need a reply as such. Charlotte had only sent it so Arte had her number — hadn't she? But why would Charlotte want Arte to have her phone number if she didn't want her to contact her? She had said 'anytime'. Was that not an open invitation?

Arte opened her phone and looked at the message for the hundredth time. The words were still the same as the last time she'd looked.

I'm looking forward to showing you my place.

By 'my place', she clearly meant her hotel, not her penthouse, didn't she? With two glasses of wine inside her and a craving for some interaction, Arte pressed her fingers to the phone.

I'm looking forward to dinner very soon.

She regretted it the instant she pressed 'Send', but there was no going back as the word 'Read' appeared underneath the message. Her heart pounded, and she patiently waited for a response. Any reply was better than nothing, even if it was Charlotte laughing at her attempt at conversation. She hated text messages; it was always preferable to read people and situations in person.

Fifteen agonising minutes later, her phone pinged as she was shaping herself around Rodin in bed.

I'm looking forward to seeing you *very soon.*

Arte's heart almost stopped in her chest, making her cough. Had Charlotte one-upped her in a single message? Not that she was complaining. Why hadn't she thought to make her message more direct and state she was looking forward to seeing Charlotte? Sod dinner.

Should she respond or leave it there? How could she respond to that without sounding like a rambling idiot? She could send a smiling emoji. That would be enough to say she appreciated the comment, though something told her Charlotte wasn't the type of woman who responded well to emojis. Realising she was overthinking the entire non-conversation, she pushed the phone out of reach to stop herself from replying and went to sleep.

The short yet sweet interaction powered her through the rest of the week, and by the end she was exhausted but pleased with her achievements. A weight had lifted from her shoulders to have broken the back of the work. She had one important task left that couldn't wait: she had to pack for her stay at Beaufort Mayfair and dinner with Charlotte. A dinner, she had to remind herself, that was most definitely *not* a date.

Packing turned out to be the greatest challenge she'd faced all week. Not one to concern herself with her appearance, she suddenly felt compelled to care and make a good impression. She was unsure of the dress code for dinner, but she knew her dungarees wouldn't make a great match for such a place.

Deciding it was best to have clarification as to the dress code, she texted Freddie. His reply with photographs of beautiful dresses did nothing to allay her fear that she was far from being a suitable dinner guest at a classy hotel. They were all incredible, and the last image had her zooming in on a sleek, black, sleeveless jumpsuit. It wasn't a million miles from a pair of dungarees, except for the part that would leave her naked from her midriff upwards, where the material parted to cover the breasts. From there it went over the shoulders and crossed at the back. It was gorgeous, up until the moment she spotted the price.

She tapped at her phone. *I can't afford that. I could buy a new bathroom suite for that.*

Don't worry. There is a budget for your wardrobe.

There is?

Of course.

But this is for dinner. We won't be filmed then, will we?

No, of course not. Dinner is for the two of you, alone. You have the best table in the restaurant reserved. You'll be able to take in the bright lights of London when you're not drooling over my employer.

Very funny!

He hadn't contested the point that this outfit was for dinner and not the show. She was too in love with it to push the question any further.

I'll have it sent to you tomorrow. Send me your dress and shoe size.

Shoe size?

I'm assuming you don't have matching shoes.

Okay, thanks, Freddie. I appreciate your help.

All she had to do now was hope Charlotte appreciated it as much as Arte hoped she would.

Arte stared out of the window and up at the city she'd not visited in years. From the back seat of a luxurious Mercedes S-Class, with only a silent chauffeur for company, she took in her surroundings. The cityscape had grown taller and more metallic than the last time she visited. It had lost a lot of its charm. Living in the countryside for only two weeks, she'd already become accustomed to its peace and serenity after leaving the hectic streets of Rome.

As they pulled up to the hotel, Arte tapped out a message to Freddie to let him know she'd arrived. She put her coat on and gathered up her belongings as the chauffeur opened her door. The Beaufort Hotel logo emblazoned on his jacket caught her interest as she exited the car.

"You work for the hotel?" Arte asked, having presumed he was sent by the production company.

"Yes. Miss Beaufort requested I collect you and deliver you safely to her door, Miss Tremaine."

"Thank you," Arte replied.

He nodded.

"Do you collect all the hoteliers from the show?" The words had come out before she could stop them.

"You're the first."

"Are you new then?"

The chauffeur removed his hat to reveal a balding head, which he proceeded to scratch. "I've been working for Beaufort for nigh on forty years. I was Miss Beaufort's father's chauffeur."

"Oh. What was he like?"

"He was a great man and an even greater employer. Sadly, he was taken too soon." Putting his hat back on, he said, "I have no doubt Miss Beaufort will be even greater."

Arte nodded, having no doubt too.

"I'd best be getting this cleaned," he added, examining the mud spray along the side of the Mercedes. "Miss Beaufort doesn't appreciate a dirty car."

Arte chuckled. "That I know. I'll leave you to it. Thanks again."

She stood on the pavement, absorbing the knowledge that Charlotte had sent her driver to collect her and had not done that for anyone else. She was to be delivered to Charlotte's door. Her bedroom door? Arte allowed her mind to wander for a moment. What would her bedroom look like? It would be immaculate, she was sure of that; not like the chaos of her own. Her sheets would be silk… And just like that, an image of Charlotte in nothing but a silk slip came to mind, beckoning Arte to join her under the sheets.

Yep, that's enough.

Daydreaming like that was not appropriate for the pavement. She stared up at the hotel. The cold, metal box she recalled from the photographs stood before her in all its glory. It was an intimidating sight, and a far cry from her little country hotel. Arte didn't envy the weight of responsibility Charlotte must have felt from owning fifteen of them.

With no Freddie in sight, she walked inside, thanking the doorman as he held the door. Having only looked at the exterior photos online, she was taken aback by the grandeur that met her in the lobby. It may have been a metal box on the outside, but the interior was a warm, welcoming space, even at double height. The walls were tastefully styled in contemporary oak veneers and offset with bold wallpapers, blending seamlessly with elaborate brass-and-glass chandeliers. Teal velvet covered crescent-shaped sofas; their tapered wooden legs stood on a two-tone marble floor, bringing the styles together in a contemporary nod to Art Deco.

She made her way over to the reception desk, and a young man greeted her with a wide, cheerful countenance.

"Checking in, madam?"

"Yes. My name is Arte Tremaine, erm… *Hotel SOS.*"

"Oh, yes, I can see you here. We have you in one of our standard roo—"

A breathless Freddie appeared by Arte's side and scooped her into a hug. "Sorry, I was stuck on a call." Letting her go, he spread a grandiose arm to indicate the space around them. "Welcome to Beaufort Mayfair." He leaned over the reception desk. "Tom, Miss Beaufort has requested you upgrade Miss Tremaine to a luxury suite," he whispered loudly enough that Arte could hear. "Room 96 is available."

Tom looked at his screen. "Of course. Parking pass?"

"No need. Donald collected her."

Tom shot a look at Arte as if now taking her in as a person of importance. Freddie held out his hand, and Tom placed a keycard into his waiting palm. He slowly retracted his hand, sliding his fingers along Freddie's skin. Arte blinked and then bit her lips to stop a grin from giving away what she'd seen.

"Thanks," Freddie said softly, "and she'll be joining Miss Beaufort for dinner this evening. Double-check the reservation please; her usual table."

Tom tapped at his keyboard. "Confirmed."

Picking up her bag, Freddie said, "I'll take you to your suite."

Arte was about to protest and insist a standard room was fine — it would be more than fine considering the level of decor she'd already seen — but thought better of it. If Charlotte wished for her to have a particular experience during her stay, then she didn't want to appear ungrateful.

They stood by the elevator only momentarily before it chimed and let them in.

"When will I see Charlotte?" Arte asked as Freddie pressed a button. "Or should I be calling her Miss Beaufort?"

"You are keen," Freddie said, catching her eye in one of

the lift's many mirrors. "Lucky for you, so is she. She requested I take you up to see her immediately. When she's in the office or at a hotel, we have to call her Miss Beaufort. As for what you call her, that's between you and her." He gave her a wink in the mirror.

Choosing to ignore his connotation, she asked, "Up? She's here then?"

"Yes, she's with the production crew in one of the meeting rooms upstairs. We'll drop your bags in your suite, and I'll take you up. With Charlotte's change of position at headquarters, her schedule is tighter than we'd like, so we'll only be filming until lunchtime, after which Charlotte has insisted I take care of you and show you everything Beaufort Mayfair has to offer. You can expect a light lunch and spa treatments, followed by afternoon tea with some direct questioning from yours truly about exactly what went on when Charlotte stayed the weekend."

"Ah, I wondered when that would be coming." She shrugged and hoped her cheeks didn't colour as she said, "There isn't anything to tell."

It was true — there wasn't much to tell. They'd sorted out their differences, got to know each other a little… no, a lot better, filled an entire skip, and exchanged numbers. It was nothing to write home about and certainly nothing that needed sharing with Charlotte's assistant without her knowledge. Arte absolutely hadn't stroked Charlotte's hand, enjoyed the feeling of their bodies being pressed against one another, or lain beside her on a bed whilst thinking about touching her.

"I don't believe that for a second," Freddie said with a nod at her reflection.

In the mirror, Arte could see a dreamy smile adorning her face. She quickly let it fall away.

Where had that come from?

After Freddie showed her around the lavish suite, which included a separate sitting room with a dining area, the plushest marble bathroom she'd ever seen, and even her own butler, they returned to the elevator. Arte stood nervously in front of one of the mirrors, giving herself a quick check-over whilst trying not to draw attention to herself.

Her heart began to pound in her chest at the realisation she was minutes from seeing Charlotte again. Her palms began to moisten. She wiped them on the smartest pair of dungarees she owned, having disguised them as jeans by wearing a jumper over them.

"Nervous?" Freddie asked as he checked his phone.

Arte managed a nod. *Did nothing escape him?*

"There's been a change of plan." He hit the top button on the elevator panel. "Production has finished their meeting and left to set up. Charlotte will see you in her lair."

Her lair.

The nerves dissipated a little, replaced by intrigue and excitement at the thought of being granted access inside Charlotte's inner sanctum.

CHAPTER 18

Charlotte paced the floor of her luxury penthouse study at Beaufort Mayfair, surprised by her nervous disposition. She didn't *do* nervous, not since she'd performed on stage as Annie at age seven. Her father had found her five minutes before curtain-up, concerned for her after she'd cried in the car on the way to the theatre. He had explained that nerves were there to self-sabotage and that Beauforts always succeeded, so it was inevitable that she would too. Taking her hand, he told her to put all her nerves into her palm and make a fist, then to hold her head high and to never look at her fist. Bizarrely, it worked.

It felt like a lifetime since she'd left Arte's, despite it being one of the busiest weeks of her life. She'd purposefully kept it that way to steer her thoughts away from the distracting hotelier. The highlight of her week had come in the form of a late-night text from Arte saying she was looking forward to dinner. Having drunk the majority of a bottle of wine at the time to numb her day in the office, the message had lifted Charlotte's spirits to no end. What she had hoped would be a conversation starter — a reply that she was looking forward to seeing Arte — was met with no response. She'd waited an hour for something, anything, before finally turning in for the night, disappointed. By that time she'd finished the bottle of wine and run every scenario in her head as to why Arte was not responding. She had convinced herself that Arte was asleep and would respond in the morning, but she was met with further disappointment the next day.

A cold shower snapped her out of her pathetic state, a state that definitely wasn't pining. She'd simply clicked with someone, that was all. It was the high of finding someone in life that you hoped would remain part of it. But if that was the case, why the hell was she pacing her room now, knowing Arte was about to enter it?

The clicking of her suite door came from the hall. Charlotte rushed to her desk and opened her laptop, proceeding to type on the keys as if she was busy working. She closed the lid and then her eyes.

What am I doing?

Hearing the study door open, she got up and was greeted by Arte's beaming face.

"I have Miss Tremaine for you, Miss Beaufort," Freddie announced.

Charlotte realised that, although she'd thought of little else other than the moment she would see Arte again, she was not prepared for it in any way. She found herself walking towards her with rather too much enthusiasm for someone who was trying to play it cool, though she was surprised to find Arte striding towards her at some pace too. They stopped short of one another, neither seeming to have a plan beyond that point. Clocking the smirk on Freddie's face, Charlotte held out her hand to Arte.

"Welcome to my domain, Miss Tremaine." She groaned internally.

I did not just rhyme.

A smile evaporated from her face, a good thing, too, as it was beginning to make her cheeks ache. The twinkle in Arte's eye as she took her hand suggested she found amusement in Charlotte's words of welcome. Or was it in something else?

Catching her PA regarding their conjoined hands, she said, "Production is setting up in 107, Freddie. Go and oversee them, will you? You know how I like things."

"Of course."

"We'll join you shortly."

As Freddie left them, Arte released herself from their firm handhold and almost ran to the floor-to-ceiling glass window, having spotted the view. She stopped short of placing her hand on the glass, much to Charlotte's relief.

"Wow, it's spectacular!"

"You'll be able to enjoy more of it at dinner. The restaurant is two floors below, something I insisted on when I remodelled the hotel a few years ago."

"You can see the whole city," Arte said, her head panning the view.

Feeling the need to reduce the distance between them, Charlotte joined Arte by the window. "Indeed. And may I ask what you think of the hotel?" she asked impatiently. "The view, although spectacular, isn't my achievement."

"For a cold, metal box, it's pretty impressive."

"Pretty impressive? Is that all?"

Arte turned to face Charlotte, looking directly into her eyes. "It's beautiful." Her face flushed with a tinge of pink. "One might say it's a work of art."

Charlotte felt her body tingle as Arte appeared to look her up and down. "It may be a little harsh on the outside, but that doesn't mean it has to be on the inside."

"Are you talking about your hotel or yourself?"

Charlotte narrowed her eyes playfully.

They stared at one another for a moment, taking each other in, until Arte said softly, "It's nice to see you again."

"Likewise, and I see you've forgone the dungarees."

Arte lifted her jumper and grinned.

"Perhaps not," Charlotte amended.

Arte stepped away and examined the artwork on the walls. Charlotte watched her as she moved from one painting to the next, her pace quickening as she went. She stuttered, about to say something, then stopped.

"Do you like what you see?" Charlotte asked.

"These painting are all—"

"Emerging artists. Yes, they are. The builders of our future visual arts."

Arte pulled her attention away from the art and placed it firmly back on Charlotte, a wry smile at the corner of her mouth and a twinkle in her eye. "You really are a dark horse."

"I may not pay ten thousand pounds for a dead bumblebee, but I believe these make for a good investment."

"Not only that. In supporting a new artist you are directly contributing to the success of their career."

"Hence the sound investment. These could triple their value in a few years."

"And if they don't?" Arte asked, eyebrow raised.

Sensing she could be falling into a well-placed trap, Charlotte took a moment to consider her answer. "Then I will still own a unique and meaningful piece of art."

"Correct," Arte said, her smile lingering on Charlotte. "So, what's the plan?"

Charlotte twitched her head. "Plan?"

"Plan for this morning… filming-wise?"

"Ah, yes," Charlotte said. She'd almost forgotten that Arte was here for business, not pleasure, at least for some of the time. Dinner couldn't come soon enough.

"I'll show you one of our rooms and point out touches you may wish to introduce in your hotel."

"Oh, so we're calling it a hotel now," Arte said, returning to Charlotte's side by the window.

"Establishment," Charlotte quickly corrected with amusement. "They'll have you wheel an empty suitcase along the road outside and then enter the hotel where I'll welcome you."

"What do I say?"

Sensing nervousness in Arte's voice, she said, "Nothing. A lot of today is about getting material, which I will narrate in a voice-over."

"All nice narration, I hope. On that note, are you playing good cop or bad cop today?"

Charlotte exhaled and walked over to her desk, flopping down in her chair. Arte followed, perching herself on the desk beside her.

"What is it?"

Mike's words from their production meeting, when she'd broached the subject of going easier, came to mind. *Stick to the character! This is* my *show, not the Charlotte Beaufort Show. I have no time for wayward presenters.* His aim had no doubt been to embarrass her in front of the crew, which, to be fair, it had.

"Let's say I've suggested good cop and it has been met by a firm no."

"And if you were to be good cop, would he cancel the show because you stood up to him? Can he even do that? He's only the director."

"Mike is a petty man; I wouldn't put it past his capabilities. At the least he could get me dropped from the show."

"Why do you care?"

Why did *she care?*

Perhaps it was time to call it quits, move on from TV presenting, and focus on being CEO of Beaufort Hotels. If only she could be sure she would hold the position for more than five minutes, it might be an option. Her mother was threatening to return in a week, and with no plan to prevent it except an all-out coup — which she had little faith in pulling off — it would only result in a full breakdown of their relationship. It would undermine her position at headquarters if enough people sided with her mother, and she could do without being an unemployed divorcee.

"I'm not really in a position where I can make changes," Charlotte said, standing up. She felt Arte's hand slip into her own and squeeze.

"I know this sounds ridiculously corny, but I urge you to be the change you want to see."

"You may have grossly overestimated my power and influence, Arte."

"No. I haven't," Arte replied indignantly. "It is you that is vastly underestimating them."

Arte's mesmerising blue eyes were pleading as her warm hand squeezed again, harder this time. Charlotte felt her heart tighten, too, snatching her breath.

"We should go," Charlotte said abruptly, disliking the direction their conversation was taking and the short distance it was to Arte's tempting lips. "They'll be waiting for us."

With Arte's words weighing on her, she led the way to the elevator, where they stood side by side, waiting in silence. With mirrored walls, it was impossible not to look at each other, so following a momentary exchange of cheerful glances, Charlotte took her phone out to check her messages. It was best not to have Arte in her sight line, especially not when they were alone and in close proximity. She didn't need this particular distraction when she needed to focus on the fundamental problem that was about to present itself.

As they exited the lift, they passed a cordon; a sign beside it read 'Floor closed for filming'. Arte followed her into room 106, where make-up had set up. As she took a seat in front of the dressing table, Charlotte caught Arte's 'deer in the headlights' expression and tapped out a message to Freddie.

Seconds later he appeared.

"Arte, come with me," he said. "I'll talk you through everything."

After a quick glance at Charlotte, Arte sped from the room like she'd been given a last-minute reprieve from a death sentence. She really was a remarkable creature. Whether she would feel the same way about make-up when she looked dead on television without it, or when she reached Charlotte's age, she had to wonder. How something so simple could embolden one group of women yet strike terror into another was fascinating. Arte was lucky to have the option to avoid it. It was always expected of Charlotte, and she'd never questioned it. It was part of the routine for the lady her mother expected her to be, and it was something she wouldn't be without now.

When she returned from university in Switzerland, her mother had had a fit at the sight of her and ordered a complete makeover. She complained that the school may have taught her how to be a hotelier, but it hadn't taught her how to correctly look like one. Charlotte's shoulder-length, dark curls had admittedly become wayward, so she didn't argue. She was being given the greatest gift of a hotel to sink her teeth into, and she knew she needed to look the part for it. It was the nineties. No one would have listened to her creative ideas, grown to respect them, or embraced them if she hadn't modelled herself for the role.

Once her make-up was complete, she sought out Arte, keen to make sure she was being taken care of. She found her seated beside Freddie outside room 107, where the crew were making their finishing touches to the set. Many a hotelier had sat where she was, prepared for the humiliation that was set to continue on the other side of the wall — a humiliation in exchange for thousands of pounds' worth of renovations to their business and livelihood. This hotelier was different. Charlotte wouldn't put it past Arte to take matters into her own hands if she felt things were going too far. She'd need to prepare herself for that.

She took a bottle of water from the refreshment table, then met Arte's gaze, which was fixed on her. Her words, 'be the change', played over and over in her mind. The phrase could have come straight from her gran's hotel wall, but like most inspirational quotes, it was easier said than done.

Arte wasn't wrong, though, and as much as Charlotte didn't want to rock the boat with *Hotel SOS*, she didn't want to disappoint her either. The younger woman seemed to have such faith in her abilities. Had she been wrong to give her a glimpse of the real Charlotte? What had she been thinking, doing that? She wasn't that Charlotte now; she hadn't been for so long. Arte seemed intent on dragging her into the light and holding her up to it. The strange thing was she could feel it burning into her skin, burning Arte's goodness into her.

Was Arte also right in that Charlotte was underestimating her own power and influence? She was about to find out. Mike shot her a stern look as she and Arte entered the room. She could do this; it was nothing she hadn't done a hundred times already, even if every time the guilt of what she'd said ate into her a little more. The ratings, people's voyeuristic enjoyment in watching the distress of others — she'd enabled it. She'd never really questioned it; she had had no reason to until now. When she looked across the set to Arte, encouragement was written across her face. Her eyebrows were partly raised in question, her eyes urging, her expression supportive.

With a deep breath, Charlotte poised for the word.

"Action."

"This is one of our standard bathrooms," Charlotte began, finding her television voice, "yet it retains the feeling of luxury. The classic, white suites, when contrasted with a mid-tone tile and complemented with accents of darker marble, give the feeling of opulence. When carried out effectively, it's a style easily achieved with even the smallest of budgets. The frosted shower screens provide additional privacy but also add to the style. I would encourage you to look to this as a template." She could see Mike's agitation as he leaned in around the doorway. With only room for herself, Arte, a boom pole, and the cameraman in the bathroom, Mike would have to stay on the periphery. "A lot of hotels would use veneered wood, but I would steer clear of that in a bathroom environ—"

"Cut!" Mike yelled. "Let's draw some comparisons please, Charlotte. You know the drill."

She did. The show was second nature. She could conjure up whatever she needed. At this point, she was to demonstrate the stark contrast between her five-star hotel and that of the hotelier's shithole property. The drill was to make whichever hotelier was standing beside her at the time feel embarrassed and uncomfortable about the state of their own establishment. She was to point and sneer at their failure to do their job, for not seeing the state they had got themselves into until it was too late, and then laugh at their inability to fix their own mess without outside help. It was the equivalent of rubbing a puppy's nose in its own mess. She wouldn't do that to Arte, especially as it wasn't even her own mess.

"Cut," Mike shouted after the next identical take. "In character, Charlotte," he added firmly, his face reddening. "Let's go again and get it right this time!"

Arte fidgeted beside her. Charlotte could feel the fury radiating off her and shot her a confident smile to reassure her she was in control. Arte nodded back.

They went again, and Charlotte said her lines exactly the same way. The derogatory words about Arte's bathrooms that Mike wanted her to say wouldn't come, and never would again.

"Cut!" Mike glared at Charlotte, realising he wasn't going to win this one. "There will be consequences, Charlotte," he yelled as he stormed out of the room. "Gary, finish up this charade!"

Charlotte forced herself to keep quiet and not shout after him; staying in control of the situation was important. Getting emotional and saying things in the heat of the moment would have the opposite effect.

Gary, the assistant director, cleared his throat and suggested Arte and Charlotte move into the busy bedroom's main set. As they did, Charlotte felt a hand press into her own.

"I'm proud of you," Arte whispered in her ear.

The sensation of Arte's voice against her ear, and the touch of her hand, made Charlotte a little giddy. She wouldn't have taken the giant step to push back against

Michael if Arte hadn't urged her to reflect on her behaviour. There was so much to thank Arte for, from encouraging her to be a better version of herself, to reminding her that although some routes were easier than others, it didn't mean they had to be walked along without question. Her moment of victory wouldn't be long-lasting — in the back of her mind, she could already hear Mike's voice threatening consequences — but she tried to not let it affect the feeling those four little words were having on her body. She liked it too much.

Once they finished filming in the bedroom, the crew relocated downstairs to the lobby. Charlotte stood beside Arte at the back of a crowded elevator, still in total awe of what her encouragement had led her to do. An overwhelming urge to touch her caused Charlotte's fingers to flex. As they lightly brushed Arte's soft, warm hand, her stomach fluttered. Arte's fingers brushed back, causing goosebumps to ripple over every inch of Charlotte's skin, leaving her yearning for more.

She pursued, only to find her fingers seamlessly fitting into the spaces between Arte's, their hands fitting together like puzzle pieces finally falling into place. Her heart pounded so loudly in her chest she swore it would give her away to the rigid bodies in this tiny box, where it felt like time was standing still. The elevator doors opened with a ping, forcing them to part and dissipating the rush that had filled her senses.

The crew filmed Arte walking into the hotel, where a now tired and drained Charlotte greeted her. She knew her welcoming smile wasn't genuine, and the guilt weighed heavily on her. She didn't want to force anything for Arte.

"That's a wrap for today," Gary said. "Thanks, everyone." He shot a blank look at Charlotte which summed up everything she was thinking — What would be the fallout from Michael?

"Are you okay?" Arte asked once the crew had busied themselves with packing up.

"I'm fine," Charlotte replied a little too sharply. Immediately regretting it, she ran her hand up and down Arte's arm.

Freddie appeared beside them.

"Ah, Freddie, there you are," she said. "Please ensure Arte is looked after. I have work to do." She turned to look at Arte. A gentle glow in her eyes extended to an upturn of the lips. "I'll see you at dinner."

Hopeful that Arte understood the stress she was under, Charlotte headed for the elevator and the safety of her suite. There was a ridiculous amount of work to do before dinner, made all the more ridiculous given that all she wanted to do at that moment was slide into a hot bath… preferably with Arte waiting in it.

CHAPTER 19

Arte examined her jumpsuit in the full-length mirror. It fit like a glove. Although she was baring parts of herself that hadn't seen the light of day in public for years, it gave her a certain confidence — even without a bra. She set a few long, blonde curls into place. They suited her but were too high maintenance to ever make her consider changing her routine from a simple 'brush once and done'.

Having her hair done in the hotel's salon was Freddie's idea. He insisted she should complete her look for her 'dinner date'. That had earned him an elbow in the side. Following their delicious afternoon tea and a few hours of pampering in the spa, she wasn't going to argue about a little further extravagance. Charlotte had said to enjoy herself, and she felt the need for some restorative relaxation after the tense morning's filming.

Mike was one hell of an arsehole for pressuring Charlotte to behave in a way she didn't want to. A creeping sense of guilt made her question her own behaviour. Was she as bad as Mike for pressuring Charlotte? Was encouraging someone to be the best version of themselves as bad as pressuring them to be the worst?

Of course not.

She would at least apologise in case Charlotte had felt pressured by her when they spoke in her suite. It was best to make it clear that that wasn't her intention. Arte hoped she took the light squeeze of her hand in the penthouse as supportive rather than coercive. Although Charlotte appeared to be under a great deal of stress, Arte hoped their moment in the elevator would have at least lifted her spirits. A soft sigh escaped her lips as she recalled the touch of Charlotte's fingers as they came searching for her. How they'd brushed her skin and sent a rush of pleasure through her. How they had become entwined with her own and Arte could do nothing to stop herself from clinging onto them, perhaps a little too tightly.

She would have liked to offer further comfort to Charlotte by playing with more than her fingers, but as she'd excused herself after filming finished, it would have to wait. She was likely tucked away there now, in her gorgeous penthouse suite, preparing herself for dinner after taking a shower or a bath. Arte's mind formed an image of the latter, only to go overboard and add too many bubbles to the bath.

Damn it!

Placing her hand on her stomach, she took a deep breath and returned her attention to her appearance. What would Charlotte make of her outfit? What would Charlotte be wearing... and, more intriguing, what would she be wearing underneath?

Stop it!

She was due to meet Charlotte for dinner in twenty minutes. Unsure if she should wait for her outside the restaurant or in, she settled on being fashionably late and hoped Charlotte was there first. There was enough time to devour something cool and liquid from the minibar to calm her spiralling nerves.

Despite gorging on afternoon tea, she was ravenous and also a little tired from the spa, though it was likely Freddie's line of questioning about her weekend with Charlotte that had drained her. She had regaled him with boring snippets about their clearance work and let on that Charlotte spoke highly of him, which seemed to please him to no end. When he didn't give up pushing, she changed tactics and questioned him about Tom the receptionist. He'd blushed and agreed they should move the subject away from hotels altogether.

As she devoured a rare glass of champagne from the minibar and appreciated the bright lights of the city from her window, her thoughts fell to the art on the penthouse's walls. Knowing Charlotte not only appreciated art but collected it from emerging artists had her neurons doing backflips. There was something so attractive about a woman who appreciated art, not only because of a shared appreciation for the subject, but because she often found that other art lovers shared a similar outlook on the world.

Having finished her champagne, she made her way to the restaurant, relieved that the bubbles had worked their magic and taken the edge off her nerves. The maître d' informed her that Miss Beaufort was awaiting her at the bar.

The sight of Charlotte in an off-the-shoulder, knee-length, black dress, expertly balanced in a pair of strappy heels, was something to behold. It set Arte's heart pounding and a surge of arousal to course through her. Charlotte was more beautiful and far less intimidating than when Arte had first laid eyes on her outside Hotel Aloysius. Back then she had seen Charlotte's external beauty; now Arte saw the beauty that lay on the inside too.

Charlotte was deep in conversation with an elderly couple, oozing confidence and delight in her natural setting. It didn't stop her eyes from shifting a millimetre as Arte appeared in her sight line. Her eyes locked onto Arte's, and the tiniest of creases pulled at the side of her mouth. Neither broke their gaze until Arte reached Charlotte's side and she made her apologies to the couple that her 'dinner date' had arrived.

Dinner! Date!

Arte drew in a quiet breath to slow her heart, annoyed that the champagne had already worn off. It stood no chance against the effects of Charlotte Beaufort in a revealing dress.

Finally alone, Arte felt her host admiring every inch of her.

"You look… heavenly," Charlotte said. The tiny crease at the side of her mouth was now a perfectly formed and beaming smile.

"Thank you. As do you."

Acknowledging the compliment with a tilt of the head, Charlotte's eyes traced over Arte's outfit again. "I was sure you'd have a dungaree evening dress. I'm pleased to see you've managed to retain an element of your usual style and made it a little more… revealing."

Arte watched as Charlotte appeared to ogle her chest.

Fuck!

Charlotte turned to flag a passing waiter as Arte tried to gain control of her pounding heart. As they followed the waiter to the back of the restaurant, Arte did all she could to guide her weak legs in the right direction. She couldn't be more grateful for Freddie's thoughtful choice of footwear. Her stylish, black sandals were hiding under the wide hems of her jumpsuit. She would have killed herself in Charlotte's shoes, or at least broken both ankles, even without her quivering legs.

They took their seats at a small table overlooking the city. Looking around, Arte noticed this was one of the best tables in the restaurant. Once Charlotte had ordered a bottle of wine, Arte took no time in broaching the subject of the morning's filming as they perused the menu.

"You were incredible this morning," Arte said, testing the water to see what Charlotte made of it now she'd had time to process it all.

Charlotte's neutral reply of "Hmm" did nothing to allay her worry that she may have overstepped.

Time for that apology.

"I'm sorry if I pressured you, or if you felt pressured by me."

Charlotte looked up from the menu. "You didn't pressure me. There was perhaps a little coercion, but it was well-intentioned, wasn't it?"

"Yes. Yes, of course."

"Then let's speak no more of it." Charlotte returned her attention to the menu until the waiter returned with their wine and a bottle of water.

"Your outfit really is stunning," Charlotte said once the waiter had filled their glasses and taken their order.

You should see me out of it.

"Thank you. Freddie chose it, actually, and the sensible shoes." She dangled a leg out from the table and wiggled her foot.

Charlotte admired the sandal. "His talents have no end. I trust he looked after you this afternoon. I'm sorry I had to rush off, but I've been rather busy with my new role."

"I understand. I had a pleasant enough afternoon, despite your hotel not being a shithole. You know how I love those."

Charlotte simpered. "I see you've taken advantage of our salon." Charlotte reached forward and caressed one of Arte's curls between her fingertips. "Jules is exceptionally talented; she does my hair."

Looking down at Charlotte's hand hovering millimetres from her breast made Arte's breath catch in her throat. What she'd do to be alone now with Charlotte and that sharp tongue of hers.

"Oh, really," was all she could say. Her mind had already drifted back to the image of Charlotte in the bath.

As Charlotte's hand retreated to lift her champagne flute, the scent of her perfume lingered, lighting up all Arte's senses.

"Cheers."

Arte clinked the glass presented to her and took a

couple of large sips, in desperate need for more of its calming effects.

"So, have you been keeping busy?" Charlotte asked as she set down her glass. "How much progress have you made?"

Arte told her all about her week, leaving out the parts where she pined pathetically for her. Charlotte listened attentively.

"Have you considered getting a business loan to speed up the renovations and get you open earlier?"

"I have, but Sophie doesn't want the debt. To be honest, neither do I. We'll take the slow route. Once the interior designers have been in, we'll be operational with one room at least. I'm going to focus on spending what funds we have available to work my way through the other bedrooms."

"Ensure you don't skimp on the mattresses, carpets, or linens. Guests wouldn't know a ten-pound wallpaper from a thousand-pound wallpaper, and the only thing they notice about the lighting is if it's dusty or not working. You can pick up some decent-quality country furniture at antique shops."

Why hadn't she thought of that? It wasn't as if she was heading to IKEA, but antique shops were kind of obvious.

"Have you thought beyond the decoration?" Charlotte continued. "How are you going to get bums in beds?"

"Well, Sophie's husband is great with websites, so once I've taken photographs, he's going to do that, and Sophie's great with all that airy-fairy word stuff."

Charlotte lifted an eyebrow. "You mean copywriting?

The skill of artfully persuading another human to take a particular action?"

"That's it. Sophie has a great ability to bullshit and manipulate."

"And beyond a website? I assume you've contacted the booking sites to re-establish a partnership. That's where most of your bookings come from."

"Of course," Arte said, withholding the fact that they refused to include the hotel again until she settled the existing debts on previous bookings.

"I could ask my marketing director to give you a call and talk through some ideas."

"Yes… please. That's kind of you. Thanks." Thinking for a moment over what Charlotte was offering, she added, "Unless that puts you in an awkward position. I don't want anyone to think you are singling me out for special treatment."

Arte's cheeks burned as she realised she could have worded that much better.

Charlotte leaned forward and in a low voice replied, "Oh, if I wish to single you out for special treatment, Arte, I'm perfectly entitled to do so. I wouldn't let anyone persuade me otherwise."

"Are you flirting with me, Miss Beaufort?" Arte teased; Charlotte's twinkling eyes said it was game on. "How do you even know I'm into women?"

"I don't need to know your sexuality to flirt with you, Arte; you're an adult. If you don't like the attention, you can tell me to stop. Like you would if a man flirted with you." Charlotte repositioned herself back against her chair and took a sip from her wine glass. "Anyway, I know you like it. I have a lot of experience with body language; it's important when dealing with people."

"Oh, really? And what is my body language telling you?" Arte licked her lips, realising she may not wish to hear all the ways in which her own body was mutinously telling Charlotte how she felt about her.

"That my attention makes you a little nervous, but you like it."

That was an accurate observation, and the little eyebrow flicker Charlotte shot her did nothing to ease those nerves.

"Even your 'Oh, really?' just then was overtly flirtatious," Charlotte continued, as one side of her mouth twitched up. "So I would say you're the one flirting with me."

"Am I now?" Arte said coyly, only to realise how flirtatious that may have sounded too. "For your information, I am into women, and only women."

Charlotte acknowledged her declaration with a tilt of her head.

To Arte's annoyance, the arrival of their meals interrupted their conversation, and when the waiter was gone, Charlotte moved on to point out the illuminated London landmarks whilst they ate.

Charlotte thanked the waiter as he cleared their dessert plates. The hotel's chocolate torte really was a highlight of the menu. She watched Arte cross the restaurant and return to her seat from the toilets, giving Charlotte a delightful eyeful of cleavage as she settled in.

"There's one thing I have to know about your outfit." To be fair, Charlotte had a lot of questions about it; she had been unable to take her attention off it all evening — or the parts it wasn't covering to be accurate.

"Just the one?"

"How on earth do you…?" Charlotte pointed down.

Arte leaned forward, causing the soft candlelight to flicker gently. "It's too complicated to explain. I'd have to show you," she whispered.

Charlotte let out a quiet gasp as her cheeks tinged with pink. She was doing everything she could to not think about Arte undressing, and she was failing miserably. In need of a swift change of subject, she asked, "How's Rodin?"

"He's fine; he's at the kennels. I could have brought him to see you if only you would allow dogs."

"Dogs in a Beaufort Hotel!" Charlotte exclaimed automatically, before realising she'd fallen back into character. Arte's twisted lips told her she knew it too. "Mother wouldn't approve."

"Your mother is no longer in charge, is she?" Arte said.

No, she wasn't, though neither was Charlotte, technically.

"So, how does it feel to be CEO?" Arte asked, refilling their water glasses.

"Challenging, to say the least." In truth, the reality of running a multimillion-pound business wasn't quite living up to her expectations. "I could be CEO of anything. It's all profit and loss, spreadsheets, structuring, restructuring, and strategy. Don't even get me started on HR issues and the never-ending meetings with pointless men posturing at one another. The only way I know I'm in the hotel industry is my pen says Beaufort Hotels on it."

"That doesn't sound like much fun."

Charlotte gulped her wine, chastising herself for not appreciating its full £200 flavour as it slipped down her throat.

"Tell me about the remodelling of this hotel," Arte prompted.

That she could do for hours, though in this case, she would refrain. The last thing she wanted to do was bore Arte with the finer details of lighting choices, wallpapers, soft furnishings, and the installation of smart technology.

"When its turn came for updating, I insisted on dealing with it. I may not have been running the hotel then, but it was still my…"

"Baby?" Arte suggested.

"Still important to me," Charlotte finished, playfully narrowing her eyes. "I've kept one eye on this place since I left. Hired all management." Arte's pointed look from across the table led her to add, "And yes, I guess it does feel like my child. There. Happy now?"

"Yep," Arte replied with a twinkle of satisfaction in her eye.

What Charlotte would give for an opportunity to make them twinkle with ecstasy.

"So are all the Beaufort Hotels metal boxes?" Arte asked. Charlotte's questioning expression led her companion to add, "And tastefully enriched on the inside, of course."

"Of course," Charlotte replied with a playful twitch of her mouth. "Yes, we only deal with city hotels. Mother has a particular dislike for the countryside."

"Must be where you got it from," Arte pointed out with a chuckle.

Feeling the full effects of that comparison, Charlotte looked down at her plate. Arte reached forward and placed her hand on hers; the softness and warmth radiated into Charlotte's skin.

"Sorry," Arte said tenderly. "What do I know? I've never met her."

Charlotte admired how good Arte's hand looked atop her own, but then Arte withdrew it, leaving behind that emptiness she'd found it always did.

"I'm sure you're nothing like her." Arte reached for her wine and turned her attention to the window.

Watching her reflection, Charlotte noticed her eyes were rolling as if she were chastising herself. With a smile and the most reassuring voice she could muster, she said, "I find the countryside growing on me more and more. Maybe when I'm CEO I'll buy a couple of country hotels."

"I thought you were CEO. Has something changed?" Arte asked, her attention fully back on her host.

Charlotte waved her hand casually, realising her slip. "I mean once I'm settled in." She hated not telling Arte the full truth about her position and had regretted it ever since. It was petty to have made out she was full CEO, just to impress her and prove a point.

"Can I ask how things are with your husband?"

"You can ask. Whether I'll answer is another question entirely."

Arte's concerned face forced her to give her guest something.

"It's all quite amicable at the moment." What she meant was she hadn't heard a peep from Gideon directly, but she knew he had instructed a lawyer as he had contacted hers. "Whether it will remain so, once my mother returns from abroad, only time will tell."

"What's your mother got to do with any of it?"

"What indeed?" She forced a smile, aware that the mere mention of her mother had likely made her face fall flat. "I just mean she will have something to say on the matter."

Charlotte suspected Gideon hadn't informed his parents yet because her mother hadn't mentioned it. Gideon's mother would have been straight on the phone to discuss it with Claudette, no doubt to ask her to sort Charlotte out. The thought struck her that perhaps he had told them, and they had decided instead to close ranks. She let out a sigh. She was sick of second-guessing the situation and decided she would deal with whatever particular shitshow presented itself.

She turned her attention back to Arte. "Any more thoughts on your studio?"

"Nothing but thoughts," Arte replied, her eyes glistening in the candlelight. "It frustrates me that I can't jump straight in and that I may have to wait years… if not forever."

Charlotte placed a hand on Arte's, concerned that the shine had gone from her eyes in all but ten seconds. Arte didn't react to her touch with anything but a look of contentment, so she left it there.

"I love your enthusiasm, and I want you to realise that dream more than anything, but you have to start small. Be realistic."

"I know. I just miss sculpting and teaching; it's in my blood. I was hoping I could put it aside for a while and focus on the hotel like Gran managed to for all those years."

"Perhaps your gran's grand passion was the hotel, not the art, and yours is the reverse. It sounds like she made the right choice… for her, I mean." She'd seen her gran's art, and privately, Charlotte felt she had nowhere near the talent Arte did.

"I don't want to choose one over the other as she did. I could plough on with the barn and at least get an income to pay for the hotel."

"And have them stay with your competitors, or in a tent?"

Charlotte reluctantly withdrew her hand from Arte's as a waiter approached. The tips of her fingers cooled at the loss of Arte's warmth, but the last thing she needed was the staff talking and it getting back to her mother that not only was she divorcing Gideon, but she was having a candlelit dinner with a beautiful woman she'd been gazing dreamily at and holding her hand. She knew she would have to explain everything in time, but she wanted to be the one to choose the moment.

"I guess we should call it a night," Charlotte said, conscious of the time and the amount of work she had to do tomorrow. "I'll walk you to your room."

"Thank you." Arte stood as she spoke. "And for dinner, it's been delightful."

"Perhaps we could have breakfast together in the morning. I have this table reserved at eight."

"Yes," Arte gasped, almost erotically. She cleared her throat. "I look forward to it."

~

Arte stood up from the table only to realise how much the wine had gone to her head. She steadied herself on the chair whilst Charlotte thanked various staff members.

Sober up.

Having made it this far without making a tit of herself, she was not going to fall at the last hurdle. Charlotte led her out of the restaurant and straight into a waiting elevator as if she'd telepathically summoned it.

It had been some years since someone walked Arte to her door. The anticipation during their journey down five levels to Arte's floor felt like someone had turned up her thermostat and set the dial to swoon.

As they reached her door, Arte turned to face Charlotte and said, "Well, this is me," acutely aware that it was the line said in every cheesy romance film ever produced.

"So it is."

They stood still for a moment in awkward silence. Arte was about to say 'good night' when Charlotte looked both ways down the corridor, stepped forward, and placed one finger and then two onto Arte's exposed abdomen. Arte froze as Charlotte's eyes came to hers, seeking permission. Her skin tingled under the touch of Charlotte's fingertips as they continued to brush lightly. Working their way up the exposed skin between Arte's breasts, they came to rest on the side of her neck.

Leaning forward, Charlotte whispered, "Breathe," into her ear.

"I don't think I can." Arte's words came out as a throttled gasp. It was all she could manage. The feel of Charlotte's cheek against her own, her breath against her ear and her familiar musky scent, it lit up Arte's senses like electricity. Her heart was pounding so hard against her chest, she was half expecting it to burst out and jump straight into Charlotte's arms.

Charlotte drew back to face her. Her warm and inviting eyes, determined and unyielding, bore into Arte's, leaving her breathless again. The space between them narrowed to within an inch as Charlotte edged towards her again. She placed her hand on Arte's face and brushed her thumb against her lips, shooting tingling sensations to every nerve.

Charlotte Beaufort was about to kiss her!

A ringtone sounded from somewhere. She prayed it wasn't Charlotte's, but knowing they were alone, she waited for the inevitable.

Charlotte closed her eyes and then took a step back, reaching for her phone in her bag. "It's Freddie," she said after examining the display. "Sorry, I have to get this. Don't go anywhere. I'm not finished with you."

"I'll be right here… waiting."

God, that sounded lame.

Charlotte's lips twitched with an apologetic smile as she moved away to answer. "This better be important," she growled.

Arte chuckled, then took the moment to suck in a few deep breaths, feeling devoid of oxygen. After all, the blood in her body had rushed to one place.

Her whole body tingled at the authority in Charlotte's voice. For all her attempts to persuade Charlotte to be kinder, there was something in that stern voice that was a massive turn-on.

Charlotte began pacing the corridor, her hand gesticulating. "What! I knew something wasn't right. I'll have to go through the contract again tonight. Set up a site visit for tomorrow; I'll need to see for myself." Putting the phone back in her bag she re-joined Arte, the softness that had been all about her that evening replaced with firmness and anger.

"I'm so sorry, I have to go. Something's come up."

Arte wasn't sure what to say to that, so she fumbled out, "Oh, okay… good night."

Charlotte took Arte's hand and lifted it, placing a soft kiss on the back. "Sleep well."

She watched Charlotte stalk down the corridor, doubtful she would ever sleep well again, at least not until she'd had her way with her. Brushing the back of her hand against her lips, Arte inhaled the scent she'd left behind. If that was the closest she was going to get to Charlotte Beaufort tonight, she'd take it. As for the pulsing between her thighs, she would have to deal with that alone.

CHAPTER 20

When Arte awoke the next morning, her first thought landed on what last night could have been if not for the interruption. Rolling onto her back, her second thought fell to Charlotte Beaufort being millimetres away from kissing her. She eagerly anticipated a repeat performance and would murder anyone who interrupted them.

With that thought she leapt out of bed and headed for the shower, then packed her suitcase for departure following breakfast. With a quick call to give Jenny an approximate time for when she would collect Rodin, she headed to the restaurant with a spring in her Doc Martens.

A waiter led her to the table she had shared with Charlotte the night before. Taking the same seat she waited… and waited.

Five minutes late, she thought as she checked her phone. *That's okay, right?*

A waiter appeared moments later with news which crushed her.

"I'm afraid Miss Beaufort has been unavoidably detained and regrets she won't be able to join you for breakfast. Can I get you anything?"

"Oh, okay. Just some tea, please," Arte replied casually, trying to disguise her dismay and finding her appetite had abandoned her all of a sudden.

Relieved that her tea arrived swiftly, she drained her cup, impatient to return to her room. If Charlotte became un-detained and came looking for her to say goodbye, at least she'd know where to find her.

Waiting as long as she could in her room, she reluctantly grabbed her belongings and admitted she was unlikely to see Charlotte again — for some time at least. The car was due to collect her shortly, and she didn't want to keep the driver waiting. As she stepped out of the elevator and crossed the lobby, she took out her phone, tempted to call or text Charlotte to say goodbye.

"Were you going to leave without saying goodbye?" a stern voice boomed behind her.

Arte spun so fast she nearly gave herself whiplash. "Charlotte!" The relief in her voice must have been palpable because Charlotte's face lit up, even as she drew closer. In a lower voice, Arte added, "I thought that, as you stood me up for breakfast, you might have thought twice about what nearly happened last night."

"I'm sorry I couldn't join you for breakfast; I had an important call. And as for thinking twice about last night" — Charlotte smirked — "I can assure you I've thought of little else. All night in fact, while I was awake, dealing with a shitstorm over our latest acquisition."

"You haven't slept?"

"No time to even change," Charlotte said, looking down at herself.

"Oh, yes," Arte said, her mind drifting back to the previous night, when she had felt the same eagerness as she had now to relieve Charlotte of every stitch of fabric. "I hope you get it sorted."

"I'm sure I will, in time," Charlotte replied, surveying the lobby as she spoke.

"Are you okay?"

"I've realised there is something very important I haven't shown you yet. Come." Charlotte beckoned for Arte to follow her across the lobby, to a room beside reception, where she ushered her inside.

Arte had been sure it said 'Closet' on the outside of the door, and she was even more sure it was when she saw rows of coats hanging up on rails. As she turned to question why she needed to see the room, Charlotte answered by pressing her lips against Arte's and pulling her into her arms.

Arte didn't hesitate. She kissed her back, pushing herself so hard against Charlotte that she'd forced her back against the door. A lustful passion ached within her as Charlotte's warm and frenzied lips took everything they wanted, as if they'd waited a lifetime to kiss her.

The sensation of Charlotte's lips against her own, the taste of her, was overwhelming. She reached for Charlotte's breasts, grasping them, caressing their softness beneath the sexy, black dress. She pressed herself harder against Charlotte, pushing her thigh between her legs.

"Mmm, Arte," Charlotte moaned into her mouth with rapid, shallow breaths as she writhed against her thigh.

Arte's body weakened at the sound of her name spoken so softly, and so erotically, by Charlotte Beaufort of all people.

"I wanted to do this to you last night," Charlotte said, her hands roaming eagerly over Arte's body, much to her delight.

Light gasps escaped from her lips as Charlotte's nipped and kissed her neck, sending a pleasant tingle coursing through her body. She'd never felt such an overwhelming sense of being desired, nor had she experienced such intense desire for another person before.

"You're so beautiful," Charlotte whispered as her tongue skimmed Arte's trembling lips.

Arte wanted to respond in kind, but she was too busy, taking in the sweet taste of Charlotte.

"When can I see you again?" Charlotte asked breathlessly.

"They're filming…"

Charlotte placed a finger on Arte's lips as she kissed her jawline. "No, no. I'm not making myself clear, am I? Let's try again."

She felt herself being pushed across the room, and then the backs of Arte's legs met the side of a desk, forcing her on to it. Her weak knees were grateful for the relief. Charlotte positioned herself between her thighs, forcing them apart as she held her waist and pulled her back up to her, pressing their bodies together.

"When can I see *you* again?" Charlotte clarified before placing her lips back on Arte's and kissing her deeply.

"Oh! Erm…" Arte struggled to remember how to form

words, let alone get them to leave her mouth when it was so busy exploring Charlotte's.

"You could invite me to stay with you?" Charlotte suggested, coming up for air.

"Erm… yes, nice."

"Only nice?" Charlotte teased as she left breathy kisses against Arte's cheek.

Arte searched her brain for a better word. She only needed one; where were they all? "Exquisite?"

"A word more suited to you, I think," Charlotte said, tightening her grip again. "You, Arte, are exquisite."

Her voice was deep and desperate, making Arte feel faint, overwhelmed with the depth of Charlotte's passion.

"Will you have… time?" Arte stuttered, wondering if the rushing blood that was making her giddy had taken all her words with it.

"I'm CEO now. I'm sure even they get the odd weekend off. I don't answer to anyone, not even my mother."

Charlotte's lips found their way to her neck again as her hand lightly caressed Arte's breast, causing a groan of pleasure to escape from Arte.

"Tell me something… did you come to my hotel that weekend to seduce me?"

A light chuckle from Charlotte's mouth tickled the soft skin of Arte's neck, sending her writhing against the desk. "No. I came to make amends and get to know you. I meant what I said… I was trying to impress you when I insulted you so abominably," Charlotte said between kisses. "Not my finest moment, I'll admit. Something struck me about you the first time I saw you. The way you looked at my car perhaps… or your dungarees… or this face." Charlotte sighed and licked Arte's lips, setting her body on fire again.

A low, vibrating feeling in her pocket told her the car was waiting and Freddie was looking for her, but she didn't want to be the one to bring whatever this was to an end. Or for Charlotte to ever take her hands off her. She wanted more of their touch… and in less chaste places.

The phone vibrated again.

Arte pulled out of their kiss, hating herself for doing it. "I have to go, sorry."

Charlotte only became more frantic at Arte's words and pulled her back to her, unwilling to let her go.

"My phone… Freddie… car," Arte managed to say between their breathy kisses. "I'm sorry, I don't want—"

"That's the second time my assistant has interrupted us." Charlotte tutted, though she loosened her grip and stepped back to allow Arte to move.

Slipping down off the desk, Arte told her legs to sort their shit out before she fell over.

"Thank you for being such an attentive host. I've enjoyed my stay… particularly this last bit," Arte said her eyes glistening as she wiped her lips to remove any traces of Charlotte's lipstick.

Placing a hand against the side of her face, Charlotte said softly, "Let's do it again… soon."

"Can't wait," Arte said, feeling a heady smile break over her face. "Call me?"

"You can count on it."

Arte opened the closet door, smoothing herself down as she exited. She wasn't ready to leave Charlotte and wished she could go back inside and finish what they started.

What have *we started? What is this—*

A voice coming across the lobby interrupted her thoughts.

"There you are!" Freddie said, striding towards her. "What on earth are you doing in—"

Charlotte appeared beside Arte and closed the door. This was definitely a question for her to answer.

"Ah, Freddie. I was just giving Arte a tour of the..." Charlotte looked at the sign on the door.

"Closet?" Freddie suggested with a grin.

Charlotte flustered before saying, "Erm, yes."

"Well, now you are out of the closet... if you are ready, Arte, I will escort you to your vehicle." He held out his arm to her and picked up her bag from outside the cloakroom door.

Arte did her best to stifle her giggle at Charlotte's blushing face. Taking Freddie's arm, she made a circular motion around her lips and pointed at Charlotte, hoping it would be enough to make her check her smeared lipstick.

Charlotte nodded and gave her the slightest of winks.

"I knew there had to be more to all that anger when you two first met," Freddie whispered as they headed outside. "People only get angry when they care about the other person's opinion, and it looks like you really care what Charlotte thinks. She must have made quite an impression on you that weekend."

"Okay. I admit it: we shared a bed together..."

Freddie gasped. "I knew it!"

"...for about five minutes when we were checking

which mattresses needed throwing away," she added, immediately bursting his bubble.

She'd give anything to be back on a mattress with Charlotte now, but the souvenir of their time in the closet would have to satisfy her for a brief time at least… until the taste of her wore off.

CHAPTER 21

It had been forty-eight hours since Charlotte carried out an emergency inspection of what was due to be Beaufort Hotel's latest acquisition. It was therefore forty-nine hours, forty-seven minutes, and too many seconds ago since she'd kissed and caressed Arte like the world was about to end — not that she was counting. Although she was only a temporary CEO, she had deemed it necessary to check the contract thoroughly since it would be signed during her tenure. She was hoping she was wrong about the problem she'd spotted. When she'd queried it with her surveyor, Jeremy, she hadn't expected him to respond so late at night to confirm that she was correct.

Despite her threat to fire Freddie or anyone who had disturbed her during her evening with Arte, he had been right to call her. Regardless of her frustration at the interruption, the matter required her immediate attention. When she'd returned the surveyor's call, she was astounded to hear that the subsidence that was affecting one of the walls was thoroughly documented in his report. He, on the other hand, was shocked that she didn't know about it.

Now, she was stuck in renegotiation hell, with only one person to blame. That person wasn't even aware of what was going on, as Charlotte hadn't summoned the courage to make the call and have the conversation with her mother. The question was, had her mother missed it in the report, or seen it and ignored it? Either way it was tantamount to gross negligence and in itself was going to cause a vast number of problems — as if she needed more.

Knowing she couldn't put it off any longer, she picked up her mobile phone and spun her chair around, admiring the view from her office window. Covering the top seven floors of one of the taller skyscrapers within the City, Beaufort HQ offered breathtaking views she couldn't get enough of. With a deep breath, she dialled her mother.

"Oh, that," Claudette's voice came back casually after Charlotte had explained the problem as calmly as she could. "It's nothing that can't be fixed during the renovation."

"It's subsidence, not a decoration blemish. It needs underpinning! Not only will that cost us thousands of pounds that we've not budgeted for, but it will also put the project back by weeks, if not months. That costs us, too, and more than fixing the issue. We're lucky the sale hadn't completed already. I'm in the middle of renegotiating the terms of the contract."

"Don't you go meddling in the contract! I negotiated a good price; we were lucky to get it for that."

"Meddling! I'm doing my job. Or rather your job, as you've failed to do it properly."

A sharp sniff came down the phone followed by an even sharper reply. "I'll be on the first flight home."

Charlotte was about to query why her mother was flying at all following a mini-stroke but realised it would be pointless to question her.

"Don't bother, *I'm* dealing with it!" Charlotte hung up, disgusted by her mother's laid-back attitude to something that had cost her endless hours of sleep, multiple grey hairs, and what may have gone on to be the best night of her life. Not that up to that point in the evening it hadn't already been. Arte was so easy to talk to, a breath of fresh air, and Charlotte wanted to fill her lungs with the intoxicating blonde.

Turning back to her desk, she rested her head against her fist. It had also cost her breakfast with Arte, the thought of which had kept her going through the night as she read the entire contract to check it for further issues. Why was she even fighting to add yet another metal box to the chain of Beaufort Hotels?

Her mind drifted to the charm of the historic Hotel Aloysius, hidden away in the South Downs. If anything in the South Downs was an Area of Outstanding Natural Beauty, it was Arte. Charlotte sighed again, wondering when she'd become such a sappy romantic. There was something about Arte that made her feel things she'd never felt before, and she'd made sure Arte left the hotel knowing that. The taste and scent of her lingered on the edge of her senses.

"Hello."

Charlotte jumped. "Shit, Freddie! I didn't see you there."

"Clearly not." Freddie smirked. "You were miles away, so how could you have? I did knock. Where was it that held your attention — or should I say who?"

"No, you shouldn't. You should say 'whom'," Charlotte corrected him.

Freddie rolled his eyes as he placed a cup of tea down on her coaster.

Charlotte picked it up immediately "Thanks. I need this. I just spoke to Mother."

"Oh. Would you prefer wine, whiskey? A bullet?"

Ignoring him, she asked, "When do I next have a day free to see…" Charlotte stopped herself.

"See *whom*?" Freddie snarked.

"Oh, very well," Charlotte replied, knowing there was no use denying it when Freddie was well aware of what was going on anyway. "To see Arte. Outside of filming. I'll see her for filming next week, obviously."

Freddie sucked in a noisy breath. "I've just received Claudette's schedule from Janet for next week when the design team is there, and I've had to cancel your attendance. Mike sounded more than fine with it and said they would add it to the studio time for voice-over instead."

"What? Why?" Charlotte demanded, having marked that date in her head to be reunited with Arte.

"You have to be in Edinburgh for meetings with the northern team."

So much for a CEO calling the shots on their life. She felt possessed by an unnatural force she'd not felt before, and yet she had no way in which to seek out its further possession. She was in no doubt that Mike was overjoyed by her future absence. It was easier to control what someone said when you placed a script in front of them in an audio booth.

"You have a rather packed diary," Freddie said, caution in his tone, as he tapped at his iPad. "Looks like… yes, you have Sunday free next week."

Her heart sank at the thought she wouldn't see Arte for another week and a half.

"Make sure it stays that way," Charlotte replied. "Please," she added more softly, noting the harsh tone creeping through from her misery. She rolled her eyes, feeling a virtual pat on the back from Arte.

"Will it be an overnight?" Freddie asked, a sly grin forming on his lips. It disappeared as soon as he caught the glare from Charlotte. "So I can pop it in the diary," he explained.

"I wouldn't like to assume, but I will be taking an overnight bag. Where am I on the Monday after?"

"Here, so it's an option." Freddie tapped at the iPad. "The design team will finish before then, so you can admire their work. Then you're back for filming of the reveal on the following Wednesday."

Freddie turned to leave.

"One more thing. Have you used my business credit card? There's a purchase here I don't recognise." Charlotte tapped a pen against a statement on her desk.

Freddie scurried over and examined it. "Oh, yes… that. I kind of told Arte there was a budget for her wardrobe for the Beaufort Mayfair shoot. She was really nervous about having something nice to wear for dinner and couldn't affo—"

"Okay." Charlotte signed it and handed it to him.

"You're not mad?"

"No, why would I be? It was a kind gesture. One that will take some explaining to accounts, but I'm sure you'll manage it. If they have a problem with it, I'll cover it from my personal account."

"I'll tell them it was for a model for a photoshoot," Freddie said, jogging from the room to his desk to answer the phone.

That outfit had been worth every penny to Charlotte. She looked at her mobile, tempted to pick it up and call Arte. Just as she reached forward, her desk phone rang.

"I have Malcolm for you," Freddie shouted through.

Charlotte groaned as she answered.

Business before pleasure!

The drawing room was a stark contrast to every memory Arte held of it. Now a stripped-back shell, she wondered what her gran would make of it all and how she would have dealt with the process.

With the carpets gone and the salvageable furniture taken by a clearance company, the slightest sound echoed in the empty space. She would have to insist on large rugs to cover the walkways. She couldn't have guests in the rooms above disturbed by the sound of people walking around the ground floor.

Ripping carpets up hadn't exactly been on her list of

jobs from the interior design team, but the more she did, the less they would need to do, and the sooner she could be rid of everyone, the better. Not that the crew weren't a nice bunch of people; the catering van in particular was more than welcome. It was Mike's presence that put her on edge. Knowing he was gunning for Charlotte placed him firmly in the enemy camp, so it was going to be uncomfortable having him around the place.

With Charlotte only scheduled for one day of filming out of the three, it greatly reduced the potential for disagreements between the director and his presenter. It was disappointing for Arte not to have more days with her, but she was determined to make the most of whatever time they would have together.

She was in two minds whether to take Rodin to Jenny to keep him out of everyone's way. With little to do herself except watch the transformation, she decided she could use the company. She could always set Rodin on Mike if he got out of hand. Seeing him covered in drool would bring her some amusement.

It had been a couple of days since she'd last seen Charlotte at Beaufort Mayfair. Every time her phone rang, she'd leapt at it in the hope that it was Charlotte calling, and every time, it left her disappointed. They hadn't exactly agreed on when they would make contact again. Charlotte had said she would call — well, she had nodded that she would. That was an agreement if ever she saw it, yet she hadn't called. What was the right amount of time to call someone after you'd kissed their face off in a closet? The very thought of it brought Arte the urge to do it again.

Fuck it!

A quick call wouldn't do any harm. She could keep it casual. Assess the lay of the land.

She listened to the ringing, growing impatient to hear Charlotte's voice. Then she became racked with guilt that she may be disturbing her in the middle of something important. The last thing she wanted was to appear needy. She was about to hang up when the tone of the ring changed and then stopped.

"Arte," Freddie's voice came back. "And what can I do for you? As if I couldn't guess."

The unexpected voice threw her off course.

"Oh, Freddie. I thought I called Charlotte." She knew she had called Charlotte.

"You did; her phone diverts to me when it's off. She has back-to-back meetings today."

"Oh, okay. Well, it was nothing important. I'm sure I'll catch her soon… for filming, right?" Arte replied, trying to curb the sadness that was no doubt exuding from her voice.

"About that… I'm afraid things have changed. To be exact, Charlotte's part in the schedule has changed; nothing has for the team."

What?

"Where will she be?"

"Edinburgh for—"

"Let me guess. Meetings?"

"She's covering Claudette's itinerary until she returns."

"Wait, what?" Arte shook her head. "I thought Charlotte was the CEO."

Silence met her down the line.

"Freddie. What's going on?"

"She's not officially CEO. The board were told Claudette's on holiday, which she actually is, but she's just taking a bit of recovery time."

"Then why did Charlotte tell me she was?"

"Probably because she will be soon; it's only a matter of time. We can't foresee Claudette returning. Between you and me, she isn't at all well. I've been chatting to her PA, Janet, and even she said she didn't think Claudette was up to the task of returning. So Charlotte is effectively the new CEO. Have I convinced you yet?"

"No," Arte replied, trying to convince herself that Charlotte would have had her reasons for not making her position clear.

"Okay, well, moving swiftly on, she's free a week on Sunday. I risk execution if anything threatens that, so rest assured she'll be there. I'm on holiday then anyway, so she'll be managing her own schedule. If she doesn't turn up, don't you come hunting me down, understood?"

Charlotte had fixed a date in her diary and was fiercely protecting it. That was something. Finding her mood lighter, Arte replied, "Noted. So, where are you off to, and might I ask with who?"

"With whom."

Arte scoffed. "I didn't have you down as the pedantic grammar type."

"I'm not, yet I found myself recently schooled in it by your girlfriend."

Girlfriend! She liked the sound of it, but they weren't there yet, were they? They hadn't even spoken since they'd locked lips and caressed as much of each other as they could in the small closet. A warm, tingling sensation washed over her at the thought of doing it again, and a little more, a week on Sunday.

"I'm not going to dignify that with a response. Now tell me where you're going."

"We are off on a ten-day cruise around the Mediterranean. And by we, yes, Tom and me."

"Sounds very civilised."

"It's a gay cruise with an overnight in Ibiza. If it's civilised, I'll be asking for a refund."

Arte laughed. Her twenties felt like a long time ago, not that she had ever been a party animal. An evening with a good book or a television show about art had always been more than enough to satisfy her.

"Are you going to tell me how you two met?"

"Galop."

"I've not heard of that. Is it like Grindr?"

Freddie chuckled. "It isn't a dating app; it's a helpline for LGBTQ+ people who have experienced domestic abuse. We both volunteer there. Tom more recently."

"Oh, so he…" Arte couldn't even finish the sentence.

"Afraid so," Freddie came back, his voice sullen. "A similar experience to my own, but we're at a point now where we're looking to help others."

"That sounds great. Not what you've both been through, of course, but that survivors can help each other, and even find… love."

"Don't push it, Arte. You're not getting any more details out of me about my love life."

"That's fine. I can wait for a wedding invite."

"And on that note, I'm hanging up on you. I'll tell

Charlotte you called as soon as she comes out of the meeting."

"Please don't mention it," Arte said quickly, hoping Freddie would hear before he hung up.

"Why?"

"I don't want to look pushy or desperate. It's hardly a great look, is it? She said she'd call, so I guess she will."

"If you're sure… but I'm pretty convinced she'll want to know you called."

"Yes, I'm sure."

"Okay then. Ciao, bella."

His last words sat with her. What was once such a familiar phrase now felt strange to hear. So much had happened since she'd left Italy all those weeks ago, it almost felt like a dream. Yet the soft touch of Rodin's fur beside her on the floor and the ache in her heart for Charlotte were very real. How could she miss someone she barely knew and yet felt like she'd known forever? And why did it feel like she spent most of her time with an ache inside for the people she missed?

Alongside that ache sat mild confusion as to why Charlotte had kept the permanency of her new role from her. There also sat empathy for her; Arte knew she disliked meetings. She was likely suffocating from an outpouring of testosterone at that very moment. Arte shuddered at the thought.

CHAPTER 22

Charlotte tapped her fingers against the desk, the soothing rhythm calming her racing mind. The contract renegotiation wasn't exactly going to plan. The other side was giving little movement, considering the scale of the problem. Although they had negotiated with her mother in good faith, the issue was down to negligence on her side. Charlotte had hoped they would be a little more amenable considering the implications if Beaufort were to pull out now. There were no other buyers interested — that much she knew from sweet-talking the agent. The seller also didn't like the fact that they were now negotiating with someone new and were demanding to speak to her mother.

She gave up drumming against her desk and pressed her fingers firmly into a stress ball. There was so much to do that she didn't know where to start. The one thing she wanted more than anything else was Arte's voice to soothe the aching for her. She reached for her phone.

The speed with which Arte picked up her call did more than soothe her, it warmed her heart.

"Sorry I haven't called before," she greeted the younger woman. "I'm snowed under at HQ. By the time I arrive back at the hotel, I'm so tired. I didn't want to give you two minutes of time only to fall asleep."

"I wouldn't have minded," Arte replied. "I was beginning to think you might be avoiding me."

"Avoiding you?"

"You kind of have a history of hiding," Arte said with a light laugh.

"No, I have not been hiding," Charlotte replied firmly but playfully. "I want to give you my full attention." She yawned. "Sorry, I didn't quite appreciate how much work a CEO has."

"And what about a temporary CEO?"

Charlotte paused, her warmed heart now racing in her chest. It was time for some honesty. "It's no different."

"Why didn't you say?"

The despondency in Arte's voice made her feel sick.

"I was trying to impress you, again."

"I'm not impressed by power, Charlotte; not that sort of power," Arte said firmly. "The power that impresses me is seeing a woman being honest with herself about what she wants and taking it. Like you did when you led me into that closet and—"

"Oh, I remember." The light in her eye mirrored the gentle uplift of her lips as she placed the stress ball back on her desk. "Vividly."

Arte continued. "It's knowing something isn't right and having the strength and bravery to change it, no matter the consequences. Not lying or inflating the truth."

"It wasn't a lie, just not the full truth." Charlotte sighed. "I'm sorry. I promise to stop trying to impress you in future. I appear to be pretty bad at it when I'm trying."

"That sounds good to me," Arte replied, almost sounding relieved. "Just be you. That will impress me."

Her words stirred a gentle flutter in Charlotte's chest.

"Part of me also didn't want you to be right about Mother, yet it seems you were. She still can't give it up."

"It is okay for other people to be right on the odd occasion, you know," Arte replied, sarcasm dripping from her voice.

"I know. It hurts to think that my mother might not trust me to take over."

"Your mum's inability to have faith in you is her failing, Charlotte, not yours. Why do you care when she's been stringing you along all this time?"

"Because… she's my mother," Charlotte replied firmly, finding her voice beginning to crack.

"Exactly. She shouldn't be treating you like this," Arte proffered, her tone hardening and volume increasing. "She recognises your worth, trust me. Anyone who knows you knows you are more than competent."

Arte had voiced more faith in her than her mother ever had, and she hardly knew her. Charlotte didn't want to consider what that said about her relationship with her mother.

"Sorry," Arte continued more calmly. "I don't mean to raise my voice, but it angers me when someone I care about gets treated like that."

Charlotte swallowed hard and opened her mouth to speak, to find only a whisper escaped. "'Care about'?"

"Yes, I care about you. A lot. In fact, I don't think there is anyone I've cared about more in my life. You know… like that."

"Like what?" Charlotte teased.

She knew full well what Arte meant, but despite their flirtations and an unforgettable fumble in the closet, she was still desperate to hear the words spoken from her lips.

"You know, romantically. I hate you not being here. To have a date when I can see you and then for it to change… I understand you have work, but it hurts."

"I have Malcolm for you," Freddie called through, sucking Charlotte back into her office.

"Tell him I'll call him back."

"It's important."

"This is more important," Charlotte shouted back. Pleased to finally hear silence from her assistant, she turned her attention back to the call. "I want to be there, too, but I can't get away. I have my own job to do, and my mother's. I was due to begin my annual inspections of our hotels over the coming weeks, like I do each year, but now I have to work around her schedule, which ultimately means coming in and out of London between inspections from all around the UK. I'm sorry. This is a crucial time for me. I finally have the chance to prove myself in the role, even if only temporarily. I've been waiting for this opportunity my whole life." She wanted to add that she felt she'd been waiting for Arte her whole life, too, but felt that might be a little too much too soon. "Please trust that I haven't been able to stop thinking about our time together. I want so much more of it."

"Me too," a tender voice replied.

"My feelings for you scare me, Arte. I hardly know you, yet it suffocates me to remember a time when I didn't. Every time I think about you my stomach lurches… in a good way. My heart rate goes off the charts, and I get a little hot under the collar. I've never felt like this before, and it scares the crap out of me at the same time that it excites the hell out of me. It's like you've lit a fire within my soul, but I'm afraid of it burning me."

Silence filled the air.

"Arte, are you still there?"

Don't say I just said all that and…

"Yeah… I'm here," Arte finally answered. "It's… I'm… taking it all in."

"I don't mean to overwhelm you, but I need to be honest with you about how I feel."

"No… no… it's great I feel the same."

She does?

"You do?" Charlotte asked, thinking she must have misheard.

"Yes, especially the bit about feeling suffocated."

Charlotte laughed with relief.

"I want to be honest too," Arte continued. "I didn't want to scare you away with how I feel either."

"Arte, you can never scare me away with your honesty. All it has done so far is pull me closer to you, even if it still doesn't feel close enough. Trust me when I say if I could be anywhere in the world right now, it would be there with you."

"I'd like that. So would Rodin," Arte replied in such a way that Charlotte could sense a playful smile on her face.

She didn't want to spoil the moment yet was acutely aware of the time.

"I'm sorry… I am going to have to go now. I hoped I would have more time to talk."

There was that silence again.

"Arte?"

"I'm here. I…"

"Talk to me," Charlotte urged her.

"I don't want you to go. I don't like the moments between. They feel… empty."

Charlotte touched a stinging in the corner of her eye, only to find her finger moist.

What has this woman done to me?

"I know." She hesitated before continuing. "I may not have a lot of time to talk until I see you next; I'll be travelling a lot and working on the road. How about we text each other when we wake up and before we go to sleep? Anything between we will count as a bonus."

"Yes," Arte replied with a sniff. "I'd like that."

"Great. Give Rodin a big hug from me."

Although she felt relief to hear Arte laugh at her request, the quiet goodbye that followed left Charlotte feeling subdued as she hung up.

"Err… Miss Beaufort," Freddie's voice snapped her uncomfortably back into reality.

"Yes, Freddie, I'll call Malcolm back now."

"No, you have something more pressing… incoming… right now." The high pitch of his voice as he finished speaking forced Charlotte to look up from her desk with concern. The petrified expression on Freddie's face on the other side of the glass wall could only be caused by one person.

Taking a deep breath, she braced herself as her mother waltzed into the room.

"Mother, you're back."

Claudette approached, removing and then slapping down a pair of black leather gloves on the desk in front of Charlotte.

"Still as observant as ever I see."

Her tall, thin frame carried an invisible weight which somehow dominated the room, even though it felt a little more frail than usual.

"Now what's all this nonsense with the Curtis Group?"

Nonsense? Seriously? It was gross negligence.

"I'm in the middle of renegotiating the contract. Please stay out of it," Charlotte said politely, hopeful it would encourage her mother to respond in a similar manner.

"I will speak with them myself!" Claudette spat.

"No, you won't. It will undermine our credibility, my credibility. You're the one who misjudged it," Charlotte replied calmly, squeezing her fists under the desk.

"It's hardly a misjudgement. More an overreaction on your part."

"Overreaction!" Charlotte slammed her hand on the desk. "We've had to re-budget the entire refurbishment. It's added eleven percent to our costs. Four percent of that increase is from a miscalculation on the refurbishment of the rooms alone. I can look at a room, calculate the size, and then price it to meet our standards with 0.25% accuracy." Charlotte knew she should stop and take a breath but wouldn't allow herself to do so. She needed the adrenaline that was pulsing through her to finish her point. "You should have brought me on board with the acquisition from the start instead of trying to deal with everything yourself when you're clearly not up to the task!"

Claudette shot a stare as cold as an arctic blast at her daughter. As she took a seat in the chair across the desk, Charlotte took a much-needed breath.

"As you can see you've wasted your time returning from your… holiday," she said. "I can handle everything here."

"Well, let's hope you manage it a little better than your marriage!" Claudette tapped a finger against the desk, her long nail clicking furiously.

Any concern for her mother's health melted away as quickly as Charlotte's mouth opened in protest.

But Claudette was clearly just getting started.

"You can forget this nonsense about divorcing Gideon. He's been nothing but good to you, despite your unwillingness to fulfil your role."

Translation: 'have children'.

"Even I managed that," Claudette spat. "I told him to hold off on the paperwork."

Charlotte shot out of her chair and finally found her tongue. "You did what?! This is not your marriage and not your life! Keep your damned nose out of it!"

Claudette was taken aback only briefly. "Do you know how embarrassing it was for me to find out from someone else that my daughter was filing for divorce? From Elizabeth of all people."

Charlotte's heart sank. So the in-laws knew, and of course, Elizabeth Black had predictably informed her own mother, who was now glaring at her. She was clearly awaiting an answer to what Charlotte had assumed was a rhetorical question.

"You were hardly in a fit state for me to tell you."

Claudette shot her a pointed look. "So you at least acknowledge how terrible it is."

"Terrible for you, perhaps; it's like a breath of fresh air for me. I'm sorry you can't see that."

"You can't throw away your marriage." Claudette folded her arms. "You won't find another man at your age, trust me."

"I don't need a man to feel I'm worth something, Mother. I'm not you."

Charlotte felt a brief moment of regret as her mother's face contorted. She knew she shouldn't be stressing her out, but things needed saying, and it seemed this was the time.

"You'll live to regret this," Claudette said, leaning forward, her glare piercing into Charlotte. "It's no fun being old and alone."

"I am alone. I've been alone our entire marriage — that's why I'm divorcing him! We were never compatible, and we never will be."

"You know we'll be the laughing stock amongst our friends," Claudette said, changing tack.

"Mother, if your friends laugh at you, then they are not your friends. Why can't you see that? None of those people gives two hoots about us. We greet them with falsity. We show up to their parties and make small talk.

All the while you slate them behind their backs as they do ours."

It was like living in an episode of *Bridgerton* but without the ridiculous costumes.

"Have you met someone else?" Claudette demanded. "Is that it?"

She took Charlotte's shocked silence as agreement. "Who is it? Don't tell me it's someone we know. Not Duncan… he always has a hand sliding onto a woman's backside. He's had his eye on you for years. Don't tell me you were flattered by a quick grope."

A cackle broke forth from Claudette, sending a wave of hot rage through Charlotte. Was that really what her mother thought of her? If her opinion was already that low, it was time for some hard truths.

Taking a deep breath she said, "It's… a hotel owner, actually."

Claudette's cackle only strengthened. "Someone who owns one of those dreadful hotels you have to deal with? Oh, the depths you'll go to."

"Yes, actually!" Charlotte yelled. "It is someone who owns one of those 'dreadful hotels'. Someone who has fallen on times of hardship and needs our help, not our disdain!"

Claudette fell silent and sniffed as Charlotte took the opportunity to catch her breath. She continued more calmly.

"Not everyone can be as wealthy as we are, Mother. Sometimes others can work as hard as we do, harder even, but not have fortune befall them as we have."

"What's his name?"

Charlotte inhaled a deep breath. "*Her* name is not up for discussion."

A strangled gargle came from across the desk.

"Her? A woman?" An unsettling mirth returned to Claudette's voice. She looked at Charlotte as if she expected her to retract the statement. Her face soured in the resulting silence. "Since when have you been a lesbian?"

Charlotte inhaled and tried to contain her anger. "Two women being together doesn't necessarily mean they're lesbians."

"It did in my day."

"We're not in your day, Mother! I would have thought you'd realised that by now. The world has moved on. Either move with it or—"

Claudette stood and replaced her gloves. "I'm off to Monaco for the week. We will discuss this further on my return."

"*My life* is not up for discussion! Enjoy your holiday."

Claudette turned at the door and looked back at Charlotte with disgust. Her mouth opened to speak and then closed again as she stalked off down the corridor.

Freddie's head appeared around the doorway as soon as the elevator doors closed.

Charlotte leaned back in her chair. "I suppose you heard all that."

"Yes, and you were bloody brilliant. Also, you're five minutes late for a meeting in the boardroom." He winced. "I think they heard too."

"I expect everyone on the floor did."

"No. Lucky for you, advance warning of her arrival came up from downstairs, and everyone left to avoid her."

She chuckled wearily and rubbed a hand down her face. "Why did no one warn me?"

"As you so kindly made clear to me, you were on an extremely important call and didn't wish to be disturbed. That and you're the boss and she's your mother. You're... kind of obliged to suck it up."

"Hmm. True."

Charlotte couldn't help but find some amusement in her interactions with her mother. It felt liberating to finally give her a piece of her mind while subtly revealing her relationship with a woman. Whether her mother accepted it or not was inconsequential to Charlotte.

It was clear her mother was unfit to resume her position as CEO, a fact she would need to come to terms with, however, Charlotte was beginning to question if it was a role she truly desired. As she stood up, gathering her organiser and phone, she contemplated if there was more to life than endless meetings.

CHAPTER 23

The best part of the returning *Hotel SOS* crew was the bacon roll nestled in Arte's hands. As she stood beside the catering van, blue skies stretched out overhead on a day that would see a new chapter for Hotel Aloysius. After weeks of preparation stripping out the rooms, it was finally time for it to take on a new image. With the work on the two rooms calculated to take three days, Arte was looking forward to showing them off to Charlotte on Sunday. Following their open and honest chat about how they were feeling, she couldn't wait to see her again. Her body was craving Charlotte like a bee craved nectar.

Whilst the decorators were working on Gran's old bedroom and the drawing room, it was time to begin forging plans for the next room, which she was taking on alone. She'd already received some great cost-saving tips from the interior design team when they'd popped in to check on her progress at the end of the previous week.

"Do you want a sausage, Rodin?" Kirsty the server asked as Arte layered brown sauce over her bacon roll.

Rodin's flat head, tilted ears, and drooling mouth answered for him.

Arte chuckled. "I don't think he'd ever say no to you."

Kirsty threw a sausage in the attentive dog's direction. It didn't even touch the sides of his jowls. The woman had become quite fond of Rodin, having grown used to his lurking presence during her previous visit.

"You know, if you keep feeding him," Arte said, "he'll never leave you alone."

"That's kind of the plan," Kirsty teased. "He's adorable! I've always wanted a dog, but with this job it's impossible."

Arte shivered as a biting wind whipped around her neck.

"I don't know how you do it. What's the appeal of working outside in all weathers, for long hours, all over the country?"

Kirsty shrugged and laughed. "I guess I like feeding people, and as for the cold, with a bit of hard work and all these cookers, I don't feel it."

"It must be interesting getting to meet a variety of people. I guess you must feed a lot of famous people too."

"I do, but I treat them all the same. I don't care if they're an unpaid extra for the day or a film star on a million a day. I don't go in for all those airs and graces. Take that Charlotte Beaufort, for example; heiress to a property empire, and no doubt a multimillionaire, but the way she behaves to people like you on this show is shocking." Kirsty tutted and shook her head. "Mind you, she's always remembered her *p*'s and *q*'s with me. No doubt because she knows which side her bread is buttered — quite literally, sometimes."

Arte felt the overwhelming urge to say something to defend Charlotte. Her mind drifted to Freddie and everything she'd done for a complete stranger in his hour of need.

"Sometimes even a villain can be a hero to someone."

A perplexed expression flashed across Kirsty's face. Arte took it as an opportunity to head back to the house. She couldn't blame Kirsty for her opinion. She was simply stating facts as she'd seen them. Charlotte was everything she'd described — on the surface, at least. In reality, she was a good person who was trapped in a tricky situation, surrounded by difficult people. All Arte wanted to do was get Charlotte away from everything that forced her to be the person she wasn't.

The radiating heat from the fire hit her as she entered reception, relaxing the aching muscle she'd been trying to ignore since she'd dragged herself from her bed that morning. Rodin trotted in beside her and collapsed in front of it, not taking his attention from her hand.

She was about to take herself off to the drawing room to finish her roll when she remembered why the door was shut and there was so much noise coming from inside. Instead, she sat on the church pew by the window and gazed outside. Charlotte would be suffering even more than she was from the freezing air. If it was cold in the South Downs, it was sure to be biting at her well-toned legs in Scotland.

She checked her phone as she had every few minutes

since she texted Charlotte to say the crew had arrived. It immediately began vibrating, and she gasped with elation to see Charlotte's name on the screen.

"Hey. I was just thinking about you," Arte said as she answered it.

"Glad to hear it. I have a few minutes before I leave for my meeting. I was going to text you until I realised I needed to hear your voice."

Arte's insides went all gooey at her use of the word 'needed'.

"What's happening?" Charlotte asked.

"Well, I'm devouring a bacon roll, and Rodin is looking as disappointed as I've ever seen him."

"Poor Rodin," Charlotte replied. "Is Mike there?"

"No, Gary's directing."

A quizzical 'hmm' came down the phone.

"They're making a start on the drawing room whilst the plumbers work on the en-suite bathroom upstairs. Someone did go up earlier with a couple of rolls of wallpaper. When I wandered past to have a sneak peek, there was a lot of swearing coming from inside."

"Sounds like wallpapering to me," Charlotte said with a chuckle.

"It's weird without you here… being rude and, if I may add, looking incredibly hot," Arte said, with a snicker.

"Okay, I'm not exactly sure how to take that, but I'll assume it's your unique way of saying you miss me," Charlotte replied.

"I guess it is, and I do. They are pulling out all the stops, trying to finish before the snow reaches here. It won't stop you coming Sunday, will it?"

"Nothing is stopping me coming Sunday, even if I have to bring a snowplough."

Arte laughed, knowing full well that if anyone could do that, it would be Charlotte.

"I wish I was there now," Charlotte said with a sigh. "It's already snowing up here, and everyone is deeply tedious and desperately trying to impress me."

"Do they feel the changing of the guard, perhaps?"

Charlotte let out an even louder sigh in reply.

"Are you okay?" Arte asked, concerned.

"I'm tired from travelling yesterday, that's all. And I didn't sleep well last night."

"Tiredness comes with a yawn, not a sigh. What's wrong?"

"Oh, it's nothing. Nothing I need to burden you with."

Arte's silence spoke volumes until Charlotte relented.

"I had a run-in with Mother. We had words about this problem I've been dealing with on the acquisition. It's a problem of her making, which she doesn't see as a problem, more an overreaction on my part. Anyway, she's found out about my divorce, too, and is trying to interfere. I was planning on telling her but thought it was best done face to face, once she was on the mend. I'm guessing my mother-in-law got there first."

"I'm sorry," Arte said. Her need to wrap an arm around Charlotte had manifested itself in her wrapping an arm around herself. "I really don't understand what your mother has got to do with your divorce."

"Nothing in my eyes and everything in hers. She'll get used to it. She suggested I was seeing someone; I didn't correct her."

Arte's brain was about to freak out until she realised Charlotte was talking about her. Then it freaked her out anyway with delight.

"Oh," she replied with an attempt at a neutral tone. She needed more information before she'd decide how she felt about that.

Charlotte's soft 'hmm' came back again. Why was it beginning to turn her on?

"Did you go into specifics?" Arte asked, trying to ignore her distracting thoughts.

"Somewhat. That's when she walked out."

"Oh."

"Hmm."

Oh God, stop with the hmming.

"I'm sorry if this… us… is problematic for you."

"Nothing about you or us is problematic for me. It's problematic for other people, and that's not my problem. You are the only part of my life that feels right at the moment. You feel like a guiding beacon, Arte."

Arte made every effort to contain the squeal that was trying to jump out of her throat. "You say all the right things."

"You make it so easy," Charlotte replied softly.

"I'm not sure I can wait until Sunday to see you."

"I'll be worth the wait. I promise."

"But what happens after Sunday?" Arte asked tentatively. "Do I only get to see you every few weeks? I don't know about you, but that's going to be tough for me."

Her question brought silence, and she instantly regretted broaching the subject. The last thing she wanted was to scare Charlotte off by coming on too strong, but she was a firm believer in addressing potential issues early on. With Charlotte's schedule barely allowing her time to breathe and her own focused on the hotel, if they didn't make a point of finding time, it was unlikely to find itself.

She wanted to press pause on life for a moment, spend a weekend in the penthouse with Charlotte, visit art galleries together, take a walk along the Thames before they took in a West End show or a concert at the Royal Albert Hall.

"You still there?"

"Yes," Charlotte's soft, subdued voice came back. "I was… thinking." After another pause, she added, "We'll make it work, I promise."

Arte wasn't sure how, but a promise was a promise, and it was all she had.

"I have to go now," Charlotte continued. "I have a meeting about to start."

"Sorry."

"Why are you sorry?"

"Because I know you dislike them," Arte replied.

"Indeed I do."

"Can we speak later?" Arte asked, hopeful to hear Charlotte's voice one more time that day.

"No, not tonight," Charlotte groaned. "I have a charity dinner until late. Not one I'm looking forward to."

"Can't you get out of it?"

"Not exactly. Beaufort Liverpool is hosting it, and I'm representing the brand."

"Liverpool?" Arte asked with confusion. "I thought you were in Edinburgh."

"I am. I'll be taking the helicopter to Liverpool this afternoon. I'll return to Edinburgh tomorrow. On the plus side, I can carry out my annual inspection whilst I'm there. Likewise with Edinburgh."

"Sounds exhausting. So, what's so bad about the dinner, except the logistics and trying to stay awake? Will your mother be there?"

"No, she's in Monaco. But Gideon will be."

Oh!

Jealousy hit her square in the chest. There was no reason for it to. They were hardly going to rekindle their marriage over a couple of boring speeches and lousy dances, were they?

No, of course not.

"I'll be keeping as much distance as I can, trust me," Charlotte added, as if she sensed Arte's discomfort. "It's his family's charity, and he's representing it. We haven't made our split public yet and don't intend to until tonight is over and done with. It's the last of our appearances scheduled together."

Scheduled.

She knew Charlotte and Gideon had an unconventional relationship, but Arte didn't like how the word sounded.

"Text me before you go to sleep," Arte demanded, pushing any thoughts of Charlotte and Gideon appearing to be in love aside.

"I will. I miss you," Charlotte finished, softly.

"I miss you too."

After hanging up, Arte sought comfort from Rodin. His warm fur made her want to curl up in front of the fire for a cuddle, at least until he started licking her fingers for traces of bacon.

"Oh, Rodin," she muttered. "You always let yourself down."

She stoked the fire, threw another log on, and sat herself at the reception desk with her laptop. Plans needed plotting if she was going to get the place open.

CHAPTER 24

The latest photographs Charlotte had received from Arte were impressive. Two elegant new sofas and a coffee table flanked the fireplace. Several sets of new chairs and tables utilised the outer space to create small, intimate areas in front of the windows. It made her crave being there even more. She could picture herself and Arte curled up on the sofa in front of the fire.

Picking up her steaming mug of tea, Charlotte wandered over to one of the windows of her southwest corner office at HQ. A white blanket of snow had covered the city of London overnight, lightening the landscape, smoothing out its harsh edges and tones. It highlighted features that were normally indistinguishable. In this case, she could make out her penthouse apartment at Beaufort Mayfair in the distance. Moving to the other window, the Surrey Hills stood on the horizon, and beyond that lay the South Downs and Arte.

Arte's question of how they were going to make it work had hung over her the whole time she'd been in the north. In truth, she had no idea how they were going to find time, but with determination they could make it work. If she got a jump on her calendar and booked out weekends in the South Downs, everything would miraculously fit around it. Charlotte glumly tapped the side of her mug. She hadn't even convinced herself.

She wondered what Arte would be doing at that moment. It was early, so she was likely giving Rodin his morning walk. The thought of Rodin doing zoomies in the snow brought a hint of mirth to her lips. That she would like to see.

Her mind was less on Beaufort business and more on Hotel Aloysius of late. She envied Arte and her future. Turning nothing into something was one of the biggest thrills out there. It reminded her of when she'd looked up at Beaufort Mayfair the day her father handed her the keys. She knew if she made a success of it, one day he'd hand her another set, and then another, until one day she held all the keys. It wasn't until recently that she realised the weight of all those keys was far heavier than she'd ever imagined. She tapped her mug again, realising she was a far cry from where she'd begun — doing what she loved.

It had all happened so organically and yet felt so out of her control, even though she'd been there for every step. She'd allowed it to happen to her, driven by ambition, power, and money at the expense of her own happiness. She would have been content with Beaufort Mayfair for the rest of her life, steering it through the changes the world sent its way. Now here she was, aiming to add the weight of another set of keys to her belt within the hour.

The vibration of her phone on her desk pulled her from

her thoughts and the beauty of the winter wonderland. Her spirits lifted as she saw Arte's name on the screen.

"I was just thinking about you," she said. "I was looking at the photographs you sent last night. It looks —" Erratic, ragged tones coming back down the phone made her blood run cold. "Arte, what's wrong? Are you okay?"

"The roof."

"What about the roof?" Charlotte asked, trying not to panic.

"It's got a hole in it. There's snow everywhere in one of the attic rooms… I didn't know who else to call."

"Take a breath. I'm here for you."

"But you're not here," Arte replied through breathy pants.

"No… I'm not." How she wanted that to be different. "But I want to be, you know that."

"They only finished filming yesterday. I couldn't even catch a break for one bloody day!"

"Is it contained to the attic? It hasn't damaged any of the work they did?" Charlotte asked, suddenly panicked by the thought of the loss of those interiors and all the work the team had carried out.

"Everything else is fine, assuming the rest of the roof isn't about to fall on me. If it had rained, the new bedroom would be in ruins. Thankfully it's so bloody cold it hasn't melted yet."

"If it had rained, I doubt you would have a hole in it."

"What do you mean?"

"It will be the weight of the snow that's collapsed the roof," Charlotte said, pacing the room as frustration clawed at her. "It's quite common in historic buildings with weak timbers. Did you not get a survey done?"

"No."

"Why were you investing money inside without checking the structural integrity of the building first?"

"Because I don't know what I'm doing, Charlotte! I'm out of my fricking depth here! I've never owned a property before."

Charlotte felt the full force of Arte's frustration and what she guessed was also fear. She took a deep breath; hearing Arte do the same.

"*Hotel SOS* should know," Arte continued, more calmly. "The show invested money, too, without checking. Now I'll have to spend the money I put aside to redecorate the next room on fixing the roof. I may not even have enough to do that if the whole thing is rotten. What am I saying? I *don't* have enough. I'll have to call Sophie for help, and she'll force me to sell."

Charlotte's mind raced with thoughts. The cost to replace an eighteenth-century roof would be out of most people's reach. She hoped it would just need patching up. It was a good sign that there were no other holes.

"I'll have to ring Mike. They'll want to film this. It's going to put our schedule out; we may even have to stop production of this episode or delay it at least."

"Seriously? Is that all you care about? My misery makes for good television, does it?"

The sound of quiet sobs made Charlotte's stomach roil.

"Film the leak, Arte, not your misery," she clarified.

"Why am I putting myself through all this?" Arte sniffed. "Maybe I should sell up and go back to Italy."

The mere thought made Charlotte's roiling stomach want to vomit.

"That is, of course, your choice, but remember why you're doing this… because it's your dream, Arte. One day the hotel will be full of guests. You'll have a studio to work in and students to teach." Adding a little firmness, she continued. "No one said it was going to be easy or that there wouldn't be hurdles, okay? This is that — a hurdle, nothing more. We'll either crash through it or jump over it."

"We?"

There was such hope in Arte's voice, and as much as she wanted it to be 'we', Charlotte knew she was going to disappoint her.

"I've just got back from Edinburgh, and I'm about to go into a meeting for the final stages of negotiations on the acquisition. We're on the cusp of signing."

"Sorry, of course. You're a busy lady. I should have realised it would take more than my home crashing around my ears to pull you away from work."

Arte's tone cut straight through her, but she wasn't going to rise to it. Arte was under as much pressure as she was, and biting back wasn't going to help anyone.

"I could try and get over this evening. The roads might be clearer by then too… but then I have an eight a.m. meeting scheduled with a supplier in Beijing."

"Don't put yourself out. I don't wish to be a burden to your schedule."

"Arte," Charlotte pleaded. "I'm sorry. My heart is breaking for you." That was the truth. Not only was she gutted for her setback, but for Arte to think Charlotte would consider her a burden, that hurt. "I'll get the team to you as soon as I can. They'll sort everything; don't worry."

"Fine," Arte said through a sniff.

"Keep me posted, and I'll see you as soon as I can, okay?"

"Bye." Arte hung up.

Charlotte slammed her phone down on the desk. "Fuck!"

She hated leaving things like that. Arte was in distress, and she could do nothing but move on to the next meeting. How could being a CEO give her less power?

Malcolm was standing outside her glass office door, and with no Freddie in sight, she beckoned him in. She walked over to greet the short-statured, greying man as he entered. He reached up and placed his hands on her arms and kissed her cheek. He had been the Beaufort Hotels' lawyer since her father established the business. They had been good friends up until his death, and Charlotte saw him more like a favourite uncle than as the family's lawyer. He was also one of the few people who knew of her mother's condition and the position it put the company in.

"Good to see you, Charlotte. You keeping well?"

"As I can be juggling two jobs and a divorce."

"Ah, yes, yes. Is Jacob handling everything to your satisfaction on that front?"

They took their seats opposite one another at the desk.

"He is. Thank you for recommending him."

"He did all three of my divorces; he's a good fellow. Now, turning to the matter at hand. Your assistant is just showing the other party into the boardroom, but I thought we should discuss negotiating tactics."

"Yes, good." Charlotte said, trying to pull her focus to where it was needed.

"Property prices have taken a bit of a nosedive in the last few weeks. We should use that as a starting point. I predict they will keep falling, so let's see if we can't cajole them a little. The longer they spend trying to move us by a percentage point they could have lost double that." Malcolm passed Charlotte some paperwork from his black leather briefcase. "We're still agreed on the price."

Charlotte flicked to the back page, where she found the price they'd discussed. "Yes, and not a penny more."

"Right. Let's get this deal signed," Malcolm said, standing.

They passed Freddie as they reached the boardroom; Charlotte pulled him to one side and indicated to Malcolm that he should begin without her.

"Hotel Aloysius has a hole in the roof," she told Freddie. "Call Michael and tell him to get the team there ASAP. Then ask Jeremy to get over there too. He needs to assess the damage and the rest of the roof. Let Arte know they are on their way."

Freddie nodded. "And you too?"

"I'm rather busy here, don't you think?" Charlotte said, looking for some reassurance that she couldn't just up and leave. She didn't receive any. Freddie's gaze simply fell to the floor before he rushed off down the corridor, leaving her feeling even worse.

Voices inside the boardroom prevented her from

having any further thoughts on the subject. She forced her shoulders away from her ears and wandered inside.

Her view across the boardroom table was businessman Rafe Curtis and his lawyer, Christopher Morris. Behind them lay the snowy hills on the horizon. Having listened to back-and-forth arguing for ten minutes, Charlotte was not only beginning to lose her focus, but her patience. It was quite an experience watching men negotiate. It brought out all their worst traits: speaking over one another; posturing; bullying tactics. Seen as aggressive when performed by a woman, such things were classed as skilled negotiation tactics in men.

She tuned out, leaving Malcolm to an art form he performed with finesse. Instead, she turned her attention to the snowy hills as she focused on Arte's words that were playing over in her mind. Two to be precise. 'Burden'. 'Schedule'. She would make it clear when she did see Arte that she was not a burden; if anything, it was her schedule that was the burden. She was CEO — for the moment, at least — and what she said went. Except when it came to herself, a voice reminded her.

She sighed, not realising how loudly until Malcolm said, "You okay, Charlotte?"

"Yes. Sorry."

Why did I say that? Why do I always say that?

"You know what?" She shook her head. "No, I'm not, actually. Someone I care very deeply about is in distress, and I need to be with her."

She stood, taking in all the gaping mouths. "Gentlemen, I'm not negotiating any further. Those are the terms, take it or leave it." She signed the back page of the contract in front of her. "We both know full well that there are no other interested parties, so let's cut to the chase. We have come this far, we've both incurred costs, and Beaufort is more than happy to walk away."

She slid the contract and pen over to Rafe Curtis. "I urge you to sign."

With that, Charlotte marched back to her office. There was only one place she wanted to be and only one place she was going.

"That was quick. Are you finished already?" Freddie said as she approached.

"I am, Freddie. I so am."

Noticing her demeanour he stood and asked, "Are you okay?"

"I'm going to need some wellies. Pronto!" Charlotte said as she passed his desk and entered her office. She stopped, then backed up, adding, "And a snowplough."

"On it," Freddie replied with a wide smirk.

Charlotte glared at him. "What are you smirking at?"

Freddie shrugged coyly. "Oh, I don't know. Perhaps I like this version of you."

"This version?" Charlotte asked, eyebrow raised.

"Yes." Freddie sat back down and looked at his laptop.

Charlotte folded her arms and gave him a pointed look to say he wasn't as done with this conversation as he thought he was.

"Oh, come on." He spun his chair to face her. "You know what I mean. This version, when you allow yourself to smile at a thought, when you daydream in your office, when you hum contentedly to yourself when you think no one is listening. Ever since you met her, you've been different."

"By her, I assume you mean Arte."

It was Freddie's turn to shoot her a look. Charlotte replied with a gentle expression of contentment as she entered her office. She was beginning to like this version, too; she needed to allow herself to be it more often.

CHAPTER 25

Arte stared at the snow-covered room in disbelief. She'd woken that morning to the sound of what she assumed was a lightning bolt hitting the roof. Upon investigation of the attic rooms, she'd discovered a two-foot-wide hole in the roof and a large amount of snow piling up under it.

Charlotte had said to leave everything exactly as it was, so she'd resisted the urge to clear it. She was grateful it wasn't melting and that the falling snow had lightened a little. Freddie had called shortly after to check on her and inform her the crew were scrambling to get to the South Downs. She'd give them a few hours to arrive, and then she'd board up the hole and start shovelling the snow into the en-suite bath to melt it.

By the time she had dressed, Arte had calmed down — well, she had stopped shaking. She felt a niggle of regret for phoning Charlotte in such a blind panic. She knew she was busy and under a lot of pressure finding her way in her new role. Then a voice told her she wasn't being unreasonable. She should feel able to call her *person* and expect them to be there for her. If Charlotte was in this, whatever this was, it shouldn't be too much to ask her to show up when she was needed. If she meant anything to her, Charlotte would need to show it.

She'd considered ringing Sophie, but decided against it. She needed to be in control of what was happening — as much as she could be — and getting her involved would cede that control. Knowing Sophie, she would use it as an excuse to exert pressure on her to sell. Charlotte was right: this was another hurdle, one she didn't need to bother her sister with right now. Once she knew more, then she would decide a way forward.

Feeling the need to distract herself and with assistance supposedly on its way, Arte headed to the boiler house in search of a shovel. The snow on the driveway was going to need clearing for the production crew, though the idea of them getting as far as the snowy drive would prove to be a bigger challenge. There were reports on the news of record snowfall, with roads being impassable in places and vehicles left abandoned overnight. Digging out the drive was back-breaking work, and she was making little progress with a small shovel.

Rodin at least was enjoying the snow. He bounded around the front lawn, jumping in and out of snowdrifts as if he'd never seen it before. Arte was beginning to give up all hope of help coming when, around mid-morning, Rodin let out a sharp bark and ran towards a figure at the road. Arte didn't pay the figure much attention until she realised Rodin was far too interested in whoever it was for it to be the postman, and that he wouldn't likely be able to visit for some days. As the person drew nearer, she inhaled a sharp breath of freezing cold air.

"Charlotte! You're here!" Arte looked down, just making out the tops of Charlotte's footwear in the deep snow. "And in wellies."

As Charlotte neared, Arte could see her hair was wet and snow had settled amongst it.

"I thought it was about time I invested in some," Charlotte stuttered through chattering teeth. "I have a feeling I might be needing them."

That brought a smile to Arte's lips, until she realised how much Charlotte was shaking.

"Where's your car?"

"Abandoned in a snowdrift two miles away, with my gloves inside." Charlotte pulled her hands from her pockets to reveal they were red.

Letting the shovel fall into the carpet of snow, Arte wrapped her arms around her. She pulled their bodies together tightly, taking in the feel of her icy cheek pressed against her own warmer one. Charlotte did care about her and about Hotel Aloysius, apparently enough to risk exposing herself to hypothermia.

Needing more than a hug, she pulled back and asked, "Can I warm up those frozen lips of yours?"

"I'm going to turn around and trudge back to my car if you don't."

"That sounds life-threatening considering the state you are in. I'd best make this convincing," Arte said, moistening her dry, chapped lips.

Removing her gloves, Arte placed her hand on the back of Charlotte's head and guided her closer, determined to enjoy every moment of what was to come. When they kissed before, it had come as a surprise — a very welcome surprise. This time she was drinking in every second of Charlotte Beaufort's lips being millimetres from her own.

The intensity of Charlotte's gaze and the pressure of her frozen fingertips as they pressed into Arte's back told her Charlotte was entirely hers, and Arte willingly gave herself wholeheartedly to the woman in her arms. As their lips met, the coolness of them warmed in an instant, all inhibitions vanished as they immersed themselves in each other. Arte was so consumed her feet tingled in her boots, and this time not from the cold.

Rodin barged between their legs, desperate to be part of their embrace, and forcing them apart.

"Well, I've never been more convinced of anything." Charlotte's eyes sparkled as she wiped a tear from under Arte's. "Looks like you haven't either."

"Oh." Embarrassed, Arte turned away and dried her unexpectedly moistened cheeks. "I'm sorry, I'm just so relieved you're here. Nothing feels quite as difficult when you're with me."

"It's okay." Charlotte's arms engulfed her, almost suffocating her. Arte didn't care; the feel of her arms around her was too good to care about anything. She felt safe and warm. *Loved?* She batted the thought away, feeling foolish.

"Is your car okay?"

"It's fine. The hills around here are treacherous. One minute it's clear, and then you hit a snowdrift. I should have waited for the snowplough."

Arte laughed, then blinked at the seriousness on Charlotte's face. "You're not joking, are you?"

A subtle knowing smirk emerged from Charlotte.

"You seriously brought a snowplough?"

Charlotte nodded.

"How?"

"I have contacts and luxury hotel suites at my disposal. It doesn't take much to summon anything I require."

"Oh, so you have a penchant for bribery, do you? I'll have to keep an eye on you."

"Trust me. Any bribe I offer you won't feel like one."

Arte imagined what Charlotte might bribe her into doing. She was right. Everything she could think of wouldn't feel like bribery. She would be a very willing and eager participant.

"What about all your meetings?" she asked, feeling the need to move the subject onto safer ground, only to remember how awkwardly they had left things.

"I brought my laptop," Charlotte said, holding up her bag. "I told Freddie to move them all online. What's the point of being in the digital age if we don't utilise it? At least on a snow day."

"A laptop… and a toothbrush?" Arte hinted. "Will Madam require a room for the night?"

"Madam does if she's welcome. I'm aware it's the second time I've invited myself to stay the night. I don't think it will be the last time either."

"For someone who at one time refused to stay, I believe it speaks volumes to the level of hospitality I offer."

The corners of Charlotte's mouth turned up. "Let's see

how it goes this time, shall we? I'm finding myself in need of a whole different level of service from you."

"I'm up for the challenge, not that I expect it to be much of one. Let's start by taking your bag."

"And I'll take this," Charlotte said, scooping up Arte's free hand.

The sensation of Charlotte's icy hand against her own warmer hand brought a smile to Arte's face. As she turned back to the hotel with the hole in its roof, her heart sank for a second, until a feeling of peace settled in her, remembering she wasn't alone.

"How are things inside?" Charlotte asked.

"Wintry."

"Let's take a look. Production is clambering together; they won't be long."

"They decided to follow behind the snowplough, did they? Quite sensible."

Charlotte nudged her with her shoulder, then held up their conjoined hands. "They didn't have this waiting for them, did they?"

"No. This is only for you," Arte confirmed. "Look, about earlier. I was upset—"

"Arte." Charlotte shook her head. "I'm sorry. I should have been here sooner. You needed me, and it took me a moment to understand what that actually meant. It's not something I'm used to, being *needed* like that. Mother will return soon, and things will be easier. I promise."

Charlotte kissed the back of Arte's hand, sending a warming sensation through her cold core. A pang of sadness remained somewhere inside her for Charlotte. Having been surrounded by love her whole life and spending years teaching students who looked to her for guidance, Arte knew how it felt to be needed and wanted. She'd come to know a little of Charlotte's situation in recent months, having lost Gran and then her students as a result of that. Being encircled by mutual love, respect, and support grounded you. She could only imagine Charlotte to be floundering in a vast ocean. Arte hoped she'd hooked her well enough to pull her to shore. As for herself, she would cling onto the hope that one day she would teach again and have a barn full of eager students ready to learn from her.

"So, how did the negotiation go?" she asked, desperate to move away from her morbid thoughts. It was a big day for Charlotte too.

"I don't know," Charlotte replied casually. "I told them I wasn't budging and walked out. I'm thinking they will have signed. They'd be fools not to."

"You walked out?" Arte said in disbelief as she held the front door open for Charlotte, only for Rodin to barge in first.

"Yes, I had somewhere more important to be."

As they entered reception, Charlotte slipped her hand inside Arte's coat as she opened it and wrapped her arm around her waist. Pulling Arte against her, she kissed her passionately. All Arte's problems melted with the feel of Charlotte's lips against her own, their breasts pressed together, and their arms wrapped tightly around each other, making them one. She never wanted it to end, but end it did, leaving Arte hungry for more.

Charlotte pulled her phone from her pocket as they

hung up their coats. "Freddie has messaged. They signed," she said flatly.

"Congrats."

"Thanks."

Charlotte's dull tone concerned her. "You don't sound so pleased."

"It's great for Beaufort to add another hotel to the chain."

"But?" Arte pushed.

"But nothing," Charlotte said with a quick shake of her head.

"We'll celebrate later then."

"Of course."

Charlotte still didn't sound convinced that it was a good thing, and the half-hearted smile on her face did nothing to convince Arte either. Rodin forced his way past them on the narrow attic stairs, earning him a groan from both women. The corridor was eerily dark as they entered. The overhang of snow from the roof and the build-up on the sill partially covered the windows.

"Brace yourself," Arte said. She opened the door to reveal a thick, white layer of snow covering one end of the room. As she blinked to adjust her eyes to the brightness, she felt an arm slip around her shoulders.

"Oh, Arte, I'm sorry."

The feeling of Charlotte against her made everything feel okay, in that moment at least. It stopped as Charlotte moved further into the room and looked up at the hole in the roof. Arte watched Charlotte's face as it cycled through a mixture of emotions. It dropped as she looked back at Arte and then picked up reassuringly.

"It doesn't look too difficult to fix. I'm sure we'll have it sorted in no time. As soon as the crew get the shots they need, we'll have the hole covered, and all this snow cleared. My surveyor is on his way too. He'll be able to give us a full assessment of the whole roof."

"You think there could be more weak spots?"

"I would hope not. I'm sure they would have revealed themselves along with this one by now. There's a lot of force acting on it. It's a long time since I've seen so much snow."

"That's because you barely leave the city."

Rodin bounded from the room, barking, making them both jump.

"Sounds like everyone else has made it," Arte said, following him out into the hallway.

"He makes for a great signaller."

"The best," Arte said as she stopped at a window and peered through the narrow gap the snow afforded her. A yellow truck was working its way around the driveway. It effortlessly pushed the snow aside as two familiar-looking crew vans followed behind it.

"You really did bring a snowplough."

Arte sighed softly to herself. *Is there anything this woman can't achieve?*

"I really did," Charlotte said, joining her in looking out the window.

She turned and placed a kiss on Arte's cheek, making her long for more, for Charlotte to never stop kissing her.

"Come on," she continued. "Show me what the design team has done."

Making their way back down the narrow staircase,

Arte led her to what had once been her gran's room. Opening the door revealed a stunning, showroom-like interior. A duck-egg blue wallpaper studded with white peonies hung from the walls, its colour highlighted in the plush carpet. Matching peony cushions covered the perfectly laid, crisp, white bedding. It all worked beautifully with the new furniture, which retained a traditional touch.

Beside the window sat two wing-backed chairs and a small table. A peek into the en-suite revealed a room completely tiled in travertine with a large, freestanding bath, a separate shower, and two basins. It was the very essence of luxury.

"Wow, the photographs did not do this justice," Charlotte said, taking it all in. "Are you pleased with it?"

"I am," Arte said, beaming from ear to ear. "The interior design team said it was all Farrow & Ball, even the wallpaper."

"Only the very best for our hoteliers… thanks to a hefty discount negotiated by me."

Arte chuckled. "Is there anything that isn't negotiable with you?"

Charlotte's attention turned back to Arte and tucked a strand of loose hair behind her ear. "One thing. You being in my life."

Arte's amused expression softened and pinked. "I find those terms more than acceptable."

Their eyes locked, and the gap between them narrowed. Before Arte could ready herself for what she felt coming, Charlotte's lips were already upon hers. Her soft, warm mouth and searching tongue drew Arte into her again. She would never be able to get enough of these kisses. She wanted everyone to go away so she could lead Charlotte over to the perfectly made bed, lay her down on the Egyptian cotton duvet, and relieve her of all that restrictive winter clothing.

As they finally drew back, Arte asked, "So I take it you approve too?"

"Of the room or the kissing?" Charlotte teased.

"Both."

"Yes, they both get my full approval."

"I just need to get used to calling it the 'Camille Claudel Room', not Gran's room."

Charlotte shot her a look of bewilderment. "The Camille Claudel Room?"

"I've named all the rooms after famous female artists. At least, those that would have been famous if they weren't female. Each room will have a framed print explaining who they were."

"Retaining the family tradition of the framed print then?" Charlotte asked dryly.

"I am indeed. Camille Claudel was Auguste Rodin's student, muse, and mistress. She even contributed to many of his masterpieces."

"Let me guess: she was never credited and was later committed to an asylum."

"Yes. How did you know?"

Charlotte shook her head. "A predictable guess, I'm afraid."

"Mmm," Arte agreed.

"And the names for the other rooms?"

"I'm not going to name my room, unless 'Private'

happens to be a famous female artist. There's the Edmonia Lewis Room. She worked in Rome for most of her career and was the first African American sculptor to gain international prominence. Then the Rosa Bonheur Room. She was a nineteenth-century French artist and sculptor, and openly lesbian."

"I bet that was challenging."

"Not as challenging as breaking gender stereotypes. She had authorisation from the police to wear men's clothing. Her work is on display in the Met. Then we have the Eleanor Coade Room. She was a Georgian businesswoman from Exeter who manufactured neoclassical statues and architectural decorations. She contributed towards Saint George's Chapel in Windsor and the Royal Pavilion at Brighton."

"Impressive."

"Then we have Louise Nevelson, a prominent twentieth-century sculptor who played a key role in the development of the feminist art movement in the States. It would be rude not to give her a room."

Catching her breath, Arte looked to Charlotte to see if she was still listening. She was acutely aware she could get carried away when talking about women and art, and Charlotte's tastes appeared to trend towards contemporary art. Charlotte, however, retained not only an interest, but a sly grin on her face. Her attempt to hide it only made it more obvious.

Arte tilted her head. "What?"

"You," Charlotte said, her shoulders twitching. "You get so impassioned when you talk about art. I like seeing you like this."

Arte beamed with pride.

"So, who's last?" Charlotte asked.

"Georgia O'Keeffe."

"And what horrors awaited her life and career?"

"Her husband created a sexualised public image of her works, and as a member of the National Woman's Party, she didn't take kindly to it. She spent much of the latter part of her life trying to promote herself as a serious professional. She's considered the mother of American modernism and played a vital role in creating a significant space for female artists."

"Is she the one whose flower paintings looked like female geni—"

"She always rejected such interpretations," Arte added quickly. "But even now, we still don't understand the real meaning to her paintings. She's an artistic enigma."

"It's a nice touch to give those names to the rooms. I'm sure your gran would have approved."

"Thanks," Arte replied, unable to contain her pleasure at Charlotte's approval. "I'm sure she would have too."

As they made their way downstairs, neither realised their hands were entwined until Mike approached them in reception.

"Ah, I see. That explains a lot," he said gruffly.

Arte found herself filled with pride when Charlotte's hand tightened against her own.

"You don't have to be in a relationship with someone to see the way this programme treats its hoteliers is wrong, Michael. Sometimes it takes a little time for us to open our eyes to it. Or someone."

The warm, moist kiss Charlotte placed on the back of

her hand barely registered with Arte. She was too focused on pleasantly digesting her use of the word 'relationship'.

Mike wandered off with a look of disgust as another man approached. This time Charlotte did let go, but only to greet him warmly with a hug. Introducing him as Jeremy, her surveyor, she disappeared upstairs to show him the damage. Arte was left to take in the chaos surrounding her where only an hour before there had been silence. Now it was a hive of activity, filled with people that had come together in the worst of weather conditions to help her. They had all been brought here by one remarkable woman.

Charlotte and Jeremy reappeared within twenty minutes, finding her in the kitchen where she was making tea and coffee for the entire crew in the absence of Kirsty and her catering van. She braced herself for his summary.

"The good news is you don't need a new roof," he began. "A few of the timbers were rotten and will need replacing. You'll be able to reuse some of the tiles too. I understand funds are tight, but you're nothing without a strong roof. With investment going on underneath, you don't want to risk further damage. Scaffolding will make up a lot of the cost, so I urge you to take advantage whilst it's up to fix the hole and get the rest secured."

Jeremy promised he would forward a full report and a rough estimate for the repairs the following day. After he left, Charlotte disappeared into the dining room for her virtual meetings. She appeared briefly at the request of Mike, who thought he might as well utilise her whilst she was there to examine the damage on film. He also took the opportunity to film the reveal of the drawing room and bedroom rather than having everyone back the following week as scheduled.

Arte didn't even need to falsify her reaction to being 'presented' with the rooms by Charlotte. She still couldn't get over how perfect they were. Tears nestled in her eyes as she imagined her gran's reaction to them. She would definitely have shed a tear or two.

Mike appeared to have given in to Charlotte's more gentle approach, although he didn't look happy about it. The reveal was a more positive moment anyhow and didn't require any verbal comparisons between old and new. They would be handled with before and after shots in post-production.

By the time the crew had packed up, Mike's face had taken on a vibrant shade of red. It left Arte wondering what method of retaliation he would impress upon Charlotte — and whether he should have his blood pressure checked.

CHAPTER 26

With the roof temporarily fixed up by the crew, peace restored, and stomachs full, Arte joined Charlotte in the newly decorated drawing room. She'd scurried into it after a late dinner to finish her work whilst Arte cleaned up.

The pleasant aroma of wood smoke and new furniture hit her as she entered. Arte took her usual seat beside the fire and scooped up her almost empty wine glass, being as careful as she could with it. The last thing the new rug or sofa needed was a wine stain.

Rodin looked longingly at the empty sofa, gave it a sniff, and then lay down in front of the fire. He'd received the message loud and clear from his mistress that he was no longer allowed on the sofa, but it didn't stop him from giving Arte the sad eyes.

"Good boy, Rodin."

The dog flopped onto his side, all hope leaving him that she would change her mind.

Charlotte closed her laptop and placed it on the new coffee table. "How are you feeling now that filming is over? Ready to take on the next steps?"

"If the next steps are bankrupting myself by repairing the roof, then no. Do you think it's a sign?" Arte asked as she sipped from her glass.

"A sign?"

"That I should give up. Sell up. Move on with my life? Perhaps all this is not meant to be."

"No. It's just a blip," Charlotte said fervently. "A costly blip, admittedly, but please don't see it as a reason to give up."

"I'm not sure what else to do."

"You can't give up on your dream, that much I know. We'll figure something out."

Arte let out a sigh. "There's that 'we' again."

"We are a 'we'," Charlotte said as she tucked her legs under her and turned to face Arte. "I'm going to do everything I can to help you through this and be there for you."

Arte wanted to believe her.

"What is a dream anyway?" Arte mused. "It's only some fantastical ambition we never expect to fulfil. That's why it's called a dream."

"A dream asks you for effort in making it come true. It's transactional. Even if you don't fulfil it, you can at least have the satisfaction of knowing you tried."

"You gave up on yours easy enough."

Charlotte's frown suggested she needed Arte to elaborate.

"You told me all about your passion for working in

hotels. The rush you get from working in one — singular. I haven't heard the same passion from you about heading up a chain of hotels. In fact, I've only heard the opposite."

Charlotte's expression changed from confusion to shock, then to pain. She finally conceded. "I do feel detached at HQ, yes. Staying at Beaufort Mayfair has reminded me how much I've missed the bustle of a hotel and how much I fucking hate meetings. Whilst we're on that subject, I want you to know… you are not a burden to me."

Arte attempted to hide her sheepish face. She'd spoken that word in a moment of high emotion. Her hopes that Charlotte had disregarded it were now dashed.

"If anything is a burden, it's my schedule," Charlotte said softly, reaching out to Arte and taking her hand.

"That's good to know."

Charlotte pinched the bridge of her nose. "God knows what I'll be returning to."

"What do you mean?"

"The board are aware of what's gone on. Well, aware to the point they believe my mother went on holiday, leaving me to fix her error. There will be pushback. There may be a vote for her to stand down."

"Can they do that? I thought it was yours and your mother's company."

"In theory, they can; in practice, it's not a wise move. Although, it would be difficult for her to continue with a vote of no confidence from her own board. The threat of one may be enough to force her to leave. I just can't see her going down without a fight."

"She might surprise you, especially since she's not well. Isn't it better to walk than be pushed?"

"Mother has never surprised me. She's as predictable as the dawn."

"Can't you tell the truth? That she was ill?"

"Then they'll associate her error with being ill," Charlotte said, covering a yawn with her hand. "It won't help the situation. The fact she lied — and I covered for her — would be worse."

"I can't believe you're covering for someone who can't do their job and doesn't believe you are competent to do it."

Charlotte's long face made Arte feel like she'd overstepped. She didn't mean to present things so starkly to her.

"Have there been any repercussions from Mike?"

"No, nothing as yet," Charlotte confirmed.

"But you are expecting them?"

"Yes. The fact I've not heard anything from the production company yet is a good sign, though." Charlotte covered another yawn. "I'm about ready for bed. Where am I sleeping?"

"I thought you could try out the new bedroom, give it the once-over."

"Oh. Of course."

Was she disappointed? Arte certainly hadn't assumed Charlotte would want to share a bed with her. They weren't at that point yet, were they? Or was Charlotte's sullen face evidence that she'd like them to be? After all, who knew what would have happened at the Beaufort

Mayfair if not for the interruption? Charlotte may have given her a kiss good night, or she may have taken Arte inside her hotel room and given her everything her heart yearned for.

"I thought you might prefer your own space," Arte said.

"Perfect. I'd love to christen the room. I mean, you know, be the first to sleep in it."

Arte smiled. Charlotte was cute when she tripped over herself.

"I'll head up then," Charlotte said, getting up. "I'm dying for a hot shower. Are you coming up?"

Was that an invitation or an enquiry about whether she was going to bed too? Arte disliked the awkwardness of the early days of a relationship, the uncertainty of expectations it brought. She decided it was best to go up with Charlotte. Whatever was or wasn't on the table, she was going to at least seek out a good night kiss. Who knew where it might lead?

"Yes. I'll put Rodin out. There should be plenty of hot water for both of us to have one." Her face dropped as she realised what she'd said and how it might sound. "I mean… you know… separately."

Oh God! Ground, swallow me up.

Charlotte's eyes shimmered.

"Erm, would you like some tea?" Arte said in an attempt to divert the attention away from her slip-up. "I usually have some before bed."

"Yes. That would be nice. Thanks."

"I'll bring it to your room after I've showered."

"Thanks." Charlotte opened the drawing room door to leave.

"Charlotte," Arte said softly.

"Yes?"

"I'm so happy you're here."

"Me too. I've thought of little else since our" — Charlotte looked down at the floor and then back up again — "brief time together."

Arte's forehead furrowed. "I don't believe you've had a second to think about me."

"Well, you know. In those moments between, you're all I can think of."

The thought of penetrating Charlotte's mind at any point of the day was enough to melt Arte's insides.

Charlotte stepped out of the shower, approving of the new cubicle separate from the bath. Hearing a knock on the bedroom door, she grabbed her towel from the rail and wrapped it around her.

"Come in. I won't be a second."

She dried herself quickly. Pulling on her black silk chemise with a lace trim, she wrapped a white, fluffy dressing gown around her.

"I'm loving this dressing gown," Charlotte said as she entered the bedroom, enjoying the feel of the new carpet beneath her toes. "This 'A' is a lovely touch." Charlotte pointed to the letter 'A' for Aloysius stitched onto the front.

"That's just a sample, but I've been promised a great

price on a bulk order, thanks to you," Arte said from the doorway, dressed in light grey pinstripe pyjamas.

"Well. I'm sure you can find a way to show your gratitude."

Arte's face pinked, much to Charlotte's delight. She couldn't get enough of making Arte blush.

"I've popped your tea beside the bed," Arte said, trying to control her own mug of tea as she shivered.

"Thanks. Are you cold?"

"I'm fine; it's just a draft."

"Close the door and jump in my bed. I'll warm you up." Charlotte winked and then turned the hairdryer on, noticing Rodin slipping into the room just as the door closed.

Arte hesitated for a moment, then practically raced toward the bed whilst trying not to spill her tea.

Charlotte didn't want to be presumptuous, but she also didn't want Arte to leave. It felt like the easiest way to lure her into her bed. Not that it appeared she needed persuading.

Once her hair was dry, Charlotte removed her dressing gown and placed it on the back of the door. Turning out the main lights and with only a bedside light left on, the room took on a romantic atmosphere. She climbed in beside Arte, enjoying the unwavering gaze she cast over her body.

"You okay?" she asked Arte as she sipped her tea.

Arte placed her mug on the bedside table. "I'm just wondering how I'll make my tea last all night. I don't want to leave."

"I don't want you to leave. I'd like to wake up next to you."

Arte looked up at the ceiling. "If the fix doesn't hold and the roof comes crashing down, we're both getting squished."

"I'm willing to take the risk if you are," Charlotte said, putting her mug on the nightstand.

"Upstairs does feel like a long way away. And this duvet is so soft and the pillow so comfy," Arte said, squidging into the bed.

"And…?" Charlotte asked, hoping to lead Arte towards the one other appealing feature in the room.

"And you're here," Arte added with a smile.

"That's more like it."

Their hands met under the duvet, having reached for one another at the same time. They shuffled closer, their eyes locked.

They were still not close enough for her liking, so Charlotte narrowed the gap between them. She reached around Arte's shoulders and pulled her closer.

"You *are* cold," she observed. "Let's find a way for you to warm up. You've got a lot of work to do if you want me to rate this five stars."

"Well, I'd better get started then." Arte's hand slipped around the back of Charlotte's neck and pulled her in.

Arte's lips melted against her own. Warm, wet, and needy. Her roaming hand brushed against Charlotte's thigh, working its way up until it cupped a handful of her bare backside under the black silk. Arte's moan of pleasure at her discovery made Charlotte moan too. She'd waited so long for an affectionate touch, to feel wanted, needed. The way Arte was making her feel now, with the nips to her ear, the pulling of her hair, exploring her mouth with her tongue and her oh-so-inquisitive hands.

"I want to see you, all of you," Charlotte whispered with more than a hint of desperation. She'd waited this long but another minute and she was going to burst. She unbuttoned Arte's pyjama top, exposing her pale chest and beautiful breasts, goose-pimpled from the cool air. Her nipples stood proud, calling to her. She pressed her mouth to them, making Arte moan as she sucked and teased at them with her tongue.

Having extracted Arte from her top, Charlotte slid Arte's pyjama bottoms off to reveal her in her full splendour. She wanted to devour her right there and then, but Arte seemed to have ideas as she pulled Charlotte towards her and then rolled her onto her back. Their gentle, polite caresses became hurried as eager hands and tongues explored each other's bodies.

Charlotte writhed beneath Arte's touch, her lips twitching as words failed to form upon them.

"What are you trying to say?" Arte teased, tracing Charlotte's lips with her tongue.

"Please. Please," she gasped in reply.

Arte slipped her tongue inside Charlotte's mouth, where Charlotte sucked it, pulling her in deeper, kissing her as firmly as she held her in her arms, never wanting to let go.

"Are you begging?" Arte asked as Charlotte reluctantly let go in exchange for a breath of air.

"Yes."

"And what do you so desperately need?" Arte teased. "My mouth?"

"Yes," Charlotte moaned, trying not to sound too impatient. She feared it would only encourage Arte to make her wait longer.

Arte trailed her fingers down the smooth, black chemise, between her breasts, sending a tickling sensation through Charlotte. As her gentle fingers stroked lower, her arousal intensified, the anticipation snatching her breath away until she finally felt Arte's fingers gliding through her wetness, making her whimper.

"Here? You want me here?"

"Yes… please," she managed, her head so light she felt drunk.

Arte disappeared from her eye line, a mischievous grin spread across her face. She would remember the enjoyment Arte got from making her beg and make her pay for it at a later date. She moaned again as Arte's warm, hungry mouth devoured her, unable to remember anything ever feeling as intoxicating. Her tongue roamed, exploring every crevice and contour, sending a warm rush of adrenaline surging through Charlotte. Arte's agile fingers caressed her, finding their way inside, making Charlotte's hips buck, urging her deeper. Her lover obliged, with gentle thrusts of her fingers to match Charlotte's rhythm.

She knew she wasn't going to last long, and there was nothing she was going to do to stop it. She told herself there would be other times, plenty of other times, and she let herself go, unable to hold back anymore. Intense waves of euphoria engulfed her body, causing her legs to spasm and a sensation she'd never felt so strongly before to throb between them.

A small cry escaped her lips when she finally exhaled, suddenly feeling weightless and at the same time as if she were made of stone.

"I'm sorry," Charlotte whispered, her voice trembling.

"What for?" Arte asked as she returned to Charlotte's side and nuzzled into her.

"I didn't give you much time to enjoy yourself. It's been a while, and you have quite an effect on me."

"Oh, I noticed my effect," she said with a knowing grin. "There is no set time… only time. I plan to spend a lot more of it down there, so don't you worry."

That was everything Charlotte needed to hear. She gave Arte an affectionate squeeze. Perhaps now would be a suitable time to air something that had been playing on her mind most of the day.

"When Michael saw us earlier… holding hands… I hope you don't mind what I said. I'm aware I may have outed you and declared myself in a relationship with you."

"No, I didn't mind at all," Arte replied softly. "I loved it. Especially the relationship bit."

It was a relief for Charlotte to hear that. It had slipped out at the look on his face and letting go of Arte's hand had not been an option. She wasn't going to allow that pathetic man to make her feel ashamed. It was best to tackle the situation head-on.

"You were very brave," Arte murmured against her shoulder.

Her words filled Charlotte's heart, giving her the confidence to say, "Not brave; just me being me."

"Well, I like you being you very much."

Charlotte pulled her closer and kissed the top of her head, smiling at the low thrum of Rodin snoring from by the door.

Lying naked in Charlotte's arms filled Arte with a sense of euphoria. She was sure she could lie like that quite happily for eternity.

She traced her finger along the soft, smooth skin of Charlotte's thigh until it disappeared under black silk. She wanted to map it; to remember it once they parted. She wanted to map the rest of Charlotte, too, and as much as she loved the chemise on her, she knew she would prefer it on the floor.

Charlotte's eyes suddenly popped open. "Oh, Arte," she whispered. "I've just realised this is your gran's old room. Does this feel too weird? We can go somewhere else if you like."

"It's fine," Arte said. "The room looks so different, it's hard to see it as it once was."

It was something she was admittedly trying hard not to think about. The room had undergone such a transformation that the only familiar parts remaining were the window and the shape of the space.

It wasn't being in the room that was a problem; she was past that now. It was more what she and Charlotte were doing that felt a little odd, and the fact it was her first time having sex in the hotel. She'd never brought anyone home to meet Gran, and now that she had someone, it was too late.

Her gran would have liked Charlotte — the nice version, at least. She would have had a few choice words for the rude one. Thankfully her gran was never a prude and wouldn't have minded what they were doing. She always spoke freely about sex. She was a hippy at heart, like Arte's parents, and just like her parents, Gran hadn't batted an eyelid at Arte coming out as a lesbian. In their family, you loved who you loved, and all that mattered was your happiness. One of Gran's sayings was, "Life is too short to be anything but happy." It was probably in a frame somewhere, packed away in a box.

"Have you been with women before?" Arte asked to move the subject away from her past. She was unsure if the moistness in her eyes was from being pressed against Charlotte's chest and listening to the beating of her heart, or from thinking about her gran. She decided it was probably a bit of both.

"My first was while I was studying in Switzerland. She was a British student, too, in much the same situation as me. She's now head of her family hotel empire, one of our major competitors. They've gone global, so the UK is of little consequence to them. Then the odd hook-up in bars abroad. It's difficult to do anything when you are high profile. If you can call me high profile. I had to be careful, you know. Not that Gideon cared what I got up to, but we had a facade that had to stay strong. You could say I got used to my own company."

The thought of Charlotte pleasuring herself caused the throbbing sensation between Arte's legs to intensify.

"So no one serious then, in all that time?"

"No. It wasn't practical. I prefer to focus on work."

Arte could believe that.

"No one ever challenged me enough to want to pursue anything further or to threaten the facade. Now I've met someone who does more than challenge me" — Charlotte narrowed her eyes — "and I thankfully don't have the facade to worry about."

"And I'm so not sorry."

"Never stop challenging me. It's what makes me want to cling onto you for dear life," Charlotte said, tightening her grip around Arte.

Arte tightened her hold on her, kissing her warm skin.

"You're a breath of fresh air in what has up to now been a mundane, miserable existence," Charlotte added.

"Can I ask what made you end it that day, with Gideon?"

"I reached a breaking point. That weekend I spent with you I was due to spend at my in-laws', playing happy families."

"Wow, are they that bad?" Arte chuckled.

Charlotte smiled and kissed her head by way of response. "Then my mother was… my mother. All the time I couldn't get you out of my mind. How I treated you… and with your gran… and those dungarees and that cute beanie. Not to mention that feisty attitude on those first days of filming."

"Oh, you liked all that? I'll make a note," Arte teased, making Charlotte's face go pink.

"I have a lot of regrets about things I've said over the years, but you ate away at me."

"So you could say I was the reason you ended the charade?"

"I wouldn't go that far, no. Let's say you were one of many factors that contributed to my mood that day."

"Glad to be of service." Arte smirked. "So if you and Gideon weren't an item behind the scenes, have there been male as well as female hook-ups?"

"Let's say I've had a mixed experience. We're all different, and we all like different things. I find sex is about the meeting of two minds through two bodies. It doesn't matter what shape those bodies take."

"And what do you like?" Arte asked, stroking her hands over Charlotte's warm, inviting thigh.

"You. Very much indeed," Charlotte answered, lowering her voice against Arte's ear.

"And what would you like to do to me?"

Charlotte repositioned herself on top of Arte. She could feel Charlotte's wetness against her skin. It was almost enough to tip her over the edge.

"I'd like to do everything to you, and I will, in time. For now" — Charlotte hoisted up her chemise and pulled it over her head — "you can enjoy something you've been unable to take your eyes off."

Arte opened her mouth to speak, but with the sight of Charlotte's bare breasts in front of her, words failed her.

Charlotte placed a finger on Arte's lips.

"Don't even think about denying it. I've seen you looking these past weeks. I see everything out of the corner of my eye," she said, lowering herself down. "Go ahead, enjoy yourself."

Unable to contain herself, Arte arched herself up, scooping her beautiful girlfriend's breasts up in her hands. Her tongue teased Charlotte's pert nipples until she heard those moaning noises again. Charlotte Beaufort's sweet moans of pleasure were the most delightful things she'd ever heard.

Wrapping her arms around Charlotte, she forced them both upright, pressing their naked bodies together. With Charlotte straddled across her lap and her breasts brushing against her own, she covered her neck in firm kisses, not caring if she left marks.

"Enough. It's my turn to have some fun with you," Charlotte said, pushing Arte back on to the bed.

Her tongue trailed down Arte's neck and chest, leaving a cool sensation in her wake. She amused herself, lightly pinching Arte's nipple, making her gasp at the arousing pain. Charlotte made her way further down, to where Arte craved her to be — where all her blood had rushed to.

The moan of pleasure from Charlotte as she devoured her with her warm, eager mouth melted Arte where she lay. As Charlotte's passionate tongue explored every part of her, it was too much to contain. Her head lightened as her toes tingled. Warmth radiated through her body. An intensity was building inside her, and any attempt to put her mind somewhere else to prolong this moment was fruitless. Arte couldn't hold herself back anymore. She let the pleasure surge through every part of her, leaving her a wet and quivering mess.

Charlotte reappeared beside her with the biggest smile

Arte had seen from her. Her eyes were bright and her breaths short. All Arte could hope, as she was swept into her lover's arms, was that the strength of her feelings matched the intensity of her own. She could feel herself falling in love with Charlotte with every passing minute, and as much as that vulnerability scared her, she'd never felt such happiness in her life.

CHAPTER 27

Charlotte awoke the next morning with a naked Arte in her sights. Her slow breath warmed the cool skin of Charlotte's upper arm. She was awestruck by the sleeping beauty and how she'd pulled down her walls, firmly placing herself in Charlotte's heart before she'd even realised what was happening.

Resisting the overwhelming temptation to nuzzle into her, Charlotte slid out of bed. She scooped up her clothes and headed into the en-suite to dress for her eight a.m. meeting. Did the wheels of business ever stop turning?

After feeding Rodin, who appeared to have slept beside the bed all night, she set herself up at a table in the dining room with her laptop and a cup of tea. Trying to turn her mind to business, all she could do was think about the kind, intelligent, challenging woman she'd left behind in the warm bed.

The previous night's escapades had affirmed to her what was missing from her life, and how intimate relationships should work — with mutual gifting. Gideon had always taken. Even her one-night stands, although worthwhile, hot, and heavy experiences, had taken. It was always about what they wanted. She, too, had taken in the past. Reciprocating was simply part of the deal, but it wasn't the same. Last night had not only been mutual gifting, but also loving and tender. She was left with the feeling she wanted to spend the rest of her life offering Arte whatever her heart desired.

For now, she needed to figure out a way to help her. Arte needed money, not only to fix the roof but to complete the hotel renovations. A considerable sum. With her own fortune tied up in Beaufort Hotels, she couldn't help personally, and Arte had been clear she didn't want to borrow money. An idea struck her as an incoming video call came up on the screen. Her idea would have to wait.

It didn't wait. It consumed her as she fought to focus on the meeting at hand with their Bristol hotel. During their request for funds towards kitchen repairs following a fire, she thought of Arte. As they explained again why the fire wasn't covered by insurance, her brain whizzed through an outline of how she could bring her idea to fruition.

Finally, they finished the call.

"There you are," Arte said from somewhere behind her. "I wondered if you'd run off without saying goodbye."

The feel of Arte's arms as they reached around her shoulders filled her senses. The kiss she placed on Charlotte's cheek and then her neck as she nuzzled against it rekindled feelings from the night before.

Contain yourself.

"Sorry. I have another meeting in a couple of minutes."

"That's okay. Shall I fetch you some more tea?"

"Please."

"I haven't got much in the way of breakfast. The unexpected arrival of the crew yesterday rather wiped me out. I have some biscuits. Only complimentary packets, though."

"No problem. If they're anything like your complimentary offerings last night, I'm sure they'll taste just as good," Charlotte said, giving her a wink.

Arte's little giggle as she left the room lifted Charlotte's spirits for her next mundane meeting. By the time it had finished late in the morning, Arte had returned from walking Rodin and brought her more tea.

Taking a seat beside her, Arte said, "I've been thinking, and I'm definitely not giving up. I'll do whatever it takes to get this place up and running, even if it takes me the next fifty years."

Charlotte reached across the table and took her hand.

"I've been thinking, too, and I don't want it to take you fifty years. Why not let Beaufort Hotels buy you out? It's about time we branched into country hotels. You could still run it, of course."

Arte withdrew her hand. "But it wouldn't be mine."

"No, it wouldn't, but it would be something. We could make it into something spectacular, with the financial backing it needs."

"What about the barn? My plans?"

Charlotte shook her head. "It will be hard enough convincing the board to acquire a country hotel, let alone adding an ancillary. But I could save the hotel, I'm sure of it."

"I thought you only had metal boxes, not country hotels?"

Charlotte sensed upset in Arte, and she realised she may have made things worse, not better. "Is it not something to at least consider?" She added cautiously.

"You can't just throw your family's money around to fix my problems. Especially if you're only temporary CEO."

Ouch.

"I wouldn't be throwing anything around. It would be a sound business investment."

"Sound? Really?'

Charlotte thought it was best not to answer that. The investment wouldn't be totally sound, not with that roof, but she didn't know how else to help her. It wasn't in her nature to sit back and watch someone drown, especially not someone she cared so much about. If she could throw them a lifeline, she would.

"It would solve all your problems. Please give it some thought."

"And give up on the art studio? I'm not you; I don't give up so easily on a dream."

Ouch – again.

Arte continued. "I told you I'm not going to give up. Gran didn't, and I won't either."

Charlotte had no answer to that one. She had to admire Arte for her tenacity at least, even if it was naïve and futile.

"What choice do you have? I don't know how else to help you."

"I'll find a way. It's not your problem to fix."

"I want to help you, Arte," Charlotte pleaded.

"You said yourself that good decisions are rarely made when emotions are involved."

Charlotte closed her eyes. Had she misjudged everything? Was it too soon to be making such an offer?

"I appreciate the offer, Charlotte," Arte replied flatly. "It's just not feasible. Okay?"

The sharp manner in which Arte finished her sentence told Charlotte the conversation was over. Her offer had been firmly rejected, leaving a tension in the air that she didn't know how to clear.

Charlotte closed her laptop. "I have to head back to the city for a face-to-face meeting this afternoon, so I'll have to leave shortly."

"Okay," Arte replied as she stood up. "I'll leave you to pack."

As Charlotte zipped up her Louis Vuitton bag on the bed, a place that hours earlier had brought them both so much pleasure, she chastised herself for the way she had approached Arte's problem. Perhaps if she'd suggested it differently Arte would have seen it was the perfect solution and that she was being thrown a lifeline. Arte was stubborn and determined to see her dream through, even at the cost of everything else.

The hug she gave Arte by the car, which a member of the crew had rescued from the snow the day before, was brief and barely reciprocated. Charlotte placed a kiss on her cheek and said, "My offer will remain open."

"I've made my decision," Arte replied, folding her arms.

As Charlotte got into her car, she couldn't help but feel she'd left Arte with more problems than she'd solved.

Perhaps with time to think on it, Arte would see the sense in her offer.

Arte warmed herself by the fire, stroking Rodin's fur for comfort. She hadn't been able to warm up since her morning walk, despite a whole afternoon spent stripping wallpaper from the last of the first-floor bedrooms, followed by a hot shower. She wasn't even sure if she was cold, but she was shaking.

She felt so far detached from how she'd felt twenty-four hours ago. The night she'd spent with Charlotte had been the best night of her life. It was like nothing she'd experienced with anyone else before. Charlotte had said sex was the meeting of minds, and their minds had well and truly met, as had their bodies. Every part of her tingled and throbbed at the mere thought of it, only for the feeling to dissipate as she recalled their cold parting.

Had she ruined everything? Charlotte's offer had come as a huge shock. Not only due to its generosity — which had completely overwhelmed her — but also because Charlotte thought she would consider selling up and then hang around to manage it. It would break her heart to see the barn every day, knowing it would continue to stand empty, its role — and her dream — unfulfilled.

She may have spoken briefly about the hole in the roof being a sign she should give up, but she wasn't serious. She had only felt down about the situation. To hand over the last remaining part of her shared history with Gran and her parents would pain her beyond all belief. She would lose a place that had shaped her; a place where she now knew she belonged.

Jeremy's email with his survey report had typically filed itself in her junk folder, so she hadn't seen it until after Charlotte left. The estimate for the work wasn't as bad as she had thought, but it was still bad enough that she was going to have to call Sophie and beg for money. With a swig — or two, or three — of wine, she picked up the phone.

"How much?" Sophie groaned. "For a hole in the roof? How big did you say it was again?"

"It's not just to fix that, but to patch other problem areas and secure the whole thing. We're quite lucky it's not in a worse state," Arte said, trying to see the positive in the situation.

"I'll have to discuss it with George when he gets home. He won't be happy. We're still owed money from the estate for the funeral. I'll chase up the solicitors in the morning. How are things with you and Charlotte? Past first base yet?"

Arte remained silent, not wishing to engage in Sophie's tactics for information. It only encouraged her.

"Second base?"

"Sophie, I'm not—"

"Third?"

With no response from Arte, Sophie said, "Oh my god, have you gone all the way?"

"Sophie, we're not teenagers, okay? I'm not discussing this. Let me know, yes? Time is of the essence. It's only patched over, but Jeremy, that's Charlotte's surveyor, has said he can pull in some favours and get someone to fix it ASAP."

"She lent you her surveyor! Wow, you've gone all the way and beyond."

"Good night, Sophie."

As she hung up, she realised Sophie must have been so amenable to her request for money because she'd had a few glasses of wine, too, hence the teasing. George may be less so, not to mention Sophie, once she'd sobered up in the morning. Arte hadn't expected to be going cap in hand to them so soon. They had agreed to contribute only in an emergency, but this constituted an emergency in Arte's book. The investment from *Hotel SOS* would make it foolish to call it a day now. That was, if they even had the money.

Her phone rang in her hand, and assuming it was Sophie calling her back, she answered it without checking. She was met by Freddie's voice.

"I wanted to check you were okay. Charlotte returned in a foul mood, which I seriously hope you aren't responsible for. I expected her to return all love-struck. What happened?"

"Nothing," Arte said, exhaling noisily.

Freddie's silence indicated he was having none of it.

"Honestly, it was nothing," Arte tried to reassure him, not wanting to go into it. "A… misunderstanding."

Was that what it was?

His silence continued.

Arte relented. "She offered to buy me out."

"Wow! She has got it bad for you if she offered to take on your shithole of a hotel. What did you say?"

"No."

Did I even say thank you?

How ungrateful she must have sounded.

"Now I don't know where we stand, but I ache for her." She groaned, realising she'd said the last bit aloud.

Freddie laughed. "You two are cute together. You'll find a way to make it work. Weigh up all your options. The perfect solution could be closer than you think."

What did that even mean?

"I'll catch you when I get back from holiday," he said. "By then, you two had better be loved up again. She's recently had a spring in her step. It suits her… and me."

"Yeah, I get the message. Send some holiday photos. Clean ones. I need something to cheer me up, not make me vomit."

By the next morning, her mood had not improved. She set out early for a long walk with Rodin, despite every muscle in her body begging for a hot bath instead. She was growing tired of the aches and pains that came from physical labour. She'd assumed her body would get used to it and stop hurting.

DIY always looked so easy whenever she watched someone else doing it on television, but holding up a wallpaper stripper against a wall with one hand and scraping with the other had pulled muscles in her shoulders and back that she didn't even know she had. The lack of hidden historic wallpapers had left her deflated too.

Crossing the field, Rodin caught the scent of something and ran off. She could make him out scoffing at something. By the time she reached his side, he was already bringing it back up. He subscribed to the philosophy that it was better to eat something and throw it up than to have never eaten it in the first place. It was always best to check if something was palatable even if it did look like it had already been through something else's digestive system.

"You know, it is possible to go off a pet, Rodin."

She climbed the stile and watched as Rodin ran off across the road to see Jenny, who was crossing her courtyard. Arte followed after to retrieve him.

"Oh, Arte," Jenny said as she caught up to them. "You look like you've got the weight of the world on your shoulders."

Arte forced a smile. "Feels like I do."

"Come on in and warm up. The kettle's just boiled. I'll make you a cuppa?"

"Thanks," Arte said, following her into the office.

"So, how are the renovations going?" Jenny asked as she poured boiling water into two mugs.

"*Hotel SOS* are all finished. They were due to finish filming next week, but the snow put a hole in the roof, so they came to film that and finished up whilst they were here. You'll have to pop over and have a look at the rooms; they're quite something."

Jenny passed Arte a mug of tea. "I will. Biscuit?" She held a tin in front of Arte, and Rodin jumped at it. "Not for you, Rodin," she chided him. "We've discussed this before."

Arte declined, unsure she could stomach a biscuit.

"So the hole in the roof is the reason for the long face, then?" Jenny asked as she sat beside Arte on the small sofa, taking a bite from a chocolate digestive.

"One of them," Arte replied. "Charlotte suggested Beaufort Hotels could buy me out."

Jenny hummed. "That's a generous offer. Are you considering it?"

"No. It was kind of Charlotte, but it's not an option."

"Hang on. Why would Charlotte Beaufort offer to buy your hotel?"

Arte felt her face warming as she smiled. "We're… kind of an item." She hoped they still were, as she recalled their night together, waking in her bed surrounded by her scent.

"Okay." Jenny blinked. "That's going to take a minute to sink in."

"Before you say it, she's not the person you see on the television," Arte added, pushing the delightful memories of Charlotte aside.

"I'll take your word for it," Jenny replied, as she chomped on another biscuit. "So, what are you going to do?"

Arte shrugged. "I have lots of questions at the moment and very few answers to them."

"This place hasn't been easy, you know," Jenny said, looking around the room. "I don't make the biggest profit, but I own it; it's my home. It provides me with food and shelter. I also get to do what I love — spend my days with dogs. Nothing worth having comes easy."

Arte nodded. She understood that, and it counted for a

lot, but it was easy to say that with a functioning business, which she was far from having.

"So, what are your options?" Jenny asked.

"One, I sell it to the highest bidder, and I wash my hands of it."

"What then?"

"I have no idea. I suppose I could try and get a teaching job at one of the London universities. I'd be closer to Charlotte." If things didn't work out, she could go back to Rome, but the thought of things not working out with Charlotte — or the hotel — made her feel more nauseous.

"And two?"

"Two, I sell it to Charlotte, and she'll let me manage it."

"The way you want to?"

Arte shook her head. "No. I have plans to turn the barn into a studio and exhibition space, where artists can learn or take time out to be creative whilst staying at the hotel."

"I like the sound of that."

"Well, it wouldn't be happening under the Beaufort Hotels brand. Charlotte made it quite clear that her hands were tied on that one."

"And is there a third option?"

"Yes. I carry on regardless. I can take one guest for bed and breakfast, but that's not going to even cover the running costs of an operational hotel. I need to get the roof fixed and the other rooms ready, and that's unlikely to happen unless I win the lottery."

"Do you play?"

"No."

Jenny laughed. "I'm sorry."

"It's fine," Arte chuckled. "If I don't laugh, I'll cry."

"If your gran was here, she'd say you should do what makes you happy. What's that?"

Arte already knew the answer. She loved the hotel, and she couldn't see herself giving it up until someone prised it from her cold, dead fingers. It had the potential to fulfil her lifelong dreams, and that wasn't something to let go of lightly. She knew she wasn't exactly up to the task, but the hotel was all she had left of the past, and as much as she'd spent a lot of time avoiding it, she damn well wasn't about to lose that too.

"Gran didn't give up," she stated, "and I'm not giving it up without a fight."

"That's the spirit," Jenny said, patting her leg.

In the back of her mind, though, Arte wondered how much more fight was required of her and how much she had left in her.

CHAPTER 28

Charlotte sat at her office desk, dreaming of what else she could be doing on a Saturday… if only she had a life. Having finished her two meetings, one of which was to sack a deputy manager in Beaufort York, her stomach felt uneasy. Even though it was lunchtime, she didn't feel hungry, just nauseous. Firing people wasn't nice. It was a job more suited to her mother, something she no doubt delighted in.

She could have left already, but she'd convinced herself that things couldn't wait until Monday. Work usually served as a useful distraction for her, and she preferred the office when it was quiet. Not that she was achieving anything today, though. Her work had all been mundane and tedious except for the email she'd received from *Hotel SOS*'s production company in response to her resignation the day before. The producers informed her that they had decided to cancel the show after the current series anyway. She wasn't sure if she was surprised or not. The show had certainly run its course, and with her resigning, she had likely forced their hand.

It was the end of an era. There were elements of the show she was going to miss. Well, perhaps one — the satisfaction of a good transformation. Even with that, any initial enjoyment she had felt presenting the programme had flitted away in recent series. There was no way she would continue doing something if she couldn't do it justice.

It also felt tarnished by her mother's involvement — not that she was purely responsible for the direction Michael had taken it in, Charlotte was sure of that. Everyone involved was to blame, including her, perhaps her more so than anyone else. Being unkind to the hoteliers may have been a gradual change, but it was a recognisable one, and one made for the worse. She couldn't blame the crew for not speaking up. They had likely expected her to complain, and when she had just got on with the job, fearful of losing her own position, they followed suit.

She pushed the compliance report she'd attempted to read three times to one side, unable to keep her mind far from Arte. She wanted to give her space, but she also wanted to be with her more than anything. Walking Rodin, washing mud off a wellington boot, stripping wallpaper, stripping Arte. She didn't want her to give up on her dream, but there was no way Beaufort Hotels would go off-book and allow someone free rein with a hotel they owned. She recalled the uproar amongst the board when Beaufort Birmingham had asked to incorporate a casino. They'd even presented a good business case for it, but her mother was having none of it, stating that it would bring down the brand. Even Charlotte had to admit she'd had a point.

A note on her desk in Freddie's handwriting caught her attention. She must have missed it when she began sifting through the piles of paperwork he'd left before he went on holiday.

'Don't forget your Sunday liaison, the answer to which is staring you in the face. See you in a week?'

What does he mean by that? Staring me in the face?

She scowled at the misplaced final question mark and looked around. Her eyes scoured her desk, passing over the photo of her mother and father at a party in the eighties, with Ronald Reagan in the background. Surely he hadn't meant that. She looked out the window then, to the distant hills on the horizon, beyond which Arte and Rodin were.

Her 'Sunday liaison', as Freddie had termed it, was also playing on her mind. Was she welcome to return? She and Arte hadn't exactly left things in a good place, and with only a few brief text messages exchanged to check in over the last few days, she wasn't sure where they stood.

She could see now that Arte may have taken her offer as a sign that she didn't believe in her ability to achieve what she so desperately wanted, but being faced with selling to someone who would enable you to carry on with at least part of your dream… surely that was better than losing the place entirely to a stranger?

Even so, Arte had shut the idea down when Charlotte told her the art studio wouldn't be an option under Beaufort Hotels' ownership. Was the dream of the studio the one thing keeping her going? Dreams had always seemed childish to her. Life often had different ideas, and there wasn't always room for dreams.

Arte's words played round in her head again: 'I'm not you; I don't give up so easily on a dream.' Had she easily given up Beaufort Mayfair? At the time she hadn't felt like she'd been given a choice. Perhaps she had allowed herself to be manipulated and steered in a direction she didn't want to go in, just to please others.

Arte only *had* choices, and she'd made it clear to Charlotte that the choice she offered her was untenable. Charlotte placed her hand on her fluttering stomach. Arte was nothing but courageous, steadfast, determined, and passionate in pursuit of her dream. Charlotte envied her; she herself was none of those things.

What she'd give to be in Arte's shoes, a blank canvas in front of her and all the potential to create something special. Perhaps she hadn't fully appreciated how hard it was for Arte to go into that space, with all its memories; to tear it apart and start again. If Charlotte could clear her schedule a little, she could spend more time there, help her more, and take some of the burden. Clearing her schedule wouldn't be an easy task, though. She'd be lucky to have a day free, let alone a whole weekend. She threw her pen across the room with a growl, frustrated at what felt like an unsolvable problem.

In need of tea, she looked for Freddie, only to remember he was on holiday and, moreover, didn't work on Saturdays. If she wanted tea, she'd have to make it herself. As she made her way down the corridor to the executive floor's kitchen, she passed her mother's office, only to notice her standing by a window, staring out. She was tempted to creep past but took a deep breath instead. They, too, needed to clear the air following their last encounter.

"Mother. You're back early. How was your break?"

Claudette turned. "Ah, Lottie, you're here. I've only returned to get my affairs in order."

"You're not dying, Mother."

"We're all dying, Lottie; that's the one thing we can be sure about."

Charlotte resisted the urge to point out she was not dying imminently but knew by now it was pointless to argue. Her mother's tone was off; everything about her was off. Charlotte's blood ran cold.

"Has something happened?" She asked quickly.

"Not as such, but since my little health issue" — she gave a flippant wave of her hand — "I've come to realise that what time I have left would be better spent enjoying life a little more. So, it's all yours."

Not wishing to receive a ticking-off for requesting clarification, but still needing it nonetheless, Charlotte asked, "What's all mine?"

"Beaufort Hotels. Malcolm has the paperwork drawn up. I've signed my half over to you. To be honest, it's been a chain around my neck since your father died, but it was all I had, and I let it throttle me."

Charlotte wanted to point out that she had her, her daughter, but there was no sense in doing so.

"I'm stepping down, permanently," Claudette continued. "Effective immediately. You were right about the acquisition; I was neglectful. Though this medically enforced holiday was not my first choice, I found I rather enjoyed my time in foreign lands." A faint smile crept across her lips as she spoke. "I plan to do more of it, lots more. I've met someone, and… I'll be living in Monaco for the foreseeable future."

Her mother turned her attention back to the window, as if allowing Charlotte time to process everything she'd just heard. There were so many thoughts flying around her head that she struggled to catch hold of any of them, but one thought left her mouth quite easily.

"I don't want it."

She realised then what Freddie had meant. There wasn't anything physically staring her in the face, but in searching for the answer, she would naturally reach a conclusion she wanted to reach, deep inside. That was her answer: she didn't want Beaufort Hotels. She didn't want to clear her schedule; she didn't *want* her schedule. She didn't want any of it.

Claudette shot her a bemused look. "Of course you want it; everyone wants this."

"I don't. All I wanted was to work in a hotel, make someone's day that little bit brighter. I didn't want an empire. Somewhere along the way I changed into a version of myself that I don't recognise and that I definitely don't like." Charlotte took a breath and added, "I never stopped to think if I actually wanted any of it, and no one stopped to ask me if it was what I wanted. It was just 'my future', all conveniently mapped out for me. I would have been happy to have been left at Beaufort Mayfair; it was all I ever wanted. It's probably why I never fought you too hard for your chair; my heart was never in it."

"I was grateful for that," Claudette murmured, "but it didn't stop me from feeling your breath on the back of my neck every day."

Charlotte joined her mother by the window. They stood in silence for a moment, taking in the busy cityscape before them.

"It wasn't until recently that I've begun to question what I wanted from my life," Charlotte explained. "I love being on the ground, not up here. I love the energy, the teamwork, and the satisfaction of putting a smile on a guest's face. Not the spreadsheets, the contracts, and the endless meetings. Looking back I only went along with it to try and impress you, to be the person you wanted me to be — and for what? You're fucking impossible to impress."

Claudette turned to look at her. Charlotte braced herself for a fallout that never came. Instead, her mother lifted a hand to Charlotte's face and rested it there.

"Lottie, darling. You've impressed me every day since you were born."

What on earth had happened to her mother? If she'd known what a bit of enforced downtime would do, Charlotte would have insisted on her taking time off years ago. She would have even packed her bags. It seemed a health scare, a holiday, and a man on her arm were enough to kick the wind out of her sails and bring her back to earth.

"I am proud of you." Claudette wiped a tear from Charlotte's cheek. "In truth, I've spent my life trying to live up to what your father knew you would be, and I've always feared I wouldn't be able to. He *always* believed in you. When you arrived, he never looked at me in the same way again. It was like all his love went to you. He spoke of little else but you taking over the company and how you would excel at it. He never thought the same of me, never believed in me. When he died, I needed to show everyone I wasn't just Henri Beaufort's wife. I was Claudette Beaufort, and I was someone."

Charlotte hurriedly wiped her eyes as Claudette took a step back and returned her attention to the view.

"I took over the business and spent every day proving I could be successful, even though he was dead. I needed to prove it to myself, too, and I did. The board were against me taking over, but they couldn't stop me. I clung on, and I've been clinging ever since. Then they started talking about replacing me with you. You had shown enormous potential with your acquisitions. I hoped the television show would get you out from under my feet, but all it did was underline how impressive you were. If I wasn't CEO of Beaufort Hotels, what was I? I didn't want to be just a little old lady."

"What's changed?"

The scowl from her mother told her she should have worded that better.

"Taking a step back has given me time to reflect on everything. I have succeeded, and I have achieved what I set out to do. I need to enjoy what I have left of my life."

Charlotte was about to protest her morbidity again, but Claudette held a finger up.

"It's time for Beaufort to move into a new era, with you at its helm. You are the fresh blood it needs for the future."

Was her mother still not listening?

"No, Mother!" Charlotte's voice penetrated the room. "I'm not your carbon copy, and quite frankly I don't have the passion for it anymore." She wasn't sure now if she had ever had the passion for it or if she was simply channelling other people's. "It put Father in an early grave; it's almost done the same to you." She pointed to the imposing black leather chair behind the enormous oak desk. "I've spent my whole life staring at that chair. Father's chair, your chair, waiting for the day that it would become mine, despite your attempts to keep me from it. As it turns out, you were doing me a favour by holding me back. Recently I was shown there is more to life than maintaining an empire. Now I realise I don't want to spend the next few years working myself into an early grave behind a desk. I want to enjoy life too. I have that chance, and I'm going to take it."

Claudette turned to face her, and, to Charlotte's astonishment, she nodded. "So what do we do with it?"

"Pass the burden on to someone else — because that's what it is, at least to us. We can sell the company and live more than comfortably on the proceeds. We Beaufort women don't sit still for long. We'll find things to do. Let's find a cause we want to champion, instead of fulfilling the dream of a man we love and miss. We don't need to prove ourselves to anyone else. Not anymore."

"I suppose you still have your show to do," Claudette said.

"No," Charlotte replied. "I quit." She withheld the fact the show had been cancelled, assuming her mother would think she'd been fired.

"What will you do then?" Claudette asked, not looking surprised.

"I think I might like to move to the country."

"With that woman of yours?"

Charlotte's face lit up at the thought of 'that woman'. As much as she would have liked to confirm that was the case, it was far from it, as things stood.

"Her name is Arte," she settled on.

Claudette nodded a form of acknowledgement. It was more than Charlotte could have hoped for.

"I'm sure you'll like her. You share a similarity."

Claudette's scowl led Charlotte to elaborate. "She doesn't take any shit either." She thought back to the times Arte had called her out on her behaviour, questioned her actions, and encouraged her to do the right thing.

The hint of a smile appeared on Claudette's face again. Charlotte couldn't remember the last time she'd seen her mother genuinely smile. It must have been in the previous century, when her father was alive.

"She must be rather special if you're giving up everything for her," she said.

Was she giving everything up for Arte? No. She'd given everything up thanks to Arte. She'd made Charlotte question everything in her life that she'd never thought to question herself. She'd suggested she open herself up to the possibility that she was fulfilling someone else's dream and showed her the hurt she was causing with her behaviour.

"Well, it's all yours now," Claudette surmised, "so it's your choice. I have enough to live off until the excessive life I plan to live kills me."

"Can I ask who your new man is?" Charlotte asked.

"Baptiste Chevalier. He owns most of the casinos along the French Riviera, so I won't be short of entertainment. You should come out there; the weather is much more palatable. I'll be staying at his villa in Monaco."

The irony that her mother was seeing a casino owner was not lost on her. Charlotte fought to contain her amusement.

"How long have you known him?"

"Long enough, probably as long as you've known your… friend. When you get to our age, there is no time by which to measure our actions. We have to take what we want and do what feels right. *Carpe diem.*"

That she could understand, and her mother was certainly experienced in taking what she wanted. Charlotte could only feel pleased that her mother had found a way forward — and in a different country.

"I'll clear out of here, and you can have it for as long as it takes you to find a buyer," Claudette said, waving at the desk.

Charlotte looked back at the chair. "I'm happy where I am, actually." She found herself relieved that she would never have to sit in it, much less be found dead in it like her father had been.

"He would have been proud of you, Mother," she said. "I'm sorry if he overlooked your potential because he was too focused on mine. That was his failing."

Claudette regarded her, her face emotionless. "Yes, well. Run along now, Lottie."

Charlotte laughed internally. She would never stop being a child in her mother's eyes. She was relieved that she'd saved herself from morphing into her — or that someone else had. The cute, beanie-headed, dungaree-wearing artist had shown her another way, and not only with her words, but with her heart. She'd been right all along about her mother kicking her back down, and also when she suggested she could still surprise her. For Claudette to open up momentarily and admit that Charlotte had always made her proud nearly knocked her off her feet. She empathised with her need to prove herself to others, was that not what Charlotte had spent her career doing too?

There was one final lesson worth taking from Claudette, one about finding a way forward.

One question remained: If Arte had already rejected one offer from Charlotte, would she reject another? There was only one way to find out.

CHAPTER 29

Although music often worked in raising her spirits, Arte's playlist was doing little to lift her mood. Even the most uplifting song could feel depressing if you were in the wrong frame of mind, and not hearing from Charlotte that morning had put her there. She was supposed to be with her today, but they hadn't confirmed it during their very short messages to one another over the past few days.

Charlotte may have been enjoying a lie-in, she tried telling herself. It was Sunday, after all, but it didn't stop her worrying that she hadn't had a reply. When she realised a formidable woman like Charlotte probably never had a lie-in, it only increased her concern.

She hoped Charlotte hadn't taken her refusal of the buyout offer as a personal rejection. It hadn't been her intention to push her away; she simply couldn't accept her offer. Beaufort wasn't interested in country hotels, that much she did know. She could see that Charlotte was trying to help, but she couldn't accept anything that would mean giving up the studio.

She thought she heard a noise, even over the sound of t.A.T.u's controversial "All The Things She Said", but when Rodin didn't flinch, neither did she. The last scrap of wallpaper was coming off the wall whether it liked it or not.

As the song changed and the room fell into silence, she could hear Rodin's quiet snores in his deep sleep. Some guard dog he was. She was about to apply what she hoped would be the last squirt of steam from the wretched wallpaper remover when she heard a distant knocking. This time Rodin heard it too. He sprang to his feet and bolted out of the room. Arte followed, finding him bouncing enthusiastically at the front door.

A quick check out of the window revealed Charlotte's car parked in the drive. Arte's heart raced in her chest — until she realised Charlotte may be back to repeat her offer. The dog shot out as she opened the door, circling his new best friend and preventing her from moving until she patted him.

"Hey, Rodin," Charlotte said, ruffling his fur.

"I wasn't expecting to see you today," Arte greeted her cautiously, hugging the doorframe for support.

"It's Sunday. I said I'd be here, and here I am." Charlotte smiled, a little too enthusiastically for Arte's liking.

Arte walked into reception, leaving Charlotte and her cheery persona to follow.

"If you've come to try and persuade me to sell to Beaufort, then you've wasted your time. I can't just give up without a fight, Charlotte," Arte said, keeping her tone as neutral as possible.

She turned to find Charlotte right behind her.

"Arte, I told you I don't want you to have to fight, as much as I don't want to keep coming down here every time there is a problem."

"I understand." Arte nodded, trying to hold her emotions together. It had been lovely while it lasted.

"No, I don't think you do," Charlotte said, placing her soft hand on Arte's cheek and looking into her eyes. "I mean I want to be here when the problems happen. I want to be here with you as they happen, to solve them with you. To help prevent them! If you don't want my family's money, then how about my money? I'd like to buy Sophie out."

Arte froze, taking in the enormity of what Charlotte was suggesting and what it was doing to her body.

"I know I said that good decisions are rarely made when we involve emotions," Charlotte continued, "but I was wrong. I was using my head then, when I should have followed my heart. I should have divorced Gideon years ago, given myself a chance to live and breathe as me instead of being what everyone else wanted me to be. I'm trying to do that now. I'm listening to my heart, and it led me here to you. We are one heart, and it's beating in here." Charlotte gesticulated around the room.

It was all Arte could have hoped to hear, but it sounded a little too perfect for her liking.

"What about Beaufort Hotels?" she asked.

"Beaufort is up for sale."

She could feel her jaw drop. "What?" This wasn't just a

manoeuvre on the chessboard; Charlotte had firmly closed the chessboard and throw it in the bin.

Charlotte nodded. "I don't want to die in front of a fucking computer. That's where they found my father, and where Mother had her stroke."

"You'd rather die tripping over luggage or Rodin? Or even at the hand of an angry customer?"

Charlotte grinned. "Yes, even more so if you are there to catch me." She winced. "Okay, that didn't sound how I meant it to."

"I get it," Arte said, feeling like her heart was melting.

Charlotte held her arms out to the side. "I stand before you, a wandering soul, looking for a new home."

"You no longer have the pick of any room then?"

"I only want one room in this world," Charlotte said, closing the gap between them, "and that's whichever one you're in."

Arte leaned a leg against the reception desk to steady herself as Charlotte took her hands. "You've mended parts of me I didn't even know were broken. Now I want to help you mend this place, to do it together. I love your vision for it; I love..."

Arte's heart nearly stopped.

"...everything about it. I want to be part of it... if you'll have me. Or I can be a silent partner. If you prefer."

Arte felt Charlotte's eyes piercing into her, searching her for a response. For something.

"I don't want that."

Charlotte let go of her hands, took a step back and lowered her head. "I understand."

Arte gently lifted Charlotte's chin with her finger.

"Now you misunderstand me. I don't want a silent partner, and I don't believe for one second you could even manage it. What I'm saying is, I don't want to do it without you."

Charlotte's eyes brightened, only to dull again. "It still wouldn't be yours. Not completely."

"No, it would be ours." Her arms reached out for Charlotte whose face lit up at what she was hearing.

"And that's okay?"

Arte pressed her lips to Charlotte's and murmured, "It's even better," as she kissed them.

The softness and eagerness of Charlotte's warm mouth sent a shiver down Arte's spine. Their kiss lingered; time standing still as they lost themselves in one another.

As their lips finally parted, Arte gazed into Charlotte's eyes, her heart overflowing with affection. "Every day I get to wake up next to you is a dream come true," she whispered.

Charlotte's eyes sparkled with tears, her voice trembling as she replied, "Good, because you are my home, my happiness, and my forever, Arte. There may be one small snag, however, which might not be a snag at all if I've read her right. Sophie."

"She won't be a problem," Arte confirmed. "George wasn't at all pleased at having to contribute towards repairing the roof. He threatened to cancel their holiday, which displeased Sophie. She voiced that quite loudly last night and again at five this morning."

Their eyes met, both exuding an uncontainable sense of happiness. Arte's partly came from relief, to have someone beside her, to support her in her quest, and for that person to be Charlotte, the woman she'd fallen in love with. She had given up everything she'd ever worked for to come and share the weight of Arte's shithole hotel. The realisation of what Charlotte was actually giving up hit her then.

"Oh, but what about Mayfair, your baby? You'd give her up for me?"

"I'm not giving anything up. I'm gaining everything I want and more. She's all grown up anyway, and between you and me, it wasn't her that needed me. It's time to move on and make a new baby... with you."

Arte admired Charlotte's courage and strength so much she thought her heart would burst with pride.

"So you'll run the hotel whilst I focus on the art studio and bring in the customers?"

"If that's what you want me to do," Charlotte said, "it sounds perfect to me."

Arte sighed with relief. "I don't think I was ever destined to do it alone. Gran couldn't have done it without my grandfather. And, anyway, I'm not sure I wanted to be a hotelier any more than you wanted to be CEO. I was right, wasn't I? It really wasn't you."

"You mean the part where you called me an entitled brat?" Charlotte smirked. "Yes, you were. It's hard to admit that you've spent your entire life working towards something you didn't want. It was an available path and a way to make someone I loved proud of me. An easy way to the top if I walked it correctly, which I did."

"Blindly," Arte pointed out.

"Yes, blindly," Charlotte conceded. "It seems you know me better than I do myself."

Arte rubbed Charlotte's arms. "That's because you were honest with me. You should have been honest with yourself, a long time ago."

"You made me want to be honest. You opened my eyes to other possibilities. Until recently, there was nothing worth looking at."

Catching her meaning, Arte blushed. "And what about *Hotel SOS*?"

"Cancelled. Don't worry, I got my resignation in first, which incidentally may have led to the cancellation. I said it had become too toxic for the world we live in, and I wasn't planning on adding to it any further."

"Good for you. And what about Freddie?" Arte asked, suddenly aware she may partly be the reason he was about to become unemployed.

"I'll stipulate to any buyer that they keep him employed somewhere."

"Or we could ask him to come and work here. We'll need a deputy manager because, trust me, you will not be working the whole time. I have plans for you," she added, along with a wink.

"I'm not even co-owner yet, and you're already bossing me about," Charlotte protested.

"I'm sure it will work both ways. I'm led to believe you're exceptionally good at that, and I'm more than happy to work within your skill set. Speaking of your skills, are you leaving me again tomorrow?"

"I'm never leaving you. I'm in here." Charlotte leaned in and pressed her hand to Arte's heart.

Arte lowered it onto her breast. She could feel Charlotte's ragged breath on her, making every part of her body tingle with anticipation. She had a sudden and desperate need to feel her lips against hers.

"But yes, I will need to return tomorrow to put some things into place," Charlotte admitted. "Then I'll be back before nightfall to work from here, if that suits you? There's a lot of change coming, and I owe it to the staff to talk to them in person. I can bring my belongings. I don't have much, but I do have a rather lovely vase I'd like to bring. We could put it on this table." She pointed to the bare one in reception. "It would look very welcoming filled with fresh flowers."

"Better than my shitty knick-knacks, you mean," Arte said.

"Your words, not mine."

"So we're really going to do this? You think we'll be able to work together and be in a relationship? And so quickly?"

"I'm game if you are. Your gran and grandfather managed it for half a century, and I've worked with my mother. I'm sure I can handle working with you."

Arte squinted at Charlotte. "Did you just compare me to your mother?"

Charlotte's eyes widened. "No. You are nothing like my mother."

"Good. Speaking of which, how did she take it?"

"Oh, she's already moved on. Got herself a new man and new toys to play with it seems. Hopefully, now she has a life she'll stop meddling in mine. She's signed Beaufort over to me, and I thanked her by saying I didn't want it."

"Wow."

Charlotte let out one of her soft, thrumming 'hmms', making Arte lose focus until another thought struck her.

"Hang on, you did accept your mother's offer, though? Right? If you're intent on buying Soph out, you're going to need some capital."

"Oh, so now you *do* want me for my money?" Charlotte placed her arms around Arte's waist.

"Perhaps... Some of it, and only if it's yours. And as an investor you need to be aware of what awaits you. The roof is falling in, you know. The decor is so last century. There's a barn falling down that needs propping back up. It's not going to be like your cushy office job, pushing paper around a desk and attending meetings. I hope you're prepared for everything this place is going to throw at you."

Charlotte's lips curled. "I am well aware of the faults, and on that note, I was thinking of a name change to welcome in the new era."

"Not this again," Arte replied playfully.

"Hotel Arte. It fits well with the plans you have for it."

"*Hotel* Arte," Arte repeated. "Not Arte's B&B or Arte's Guesthouse? Or even Arte's Shithole?"

Arte decided not to rise to the creases forming around Charlotte's lips. She had to admit she was warming to the name change and it would fit well with her plans for the barn.

"It's perfect," she said. "It also means we can keep the A on the embroidered dressing gowns. But if my grandfather starts haunting us, you're dealing with him, okay?"

"Okay," Charlotte said, pulling her in for a kiss.

Arte needed Charlotte's arms around her to prop her up. Her whole body was vibrating with happiness, making her feel weak. She wasn't weak, though; Charlotte strengthened her, and together, they were a force to be reckoned with. With an investor, a lover, and a friend by her side, she knew they would create a bright future for themselves and for Hotel Arte.

Rodin jumped at them, breaking them apart.

Arte knelt to his level. "Oh, Rodin, are you feeling left out, boy?"

He panted at her and attempted to lick her face. She dodged it, having seen where that tongue had gone recently, and pulled him in for a hug instead.

"You know we come as a pair, right?" Arte said, looking up at Charlotte.

"That's more than okay with me," Charlotte said as she pulled Arte back to her feet. "As long as he knows he's not allowed to die, and that if he sneaks onto our bed, I'll kill him."

Arte laughed. "There won't be room for him on our bed with what I have in mind."

"About that — our bed, not the plans you have in your mind. We will definitely come to them later. I've had a thought. Whilst we're converting the barn into a studio, why don't we convert that old dairy next to it into accommodation for us? It will free up another room in the hotel."

"I like it," Arte enthused, though she couldn't resist adding, "Always thinking of the bottom line, Charlotte."

"I'm thinking of a bottom, but it's not a line," Charlotte

said, reaching round to grab a handful of Arte's backside. "This has far more shape to it."

"Oh yeah. Do you need something to occupy your hands?"

"Always," Charlotte replied with a smirk.

Arte leaned devilishly close, so close her lips were a breath away from Charlotte's. "Good. You can help me hang this blasted wallpaper."

Charlotte groaned as Arte pulled her from the room. "Your wish is my command, my love."

EPILOGUE

Arte relaxed into the reception desk chair and took in the space around her. It was the one room that hadn't changed much, aside from the removal of the odd knick-knacks, the addition of a new mirror above the fireplace, and a vase of fresh flowers on the centre table. Yet, somehow, it exuded a different atmosphere compared to when she'd first sat there as its new owner. It was lighter, not just in brightness, but in the sense that the weight it once held on her shoulders had lifted. Any new weight it added was now shared.

Rodin's claws clicked against the tiled floor as he paced the room. He'd heard cars arriving and the sound of people, only to find none entering his space. The closed front door was keeping the late summer heat out of the cool, tiled reception area, so he was forced to lift himself to look out of the window.

The seasons had come and gone, bringing immense change to Hotel Arte. With renovations completed by spring, the bedrooms had been at full occupancy for the entire summer. Tonight, however, they were in reserve for some of their guests, who were attending the official opening of The Tithe Studio @ Hotel Arte.

The barn renovations had lasted throughout the summer months, and the studio would be welcoming its first students in the coming weeks. The old dairy beside it was in its final stages of restoration, awaiting the laying of carpets and the fitting of the kitchen so Arte and Charlotte could move in.

Everything had fallen into place for them; her only regret was that her gran wasn't there to see what Charlotte and she had achieved.

"Ready?" Charlotte said, entering reception.

Arte perked up at the sight of Charlotte in a front-wrap, floral midi dress that she was spilling out the top of. "Always ready for you."

Charlotte's eyes shimmered in response, making Arte want to relieve her of the dress. Instead she picked her phone up from the desk.

"Freddie's just messaged to say most of our guests have arrived."

"Let's head over then," Charlotte said, holding out a hand. "I have a surprise for you. A VIP guest."

"Not your mother?"

"No. I've not had an RSVP from her, not that I'd expect one. No, an old friend, I suppose you could call her. I didn't mention it as she prefers to operate incognito. I wasn't sure if her schedule would allow, but she messaged to say she was on her way."

"Who?" Arte asked as they stepped from the hotel.

"Wait and see."

Rodin bolted off to carry out his investigations as the sound of a burbling engine pulled their attention to the top of the drive.

"Seems you won't have to wait. Here she is now."

Arte's mouth opened at the sight of a blue VW camper van making its way towards them.

"What a cute camper."

"Don't go getting any ideas," Charlotte said.

As the camper came closer, Arte squinted to get a look at its occupants. "Is that—?" No, it couldn't be. A smile curved her lips. "That's Beatrice Russell… in an old VW camper! How on earth do you know Beatrice Russell?"

"You could say we have a shared passion," Charlotte teased.

"Are you going to elaborate?"

"No. Let's greet our guests. You'll know her wife, Sydney, from her book you were reading a few months ago."

Arte steadied herself by taking Charlotte's arm. A world-famous actress and an author at her hotel.

Play it cool!

Beatrice Russell effortlessly swooped from the camper and lifted her sunglasses onto her head. Arte was sure the vehicle was something she herself would fall out of, but this was Beatrice Russell; everything she did was elegant and graceful.

Once introductions were out of the way, Arte saw an opportunity to extract more information about Beatrice's and Charlotte's shared passion from another source. "So, how do you two know each other, Beatrice?"

Beatrice smirked at Arte's question before looking at

Charlotte. "We both love a Beaufort penthouse, don't we, Charlotte?"

"Oh?" Sydney said, looping her arm through Beatrice's.

Beatrice's eye twitched. "Not at the same time, Sydney."

"No," Charlotte chuckled. "Beatrice kicked me out many times over the years when I was living at Beaufort Mayfair. Quite willingly, I might add, considering how much you were paying."

"Worth every penny. We stayed last week, in fact. I had a Gucci shoot not far from there. I'm glad to see it remains much the same, even down to the name."

"The name and reputation were what the buyer was purchasing."

Beatrice nodded. "I was quite surprised to find you'd sold up. I'll miss our late-night chats at the bar."

"Likewise, though of course you're welcome here anytime."

Arte left Beatrice and Charlotte to reminisce over Beaufort Mayfair, following after Sydney as she locked the camper.

"Sydney, your camper is beautiful," she said, stroking it.

"Thank you! Her name is Gertie."

"You named her?"

"Of course."

"I would have expected Beatrice to arrive in a Rolls Royce or something else fancy. Not that there's anything wrong with Gertie, of course. She's cute."

Sydney chuckled. "Normally we would have arrived in

something else, but we're not a million miles from here, and Bea only agrees to come out for short jaunts in Gertie. She's a little too… basic for her liking. As it's a nice day, I thought we'd stretch her legs. She gets a little stiff if we don't keep her exercised. Gertie, I mean; not Bea."

Arte laughed; she liked Sydney already.

"Whilst I have you alone," Sydney said quietly, "I want to commission a sculpture for our garden. I understand you might be able to help me with that."

"I certainly can," Arte replied as calmly as she could, even though she wanted to scream out loud at the proposition. One of her original works, in Beatrice Russell's garden!

Sydney tapped the side of her nose. "Let's keep it between you and me, though."

"Sure. Did you have anything in mind?"

Sydney looked at Beatrice and Charlotte deep in conversation. "Are you any good at masks?"

Arte followed her gaze. "Ah, a gift for Beatrice… because she's an actress?"

"Mmm, something like that," Sydney replied with a subtle chuckle.

Arte looked to Charlotte, knowing immediately what Sydney was getting at.

"Well, you're in luck. They are my speciality. I have one on display in MAXXI in Rome, in fact."

"Impressive. We visited the museum last October whilst we were there for the premiere of Bea's last film."

"I loved that film!" Arte chirped, only to be embarrassed by her own enthusiasm.

So much for playing it cool.

Sydney's eyes crinkled with amusement. Arte told herself the author was likely used to people behaving strangely around her and Beatrice. It must be tiring, being famous and not being able to just be yourself. Her thought made her eyes drift to Charlotte, who quirked her lips into a playful smile making Arte feel all gooey inside.

"It's great that you could come," Arte continued, trying to sound less like a crazed fangirl this time. "It must be difficult finding time to do everyday things."

"It is, but I wouldn't change it for anything. It's a life that takes some getting used to, I can tell you that much." Sydney's gaze drifted to Beatrice again, who met her with a sultry stare. "She's turned my life upside down — in a good way, if you know what I mean."

"I do," Arte replied. She'd once groused that Charlotte could not be judged by her lovely cover; now she wouldn't change Charlotte's torn pages, dog-eared corners, or tea stains for the world.

"Bea was quite insistent that we check out Charlotte's latest project," Sydney said as they followed their partners around the side of the hotel. "It's great that they support each other's endeavours."

"What do you mean?"

"Charlotte's donation to Bea's charity — her drama school for LGBTQ+ children."

Arte nodded, pretending she knew all about it. Charlotte's generosity didn't surprise her one bit. The amount of money Beaufort Hotels had sold for was eye-watering. Charlotte could have lived off it lavishly on a beach in Barbados for the rest of her days. Instead, she'd not only invested in Hotel Arte and worked hard every day, determined to help her partner bring her dream to life, but she'd apparently given some of it away to help others.

"Congratulations on your book, by the way. It was remarkable."

She'd found a copy amongst her gran's belongings. The bookmark was halfway through, and when she decided to read it and finish it for her, she'd become quite engrossed in the tragic tale.

"Thanks," Sydney said. "I have a new one out soon."

"Then congratulations again! I look forward to reading it. Would it be too much to ask you to sign my copy? Only if you have time, though. I don't want to put you out." Arte stopped herself, realising she was rambling. "Sorry, is it annoying when random strangers ask that sort of thing?"

Sydney laughed. "No, not at all. I still can't get used to people asking. It takes me a minute to remember I'm an author."

"I get that. I often forget I have a piece on display in the MAXXI, but then again, I don't get asked for autographs to remind me."

"Any plans to bring the piece home?"

"Charlotte suggested that. She thought it would make a nice centrepiece for the studio, but I think it's best that it, and everything it represents, stay there."

It was time to make new pieces, not add to old, Arte thought. Her grief remained, but her relationship with it now felt different. Whether she decided to work that into her next piece was a question for the future.

~

Deep in conversation with Beatrice, Charlotte led them along the gravel path to the old tithe barn, which was abuzz with activity. A mix of grassy areas, white shingle, and abundant flower beds created an inviting, landscaped space to relax on the outdoor furniture.

Sunshine streamed in through the large, glass doors, filling the newly refurbished Tithe Studio with light. Staff members were milling around with silver trays, handing out drinks and canapés to excited guests. It was full to the rafters, quite literally, given the mezzanine floor that extended out along the back wall where people were admiring the hanging artwork and sculptures on plinths.

The mezzanine filled one side of the barn as Arte had always envisaged, with a wooden staircase descending to the entrance. A glass wall separated the space underneath from the rest of the open-plan structure. It was attracting attention as guests admired the workshop area, with its rows of benches, sculpting equipment, and other art tools.

Charlotte spotted Tom behind the temporary bar as she entered. His reassuring nod told her that everything was going as planned, and she finally felt able to relax. This party was the culmination of weeks' worth of planning for both her and Arte. A waiter stopped by to offer them all a glass of champagne. Charlotte devoured half of hers in one swoop, letting out a breath she felt she'd held in for too long.

"What a phenomenal space you've created!" Beatrice said, taking in the room. "It takes a creative vision to transform it into something so versatile."

"That's all down to this one. A vision she's held from childhood," Charlotte remarked, exuding pride in Arte's direction.

Arte tried to take her hand, but it was clenched in a tight fist. She was keeping her nerves in there like her father had taught her. Arte pushed her thumb inside and forced her hand open, taking it in hers.

"There's no need for nerves today," she whispered into her ear.

Arte didn't know the real reason why she was nervous, or what she had planned, so she just gave her hand a squeeze back.

"I adore these beams," Sydney said, arching her neck to take them in. "And the way you've incorporated the modern design to contrast with the original features."

"Sydney's a sucker for an original feature," Beatrice added with an affectionate smile.

"Me too," Arte said.

"I guess we should get this party started." Charlotte tapped her glass to get everyone's attention.

The room fell into silence.

"Thank you, everyone, for coming," she said. "I'm going to pass you over to my special guest, Beatrice Russell, who is going to say a few words and officially open The Tithe Studio for us today."

Surprised gasps and then applause came from around the room as the crowd realised they were in the company of a world-famous actress.

Beatrice expressed her gratitude to the audience with light nods of her head. "Thank you, Charlotte. Well! What a space we have the pleasure to be in this afternoon. Arte and Charlotte have worked immensely hard to bring the artistic community together in this inspiring and creative space. The symbiosis between The Tithe Studio and Hotel Arte, as they feed one another and work in harmony, reflects Charlotte and Arte's relationship. One could suggest neither works well without the other, nor can one live without the other. So whether you want to purchase or display a work of art, need a week away from daily life—"

"Or two," Charlotte cut in loudly, causing a titter of laughter to lift from the audience.

Beatrice grinned and continued. "A guiding hand from its resident artist, or simply a night's rest in a Boutique Hotel Award winner, you'll find it all here at Hotel Arte and The Tithe Studio."

"Did you write that for her?" Arte whispered in Charlotte's ear as everyone gave a hearty round of applause.

"Essentially yes; she added her unique spin."

"I particularly liked the bit about us."

"Me too," Charlotte said, popping a kiss on Arte's cheek. "That was all me."

Beatrice raised a glass. "Let us wish The Tithe Studio and Hotel Arte every success for its future."

The room filled with a 'Hear, hear!' followed by rapturous applause.

"Thank you, Beatrice," Charlotte said, giving her forearm a pat.

"It was my pleasure," she replied. "Sydney, let's take a look at the art."

As they sauntered off, hand in hand, Charlotte froze on

the spot as she heard "Lottie" being called from behind her.

"Mother? I didn't know you were coming." Charlotte said as Claudette Beaufort approached and kissed her cheeks. She flashed a smile at the handsome Frenchman, Baptiste, who had become a permanent feature at her mother's side.

"You invited us," Claudette replied. "Were we not supposed to attend?"

"An RSVP would have been nice."

"Arte, I take it? It's nice to meet you," Claudette said, ignoring her daughter.

"Likewise. Thanks for coming," Arte replied. She held out a hand to Claudette who looked at it momentarily before giving it the lightest of shakes.

"We were in London for the opening of one of Baptiste's new casinos. We saw Gideon there. Charlotte, did you know his fiancée is pregnant? They are expecting their little arrival in three months. Elizabeth is over the moon at becoming a grandmother again."

"I'm delighted for him." Charlotte wasn't even pretending. She was genuinely pleased her ex had found happiness and started the family he always wanted. She should have regretted not divorcing him sooner, but if she had, it was unlikely she would be standing in this beautiful room, which encompassed everything she loved about the woman beside her. It was more surprising that her mother was still in contact with her ex-mother-in-law, but their type tended to stick together — or at least struggled to avoid each other.

"You must show me around your hotel before we leave," Claudette said.

"Of course. We must mingle now, Mother. Please excuse us."

Charlotte steered Arte away.

"You know," Arte teased, "I don't know why your mum has such a bad reputation. She seems nice enough."

Charlotte laughed. "This is Claudette 3.0. It's an upgrade from 2.0, which needed avoiding at all costs."

"And 1.0?"

"1.0 was a long, long time ago," Charlotte replied with a gentle sigh. "A different era, one might say."

Arte rubbed her arm. "Your dad would be proud of you."

"I know."

"You may not have walked the exact path he paved for you, but choosing your own path led you here, to me. Out of all your achievements so far, I think that's the most commendable one. I know myself it isn't easy to change direction, and yet you did."

"It was easy, really," Charlotte replied, leaning forward and whispering into Arte's ear, "I looked at the path ahead and realised you weren't at the end of it. That's when I knew I was on the wrong path."

A throat cleared behind them, pulling them from the moment. Charlotte turned to see Sophie and George with Jenny.

"Congratulations!" Jenny said, giving Arte a hug. "Your gran would have been over the moon at what you've accomplished here, Arte. The amount of work you must have put into this barn and the hotel…" She shook her head in wonder. "You deserve every success."

Arte slipped an arm around Charlotte. "I won't deny it's been a difficult year so far, but we got there together. Charlotte has the hotel to focus on, and I have the studio."

"I'm grateful to you for relinquishing your half," Charlotte directed at Sophie.

"Oh, I was more than happy to. As was George."

George blushed as he looked at Charlotte. "Well, it was a hell of a weight off, let's just say that."

"We're pleased for you, Arte; for both of you." Sophie pulled her little sister into a hug. "Gran would be proud, as would Mum and Dad. As am I."

A tear threatened to fall from Charlotte's eye at Sophie's words, so she couldn't imagine what they were doing to Arte. Those words and that hug must mean everything to her. It was surprising Sophie had managed to find them, let alone make them audible.

"And I love that you have framed your original sketch for the barn," Sophie added, pointing to where it hung on the wall, taking pride of place alongside the childhood drawing of her grandparents that used to sit on the reception desk.

"Thanks, Soph," Arte sniffed as she subtly wiped a tear from her eye. "Charlotte had it framed for me. She loves framing things."

Arte's sniffs morphed into a playful smirk.

"Yes, quite famous for it," Charlotte replied, playing along. "I believe it's time we raise a glass to your gran, Arte."

As she led Arte away, Charlotte spotted Rodin

bothering Sydney and Beatrice, who were engaged in conversation with some locals near a table of canapés.

"Come, Rodin."

The dog hesitated, as if weighing up his options: follow his mistresses or stay where the food was. It wasn't a difficult choice, and he promptly sat.

"I'll watch him. I love dogs," Sydney said, dropping to her knees and fussing over the black Labrador, who was lapping up the attention from his newfound friend. "Can we get one, Bea?"

"You know full well our schedule doesn't allow for pets, Sydney."

She squinched her face, "What about a really small one?"

Beatrice chuckled. "You can have a goldfish. I'm sure that won't be too taxing for Mrs Clarkson."

Sydney curled her lip and buried her face in Rodin's fur, much to his delight.

Charlotte only felt relief that her new schedule did allow time for Rodin, but more importantly for Arte too. She couldn't imagine being beholden to a strict timetable again. Now that the renovations were all complete, she was looking forward to the simpler life of running just one single hotel.

She and Arte made their way outside and followed the path around to the front of the hotel.

"So, what do you make of my trinkets now?" Arte asked as they reached a large, metal owl sculpture, standing proudly on a plinth in the centre of the front lawn.

"I think your trinkets are 'art'," Charlotte said, giving

her a hug. "I especially like the eyes."

"You don't think it's weird to have Gran's ashes immortalised in glass?"

"I think this way, someone is keeping an eye on you, and who better to do so than your gran?"

Freddie exited the house then, speaking into the microphone of a wireless headset.

"Freddie and Tom are doing a great job," Charlotte said, giving him a wave as he strode towards Tithe Studio. "It was a good idea of yours to take them both on."

"It was," Arte agreed. "He said their house in town would be available to move into tomorrow, so we'll have the place to ourselves."

"We own a hotel, Arte. If we have the place to ourselves, we've gone wrong somewhere."

"True, and it's not just a hotel. It's a Boutique Hotel Award winner, thank you very much."

"That award is all yours," Charlotte insisted. "It's your vision that's guided us here. You've worked so hard to make this place what it is now, and even at your lowest point, when you wanted to give up, you didn't. You found the strength and resilience to keep going. Meanwhile, some of us didn't even realise our dreams were someone else's."

"Some of my strength came from you, you know. You encouraged me every step of the way and tried to find a way to help me succeed. And you had a hand in the financial side, don't forget, so we can chalk it up to a team effort, I think."

"Perhaps, but even you had a hand in that. I wouldn't be here if your sweet nature hadn't let me stay that weekend. You made the effort to see the good in me. You called me out on my bullshit more times than I care to remember, you challenged me on everything you didn't agree with, and you taught me how to be a better person."

Arte shook her head and wrapped an arm around Charlotte's waist. "You were always a better person. She was just trapped inside this beautiful, sexy body." Arte reached down and lightly pinched Charlotte's behind. "I only had to tinker a little and tease her out — and I particularly enjoyed the tinkering," she whispered into her ear.

"Well, I am at that age when I need to be tinkered with regularly," Charlotte joked. "There's always something going wrong that needs attending to, and I'm a great believer in preventative maintenance."

"I'm always up for a bit of servicing, as long as I can find the time. I already have a private commission from Sydney."

Charlotte pulled her into a hug. "Congratulations, my love. I'm sure there will be many more."

"I hope so. I also checked online earlier; all my art classes are fully booked. I can't wait to start teaching again."

"I know. They snapped up all the bedrooms, too. Your plan has come together exceedingly well. You know, now that we have a brand-new, state-of-the-art kitchen, we could think about running other events in addition to your exhibitions and art classes."

Arte groaned and polished a smudge off the owl sculpture with her sleeve. "You're not suggesting we do weddings, are you?"

"I was thinking we could do one… see how it goes."

"No. I've said all along I won't do weddings."

"How about one wedding?" Charlotte repeated more firmly.

Arte's attention snapped around to Charlotte. "Wait. Are you—?"

"Asking you to marry me?" Charlotte smirked. "Sounded like it, didn't it?"

Arte shot her an indignant look. "Well, not in any way I've heard it said before."

Charlotte took Arte's hands in hers. "Arte, I love you more with every passing day. I can't imagine a life without you in it. I want to grow older and greyer with you."

A wave of pure elation washed over Arte's face as a tear fell from her eye. "I love you too."

"So, will you marry me?"

"Of course I will." Arte leapt into Charlotte's arms, hugging the breath from her. She branded her with a kiss, then pulled away to say, "On one condition."

"Which is?"

"I can wear white dungarees at the wedding."

Laughter bubbled from Charlotte. "You can wear anything you like! My preference would be nothing, but that's only a suggestion. I'll leave it entirely up to you."

Arte turned to her sculpture, her face brimming over with happiness. "Here's to you, Gran, for leaving me your shithole of a hotel."

Charlotte laughed and raised her glass along with Arte. "To your gran, for leading me to your shithole of a hotel, and to your tenacious granddaughter, whom I will cherish for the rest of my life."

With that, she pressed a soft kiss to Arte's smiling mouth.

A phone beeped. Arte retrieved hers from her pocket. "We have a new review, from a *B.Russell*."

"What does it say?"

"It just says, 'Very good,'" Arte answered, confused.

Charlotte laughed.

"What's so funny?"

Charlotte wrapped an arm around Arte and squeezed her tightly. "It sounds exactly like Beatrice."

"If you say so, Lottie."

"Oh," she mock-growled, "don't you even think about calling me that!"

Arte laughed and looked up at Hotel Arte.

"What are you thinking about?" Charlotte asked.

"How happy I am at what we've achieved, what a beautiful home we have, and how I can't wait to call you my wife."

"Let's head back to the barn," Charlotte suggested. "With any luck we can turn this into an engagement party. It will save us a small fortune."

Arte nudged her with her shoulder. "You're such a romantic."

"I know." Charlotte interlaced her fingers with Arte's and led her back to the waiting crowd.

THE END

Keep turning for a free book!

REVIEWS

If you enjoyed this book, please consider leaving me a review on Amazon, BookBub or Goodreads. Just a rating or a line is fine. Reviews are life-blood to authors, boosting visibility and connecting new readers with our books.

AMAZON REVIEW LINK

JOIN MY READERS CLUB

If you'd like to hear about my new releases, sign up to my newsletter and receive a FREE sapphic romance, *The Third Act.*

At the suggestion of her daughter, Amy, widowed Fiona attends an art course at the local college where she meets the confident, inspirational teacher, Raye.
Raye awakens feelings long suppressed, but as Fiona rediscovers her sexuality, fear grows over how Amy will react.
Can Fiona find the courage to follow her heart, or will she be destined to spend her third act alone?

5 Review*
Absolutely loved this book! Great story line, well developed characters and beautifully crafted. It is really refreshing to see the older lesbian represented for a change!
www.emilybanting.co.uk/freebook

ALSO BY

BROKEN BEYOND REPAIR

A South Downs Romance Book 1

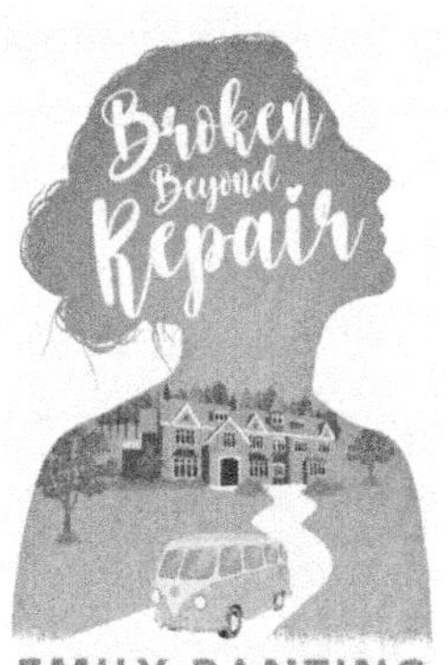

GOLDIE WINNER 2023: THE ANN BANNON POPULAR CHOICE BRONZE AWARD

GOLDIE FINALIST 2023: CONTEMPORARY ROMANCE LONG NOVEL

WINNER OF THE LESFIC BARD AWARD 2022: ROMANCE

WINNER OF THE LESFIC BARD AWARD 2022: COVER DESIGN

WINNER OF THE QUEER INDIE AWARDS 2022: CONTEMPORARY ROMANCE

An age gap, celebrity ice queen romance that will pull at the heart strings — even the icy ones!

Sydney MacKenzie, personal assistant to the rich and famous, is looking forward to a well-earned break to go travelling in her beloved VW camper van, Gertie — that is, until Gertie cries off sick. When her boss calls in a favour, one that will pay Sydney handsomely and put Gertie back on the road, she can't refuse.

Internationally renowned actress Beatrice Russell — adored by her fans and despised by those that know her — is splashed across the tabloids, all thanks to her broken leg. She limps back to her palatial English country estate to convalesce for the summer, where she finds herself in need of yet another new assistant.

Enter Sydney, who doesn't take kindly to the star's demands, attitude, or clicking fingers — much less her body's own attraction to the gorgeous diva. If not for that, and Gertie's worn-out engine, she would leave tomorrow. Or so she tells herself.

As the summer heats up, the ice queen begins to thaw, and Sydney glimpses the tormented woman beneath the celebrity bravado, drawing her ever closer to the enigmatic actress — sometimes too close.

Can Sydney reach the real Beatrice and help heal her wounds before the summer ends and she returns to filming in the States, or is the celebrity broken beyond repair?

ALSO BY

THE NUNSWICK ABBEY SERIES

4.5* Rated Series

LOST IN LOVE (BOOK ONE)

A heart-warming, quintessentially English village novel, centred on the ruins of Nunswick Abbey…

Historical tour guide Anna Walker is determined to make a good impression on her new bosses, but juggling a full-time job with caring for her ailing father is putting her own health – and potentially his – at risk.

When she meets Dr Katherine Atkinson, a charming yet intimidating new arrival to the village, Anna is infuriated by the doctor's attempts to convince her that her father needs professional, full-time care. She's even more frustrated by her growing attraction to the classy, wealthy doctor.

Anna's determination to prove she can cope forces Katherine to divulge a painful event from her past that still haunts her, hopeful it will make Anna see sense before it's too late.

With Katherine's heart lost to the past and Anna's overwhelmed in the present, can the two women help each other overcome their struggles and move forward? Will a curtain-twitching busy body curtail any blossoming attraction before it even has a chance to bloom?

Anna and Katherine's story continues in book two, Trust in Truth, and book three, Forgive not Forget.

PRAISE FOR THE SERIES

This is one of the best books I've read in a very long time. I laughed out loud, cried, and even became indignant at one point. I love a good age-gap slow burn and this checked all the boxes!! Well done!!

LOVED this quintessential English romance novel!! Beautifully written, the plot is tight and the main characters - and those around them - precisely drawn. It gripped me from the very first page and I finished it less than 24 hours!

I do not think there is a heart string left that this author didn't strum. I am a mess of happy and sad and just all out of sorts hahaha. Superb writing. Everything the characters feel, you are going to feel so maybe a few tissues, a pint of ice cream and a hug from a friend should be added to your list of things you'll need after this book.

I rated this book 5 stars because it's absolutely breathtaking, the atmosphere of the quaint little village with the ruins of an abbey is such a beautiful picture and reminds me of a town near to where I grew up. It's so hard to find sapphic books in general and it's even harder to find one as good as this! I'm in love with Katherine and Anna's relationship and I'm so excited to continue the series. Also this was such a fun book to read that I read it in 1 day and I'm usually a slow reader.

PURCHASE HERE

Made in the USA
Monee, IL
05 September 2023

42211796R00236